THE CHIRAL AGENT

ALSO BY LL RICHMAN

The Biogenesis War Series

The Chiral Agent

The Chiral Protocol

Chiral Justice

Chiral Agent/Chiral Conspiracy audiobook set

Chiral Protocol/Ambush in the Sargon Straits audio set

The Biogenesis War Files: The Early Years

Operation Cobalt

Ambush in the Sargon Straits

The Chiral Conspiracy

— BOOK 1 —

THE BIOGENESIS WAR

THE CHIRAL AGENT

LL RICHMAN

THE CHIRAL AGENT
Published by Delta V Press
The Biogenesis War™ is a registered trademark of L.L. Richman
Cover copyright © 2020 L.L. Richman

ISBN-13: 978-1-7373636-0-6

0 9 8 7 5 4 3 2 1

Produced in the United States of America

CONTENTS

The supreme art of war is to
subdue the enemy without fighting.
~ Sun Tzu

PROLOGUE

In the twenty-second century, humanity reached the stars.

With colonies established throughout the Sol system, pioneers hungry for new ventures traveled beyond its borders to nearby Alpha Centauri. There, they planted the first seeds of what would become three independent star nations—two around its binary stars, a third orbiting nearby Proxima Centauri.

Not long after, a theoretical form of propulsion became a reality. The experimental new drive's Casimir bubble magnified the Scharnhorst effect, allowing velocities up to three times the speed of light.

A brave band of explorers took a chance on the new tech and launched a pair of colony ships toward the binary stars of Procyon and Sirius. Their descendants flourished, forming the Geminate Alliance.

While the Scharnhorst drive made it possible to reach stars as distant as Sirius and Procyon, travel between the fledgling colonies and their parent star was still measured in years. The Geminate settlers were on their own, and they knew it.

Three hundred years passed. In the mid-twenty-fifth century, a pair of Alliance scientists discovered a way to fold spacetime, bending the compactified branes that were stacked within the Bulk of extradimensional space. Thus, the Calabi-Yau gates were born.

These specially tuned, 'pair-partnered' gates provided instantaneous travel between star systems, regardless of distance. For the first time, far-flung civilizations reconnected in real-time, and true interstellar commerce became a reality.

Those back in Sol had formed a loose association known as the Coalition of Worlds. The Coalition eagerly embraced the Alliance's gate tech. Treaties were signed, leases granted, and soon, the Geminate government had gates at each heliopause.

A robust and vigorous trade developed between the settled worlds, ushering in a prosperous new era for every star nation involved—with one exception: Akkadia.

The star nation orbiting Rigel Kentaurus had built an export economy around handcrafted materials whose value was based on scarcity, forced by Scharnhorst limitations and slow trade routes. This was utterly disrupted by the gates.

Akkadia plunged into a recession. Desperate circumstances allowed an oppressive regime to wrest power from its premier. The planet went from an artisan's enclave to a totalitarian government.

The current Ministry of State Security was rumored to have its hooks in every star nation from Terra to Sirius. It stole tech where it could, sabotaged when it couldn't. Such actions propelled Akkadia into a state of cold war with the rest of the settled worlds.

And then the Akkadian premier set his sights on the Geminate gate tech.

The Alliance has no idea how far Akkadia is willing to go to achieve this goal. They're also unaware how thoroughly they've been compromised, but they're about to find out....

PART ONE:
DEADLY DISCOVERY

SPECIMENS

ADVANCED ISOLATION LAB
DEGRASSE RESEARCH TORUS
VERMILION, LUYTEN'S STAR
GEMINATE ALLIANCE

THE SPECIMEN CASE was unlike any other. Tucked away in deGrasse's Advanced Isolation Lab, it was disguised as a large gray shipping crate, purposely mislabeled as cleaning supplies. One look inside instantly dispelled that fiction.

It contained no solvents, no soaps. Yet neither was it a standard sampling container. There were no compartments designed to isolate biological material, laid out in neat, sterile rows.

Peering inside was like falling into a looking-glass microcosm teeming with native life. The case was segmented into four terrarium-like vivariums, each biosphere host to its own species: insect, arachnid, rodent, reptile.

It was unique in another significant way. The biospheres within were engineered from unique molecular building blocks found on Vermilion, the sole habitable planet orbiting Luyten's Star.

The life found here was distinct from anything else humankind had discovered in all their centuries-long exploration of the universe. Experts in the settled worlds claimed such things were an impossibility; they couldn't exist.

And yet, they did.

When reports first made their way to Alliance headquarters in Procyon, the decision was made to place Luyten's Star under interdiction. The discovery was deemed too dangerous, too easily weaponized. Until Geminate scientists could fully decode what they'd found, all information pertaining to the discovery had been classified, reports redacted.

The Navy's premiere research station was secretly relocated to Luyten's Star and placed in orbit above Vermilion. DeGrasse was staffed by a small team of civilian researchers under contract to the Alliance. These were recruited by the Navy's Advanced Research Agency, and sworn to secrecy about their work.

The decision to interdict Luyten's Star had been made in the hope that news of the discovery could be contained, the sensitive information hidden from the prying eyes of Alliance enemies.

They failed.

A MATTER OF STATE

MINISTRY OF STATE SECURITY
CENTRAL PREFECTURE, ERIDU
AKKADIAN EMPIRE (ALPHA CENTAURI)

CITIZEN GENERAL CHE Josza stood quietly at attention, waiting for Akkadia's Minster of State Security to acknowledge him. It was always this way. Being granted an audience with Rin Zhou Enlai was an intricate social dance, the delay intended to build both anticipation and fear, in equal measure.

From where he stood just inside the entrance, Che could feel the weight of the room. The minister's office was at once both spare and ornate. The few furnishings allowed were priceless, dating back to the original colonists, and displayed with the reverence afforded such valuable pieces of Akkadian history.

As he waited, Che pulled up the roster of the newest recruits on his implant's overlay. He mentally flipped through them, approving some and deferring others.

He'd gone through five reports before the minister took note of him. He dismissed the overlay when Rin Zhou raised a hand and gestured him forward. As he neared, the Synthetic

Intelligence embedded in his head automatically submitted his security token. This allowed him to cross her personal perimeter and live.

He stopped in front of Enlai's desk, and her head snapped up, the gesture oddly birdlike. Her eyes bored into his with the cold scrutiny of a raptor.

Che matched her, expression for expression, chin slightly raised.

Challenge accepted.

She relaxed back and nodded, eyes glinting in brief amusement, acknowledging the silent interplay.

"Citizen General." Her tone was crisp and flat, with little inflection.

"Citizen Minister," he responded.

Rin Zhou motioned for Che to take a seat. "I see the samples from Luyten's Star are being secured."

Che nodded as he lowered himself into the indicated chair. "They are."

He waited patiently while the minister read the report from their agent in the Geminate Navy. Rin Zhou hummed, one finger tapping rhythmically on the edge of the desk, and then her hand stilled. Her gaze landed thoughtfully on him once more, eyes narrowing as her finger resumed its soft tapping.

Che resisted the urge to shift uncomfortably under the minister's regard. He couldn't tell if she was actually studying him or if her thoughts were elsewhere. When he couldn't stand it any longer, he spoke.

"If you don't mind me asking... what's so important about these samples?"

One of the minister's eyebrows rose in polite disbelief. "They would be important simply because the Geminate Alliance thinks they are. Need I remind you that, despite their relative youth, that star nation has consistently outperformed the rest of the settled worlds in scientific innovation?"

He grimaced. "No, you do not."

Rin Zhou studied Che silently, the moment extending

uncomfortably long. Abruptly, she stood.

"Come, Citizen General Josza. Walk with me."

Che's stomach churned at her unexpected formality, but he kept his face impassive, inclining his head agreeably. He rose and followed the minister to the massive clearsteel window that stretched across the far side of her office.

Rin Zhou ran a finger down the window's side seam and it retracted, allowing in a rush of sweltering heat. She stepped out onto a balcony that faced south, toward Eridu's equator. Che followed, already feeling the sweat beading his brow.

He saw a strand of silver shimmering in the distance, rising to disappear into the atmosphere—Eridu's main space elevator. Before it, countless buildings rose, home to most of the planet's population.

They were clustered together, dull gray facades seeming to huddle protectively against the elements in one densely populated swath that ran between the elevator and Rin Zhou's private balcony, atop the Special Administrative Building.

To the left, through the haze of heat and graphite dust that seemed to cling to everything in Central Prefecture, Che could just make out the silhouette of the State Assembly House. A rope of white curved gently from behind the government building, the maglev line the only public access Akkadian citizens had to their government seat.

Che's eyes followed the line as it snaked its way down the hill toward them, gleaming in the late afternoon sunlight. It paralleled Rin Zhou's balcony before swooping low to meet the ground, the nearest station a mere half kilometer from where they stood.

A train pulled up to the platform as he watched, disgorging a mix of native Akkadians and a few visiting dignitaries and businessmen. The latter were easily recognizable by the faint blue glow that emanated from the narrow headsets they wore.

The filters were a necessary evil. Natives like Che had genetically altered respiratory systems that allowed them to breathe, despite the toxins in Eridu's air. Off-worlders had no such modifications.

That same air was the reason a protective ceramic alloy coated all outdoor surfaces, a deterrent to the corrosive atmosphere. It was the only way to build structures that would last, given the amount of sulfuric acid in the air, despite the terraformers' best efforts.

Rin Zhou turned to face west, and Che surreptitiously swiped at his brow before following her gaze. Stretching out before them were the walls that bordered Central Prefecture. Beyond that were the rock-strewn grasses of the Hohen Savannah.

The minister looked over her shoulder at Che, one brow raised in invitation, before returning her gaze to the view. He stepped up beside her, his hands coming to rest on the half wall that ran along the balcony. Beside him, Rin Zhou lifted an arm to shade her eyes from the glare of the star, Ebla, riding low upon the horizon.

As near the equator as they were, there would be very little twilight, Che knew. Darkness would follow swiftly on Ebla's heels, though it wouldn't be absolute. Ebla's sister star, Zoser, was at periastron, and would cast a bright glow across the Akkadian landscape of Eridu once it rose in a few hours.

"What do you know of our history, Che? Tell me."

For all that the words were spoken in a careless, idle tone, he knew a command when he heard it.

"Nothing beyond the basics that any Citizen knows, I suppose. I'm a soldier, not a historian," Che stated, looking down at the residue of graphite powder on his fingers.

The stuff was ubiquitous on Eridu, had been for as long as he'd been alive. The dust was left over from the seeding of hydrogen and iron aerosols into the planet's proto-atmosphere. It had been done to mitigate the density of the carbon dioxide in the air during early terraforming.

Che began to brush the powder off his hands and then froze when it abruptly registered that there was silence between them. He looked up, mentally cursing his distraction when he saw the minister regarding him expectantly.

He searched for something innocuous to say that wouldn't cause him to lose status.

"My value to the State lies more with the Junxun than it does to the past," he reminded her, allowing a hint of self-deprecation to leach into his voice.

The Junxun was a deliberate draw, a reminder that the compulsory classes were his responsibility. Part indoctrination, part boot camp, they functioned as a crucible, refining the raw recruits until their strengths could be identified and catalogued, their usefulness to the State clear.

Che excelled at this, mining each new group carefully and finding the truly gifted, honing them into weapons the State could wield. Rin Zhou knew it, too.

"I suppose the State's military is less about the past and more about tactics," she conceded. "But indulge me, please, old friend."

Old friend. Che knew there was no such thing in Akkadian politics.

Rin Zhou sank one hand inside the pocket of her uniform jacket and pulled out a portable holo. She thumbed it on just as the sun, Ebla, gave up its last light with a sharp flash of green on the horizon.

A three-dimensional representation of the Alpha Centauri system sprang into being before them, partially obscuring Che's view of the maglev station below. Shadowed figures played out behind the projection, government workers hurrying home at second-shift change.

"I'm sure you're aware of the struggle we had when we first came to Eridu," she began, "so I'll not bore you with the details. The terraforming failures forced us to overcome obstacles neither Giza nor An-Yang ever had to face."

Che nodded at her mention of Akkadia's sister colonies, established around the system's other stars.

"You must also know, or have at least heard rumor, of the attempts my predecessor made to alter the balance of power

within the Coalition so that we would have a more...
egalitarian footing with other star nations."

Che nodded again. The Coalition of Worlds wasn't a
governing body per se. Its goals were the advancement of
peace, collaboration and harmony between the settled worlds.

Its members hailed from the nations that inhabited the Sol,
Alpha Centauri, and Proxima Centauri star systems. There
were eight governmental bodies represented, all supposedly
equal.

Everyone knew this for the polite fiction it was. Some
within the Coalition were more equal than others. The
sovereign nations inside the Sol system—humanity's
birthplace—held the lion's share of the influence.

The disparity this represented in both trade and commerce
was something Akkadia had been battling since Eridu had first
been colonized, centuries ago.

Che waited for her to continue. When it became apparent a
response from him was required, he picked his way through
words with the same care he would use to cross an active mine
field.

"If I recall, the last attempt didn't target the Coalition. We
went after the Geminate Alliance's gate tech, did we not?"

The young upstart star nation that had colonized the Sirius
and Procyon binary systems had invented a way to travel
instantaneously from one star system to another.

In order to protect their intellectual property, the Alliance
negotiated leases at each star system's heliopause, and then
built and staffed the Calabi-Yau gates themselves.

No one was allowed near the gates, and they were policed
rigorously. Che suspected there wasn't a planetary
government that hadn't tried to duplicate or acquire the tech.
None had met with success.

Rin Zhou nodded in approval. "We did," she replied. "We
failed."

There was a bite to those last words, emphasized by the
sharp click of the holoprojector as she flipped it closed and

pocketed it.

Che broke eye contact, returning his gaze to the horizon. He fought the urge to clear his throat, instead settling on a noncommittal sound.

"I heard rumors a Sol corporation was close to delivering a competitive alternative," he said after a moment's silence.

"The Ministry heard those same rumors," Rin Zhou confirmed. "My predecessor assigned our people to shadow the company's top scientists. When the opportunity arose, we acquired them."

Che knew what that meant. He taught the tactic to his most promising students. Though specific methods could vary, in the end all roads led to the target being arrested on false charges, while traveling abroad.

Abruptly, he realized why the story felt familiar. He'd seen the reports. Two heavily redacted documents had come across his desk as case studies, to be given to his students.

"We arrested one for industrial espionage, the other for possession of an illegal substance we planted on her," he murmured. In both situations, the scientists had been told they could work off their prison sentences by providing services 'for the good of the people.'

Rin Zou's expression turned sour. "It was hastily executed."

Che stiffened; he couldn't help it. She noticed, of course. Amusement flashed briefly across her face and she held up a hand.

"Not the arrests themselves." she clarified. "Your Junxun performed satisfactorily. The order to take the scientists was premature. The corporation's claims were nothing more than hype. A rumor, leaked to benefit its stockholders."

Her hand dropped, her expression turning cold and hard.

"And then the minister doubled down on his mistake. When they failed to produce anything of value, he attempted to force productivity by threatening their families back in Sol. Terra petitioned the Coalition for sanctions against Akkadia."

Che's eyes widened in understanding. He'd heard Rin

Zhou's predecessor had been disavowed by the Premier; now he knew why.

Soon after, the minister had quietly disappeared and Rin Zhou promoted into the position.

Part of him privately wondered if Rin Zhou would have been so hard on the man had he not been exposed to the Coalition for his actions.

No... Che came to a sudden realization. *It was Rin Zhou herself who leaked the news to the Terrans.*

Che's thoughts were interrupted by a soft chime. Rin Zhou's head lifted, eyes narrowing for a moment, before she nodded once in satisfaction.

"Come." She gestured Che back toward the cool embrace of her office. He followed her, welcoming the respite the crisp, clean air provided.

The minister directed him toward a deceptively cozy seating arrangement where the wait staff stood, ready to perform the ritual grind and pour of coffee.

As he settled onto a low pillow across from his superior, the barista carefully weighed the freshly roasted beans and then proceeded to hand-grind them. Che waited as she presented the grind to the minister, who waved a hand over it on a slow inhale. Rin Zhou nodded her approval, and the barista began the gentle pour of heated water over the grounds.

He felt a presence inside his head. A quick look at his overlay showed Rin Zhou had initiated an encrypted connection to his wire. Clearly, she wished to continue their conversation without being overheard.

{Our current situation is untenable.} Rin Zhou's mental voice was crisp. *{Despite the Premier's assurances to the people, Akkadia is on the brink of financial collapse. Our debt continues to grow, despite the redistribution of national resources.}*

Che's eyes tracked the barista's movements as he processed Rin Zhou's words. The barista drizzled the water over the fresh grounds with a slow, fluid weave of her hand. The aroma of a rich, full-bodied coffee wafted toward him.

{If we are to survive, it will be through interstellar expansion,} the minister continued. *{Akkadia must become the leader of a New Coalition.}*

The concept was bold, brazen. Ambitious. He had no idea if it was attainable. Then again, it wasn't his place to make that determination.

Che sat in silence, sipping at his coffee while the barista completed the ritual, bundled her equipment, and exited the room. He waited for the room's systems to flash secured readiness, and then he spoke aloud.

"What would be required," he began carefully, "in order for such a bold plan to succeed?"

Rin Zhou's eyes glinted as she looked at him over the rim of her cup. "Exclusive access to Geminate gate tech."

"But I thought— I mean...how—?" Che stuttered, shocked to hear her voice the same goal that had meant the death of her predecessor.

Rin Zhou smiled. "The art of espionage is finding that which your opponent fears the most, and using it against them. There are any number of ways in which we might hold the Geminate hostage in exchange for their tech."

Her smile widened, became predatory. "If your assets in Luyten's Star are to be believed, these samples we'll soon have in our possession will do the job quite nicely... as long as no one gets in the way."

PART TWO: AWAKENED

INCINERATOR

LOCATION: UNKNOWN

"HOLY—! SARGE... IT's alive!"

The exclamation pierced through the fog that cocooned Micah's mind. Distantly, it registered that he was lying on his back, somewhere cool and dark. With effort, Micah pushed against the mental haze that clung to him like a sticky web. His limbs felt leaden, his eyes refused to open.

A second voice joined the first.

"Of course it's alive," the sergeant responded. "It's biomatter. Living tissues and shit."

The sergeant's gruff tone reminded Micah of his drill instructor back at OCS—the kind of person who didn't suffer fools or idiot officer candidates.

The sergeant wasn't done. "Just do what the eggheads in research ordered and burn it." He barked the order, his voice growing louder as he neared Micah's location. "Or do I need to shove my boot up your ass to get you to do your job?"

"But I have neural activity on scan," the first man protested. "That's a *person* in there, Sarge, not biomatter. Already sent a ping to let Doc Janus know." Agitation was replaced by urgency as his voice drew near. "Hey, grab the emergency kit by the door, willya? I've got to get him out of there."

The sergeant sighed. "Dammit, corpsman. Why'd you have to go and run a scan?" His tone was a mixture of annoyed and tired. "Couldn't you have just done as Janus ordered? Now *I* gotta do as he ordered."

Those words stirred a vague sense of unease in Micah. It turned to alarm when he heard a firearm being unholstered. He fought to throw off his stupor, to reach out, call a warning.

"Sarge? What... wait—" The corpsman's words cut off at the sound of a directed energy weapon being discharged. Micah's gut clenched; he knew what that meant.

"Sorry about that," the sergeant muttered. Footfalls closed the distance as he stopped in front of the dead corpsman. "You were a good kid, too."

There was a grunt, followed by a soft scraping noise, and annoyance returned to the sergeant's voice.

"Well, hell. Now I have two bodies to deal with. You damn well better be good for the credits, Janus," the man muttered, "or I might have to pay your pogue ass a visit, too."

Janus. Micah forced his mind to latch onto the name. Not that he was in any position to share—

In a moment of clarity, he recalled the evanescent wave nanocircuitry wired into his neural net. It was something every Alliance citizen received when they came of age.

Micah's wire had been upgraded when he joined the Geminate Navy. The implant was military-issued and encrypted, allowing him to connect to any secured network. He reached mentally for it, cursing his drug-induced fog. His thoughts were clumsy, his implant a slippery and elusive thing.

A thundering scrape of metal above his head interrupted his attempt to connect with the dormant unit. His brain nudged at him, the sound vaguely familiar. Something landed with a dull thump overhead.

The corpsman's body.

A spike of adrenaline cleared his thoughts, and he realized

what his subconscious mind had been trying to tell him. He knew now where he was being held: inside an incinerator.

His limbs twitched as he strained to overthrow his paralysis. He had to get out before the thing fired up.

Easy there. You'll be fine.

The thought startled him, seeming to come from nowhere, but he'd run out of time to analyze.

With a deafening roar, the incinerator fired up. All around him, the inferno raged, heat building in the darkness until he knew no more.

* * *

"Shit. He's not dead."

Micah jolted back to awareness as the words brought memory flooding back. He was still supine, still in complete darkness. He was as surprised as the voice sounded to find himself alive.

From what he could tell, his situation hadn't changed, although he seemed to have a clearer head this time around. He had no idea how long he'd been out, but he remained unable to move, to speak, or even to open his eyes.

The voice sounded again. It was the sergeant from before.

"Now what do we do? Janus said we need to scuttle all the evidence before fifteen hundred hours."

His query was met with a curt response.

"Then kill him again, soldier. And this time, check your work."

The new voice was female, her words chilling. They galvanized Micah; he fought for mobility, to no avail.

The sound of soft footsteps heralded her departure, followed by the sergeant's softly muttered, "Damned Akkadian. I didn't sign up for this shit."

The man began to move toward Micah's location, but was brought up short when a resounding clang sounded in the distance. The noise elicited a string of curses from the man, the words fading with distance as he ran to investigate.

In the next instant, Micah felt a slight breeze caress his skin. Within seconds, his mind was much more alert than it had been mere minutes before, when he'd clawed his way to consciousness. His arm bumped against a smooth surface and he froze, arrested by the knowledge that he could now move.

This was a significant improvement.

He turned his attention to his surroundings—to finding a way out of his confinement. The cushion of chill air around his face suggested close quarters. He reached a cautious hand up and met resistance, ten centimeters above him. The cold leaching from it into his palm suggested some type of metal.

He pressed his other hand beside the first, then slid both apart, using the movement to measure the space that held him. Another twenty centimeters and both hands stopped, having found the sides of his prison.

It suddenly registered that *he* was cold.

Where the hell am I? he thought.

There was the briefest of pauses, and then an answer sounded inside his head.

Base Morgue. Level -10. deGrasse Torus. Luyten's Star.

The words jolted him. These weren't his thoughts. He knew this with certainty, but *how* he knew escaped him, since they hadn't come across his wire. After almost two decades living with the unit embedded in his skull, he'd become used to feeling the presence of the neural implant. It was always there in the back of his mind, like subliminal white noise.

Until now. Its silence was glaring, and yet a voice was unmistakably there.

Deal with it later, Case, he told himself. *Survival first.*

He ran his hands blindly along the seam of his prison walls, seeking a way out. His fingers stilled momentarily as it came to him that his wire wasn't his only nonfunctioning implant. His optical augments weren't working properly, either.

He should have been able to scan the area on all EM bands, the coolness of the metal above him registering in muted blues and purples. Instead, he was enveloped in an unrelenting blackness.

Now would be a good time to leave.

With this newly transmitted thought came movement. The darkness split above his head, broken by a shaft of light. His eyes slitted shut in response to the sudden brightness. The light played down his torso as the platform on which he lay slid out of the wall—a wall of identical drawers, each the exact dimension of the space that confined him.

And then it hit him. He wasn't just in the base's morgue, as the voice had indicated. He was on a freaking *slab* in the morgue. In one of its self-contained storage units, each of which could be individually incinerated.

Which explains why I'm still alive, he realized. *Somehow my unit must have malfunctioned.*

He turned his head, eyes darting about the room. He was alone, the sergeant nowhere to be seen. Expelling a breath, Micah sat up. The chill air hit his naked flesh as he assessed his condition.

Get dressed.

The mental words were punctuated by the sound of a locker opening against the far wall. Micah gripped the side of the platform, the sharpness of its metal edge grounding him as he considered what to do.

Shaking his head, he hopped down from the cold, steel surface. As he strode toward the locker that sat invitingly open, thanks to his mysterious benefactor, he reviewed what he could recall of deGrasse. He knew the morgue was on the military side of the torus. He'd been here once before, to...

His mind hit a blank wall.

Frustrated, he grabbed the boots that sat atop a folded flight suit, dropping them to the deck beside his bare feet. He reached for the clothing but then froze, fingers wrapped around the fabric, when he saw the weapons the suit had hidden. A pulsed energy sidearm lay beside a sheathed tanto knife. The first was a civilized weapon; the second held a lethal edge.

Micah's eyes narrowed as he studied the blade. The tanto's carbyne edge could likely cut into bulkhead, though he'd never had occasion to test its capabilities. In the skilled hands of an operator, the weapon would be swift, efficient, and brutal.

An unspoken mental nudge spurred him back into movement. He shrugged into the standard issue flight suit, stripped of both rank and nametag.

He left the tanto for now. Grabbing the sidearm, he clipped it and the spare batteries to his belt, then shoved his feet into the boots, tucking his pant legs into the tops and sealing them.

He stood—then froze, attention arrested by his reflection in a nearby mirror. His face...

It looked wrong, somehow. He raised a hand, running it through his dark, short-cropped hair in confusion, stiffening as realization came to him.

Micah was left-handed, and yet he'd reached with his right. His hair, which stubbornly grew in one direction, now fell to the wrong side. He leaned closer, noting other subtle irregularities in the face that had stared back at him for the past thirty-five years.

What the—?

They're coming. Leave now if you want to live.

The words were followed by a panel sliding open in a nearby bulkhead. Across the room, Micah heard the pounding of feet in the passageway leading to the morgue. The sergeant was returning, and he wasn't alone.

Leave. **Now.**

There was a sense of urgency to the words that propelled him forward. He spun, lunged for the tanto blade. Palming it, he slammed the locker door closed and turned to face the yawning blackness.

"Who the hell are you?" he demanded, slipping though the panel. It slid shut behind him, darkness enveloping him once more.

An image appeared in his head, a mental construct of a lab

he knew he'd never seen and yet somehow recognized. Abruptly, he realized the feeling of familiarity wasn't coming from him. It emanated from the same place as the foreign thoughts that he now understood were being pushed to him from... someone else.

Your destination. Hurry.

"Who *are* you?" he repeated as he followed the mental nudge that urged him forward.

There was a pause. The response, when it came, had him reaching for the bulkhead to support himself, his mind spinning in confusion.

I am you.

DIRECTIVE

ADVANCED ISOLATION LAB
DEGRASSE RESEARCH TORUS

THE DOORS OF the Advanced Isolation Lab parted, admitting deGrasse's senior biochemist, Clint Janus. Tall and sinewy-lean, the man had the look of a swimmer, or one born to a lower gravity habitat.

Ordinarily, someone of his stature would stick out on a military base. Here on the torus, where scientific and civilian personnel worked alongside the hardened bodies of Alliance Navy and Marines, Clint blended seamlessly with the researchers, exactly as he was meant to do.

Everything about Clint Janus had been carefully crafted for appeal. His appearance had been subtly altered to suggest capability, intelligence, and trustworthiness. His upbringing had been shaped with care, his career path chosen for the good of the star nation he was born to serve.

When the Akkadian Empire saw the need for an asset to infiltrate the upper echelons of the Geminate scientific community, Clint Janus's handlers had thought nothing of shifting his vocation from pre-law to biochemistry.

Clint hated biochemistry.

That distaste was eclipsed only by the healthy fear he held for his handlers. Akkadian assassins were not the kind of people one crossed and lived to tell the tale. Therefore, Clint applied himself to his studies without complaint.

The charisma he'd been trained to project in preparation for his legal career was a bit of a rarity in the hard sciences, and he used this to his advantage.

More than once, a professor had been on the verge of failing him. Clint's charm bought him the time needed to convince his fellow students to help him pass.

Over the years, he'd dutifully worked his way through the private sector, a sleeper agent waiting to be activated. And then deGrasse's lead biochemist position became available.

DeGrasse Torus was one of the Geminate Navy's most versatile and unique research stations. Owned and operated by NARA, the Navy's Advanced Research Agency, deGrasse moved wherever the Alliance needed it most.

Those assigned to deGrasse for a tour of duty were required to hold a mid-tier or better security classification, for it was within this station that some of the most cutting-edge military advances had been developed. And it was behind its walls that the few truly perilous threats to the Alliance had been thwarted.

Clint was far from the most qualified to work here. He knew it; his handlers knew it.

That didn't deter them. They eliminated the deGrasse biochemist whose position Clint would fill, and then made the competition... disappear.

When the job offer came, Clint acted suitably honored to have received such a plum assignment, demurring modestly when congratulated.

He knew full well that the opportunity had been engineered. This was the inauguration of his first large-scale mission.

Now, that mission was at risk of falling apart—and all

because of a single missive.

As the lab's doors closed silently behind him, Clint tossed a hard copy of the directive he'd just intercepted onto a nearby table with an agitated flip of his wrist. Long legs ate up the distance between the lab's entrance and the spinward bulkhead as he paced, his mind turning over the memo's contents.

The blank white sheet sat innocuously on the table's surface, its very presence mocking him. Physical memos were almost unheard of in a reality that relied upon wire traffic. They were employed only when there existed a need for extreme security. The sheet was keyed to his biosignature and could only be read when his security token accessed it.

The classified memo hadn't been meant for him. His handler on deGrasse had intercepted it, rekeying the biolock to Clint's ID before it reached its intended destination.

Its contents were troubling: an immediate stop to all research, by order of Parliament. All data that had been gathered was to be submitted to Admiral Toland, the officer in charge of deGrasse. All samples packaged for transport. Everything was to be shipped back to the Geminate homeworld of Ceriba by the end of the week.

He couldn't let that happen.

Clint hastily altered that directive, substituting it with one of his own. One that ordered the data be submitted to *him*. Or, rather, his immediate superior, the Navy's Chief Scientist, Lee Stinton.

Clint would need to resolve that little hierarchy problem soon.

As for the samples... Rather than packing them for transport, Clint's revised directive ordered them all terminated.

It was this last that would cause him the most trouble, he knew. He'd ducked into this lab so that he could confront the source of the strongest resistance head-on.

There was only one problem: the doctor he was trying to

contact wasn't answering.

Clint strode to a nearby holographic display panel and stabbed irritably at its controls, transferring the connection he'd already made over his wire onto the holodisplay. He continued his pacing, waiting impatiently for the person on the other end to answer, his eyes darting to the table where he'd tossed the offending memo.

At last, an image resolved on the holodisplay. The person on the other end wasn't Samantha Travis, the doctor he'd been attempting to contact; it was a Navy med-tech who worked for her. The tech released a squirming puppy back into its cage before turning to greet him with a strained smile.

Clint's lips compressed into a thin line of displeasure at the clamor of animal noises that came through over the connection. "What is this?" he demanded sharply. "What are those creatures still doing there? And where is Doctor Travis?"

The technician's smile fell as she took in Clint's expression. Her expression uncertain, she raised her hands in a placating gesture.

"Doctor Travis had an errand to run and left me in charge. She went over the memo with me, though, sir." She tucked her hair behind her ear with one hand as she rushed on, "I know you said to have them all gone by oh nine hundred, sir, and I apologize for the delay, but don't worry. It's all being taken care of. Every animal has been adopted out; we're just waiting for shift change so the new owners can come down and—"

"I said get *rid* of them, Lieutenant. Not find them homes." Janus's nostrils flared and his face twisted in rage as he cut her off. "Those are not *pets*, they are lab specimens. Terminate them. Now. Don't make me come down there and do it myself."

The woman's jaw dropped, horror crossing her face. She inhaled sharply, an incipient protest on her lips, but Clint cut the connection.

He clenched his hands into fists by his side—long, artists' hands that had never been meant to be used in the pursuit of science. He cursed, and in one violent shove, sent the equipment on a nearby table crashing against the far bulkhead.

A figure he hadn't noticed pushed away from a shadowed corner of the lab, and he couldn't control his involuntary start at the intrusion.

"Calm yourself, doctor."

The words were not a suggestion, but Clint didn't care. A dangerous light entered his eyes as he rounded upon the one person on deGrasse who knew his full identity. His keeper. The Akkadian assassin, sent by the head of their guild to ensure he carried out his duties flawlessly for the good of the Empire.

"I'll calm down when we're safely off this shithole and the research is on its way to the homeworld," he snapped, eyes blazing in anger as they bored into the woman's dusky, expressionless face.

She'd been with him for the course of this entire mission—and he didn't even know her name.

The assassin tilted her head. The beaded braids that marked her status within the guild shifted, some blending in with the brown of her hair, others glinting a deep blood-red under the lab's harsh light.

The beads were usually kept hidden, tucked inside a thick, neat braid. Today they swung freely. A detached part of his mind wondered what kind of material they were made of, and why they didn't clatter against each other when her hair was loose, as it was now.

One bead, one kill. This woman had more than any assassin Clint had ever seen.

She studied him for a long, silent moment before gesturing to the now-dark holodisplay.

"You broke cover," she said. Her voice held mild reproof. "Clint Janus is the darling of the scientific community. He doesn't kill puppies."

Clint stared back at her, his eyelid twitching in anger. "Our orders are to obtain the research, grab the samples, and to destroy everything else." A bladed hand jabbed at the now-silent holodisplay. "Those *puppies* are creatures engineered from the research we're taking back to Akkadia. If they're not destroyed, along with everything else, the Geminate Alliance will be that much closer to recreating their work once we escape with it. And trust me, Samantha Travis is more than capable of doing exactly that."

The assassin returned his stare, her own maddeningly blank. "Your job is to reset the Alliance's knowledge base," she said. "*My* job is to ensure no samples remain."

The thin smile that creased the assassin's lips was at odds with the dead expression in her eyes. "Or are you questioning my abilities?"

Clint saw the possibility of his own death in those eyes, just as she meant for him to see. He sucked in a breath, reining the anger back and wresting control over it once more. He nodded. *Message received.*

The assassin broke eye contact, moving silently over to the drab gray crate marked 'Cleaning Supplies.'

"This is it?" she asked, one hand coming to rest on the side of the case.

"It is."

"And everything Akkadia needs can be found inside?"

"Enough for us to be able to fill in the rest."

She shot him a sharp look, and Clint's fists tightened as he remained silent, fighting to retain hard-won control over his anger. After a moment, she nodded and stepped away.

"I'll contact the ship, then, and let them know how much cargo to expect."

With that, she was gone.

ESCAPE

Maintenance tunnels
deGrasse Research Torus

AVIATE. NAVIGATE. COMMUNICATE. The pilots' maxim floated to the forefront of Micah's mind as he felt his way down another dimly lit tunnel. *Prioritize the situation based on immediate need.*

"Love to do that," he muttered. "If I just knew who the hell wants me dead, and where the hell I'm going."

It was frustrating to be without both his wire and his ocular implants. As difficult as it was to believe they were both malfunctioning, it was clearly the case, and he was just going to have to deal with it.

His assets were currently limited to a virtual map and some sort of spooky connection he had to... someone. A very cryptic someone. A person whose location he could almost pinpoint, though by what means, he couldn't begin to guess.

He closed his eyes and reached mentally for the voice, his body turning like a compass seeking its magnetic pole.

There. He had no idea how he knew, but the voice's owner could be found in *that* direction—not quite the destination being pushed at him, but close. He could feel the connection growing stronger as he drew near.

He resumed walking. The lab where he was headed was half a klick upspin from his current location. So far, he'd crawled up maintenance shafts, down one thankfully empty sewer pipe, and made a mad dash across a back alleyway.

That last had been his only exposure to the 'open air' of the torus's main level. He knew this was by design. What he didn't know was why he was being chased.

As he shuffled along in the dark, he took a closer look at the map the strange voice had pushed into his head. The structure he was currently passing beneath was filled with row upon row of offices. A label he missed earlier jumped out at him, and he swore.

The offices housed signals specialists and security analysts. He was in military intelligence territory. Access to these levels was restricted to those with highest clearance. Way the hell above his pay grade.

Micah realized abruptly that even if his wire had been working, there was a good chance that it would be blocked.

"Want to tell me why I'm jeopardizing my career by sneaking into areas where I'm not cleared to be?"

No talking. They'll track you.

Fantastic, he thought. *They probably think I'm an Akkadian spy or something, here to steal top secret intel.*

No, the voice returned. *You're here because **you** are Top Secret.*

Micah stilled. He hadn't spoken aloud. The words remained seared into his brain even as the mental voice faded. He cautiously reached out, pushing his thoughts toward the voice.

Are you...reading my mind?

Yes. The one-word response chilled him.

How?

Later. Right now, focus on staying alive.

The reminder that someone wanted him dead brought him up short.

Why me? Who would want me dead?

The mental voice cut him off.

Later.

He sensed the impatience behind the word. A map appeared once more—the same one he'd been following since leaving the morgue.

C'mon, Navy. Hustle.

Those three words, sent in that order, gave Micah pause.

Only one person he knew called him that. But Jack was… he was—

Elusive memory crowded at the edges of his mind.

Jack?

Later. Thoughts can't be traced, but your biosignature can.

The thought faded more quickly this time, spurring Micah forward. He banished the cobwebby memory fragments teasing the edge of his consciousness and focused on the task at hand.

His mission.

Copy that.

Decision made, he broke into a stumbling run, hand trailing blindly along the tunnel's wall, feet carrying him swiftly and silently toward his destination.

He'd grill Jack on his cryptic mental connection once he arrived.

Assuming it *was* Jack on the other end.

LOOSE ENDS

ADVANCED ISOLATION LAB
DEGRASSE RESEARCH TORUS

WITH THE ASSASSIN gone, Clint could breathe once more. He relaxed his fists on an explosive exhale and stepped up to the crate containing the biospheres. A thin, satisfied smile ghosted across his narrow features as he rested his hand atop the unit.

He was so close to the completion of this mission, he could practically taste it. Duping the Alliance had turned out to be a more satisfying pastime than he'd anticipated.

He spared the empty lab the briefest of glances before turning back to unlock the case. It had been sealed with the highest security token available—one he'd stolen from Admiral Toland the first week he'd arrived.

Acquiring the case had been a difficult undertaking; deGrasse had strict guidelines about the materials brought up from Vermilion's surface. Samples retrieved from the planet below were studied and meticulously catalogued, the findings sent to the Geminate Alliance's Department of Advanced Research back in Procyon.

Except for the ones within this case. The biospheres inside

had been created by siphoning material from each of deGrasse's labs. The plants had originally been harvested from the planet the torus orbited, the animals cloned from its rich ecosystem.

Pale green eyes swept the case's interior in a cursory inspection before quietly resealing it. With economic motions, he moved toward a shelf of stored robotic drive units and selected one that was large enough to accommodate the crate.

The drive units were ubiquitous on space stations like this one; the mechanical workhorses efficiently and automatically routed material throughout deGrasse on a daily basis. This one would deliver the sample case to Clint's office, with no record of its transit being noted, thanks to one set of carefully greased palms.

Clint found it curious that despite all the tech available, advances that had enabled Terrans to populate distant stars, his best assets often weren't tools. They were people. Human intelligence, or HumInt, remained a valuable resource, even centuries after humanity's Sol system diaspora.

Greed was still greed, regardless of the progress a society made, and it seemed there was always an enlisted grunt who could be found willing to run a side hustle for a little contraband. It was a convenient way to smuggle information, weapons, drugs...and the occasional sample case, masquerading as a supply crate.

One such person had made sure that neither the case nor the robotic drive unit Clint had just selected would show up in deGrasse's database. The torus's security system had been instructed to ignore both, should they show up on scan.

He set the robotic unit aside when his wire signaled an incoming transmission. One look at his optical overlay told him it was another Geminate asset he'd managed to turn with the promise of a few credits.

{Hey, doc. Ran into a bit of a roadblock. You know that third corpse you brought down to us?} the master sergeant's voice sounded in his head. *{Turns out he was still alive.}*

Clint tensed at this unexpected news, but before he could respond, the sergeant continued.

{Don't worry, I'm taking care of it. One of the corpsmen found out about it, though, and I had to get rid of him. That's going to cost you extra.}

Annoyance surged inside Clint. *{I paid you to dispose of a few bodies—discreetly. What part of those instructions did you fail to understand?}*

The sergeant's mental voice grew hard. *{Shit happens, doc. Deal with it.}*

{Fine,} Clint bit out after a beat, *{but get it done quickly. And no more mistakes.}*

He severed the call, then established an encrypted connection with the assassin and updated her with the news. She responded with a simple ping. But he knew her—at least as much as anyone *could* know an Akkadian assassin. She would check up on the sergeant.

He had just knelt to attach the robotic unit to the case when the sound of footsteps rapidly approaching caught his attention. Rising, he turned and reached for the weapon hidden beneath his lab coat.

The footsteps were those of Clint's immediate superior, Lee Stinton. The chief scientist came to an abrupt stop, surprise on his face when he saw Clint standing beside the sample case. It quickly morphed into anger when he spied the robotic unit sitting beside it.

"Want to tell me where the hell you think you're going with that?" The chief scientist's voice was low, but it was filled with outrage.

As he strode forward, Clint held up one hand while at the same time tightening his grip on the pistol at the small of his back. He waited to see what the other man would do.

It came to him that the sergeant had handed him an unexpected opportunity. The news about the not-dead corpse changed things. It changed everything. Stinton was now no longer critical to the completion of Clint's assignment.

A pleasurable anticipation suffused him, and he relaxed his hold on the pistol as he mentally triggered the lab's isolation mode. This sealed the two of them inside, creating an impenetrable air-gap between them and the rest of deGrasse.

Unaware that Clint had just cut them off from the rest of the torus, Stinton's face drew into thick scowl, forehead drawing down over bushy brows.

"We agreed that the best place to keep this away from prying eyes was to store it," Stinton's blunt-tipped finger jabbed at the empty space it once occupied, "right *there*."

"We did," Clint agreed in a pleasant tone. He smiled and struck a casual pose, one palm resting lightly against the case. "I'm afraid there's been a small change of plans."

Stinton narrowed his eyes. "What do you mean, 'there's been a change of plans'? The plan was that you'd help me with my side project, and in return, you'd get samples from Vermilion for your pharmaceutical company."

"That little side project was the cloning of a human. That's illegal in the Geminate Alliance, or have you forgotten?"

Stinton brushed a meaty hand through the air as if dismissing that inconvenient truth. "When they see the results, and how humanity can be helped by it—"

"They'll what?" Clint cocked an eyebrow at Stinton. "Forgive the killing of Navy personnel so that your obsessive research could be realized?"

Stinton's expression turned stern. He crossed his arms, one heavy-browed eye narrowing in an angry twitch. "Don't think you can blackmail me, Janus. Those cadavers were from a naval incident. A collision took the lives of those pilots."

Clint shook his head in mock dismay. "You can't be that naïve, Lee. Ships like the Helios and Novastrike fighters have Synthetic Intelligences equipped with the most advanced anti-collision protocols known to humankind. They're far too sophisticated to have allowed a crash during a simple practice sortie like that. At least, not without a bit of sabotage."

Stinton blanched. His head shot back as if Clint had

delivered a physical punch.

"Sabotage?" The older man blinked, stunned. "I— No one was supposed to get hurt..."

"*You* approached *me*, doctor. You were the one who argued that sometimes rules have to be broken to achieve true scientific advancement."

Clint suppressed a smile as the man sputtered a denial. Even now, the scientist didn't see he'd been played, how Clint had maneuvered him into asking for help in acquiring those cadavers.

"Your personal research project now has the blood of three innocent Navy pilots attached to it." Clint chose his words for maximum effect. "So you see, Doctor, you're in no place to dictate to me what I can and cannot do."

Stinton's shock morphed back into anger. "You're threatening me, is that it?" he said, his head lowering like a bull readying to charge. "Well, you can have your damn samples, but only when I'm good and ready. I haven't managed to successfully clone a human using the molecular material we've found here in Luyten's Star, so I'm not done yet."

Clint shook his head, a slow smile forming on his lips. "Actually, you are," he corrected. "I intercepted a call from the morgue a few minutes ago. Your latest experiment's demise was slightly exaggerated, it seems."

Stinton straightened, eyeing Clint cautiously. "Are you saying that last pilot we cloned *lived*?"

"It would appear so."

As Clint waited for Stinton to digest the information, he considered his choice of weapons to use against the man. The pistol was certainly the easiest—a quick, clean kill. But where was the fun in that?

He fingered the items in his pocket. The nanoinjector contained a few useful agents, including a neural paralytic. As his hand closed around it, his mind replayed the months spent in obsequious obedience to the man standing before him. A faint smile traced his lips, and he released the injector, wrapping his hand around a pointed, chisel-tipped stylus instead.

A thread of visceral anticipation wound through him as he faced Stinton, the stylus now fisted in his hand. There was something personal, almost intimate, about a kill using a blunt instrument. So much more satisfying than a precision tool...

"What do you mean, 'it would appear so'?" Stinton demanded, drawing Clint's attention back to the conversation. "Either he lived or he didn't. Which is it?"

Clint shrugged. "The hospital corpsman who contacted me sounded a bit shaken when he thought he'd been about to incinerate one of the Navy's finest. I didn't press for details."

I also didn't let it stand, either. I suppose it was a good thing the master sergeant was there to take care of things, after all...

He saw Stinton turn and eye the door. "This... this changes everything."

"You're right." Clint stepped forward, a smile curving across his lips as he pulled the stylus from his pocket and began to slowly advance toward the man. "It does."

A STAGED ACCIDENT

CLINT LOOKED UP from the red-stained water pooling at the base of the lab's sink. His mirrored reflection stared back at him, light green eyes so pale they were almost colorless. He reached up and swiped at a spatter of blood—Stinton's blood—that had landed on his left cheekbone.

He hated what he had to do next, but time was his enemy. He reached out once more to the assassin.

{I could use a little help. Stinton's dead.}

There was a long pause, although Clint could tell the woman had received his message. Finally, her voice sounded inside his head, the words cool, clipped.

{What have you done?}

Clint bristled at the censure in her voice.

{I had no choice. He came in after you left, found me packing the samples for transport.}

He waited for her response, but she remained silent. It was a tactic she was fond of using, to draw more information from him. He cursed his inability to hold out, but the stress inside him was building, the fear that he would be discovered too great.

{Look, it moves our timetable up, but not by much. Everything changed when we discovered Micah Case was alive.} The words tumbled from his mind in an angry rush. *{The mission's complete. You're the fixer. So get down here, dammit, and fix it.}*

No sane person provoked an Akkadian assassin. Before Clint could think too hard about the things he'd said to her—or worse, open his mouth and dig a deeper grave for himself—he closed the connection. Grabbing a nanofiber cloth, he began swiping at the spray of blood that coated the lab's doors while he awaited her arrival.

He had no idea how the assassin always managed to arrive within minutes whenever he pinged her. In the past, it had annoyed him to think she was monitoring him so closely. This time, he only felt relief when, at the five minute mark, a command sounded over his wire.

{Open,} the assassin's voice ordered, causing Clint's hand to freeze mid-swipe. He stepped back, releasing the lock.

When the doors parted to admit her, the assassin paused just long enough to identify a clear spot on the deck before leaping lithely over the spreading pool of blood that blocked the entrance.

The feeling he always had in her presence, that of being weighed and found wanting, surged within Clint as she surveyed the carnage. His hands itched to do to her what he'd done to the chief scientist, but self-preservation held him in check. He was all too aware he was no match for an Akkadian assassin. Since Clint was rather fond of living, he held his tongue

Her survey complete, the assassin pivoted to face him. "Did you at least manage to keep him from calling for help while you—" her lip curled as she glanced down at the bloodied corpse, "—had your fun?"

He was the one with the advanced degrees. *She* was nothing more than an instrument of death. And yet her tone put him in his place as if he were a recalcitrant schoolboy.

"Yes," he hissed, hating the feelings of inadequacy she could so easily conjure in him. "I'm not stupid."

Her expression told him she held a different opinion, but she let it drop. "Is there anything within this lab that is volatile? That could legitimately be blamed for an explosion or fire?"

Clint took his time surveying the room, though he already knew the answer. "Not really, no. Why?"

An expression of distaste crossed her face. "Fires are a much more effective tool for destroying evidence," she said absently as she pivoted to face the back of the lab. Inclining her head toward an alcove, she pointed to the bulky machine installed inside. It had an attached gantry arm, protruding two meters from a thick, rounded base.

"What is this?"

Clint followed her eyeline. "That's a polarized DBC prototype."

"Expendable?"

"Yes." He waved a hand. "I have the schematics. We can build our own."

"Very well." She strolled toward the alcove, studying the prototype's gantry arm. "Tell me about it," she instructed as she began a slow perusal of the unit.

"At its core, it's an altered DBC."

"DBC," she repeated.

"Yes, digital-to-biological converter. It can print complex biological material from detailed molecular diagrams."

She leveled cold eyes at him. "I know what a DBC is, Doctor." "Right. Well." He coughed, cleared his throat. "This prototype prints with a bioink created from a special hydrogel. The hydrogel is infused with stem cells, harvested from a preselected host. You *do* know what stem cells are, right?"

The words just slipped out, and instantly he wished he could call them back. The way she fingered the carbyne blade sheathed at her side suggested she was entertaining the thought of making sure he could never say them again. He averted his gaze, rushing through the rest of his explanation.

"At any rate, this DBC routes through a two-stage 3D printer. The first stage prints molecules rapidly and continuously. They're then sent through an optical centrifuge. Short pulses of polarized lasers induce a highly excited, specific rotational state in the molecules."

"You mean it reverses their chirality."

He blinked. "That's... what I said."

Impossibly, her expression hardened even more. "No, doctor. You used more than a dozen words to describe what I summed up in three."

Clint's anger surged. "I'm a scientist." He shoved a finger in her direction. "You *made* me a scientist. That's what we do."

She ignored his accusation, her gaze returning to the unit.

Clint took that as his cue to continue. He gestured toward the back of the alcove.

"Both the first stage of the printer and the optical centrifuge are housed in the rear part of the machine."

His hand swung from the rear of the unit to the heavy, two-thousand-ton gantry arm that swung around the unit's isocenter.

"The altered molecules are then used as the foundation for the NICE bioink for the second stage. That's where complete, chirally modified cellular structures are printed, based on the material we want to replicate."

The assassin pinned him with a look. "A nice ink. Next, you're going to tell me this is a friendly printer?"

"Not nice," Janus corrected sharply. "N-I-C-E. Nanoengineered ionic-covalent entanglement."

The warning in the assassin's eyes told Clint he was done with his lofty exposition.

"In other words," she said, her tone soft yet icy, "it makes chiral copies of normal plants and animals."

He opened his mouth to clarify, but then began to nod

rapidly when she took two deliberate steps toward him. He had to force himself not to shrink at her approach.

"*Wǒ bú zài hū,*" she snapped. "I do not *care* what it can do. The only thing I care about, doctor, is whether or not you can make that thing swing freely."

She pointed to the gantry arm.

His mouth opened and closed. He swallowed, then nodded.

She pierced him with a severe look. "Good."

Her gaze swept him from head to toe, not bothering to mask her disgust as she tilted her head to indicate the carnage by the lab's entrance.

"Bring me the body, and then go clean up your mess."

The muscles in Clint's jaw bunched at her dismissal. Though it rankled, he did as instructed, depositing the body just inside the room. He then jogged back to the front of the lab and begin cleaning off the blood that stained deck, doors, and bulkhead.

Once done, he rejoined the assassin.

She looked up at him from where she knelt, adjusting Stinton's corpse. She moved the body three more times before she was satisfied with the results. Rising on silent feet, she stepped back, the expectant look on her face telling Clint the rest was up to him.

They retreated to the alcove's entrance. He powered up the machine, taking care to use Stinton's own security token to activate it, and then glanced over at the assassin.

"I'm bypassing the unit's safety lockouts now," he informed her. "That should allow the gantry head to swing freely."

The assassin's head tilted up in silent acknowledgement. "Do it. And let us hope that your machine does enough damage to mask the injuries you inflicted."

Clint pressed his lips together to prevent himself from commenting. He merely nodded and sent the command for the final lockout to disappear.

For an instant, the gantry head hovered in midair, perfectly balanced. In the next moment, it began to sway. And then it toppled, gathering speed as it neared the deck, slamming into

Stinton with the force of a maglev train at top speed.

UNLIKELY EVENTS

MEDICAL CENTER
DEGRASSE RESEARCH TORUS

ADAHY "ADDY" MASON sat at her desk inside deGrasse's medical center and stared at the charts she'd thrown up onto her holo display.

The cases were closed, the patients deceased. The charts on the right were two weeks old, and detailed the treatment of a pair of pilots involved in a collision.

The first pilot, a Navy lieutenant, had been dead on arrival. Although they'd fought fiercely to revive her, they'd been unsuccessful.

The second pilot was another matter. When she'd left the clinic that night, he'd been in guarded but stable condition. Inexplicably, three hours later, the man was gone.

As for the third chart—

A knock sounded, interrupting Addy's thoughts. She looked up to see Gabriel Alvarez, deGrasse's chief of security, leaning against the door frame of her office.

"Got a few minutes?" he asked, and Addy nodded, gesturing to a nearby chair.

"What's up?" She pushed away from her desk to face him.

He tilted his head toward the holos she had on display.

"Those the reports on the pilots who died?"

She nodded again.

"Awfully high death rate on deGrasse these days."

Though the words seemed innocuous enough, the look he shot her suggested that he might harbor his own doubts about the reasons behind them.

Addy's lips pressed into a thin line.

"Unusually high," she agreed, voice rough with frustrated anger.

Gabe motioned to the reports.

"I've found that if you talk things over with an objective third person, they can sometimes surprise you by spotting things you might have overlooked yourself."

She blew out a breath.

"There's no new information, though I wish there were. These are the same reports I sent you. Nothing's changed since we last talked."

Gabe shrugged. "Sometimes it just takes times for things to gel," he tapped the side of his head, "up here."

She shot him a look that held little hope, but shrugged and turned to face the reports once more.

"Okay, then. From the top it is."

Tapping the first one to enlarge it, she flicked a finger down its length to scroll the document to the beginning. Stopping at the header, she began to read.

"At sixteen hundred hours local, we were notified by deGrasse Space Traffic Control that there had been an incident, and wounded were incoming. Samantha Travis and I were the attending physicians. I took the Navy lieutenant, and she took the Marine."

She paused when Gabe crossed his arms and frowned.

"I know we discussed this before," he said, "but Travis isn't a member of your team. She's one of the researchers. You told me she had a medical background, but—no offense—why was she down here? Are you sure the Marine's death wasn't due to operator error?"

Addy shook her head firmly.

"It wasn't, I can assure you. You're right about Sam being one of the scientists. But she's also a practicing physician at one of the top research hospitals back in Procyon. Sam heard the news on the torus's pubnet, and contacted me, offering her assistance."

Addy crossed her own arms, unconsciously mimicking Alvarez's stance.

"I'd trust her with any of my patients. I'd put my own care in her hands. She's just that good."

Gabe shot her a brief smile. He lifted his hands, palms out, as if to forestall any additional protests.

"Got it. No worries. Just had to ask." Lowering he hands, his eyes shifted back to the report. "Go on, then. You mentioned the two vics. If I recall, Ettinger was the Navy lieutenant, and Campbell the Marine, right?"

She nodded confirmation to his query.

"The lieutenant was DOA, although with current medical practices, death isn't necessarily a permanent thing until all brain activity has ceased, and that usually occurs within seven to ten minutes."

Gabe's eyebrows rose. "Didn't know about that. Good information to have." He coughed a self-deprecating laugh. "Okay, well, there's not much I'd be able to do with it, except get the victim to you as quickly as possible."

"We're not always able to resuscitate," she cautioned, "although we give it our best shot. In this case, the damage was too extensive. We lost her."

"Hmm." Gabe shook his head. "Even with all the medical advances, the nano available—"

He cut himself off as she, in turn, shook her head.

"It's not the silver bullet everyone seems to think it is. Sure, nanotech can work wonders, but it has its limits. The very word itself gives you the first clue."

She smiled at his raised brow. "Medical nano is *tiny*. That means it takes a lot of it to make a difference, especially if the nanorobotics in play are performing a task, not just delivering a medication. If the damage they're set to repair is too systemic..."

Comprehension flowed into his eyes as she let her voice trail off. She turned away, her explanation reminding her of how very extensive Ettinger's wounds had been, beyond her ability to counteract.

Failure to save the pilot felt just as raw as her very first loss, despite the years of experience which had led to her current role as deGrasse's chief physician. They never seemed to get any easier. To be honest, she hoped they never would.

"And the Marine. Campbell?" Gabe prodded after a moment of silence passed between them.

Addy returned her focus to the report hovering before her.

"He and Sam arrived on deGrasse on the same transport. She knew Jack, had struck up a friendship with him on the way here." Addy shook her head, remembering. "She was determined to save him."

A gesture brought up Campbell's personnel file, linked to the report. The image of a stocky, auburn-haired man appeared. He had the typical, well-muscled build of a Marine. The man looked fit and healthy, a far cry from the last time Addy'd laid eyes on him.

"Jack Campbell had no preexisting or hidden conditions that might have contributed to his injuries," she said. "His back had been broken in several places, he received numerous contusions, suffered a fractured femur, and his spleen had ruptured."

Gabe whistled. "I remember that from the report. That collision had to have been intense to have done that kind of damage."

His attention swerved from the holo to her.

"He had a standard pilot's lattice, didn't he?"

"Yes, the injuries occurred in spite of it," she confirmed,

pulling up a scan of the man's torso.

Pointing to a network of filaments that permeated the patient's organs, she said, "Campbell had the same standard-issue SmartCarbyne nanofloss issued to all military pilots. It's woven throughout their soft tissues. It's what kept him alive. And honestly, when we left that night, he was doing just fine."

"Until he wasn't."

Gabe's statement landed harshly between them. Addy looked up, expecting from his tone to read censure in his eyes. There was anger there, but she realized it wasn't directed at her when he spoke again.

"Clint Janus was the one here with him when he died." The words were flat and hard. Addy wondered suddenly if she and Sam weren't the only ones who disliked the man.

"Yes," she said cautiously, feeling her way through her next statements. "You know he showed up shortly after the medics brought the two pilots in."

Gabe's expression was impassive. "I didn't realize he had a medical background, too."

Addy shrugged uncomfortably. "I didn't really have the time to check his record. Each patient had an attending physician, so his role was both secondary and under supervision."

She fiddled absently with a stylus on her desk. "He offered his services in any capacity and frankly, since we were in an all-hands-on-deck situation, I was happy to have the help," she admitted. "He basically functioned as a highly overqualified errand boy, schlepping whatever the surgeon needed from medical stores."

"No suspicious activity?" Gabe pressed.

"Was his behavior completely out of character? Yes. Suspicious? Not really." She shook her head, positive of these facts, at least.

It had been natural to suspect Janus when she learned of Campbell's demise. She'd grilled everyone who'd been in the operating theatre that day; none had witnessed him doing anything remotely questionable.

"Okay, then." Gabe bent forward and braced his forearms on his thighs. He looked up at her from beneath lowered brows. "Would it be accurate to say he returned to the clinic in the wee hours of the morning, when you had a skeleton crew?"

Addy waggled her hand. "I wouldn't call it skeleton. We were staffed appropriately for the patients currently in our care."

"Yet Janus was the one who told you Campbell was gone." It was a statement, not a question, but Addy nodded anyway.

"He pinged me an hour before my alarm went off. Said he'd stopped in to check on him before heading to the DFAC for breakfast," she said, using the Navy's term for the torus's dining facility. "According to him, Campbell coded while he was there. He claimed he was unable to resuscitate him."

"Bit odd, don't you think?" Gabe sat back, pinning her with an inscrutable look.

Addy grimaced. "More than a bit. Janus has never, not once, stooped to doing that kind of menial work. Just my opinion, but I think he considers caring for deGrasse personnel—hell, anything other than his precious research—to be beneath him."

"But he came when he heard. Pitched in."

She nodded. "He was actually useful, too. Something that truly surprised me."

Addy's finger hovered over the line in the report where Janus had turned Campbell's body over to the morgue himself. Something about the whole thing rang hollow to her.

"Janus has to have an angle," she murmured. "There has to be a reason behind his out-of-character helpfulness that night. But damned if I can figure it out."

Her eyes tracked to the final report, this one from just last week. It was of another in-flight accident, and it involved only one pilot.

"Then there's Micah Case." Gabe's comment told Addy he'd noticed her attention shift. "There's almost four weeks between the first crash and that incident."

Addy tapped on the date. He was right, of course. She hadn't needed the document to confirm it. The dates were seared into her brain, two failures, one right after the other. Unless...

"Just enough time to throw suspicion off, if there really is a connection." Her tone lifted at the end as she let the unspoken question settle between them.

Gabe shook his head. "I just received the initial report back from the second one. Findings suggest metal fatigue is to blame for his spacecraft's failure."

Addy had a hard time deciphering his expression.

"So, not pilot error, as was the case with the first accident," she said.

He shook his head. "Doesn't look that way, no."

"Still. Two accidents in little under a month, whereas before the torus had boasted a flawless record."

"Janus wasn't around when this one died, was he?"

Addy began to shake her head then paused, thinking back. "Actually, he was, but Sam told me she refused to let him anywhere near the patient."

"And still, he died."

She nodded and felt a surge of uncertainty as she met his gaze. There was no way she was going to tell Gabe about Sam's odd behavior the next morning, how her colleague danced around specifics, claiming she was too upset to discuss the situation at the moment.

Something about the stiff way Samantha Travis had held herself set off alarms in Addy's head, but until she had a moment to question Sam more thoroughly in private, she'd keep her unease to herself.

Addy returned to the first report, eyes seeking the line that stated Janus had taken Campbell's body to the morgue.

"Now, why would he do that, I wonder?"

"Do what?"

She highlighted the section of the report and enlarged it for him.

Gabe narrowed his eyes. "Addy, I need you to think back on

that morning. You spoke with everyone who was there when Janus arrived. I know he didn't say or do anything unusual, or they would have reported it. But is it normal for a body to be sent to the morgue this quickly after death?"

Her mouth twisted. "Actually, yes. Completely within scope."

Gabe steepled his fingers, brought the tips up and tapped them against his chin, his eyes locked with hers.

After a moment, he said slowly, "And what about after a body arrives at the morgue? What's the procedure there?"

Gabe interrupted himself, sitting up abruptly and holding a hand up in a 'wait' gesture that told Addy he was receiving an incoming call. His face darkened, and he stood.

"I have to go. Looks like you're going to get to play medical examiner today, doc." His eyes cut to hers, their expression grim. "They've found another body."

AID AND ABET

MEDICAL RESEARCH LAB 1A
DEGRASSE RESEARCH TORUS

{MICAH'S ON THE move.} The voice came unexpectedly over Samantha Travis's wire as she raced to pack the supplies her patient would need to survive.

Startled at the intrusion, she tripped and reached instinctively to brace herself, forgetting the crate in her hands. It fell, spilling its contents across the deck.

Blowing out a sharp, annoyed breath, Sam lunged for the duffel she'd set out, tagging her hand against the hard edge of a countertop in her haste. She shook off the sting with a stifled curse.

{Tell him to hurry,} she shot back in response as she bent to transfer the scattered bioplas packets from the spilled crate into the duffel.

{Can't. You know that. He has to stay out of sight, or they'll find him. If they do, they'll make sure they finish the job this time.}

{I know. I know,} she replied, shoving visions of the morgue's incinerator to the back of her mind. She didn't have

time to deal with that right now.

{I've had to send him crawling through sewer pipes, for stars's sake.}

She didn't respond to the voice this time, just continued filling her hands with the last of the spilled packets. Swiping her hair out of her face with one forearm, she stuffed the last of the packets in with the rest and then pressed the bag's closure, not taking the time to watch as it sealed itself.

The voice sounded in her head again, insistent.

{He won't know you, doctor.} The words were harsh, a warning. They lingered in her mind long after the mental voice faded.

"I know that," she snapped aloud, propelling the duffel toward the lab's entrance.

She raced toward the back of the room, where cylinders of nano formation material and molecular bricks were stored.

A quick, careless sweep had them tumbling into a second bag, bricks and cylinders clattering as they fell. This she sent sliding across the deck to join the duffel.

*{He's just outside. You have to go. **Now**.}*

Sam didn't bother with a response. She bent to palm a stray brick that had missed the bag. Dropping it absently into a lab coat pocket, her gaze danced anxiously across the room one last time.

{He's already been spotted once since escaping the morgue. If they see him again...}

She blew out an impatient breath as she shoved away from the storage area, the voice spurring her into action. Sam understood the risks, knew better than most the dangers the man faced if caught.

{How about a little assistance in that department?} she asked. *{A distraction, maybe? Or something to help mask our departure?}*

Her eyes snagged on the last digital-to-biological converter, maglocked to the wall behind the remaining portable surgical suite. Sam veered toward it, intent on adding the DBC to her cache on her way out.

The miniature DBC would allow her to print medical supplies and pharmaceuticals on demand, using the stash of molecular bricks she'd just packed. Where she was going, she'd take every advantage she could get. She pocketed it, sparing one last, longing glance at the surgical suite as she passed by.

She'd hated to leave the suite behind, but the absence of such a large piece of equipment would have been too difficult to hide in the days leading up to this. Thankfully, deGrasse had an older model kept in storage as a backup; they'd opted to load this one onto the ship instead. It would have to do.

The lights in the lab abruptly cut out, and Sam stumbled to a halt. Her optical implants automatically cycled to a more optimized setting, using the fading residual glow from the wireless charging strip to throw the lab into an eerie green twilight.

{Better?} the voice asked in amusement.

{That'll do,} she replied, as she started for the lab's entrance.

She'd made it halfway when the charging strip's faint illumination faded. This time, the darkness was so complete, not even her optical implants could overcome it. She kept moving, hands splayed before her to feel her way past any obstacles, as she crossed the last few meters.

Her foot connected with something soft that clanked. The formation bricks. She'd made it to the door.

She felt around for the manual release and the door slid open with a groan, emergency batteries laboring under the load. Red light filtered in from the corridor the moment the doors parted.

She wedged a hand into the space between them and began to push, bracing a shoulder against the heavy doors to widen the opening. A hand came down between her shoulder blades and she jerked back, twisting reflexively to evade the perceived threat.

Emergency lighting in the passageway revealed the figure

of a man. He hesitated for a brief moment, his eyes meeting hers in question. She sucked in a hard breath and nodded. He turned to finish what she'd begun, large hands making short work of the halfway-open door.

Sam's wire pinged, identifying the man limned by the pulse of red passageway lights. She knew what the database embedded in her head had done; it had run the silhouette's bio signature against that of known base personnel. Her jaw tightened as she read the label, hating the overlay's annotation.

CAPTAIN JONATHAN MICAH CASE. ALLIANCE NAVY, SRU. DECEASED.

Like hell he is, she thought fiercely as he turned to face her.

Micah's voice reached her in the darkness. "Are you—"

"Come on," she interrupted, shoving the duffel into his hands. "It's not safe here." She bent to retrieve the pack. She straightened, slinging its strap over her shoulders as she slid through the parted doors. "This way."

ACCIDENT INVESTIGATION

ADVANCED ISOLATION LAB
DEGRASSE RESEARCH TORUS

HALF A KILOMETER away, in the torus's research complex, the discovery of Lee Stinton's body had turned the Advanced Isolation Lab into a warren of frenzied activity.

"Coming through," Gabe announced to the gaggle of onlookers hovering around the holographic 'Police Line—Do Not Cross' banner at the lab's entrance. He deactivated the ticker and pushed past them, Addy at his heels.

"Hold up a second," she called out, snagging his arm just as he walked through the open doors. A quick glance down the corridor told him the instructions Addy had shouted to her medical team as they ran from her office had been implemented. Medics were coming in fast, laden with supplies and pushing a maglev gurney.

"They made good time," he said.

Addy shot him a glance. "In emergency medicine, time is

everything."

"They do realize Stinton's dead, don't they?"

She exhaled—a quick, sharp breath. "Time's a factor when you're gathering forensic evidence, too."

He nodded, pleased to see that her people recognized that.

Now wasn't the time to enlighten Addy about his true rank in the Alliance Navy, nor his official title as a criminal investigator. They hadn't exactly come out and said that Gabe's assignment was an undercover operation, but he found it telling that the Navy's Criminal Investigation Command had altered his work history on the public military net.

Gabe's superior had told him Admiral Toland had specifically requested an NCIC operator for deGrasse's chief of security. He wondered if Toland was prescient, or if she'd just known news about the research in Luyten's was likely to leak and draw unwanted attention.

Either way, his highly-trained, analytical brain was telling him this temporary assignment was no longer simply Toland's insurance policy. The situation now warranted an official NCIC investigation.

Now that the medical team had made it past the onlookers, Gabe reactivated the police line tape and turned for a slower, more thorough survey of the room.

The security officers were gathered just outside an alcove, with a fireteam of four Marines in powered armor. Beside them stood Clint Janus. Gabe's eyes narrowed as they landed on the man. He glanced at Addy, wondering if she'd noticed Janus's presence yet. The slight flicker of an eyelid told him she had.

The officer in charge signaled to Gabe. He lifted a hand in silent response, then turned to Addy and tilted his head in the direction of the group. She nodded, falling into step beside him.

"Sir," the officer greeted, then gestured to the Marines in powered armor. "I called in a fireteam to help with the removal of the body. Doctor Janus said the printer pinning

Doctor Stinton is too heavy to displace otherwise. I didn't think you'd want to trust the machine's interface to do it, given the circumstances."

Addy eyed the scene. "I'll need to take a look first, but yes," she said, "that sounds like a good call."

One of the Marines stepped forward. "We'll be your muscle, ma'am. You just tell us how you want that thing moved, and we'll do it for you."

Gabe peered around one of the Marines to get a glimpse at the mangled remains of deGrasse's chief scientist, flattened beneath the gantry arm. Motioning everyone back, he said, "Let's give the doctor and her team some room."

He waited while Addy waved her medics and their gurney over and retrieved a few pieces of gear. When she stepped into the alcove, Gabe followed.

It appeared that Stinton had been facing the gantry arm when it impacted him. He found that strange. Surely the scientist would have noticed the thing swinging toward him and tried to evade. The blow shouldn't be so head-on...

He saw Addy stiffen, her body held frozen for a moment as if in shock. Then she moved, releasing a microdrone. It flew to Stinton's approximate center of mass and began rotating around the dead body, progressing slowly outward.

Once she confirmed the drone was behaving as she'd programmed it to do, Addy began skirting the area. Her actions were careful and deliberate.

He stepped up beside her, resting one hand lightly on her elbow, the action enough to generate a direct, peer-to-peer connection.

{What is it?} he asked, his eyes taking in the blood spatter pattern and the position of the body, and wondering if she would confirm his suspicions.

She sprayed a nano coating on her hands, the action gloving them and protecting anything she touched from contamination. She shot him a side glance.

{Spray pattern is consistent with how the machine impacted

the body. But Gabe...}

Her eyes flickered to the people around her, before drilling into his.

{We have a big problem here.}

* * *

Addy felt Gabe's hand on her arm tighten in warning, and then he interrupted her.

{Not a word, Mason,} Gabe's mental voice held caution as he lifted a holorecorder with his free hand and thumbed it on. With a murmured, "Need to record this, doc," he trained his eyes back onto the scene before them.

{Focus, doctor. Eyes on the machine.} His tone was terse. *{I need you to keep your shit together, okay? You can't act as if this was a murder scene.}*

She turned to face him, startled. *{You see it, too, then.}*

A warning light flashed in his eyes, causing her to turn and stare unseeingly at the machine in front of them.

{There's not nearly enough blood to account for his death,} she said. *{A man Stinton's size should have had over five liters of blood in him. I can tell just by looking that the blunt trauma insult would have expelled more than what we see here.}*

Gabe sent her a mental nod. A gentle nudge had her continuing their perimeter walk while he rotated the camera to catch the scene from all angles.

{I know. Look—} He hesitated, glanced over at the alcove's entrance before returning his gaze to the camera. *{The last thing we want to do is cause panic to spread. You saw how upset the lab techs were when we arrived. Tensions are high; let's not add to that just yet.}*

Addy shot a glance over her shoulder at Clint Janus. When she returned to face the corpse, she caught a knowing look in Gabe's eyes.

{Disliking someone isn't evidence,} Gabe warned, as if reading her mind.

{I'm not the only one, you know,} she retorted. *{Samantha Travis suspects him, too. We discussed it after the first accident, but neither one of us could find anything he did wrong. At least, nothing we could point to.}*

{Just... try to act as normally as you can around him. If you don't think you can, then avoid engaging with him, okay?}

She sent him a small chuckle. *{Avoiding the man is one thing I can do. With pleasure.}*

Straightening, Gabe snapped off the camera. "Got what I need. What do you think, doc? Ready for the Marines to do their thing?"

Addy consulted the drone and saw that it had gathered all the measurable external data possible: distances, air composition, surface composition and so on. She knelt beside the wall where a small spattering of blood had reached and aligned a small device between its surface and what she could see of the top of Stinton's head. The device measured the distance and captured several additional data points.

Nodding, she stood. "Ready," she said, and followed Gabe to the alcove's entrance. Releasing the nanosheath that gloved her hands, she stepped over to the gurney to wait for the Marines to finish with the gantry arm. As she did, she caught Janus staring at her. The supercilious expression on the man's face made her forget everything Gabe had just said to her. Anger swept through her and she returned his cold stare.

* * *

Clint's eyes narrowed at the angry look the doctor was sending his way.

Officious bitch.

He knew Adahy Mason. She'd been the attending physician the night of the accident involving the Navy pilots. She'd made the job of acquiring the corpses almost impossible, not least because she'd managed to save Campbell.

After the trouble he'd gone through to stage the accident,

the damned Marine had refused to die. He'd had to use extraordinary measures to harvest that second corpse for Stinton. At least the Navy lieutenant had had the decency to stay dead, despite Mason's attempts to resuscitate her.

A familiar smell teased Clint's nose as the gurney floated toward him. It was a particular aroma, slightly metallic, catalyzed by human blood when it came into contact with human skin. He shelved the pleasant memories it evoked, knowing he could indulge at his leisure, at a later time.

For now, he had a job to do, though not the one the Alliance had for him. It was time to focus the civilian science team back onto the task of destroying samples and purging their files.

They stood, gathered at the lab's entrance as if frozen, shock writ plainly upon their faces at the sudden demise of their leader. A few showed a morbid fascination he understood all too well.

The accident site had been every bit as gory as he could have hoped, Stinton's body barely identifiable. He found himself amused by those individuals, as they craned their necks for a glimpse of the DBC prototype's blood-spattered, fallen gantry.

His eyes flicked to a corner, where the assassin stood. She was dressed in the unassuming coveralls of an engineering technician, awaiting her turn to service the malfunctioning machine.

Her job was done for the moment. It fell on him to obtain the last remaining bits of research material from the scientific teams. Clearing his throat, Clint stepped forward, the movement garnering the attention of the assembled scientists.

"All right," he began, spreading his arms and schooling his features to exude a compassionate yet firm authority. "Let's give the medical team the space they need to do their jobs. Please return to your stations and resume your work. We still have a deadline to meet, and samples to space."

There was a sharp intake of breath from one of the junior scientists. "About that order to destroy all the samples," she ventured timidly. "Doctor Stinton wouldn't want—"

"We're civilians, not military," Clint cut her off, then forced a smile to soften the blow. "If the Navy says to shut down, then we shut down." He took a moment to establish eye contact with the ones who looked the most recalcitrant. "Let me be clear. All data, all copies, must be wiped after you deliver the information to me. This is not negotiable. Understood?"

He saw it in their faces; none truly had the heart to oppose him. The assassin had been correct; the shock of a death always made people more pliable. Still, he thought it prudent to offer an olive branch, however false it might be.

"New samples can always be gathered from the planet surface when we return," he said, injecting soothing reassurance into his voice. "And we *will* return."

The lie slipped easily from his tongue.

"The truly irreplaceable part of the work we've done here on deGrasse is your research. So please. Gather your materials—quickly, and send your findings on to me before second shift."

Faces stared at him blankly. Impatience threatened to slip its leash. He clapped his hands together sharply. "*Now*, ladies and gentlemen. That was not a request."

Biochemists, nanogeneticists, laboratory technicians—they all jumped as one at the noise, like a flock of birds at the sound of a gunshot. Within moments, the passageway had emptied.

The Akkadian assassin's voice sounded inside his head, interrupting his musings. *{Sharp words, doctor. Persist, and you jeopardize your cover and endanger the mission.}*

Clint's annoyance overrode the unease he felt to find the assassin had approached him from behind—noiselessly. He fought the urge to shake off the hand that touched his arm.

{I think even the most congenial of people would be allowed a bit of temper after seeing a 'close colleague' dismembered, don't you think?} he shot back.

When she didn't respond, he looked over to find she'd retreated once more. Unnerved despite himself, he glanced at the time stamp on his overlay. It was already noon, station time.

Just a few more hours, he thought, *and I'll be able to wash my hands of the lot of them.*

He turned to find the medical doctor studying him through narrowed eyes. He returned it with one of his own.

"Please don't let us keep you from your work, Doctor Mason," he said smoothly, and with an arched brow. "I'm sure you have forms to submit or tests to run…"

Her lips compressed in displeasure and she exchanged a look with deGrasse's security chief, who shook his head, eyes grazing Clint's briefly before returning to Mason.

"You go on ahead with the body, doc," the man said, rising from his crouch beside the blood-stained deck. "My team'll be finished in a few. We'll send you everything we find."

His words drew Clint's attention to those crawling around the gantry arm, taking measurements and gathering samples. He failed to notice the suspicious look Mason threw his way, and the subtle, warning head-shake the security office sent her in response.

"Very well, then." The doctor's response was terse. With one last look at the alcove that housed the polarized DBC prototype, she eased away from the scene of the incident. Pausing at the lab's entrance, she added, "I'll be in medical if you need me."

With a nod, she was gone.

ON THE MOVE

RESEARCH WING
DEGRASSE RESEARCH TORUS

THE WOMAN MICAH followed had the build of someone raised planetside. Ceriba, maybe. Or Beryl, if she hailed from Sirius. She looked vaguely familiar, but he couldn't tell if that feeling was coming from him, or if it emanated from the strange voice inside his head.

She strode down the poorly lit, steel-reinforced passageway with a confidence and determined urgency that told him that her optical implants were working just fine.

There was only one problem: she was headed away from the nearest lift, which in turn, would lead them to the torus's flight deck.

Just as he was about to point this out to her, she stopped abruptly. He barely managed to avoid plowing into her.

"Sorry, optics are offline," he began, bracing one hand on the bulkhead's smooth, cool surface while reaching out to touch her shoulder with the other.

She cut him off, twisting suddenly to place her fingers against his lips.

"People up ahead."

Her voice was low, a mere breath. He paused, listening, but heard nothing. She pressed them both back against the wall and waited.

Finally in the distance, he heard voices. Sharp, urgent commands followed by footsteps pounding the deck. Searching for him? The sounds faded and she urged him forward with a tug on his flight suit.

"We're going the wrong way," he tried again. "Ships are docked in the other direction, if we want to—"

"Not all of them, Captain," came her terse voice.

He tripped then righted himself. "You know me?"

"Not *now*," she hissed, breaking into a trot. "We have another half kilometer to go before we reach the access hatch. If they catch you, you're dead. Understand? Now, come *on*."

* * *

Sam knew the man behind her was operating without any of the enhancements the Alliance Navy gave to their service members. At the moment, he was at an even greater disadvantage then the average human. He was currently operating only with the basic DNA Jonathan Micah Case had been gifted when he was born.

That meant it was up to Sam to get them safely to the hatch and off the torus.

"No sweat," she muttered as she made a fast left into a cross stub that would intersect with the outer passageway.

The Rim Passage was so named because its bulkhead was fused to the dense, composite-alloy regolith that shielded its inhabitants from the dangers of high-energy particles and ionizing radiation.

Used only by maintenance personnel, the area was usually deserted—or so she'd been told.

A few meters down that passageway was a little-used service hatch, and it was there that an escape craft awaited them. She hoped to hell its pilot was as skilled as he claimed to be.

The deck vibrated under the soles of Sam's boots as a blast struck the torus. She inhaled sharply and jolted to a stop, head cocked.

The man behind her wrapped a steadying hand around her arm. When she started to move once more, his hand tightened in a warning squeeze. She looked up to meet his concerned eyes.

"That… was an explosion."

UNDER ATTACK

EN ROUTE TO MEDICAL
DEGRASSE RESEARCH TORUS

THE MOMENT HE could break free from the investigation, Gabe went in search of Addy.

The lift from the laboratory deck dumped him out into deGrasse Park. It was the only true open area on the torus. From here, one could see through the clearsteel 'roof' that ran along the inside of the ring, half a kilometer away.

Its transparency wasn't for aesthetic purposes. At night, all that could be seen were a network of struts that connected the torus to the five fusion-powered generators at its center. These rotated the ring, providing artificial gravity.

During deGrasse's day-cycle, a series of complex mirrors directed the rays from Luyten's red dwarf down into the torus, bathing the park in golden light.

He'd always thought it was a stretch to call the area a park, no matter how they'd tried to dress it up with a fountain at its center.

They even ringed the damn thing with park benches.

Shaking his head, he turned toward the clinic. It sat

opposite the open-air park, which in turn sat between the research complex and the common area that housed the DFAC, a handful of smaller shops, a coffee house, and even a small pub.

As he strode across the small greenspace, he looked up, eyeing the light pouring in from above to gauge the time of day. He had a habit of doing that whenever he was planetside, even though it was just as convenient to consult his wire.

He could tell it was nearing the end of first shift.

Wonder if I can talk Addy into dinner? We could discuss the case over the meal.

Just as he neared the complex that housed the torus's clinic, he heard a series of rolling, low frequency rumbles. They were accompanied by a slight shivering of the deck beneath his feet.

That felt like an explosion.

He pivoted slowly, trying to pinpoint the origin of the sounds.

An icon flashing on his HUD warned him of an incoming call.

His eyes narrowed when he saw the ID attached to it.

Colonel Nate Fraley was Admiral Toland's second, the man responsible for the torus in her absence. Fraley was also the only other person besides Toland who knew Gabe's true identity.

{Alvarez.} Fraley's voice was gruff. *{Marines are in pursuit of two suspects. They have eyes on, and are rounding them up now. Need you to take point on this.}*

{What are they suspected of doing, Colonel?}

Gabe turned back toward the clinic, pushing aside his concern over the rumbling sound as he focused on the information Fraley was sharing.

{Anonymous tip linked them to Stinton's death,} the colonel's replied. *{You know procedure. I'll have the Marines hand them off to your people once they're in custody. Interrogate them, see what they know. Innocent people don't run from Marines, Alvarez. You know that.}*

Gabe wasn't certain he entirely agreed with Fraley's assessment, but refrained from commenting.

{We'll take care of it, Colonel,} he assured the man instead, then took a gamble. *{Any connection to what I just heard coming from the research sector? Sounded like an explosion.}*

{Too early to know,} came the colonel's quick reply.

His evasive tone reminded Gabe of those times when someone outside the investigation asked him a question about an ongoing case they weren't cleared to know about.

{What about the suspects? Have they been IDed?}

{They have,} Fraley sent. *{You know that pilot flying the Novastrike that broke up in flight last week? Seems the news of Micah Case's death was a bit exaggerated. He's been spotted with one of the scientists, a Samantha Travis.}*

{Travis?} Gabe pulled up short, startled.

Shit. Addy's going to be pissed.

To Fraley, he said, *{That can't be right. Can you patch me into their combat net?}*

{Already done,} Fraley assured him, and Gabe saw an icon flashing on his HUD, awaiting his approval to complete the connection. *{Wish I could say they're wrong, but I saw some of the footage from one of the Marines' feeds myself. It's them.}*

Gabe sent a mental whistle.

{Things just got a lot more interesting.}

{Damn straight,} Fraley responded curtly, and then just as abruptly dropped the connection.

Not looking forward to the conversation ahead of him, Gabe strode through the clinic's entrance—just as the deck beneath his feet heaved and a loud explosion reverberated through the exterior bulkhead half a block away.

EVASIVE MANEUVERS

UNDERGROUND PASSAGEWAY
DEGRASSE RESEARCH TORUS

WHEN THE DECK settled once more beneath Sam's feet, the man in front of her released the steadying hand he'd laid upon her shoulder. The pilot shot her a penetrating look. "You sure we'll be safe, wherever we're headed?"

He had a point. She held up a hand and reached out to the voice.

{Is the torus under attack?}

After a beat, the voice responded. *{It is, but not near your location. Shouldn't be a factor.}*

Another detonation, closer this time, slammed them both hard against the passageway's bulkhead.

*{Are you **sure** about that?}* she began, but severed the connection when a shouted "Freeze!" sounded from behind them. She looked frantically around for an exit to duck into but saw nothing but smooth bulkhead around them.

The man at her back swore, then she was abruptly shoved to one side, his frame covering hers. The man jerked slightly and a cold, burning sensation ran down her left arm.

A frisson of fear spread through Sam as realization set in. Someone was shooting at them.

* * *

THE WEAPON THAT had been fired at Micah and the woman he was shielding missed them both, though just barely. As the pressure wave dissipated down the passageway, Micah chanced a glance behind them. The shot had come from a compact ultra-short pulse pistol, or CUSP, held in the hand of the first of two Marines just rounding the corner.

Micah suspected it wasn't his quick action that turned the shot into a glancing blow. More likely, the Marine's aim had been hasty. He doubted the next one would miss.

"Go! Go!" He dropped the duffel she'd given him to carry and drew his own pistol, pushing her toward the intersection. He silently willed the woman onward as he fired back at the Marines, but the woman with him resisted. She scrambled for the bag he'd abandoned, but he yanked her forward, jinking left to avoid the next pressure wave from the two in pursuit.

Thankfully, the Marine shooting had widened the beam in an attempt to better hit their now-moving target. It weakened the pulse, leaving a cold burning sensation in its wake as Micah shielded the woman from another blast.

"We *need* what's in that duffel!" she hissed, struggling against his hold.

"We *need* to stay alive," he shot back, dragging her forcibly forward and doing his best to make their track as erratic as the passageway would allow.

They only had another two meters to go. He thumbed his own sidearm to wide dispersal as he ran, but before he could return fire, a loud crack echoed in the confined space, followed by a muted *thwack*.

Shit, they're not fooling around!

Micah knew that sound. It came from a small caliber firearm, the kind that could be safely discharged within a structure like deGrasse.

The bullet spent itself harmlessly against the bulkhead, the softer metal's kinetic energy dissipating upon impact as it flattened the projectile against the surface. The weapon might not pose a threat to the torus, but it could easily tear through the more delicate medium of human flesh.

He urged the woman to a faster pace.

They'd just reached the corner when a whine reached his ears and a pressure wave from the Marine's CUSP hit his leg. Micah lost his footing, the EM pulse causing searing pain to trace down his right side.

The Marine wielding the small-caliber pistol took aim once more, and he willed his body to move, the woman with him reaching to pull him clear of the intersection. Another crack sounded, and Micah felt a stinging sensation slash across the side of his head. He lifted a hand to his forehead and it came away slick with blood, the bullet having creased his temple.

Blindly, he aimed his pistol around the corner and pulled the trigger, hoping the return fire would keep them back long enough for feeling to return in his leg.

"I'm a doctor; let me see." The words were hastily whispered as the woman crouched beside him.

He shoved her hand away. "No time. We have to move."

He levered himself to standing with the woman's assistance as another hail of bullets spattered against the deck. He got off another shot with his own weapon, and then turned to the woman.

"Come on. Let's go."

He pulled at her arm, but she resisted. Her gaze drifted back to the intersection.

"Good thing we're in a rotating torus. The physics of rotation makes it harder to hit what you're aiming at."

Unfortunately for Micah and his mysterious companion, the people after them were highly trained Marines. The processing power in their implants made live targeting solutions an easy thing.

"Yeah, well, *we're* who they're shooting at, so can we save the science lesson for later?"

He'd be willing to bet that *their* wires, unlike his, were fully functional, too.

Once more, he urged the woman farther down the passageway. Instead, she wrenched herself free and stepped back toward the intersection.

* * *

Sam knew they had to get that duffel back, or the man with her was going to die. She saw the streak of blood across his temple, the gash shining black in the red emergency lighting. He was struggling to stand, his leg refusing to respond after the CUSP's EM pulse set the nerve cells in his leg on fire.

A burning fury lit her from within. This had to stop—now. Scrambling to her feet, she pulled out of his grasp and stepped toward the intersection.

"What the hell do you think you're doing?" she called out to the Marines around the corner.

"Come out with your hands up!" one of them shouted back. She felt a hand on her shoulder and turned, frowning at the man behind her.

"See one, think two," he murmured. He must have caught her look of confusion. "Marine fireteam's made up of four people. If there are two here, then it's likely the other two are circling around to come at us from behind."

She shifted, the movement causing her lab coat to fall open. The contents in her pocket made a soft clunk as it connected against the bulkhead behind her. Her hand automatically reached down to still its movement.

"Maybe I can talk some sense into them, or at least delay them long enough for you to make it to that hatch." She tilted her head to indicate the passageway, ignoring his look of incredulity.

She turned, her fingers absently reaching for the digital-to-biological converter inside her pocket. Instead, they came into contact with the spare brick of molecular material she'd shoved inside, along with the DBC.

Sam froze as an idea came to her.

"Wait…" Twisting, she glanced back at the man, holding up a finger as she mentally reached out over her wire.

{Hey. You still in contact with our friend?}

{Yes,} the voice replied.

{Tell him to stay put, but be ready to haul my unconscious ass to that hatch as soon as I make my move. Got it?}

She didn't wait for a response. Unslinging the bag of formation material from around her shoulders, she let it fall to the deck before moving closer to the corner that separated them from the Marines.

"Stand down!" she called out from her still-hidden position. "I'm Doctor Travis, Samantha Travis. Part of the deGrasse research team. Why are you shooting at me?"

"Sorry, ma'am." Funny, the Marine's tone didn't sound apologetic. "Just following orders. The person with you is wanted for questioning."

Sam glared at the overhead. "And that justifies the use of firearms? Against a civilian? Are you *kidding* me?"

She should have seen it coming. The ones who had experimented on the man behind her had tried twice to bury the evidence by eliminating him. He was living proof of their misconduct; they'd have no intention of letting him walk away a free man. She couldn't let that happen.

"Look, there's no need for force," she said firmly as she stepped out into the intersection.

Weapons snapped up and she froze.

"Okay, okay," she said, one hand rising slowly. "Just calm down, now. I'm no threat. Don't shoot."

Sam heard the man with her suck in a sharp breath and take an involuntary step forward, but trusted the voice inside his head to take care of things on that end.

"Hands up, doctor and don't move," the older Marine

ordered.

"Look," Sam tried again, "I suggest you rethink your actions here. Who ordered this man hunted down?" She remained still, one hand up in a gesture of surrender, her eyes locked onto the weapons aimed at her.

"Ma'am, we need you to step away from the person with you."

"I can do that," she said easily as she began to step slowly toward them. "But again, is this the wisest course of action right now, when we're evidently under attack?"

As if on cue, the torus shuddered once more, a reminder that they had a bigger problem to worry about. She staggered a little as the deck beneath her feet shifted, then resumed her slow walk toward them, her hand still out.

The other remained in her lab coat pocket, fingers keying the digital-to-biological converter's activation sequence by rote memory. The unit awakened, handshaking with her wire interface.

As she walked, she tried once more to reason with them as she called up the DBC's database on her HUD and searched for the formula she needed it to create. Taking a guess, she added, "Doctor Janus is *not* in charge, Marine."

One of the figures shrugged. "My sergeant said he was. Gotta follow orders, ma'am. You understand."

Bingo. She shot them a stern look. "Even when those orders are to fire on one of your own people, *inside* the torus?"

The Marine ignored her and gestured with his weapon. "Hands up where we can see them, please. Both of them, doctor."

She was close now, only two meters separated them. The formula flashed on her overlay, the icon flashing its query to execute. Pressing the DBC's maglock against the molecular brick, she removed her hand from her pocket as she mentally toggled the icon.

The younger Marine glanced over at her partner, who nodded for her to secure Sam. She holstered her CUSP and reached for Sam's arm. Sam sidestepped toward the male Marine. The proximity map projected by the DBC's program now included all three of them. Just as the male made contact with her shoulder to shove her back toward this partner, the unit turned red.

It was the last thing Sam saw before she lost consciousness.

* * *

Micah couldn't believe it when the idiot woman stepped back out into the cross corridor. He shot out an arm, ready to yank her back to safety when the voice interjected.

No! Let her go. She knows what she's doing.

Didn't look like it to Micah. He knew—*knew*—there were at least two more Marines coming for them. They were on a very short clock.

We don't have time—

Just be ready to grab her, and the bags, and run.

Micah blew out an impatient breath and ran his hand through his closed-cropped dark hair, the coiled tension in his body ratcheting up a notch at the forced inaction.

What's she going to do, incapacitate them both, all by herself?

A thread of amusement wound through Micah's mind.

Something like that, yes.

Annoyed, Micah swiped at the blood dripping into his eye from the bullet's track across his brow. It worried him that even his medical nano wasn't working. The wound should have clotted by now.

His head snapped up when he heard muted thuds coming from the cross corridor. Closing the distance to the corner in a quick leap, he raised his CUSP and chanced a look. The sight of three bodies slumped on the deck, out cold, had him stepping out into the corridor. He pulled up short when the voice interceded.

Hold while it dissipates.

Assuming the 'it' the voice referred to was some sort of airborne agent, Micah spent the time waiting for the all-clear trying to regain feeling in his still-tingling leg. Massaging the much-abused limb, he kept his head on a swivel and his weapon drawn. Not that his limited eyesight was of much use in these conditions. But the area behind the slumped pile of bodies and the Rim Passage both remained empty.

Clear. Grab her and go. Bring both bags.

Micah launched himself forward, pausing at the duffel.

This stuff really that important?

Yes.

He looped the strap over his head, then lifted the doctor into a fireman's carry before stepping up to the intersection, CUSP once more held at the ready. A quick glance assured him the passage remained clear.

He dipped to scoop up the second bag, surprised to find it so heavy.

What's in here, a load of bricks?

Micah's mental comment elicited a surprised laugh from the mystery voice, nothing more. He shook his head, his attention returning to the passageway that stretched out before him.

The hatch?

Six meters ahead, on your left.

Tightening his hold on the unconscious woman, he moved toward the hatch. It was cycling as he arrived. He slid through the opening just as the thud of running footsteps sounded in the distance.

The other half of the fireteam was closing in.

Too close, he thought to the voice inside his head as the hatch sealed. *Any idea if we were seen?*

There was a pause, then an uncertain reply: *Don't think so.*

Micah didn't like the sound of that, but all thought fled as he turned to face the open outer hatch. The hull waiting just beyond belonged unmistakably to—

*What the hell, Jack? That's my **ship**!*

PART THREE: DEPARTURE

WRAITH

GNS *WRAITH*
OUTSIDE DEGRASSE SERVICE HATCH

MICAH CARRIED THE unconscious woman through his ship's hatch and shut it behind him. As he did so, he mentally reviewed what had just happened. If awakening in the station's morgue wasn't a clear indication that someone wanted him dead, sending a Marine fireteam after him with weapons hot sealed the deal.

He wished he knew who was gunning for him, and why, but his mind was drawing a blank. He had no idea what the hell was going on. No briefing, no mission parameters.

A quick glance around informed him that both the cockpit and crew cabin were empty. *Wraith*'s aft cargo doors were closed. His co-pilot, flight engineer, and crew chief were nowhere in sight.

"Jack?" he called out, but there was no answer from the big Marine whose voice he was certain he heard in his head.

"Yuki? Will?"

Neither crew chief nor flight engineer responded.

Micah dumped both bags and settled the unconscious

doctor into Will's station, cursing his inactivated wire once more. He did another quick visual sweep while his fingers automatically ran through the lock-and-web sequence that would secure her into the seat. He saw nothing out of order.

"*Wraith*, monitor vitals at flight engineer's station," he called out to the ship's Synthetic Intelligence.

When the SI chimed an affirmative, he blew out a relieved breath. Since someone apparently had a kill order out on him, he'd been worried his ship had been updated with orders to report his whereabouts to the station Marines, should he show up.

He straightened and stepped forward into the cockpit, eyes scanning the readouts currently on display. On the holo, he could see a swarm of ships exiting deGrasse in a way that suggested a station evac.

He reminded himself to follow up on that shortly. If that was indeed what was going on, it could be beneficial. The sensor clutter would help mask their own departure.

The Helios shuddered slightly as another explosion rocked the station. Micah plunged his hands into *Wraith*'s holo interface and, with a gesture, released the clamps that connected them to the torus.

They floated away at a hundred meters per second, the tangential velocity deGrasse's rotation imparted to the craft. No longer under centripetal acceleration, he felt instantly lighter, the ship sloughing its apparent gravity like a balloon whose tether had been snipped.

He started to slide out of the pilot's seat when a mental nudge pulled him up short. The voice he swore was Jack's returned.

Before you leave, have the ship run a full bioscan on you.
Micah blinked at the suggestion.

"Now's not really the time—"

Do it. Your wire's not the only thing out of commission. Your lattice is, too. You're going to have to take care how you fly this thing.

Every military pilot had a smart lattice of carbyne nanofloss woven throughout his body. The SmartCarbyne reinforced bones, strengthened muscles, protected organs. An accelerometer embedded in a pilot's wire fed data to nanosensors embedded within the lattice, signaling it to automatically harden during high-g acceleration, the kind pilots often experienced during combat.

With his wire out of commission, Micah had no way to determine if the lattice worked, short of the bioscan the voice suggested. He initiated the scan, his mouth thinning as the results hovered on the holodisplay before him:

No detectable lattice.

"You're right. That's going to limit our maneuvering capability."

Best to batten down, then.

He nodded reluctantly. "In a minute. Since we're without crew, I need to do a quick check and secure the cabin." He held up a hand to forestall any protest, and then wondered why he did it when no one was there to see. "I'll make it fast. I'm stubborn, not stupid."

The other man made a derisive noise. *Grab the med kit while you're at it. You're still bleeding.*

Micah's hand automatically went to his still-seeping head wound as he stood. Somewhere within the past few minutes, he'd gotten used to swiping the blood away from his eye and hadn't even noticed. He grunted and moved aft toward a starboard storage panel, to access the ship's med kit.

"Keep talking," he instructed as he flipped open the case, stocked to triage injuries far more severe than his. "Who's attacking us?"

There was a beat of silence. Then the voice returned, sounding amused.

We are.

Micah froze, his hand on the nano injector. "Come again?"

Stop dripping all over the ship.

He growled and pressed the injector to the site of the injury on his temple. He could feel the open wound scabbing over as tissue nanotransfection agents worked to regenerate the traumatized skin.

"Explain," he demanded. "What do you mean, 'we are'? We're attacking the torus?"

I used Banshees to plant low-yield grenades on the torus's exterior. Maximum confusion, minimal damage.

Banshees were stealthed drones, part of a Helios's standard weapons load. *Wraith* carried two hundred fifty of them under normal conditions.

A mental image pushed its way into his mind. He recognized the feed from *Wraith*'s external sensor suite, as it registered dozens of Banshee drones. As he watched, the tiny ships dipped and whirled in an intricate dance, attempting to evade the Novastrike defense fighters deGrasse had unleashed against them.

Micah groaned as he saw one of the drone's icons wink out of existence. Moments later, another Banshee began a strafing run.

"Aw, c'mon, Jack! You got a death-wish? We can't fire on an Alliance installation!"

They were a distraction to buy you two time to get out of there, the voice explained. *The torus's self-healing protocols will repair most of the damage within a single week. They figured it out almost immediately, which was why you found yourself face to face with a Marine fireteam.*

"Well, yeah. I'd imagine they would." Micah's voice dripped sarcasm. "Way to go, asshole. You just bought us a one-way ticket to a court-martial."

There was a long silence. Micah received a sense of exhaustion and realized the voice's explanation had been the most he'd heard from Jack at one time.

"Hey, you okay?" he ventured after a few more moments had passed.

Don't get your panties in a wad. Worry about yourself, not me.

Micah grinned involuntarily at the classic Jack-style comment.

The Banshees have been recalled, the voice continued. *They'll begin to rendezvous with the ship in fifteen.*

Micah chewed on that as he snapped the med kit back into place. He glanced over at the still-unconscious doctor.

"Any idea how long she'll be out?"

He felt a mental shrug.

Could be minutes; could be hours. She didn't say.

Micah nodded, and then ran a quick check for loose items before returning to the pilot's chair, hands automatically reaching to secure the webbing that would hold him in place.

His eyes sought the cockpit's SyntheticVision display, the array of holoimages providing an immersive view of the ship's immediate surroundings. Once he saw that *Wraith* was, indeed, clear of the active area, he relaxed back into his seat.

"Okay, our destination is Luyten Gate," he said, pulling up the system map and tapping on the gate icon at its astropause. "*Wraith,* maintain heading, thrusters only, until we're a thousand klicks from the station."

The system flashed compliance.

He glanced at the growing clutter of ships on the holo. With a gesture, he zoomed in, noting the number and type of vessels, and their dispersal pattern. Oddly, one of them looked like it was on a heading outsystem. He circled the mass of ships, then dropped an icon tag on the departing spacecraft.

"Let me know if the departing vessel changes course. And if any of the ships in that field get within a hundred kilometers of our location."

He continued to scroll through data, then paused, his attention snagged by a cargo manifest. Frowning, he moved the manifest to the main screen, expanding it to show more detail.

None of this made any sense. *Wraith*'s hold read like a

medevac triage unit, but he didn't recall being deployed on a Combat Search and Rescue mission. CSAR had turned many a Helios into the equivalent of a spaceborne hospital as the ship's crew infiltrated hot zones and military medical personnel evacuated soldiers wounded behind enemy lines.

But *Wraith* wasn't on such a mission, not that he could recall. Even if they were, what call would there be for such an operation within Alliance borders?

A noise in the crew cabin pulled his attention away from the mystery of the manifest. In an instant, he knew he and the doctor were no longer alone. A flick of his finger brought up the feed for the main crew cabin on one of the lower screens, his torso blocking it from view.

It showed a figure traversing the starboard bulkhead, the movement deliberate and furtive. The figure was small, female—and armed. She wore a tactical vest; a pulsed, short-barrel combat assault rifle, or P-SCAR, hung on a single-point sling around her neck.

It seemed they were under attack—from within.

STOWAWAYS

GNS *WRAITH*
OUTSIDE DEGRASSE SERVICE HATCH

MICAH'S INTRUDER WAS nearly to the flight engineer's cradle. The woman's attention was split equally between the cockpit and the unconscious doctor. The way she handled the rifle hanging around her neck didn't suggest an easy familiarity with it.

That, in itself, could pose a problem. Startling a person who didn't know how to handle the weapon they wielded was a recipe for unpredictable, often deadly, results. Micah knew his best option was to close the distance between them as rapidly as possible and get inside the intruder's line of fire.

Micah reached for the tanto blade sheathed at his waist and planted his feet against the base of the pilot's cradle. In one coordinated move, he jackknifed out of the seat and launched himself toward her.

The woman reacted quickly enough, turning to meet Micah's rush head-on. Dark hair fanned out around her, arm lifting instinctively to block the blade coming toward her. Recognition flickered in her eyes, along with a wariness he didn't like.

The P-SCAR on the sling around her neck swung to one side, weapon forgotten. She would have gone spinning away had Micah not pulled her toward him with a grappling hold. She froze when she felt the naked carbyne blade settle against her neck. His other hand snaked out and latched onto the weapon; a quick glance showed the pulsed rifle was safetied.

"Who are you and how the hell did you get access to this ship?" he growled, unclipping the P-SCAR from its sling. When she didn't immediately answer, he increased the blade's pressure; a drop of blood beaded where its sharp edge met her flesh.

She pulled against his hold, seeking to ease the force of the knife resting against her jawline. She swallowed convulsively, then in one breath, seemed to recall herself. Her spine straightened in anger, dark eyes narrowing.

"*You* gave me access!" she hissed the words at him, pulling against him once more.

She put up a good front. He could tell she was wound tight, felt her pulse beating rapidly under his fist that held the knife. Yet after that initial reaction, she refused to show fear.

Their floating bodies connected abruptly against the bulkhead that separated the cabin from the aft cargo hold. The jolt caused the tanto to slice deeper into the skin beneath her jaw. Feeling guilty, he jerked the blade away from her, the action causing the blood globules on its edge to float into the air around them.

She flinched, more in reaction to the sight of her own blood, Micah knew, than because of the pain. The blade was so sharp that it would take a moment for her to begin to feel—

"Ow, dammit!" She glared at him, her hand going up to cover the wound.

"*Wraith*," he called out to the SI, his eyes drilling into his intruder, "release containment nano, cargo bay bulkhead, starboard side."

The SI acknowledged and, from the corner of his eye, he caught a flicker of light as a haze of glittering specks leached from the bulkhead to envelop the floating droplets. A slight breeze grazed his cheek, the ship directing the airflow to recall the nano. Soon it would absorb back into the ActiveFiber coating that layered the ship's bulkheads.

The woman he held captive twisted in an attempt to once more break free; she stopped when he tightened his grip. He suppressed a shaft of envy when he saw that her body's medical nano seemed to be working just fine; it had already stopped the bleeding and begun to heal the wound.

"You haven't told me who you are yet," he reminded her. "And I never gave you access to *Wraith.* Believe me, I'd have remembered that."

She remained stubbornly silent.

To draw her out, he deliberately stropped the tanto's blade against the sleeve of his flight suit, the self-cleaning fabric absorbing the remainder of her blood. The suit would break it down into its constituent components of water, salt, and proteins, shedding the water molecules back into the atmosphere and retaining the rest to refresh the suit's nano reservoir, as needed.

The woman's eyes remained transfixed, arrested on the movement of his hand.

As the last of the blood disappeared into the fabric, she sucked in a breath and shook her head, the spell broken. She stared intently at him for a long moment, then nodded, apparently having come to a decision.

"Okay. Sam said recent memory might be an issue," she muttered under her breath. Micah's brow furrowed at that, but before he could ask her what she meant, she continued.

"My name's Harper Kinsley. I'm an analyst for Alliance Military Intelligence," she clarified, one hand reaching cautiously up to unseal the top of her tactical vest and reveal the Mil-Int insignia displayed on her uniform. "Sam's a friend from college. I've been helping her with—"

Harper abruptly fell silent.

"With what? Breaking me out of the morgue?" Micah made

a frustrated sound as he gave her shoulder a small shake, but then he released his hold on her. "What in hell's going on here? And why do they want me dead?"

"One thing at a time," she said. Before she could continue, a groan came from the flight engineer's cradle. The doctor was regaining consciousness.

"Sam!" Harper snapped her head around and then pushed off, shooting across the cabin over to her friend. She overshot, slamming awkwardly into the bulkhead before recovering and twisting back around. "Damn, zero-g sucks."

Micah stifled a grin at that pronouncement. Rarely had he ever seen anyone quite so awkward with weightlessness as Harper. It was apparent the woman spent most of her time at a desk, either planetside or on a station with artificially generated gravity.

Sheathing his blade, he followed her over to the cradle, one hand reaching up to snag the holopanel above the flight engineer's station to arrest his motion.

The doctor blinked, staring unseeingly at her surroundings. She shook her head, struggling to throw off the sedative, and the motion caused her short hair to float gently around her face. He could tell the moment memory returned. Her gaze sharpened and her eyes darted about the cabin until they fell on him.

She smiled. "Guess we made it, then," she said.

"Guess we did, doc," he agreed. "Want to tell me what's going on, now? And why someone from Mil-Int is on my ship?"

"I told you," Harper shot back, her tone acerbic. "You gave me access."

"Not possible. We've never met."

"Not true," she countered quickly. "You, he... Well, that is—" Her voice cut off and she turned to look pointedly at Sam.

* * *

{Look, you got me into this,} Harper's voice sounded sharply

in Sam's head. *{**You** answer him.}*

Sam worked to hide her amusement at the analyst's aggrieved tone.

{Has he been back there yet?} she asked Harper, shooting a glance at the closed cargo bay, and her friend responded with a minute shake of her head.

{No time. Soon as I felt the ship move, I popped my head out and saw you here. I could tell through my wire that you were still alive but when I tried to sneak out to check up on you, someone got the drop on me.} Her voice turned wry and Sam saw her reach up to finger a recently-healed cut.

{He did that to you?} Sam asked in surprise and Harper shrugged.

{He caught me off guard. You said he might not remember anything. You were right.} Her mouth twisted, eyes glinting with unexpected humor. *{Guess I make a better analyst than I do a spook.}*

"So," the man in front of her nudged her leg with his foot to get her attention. The expression on his face told Sam he was well aware there was a conversation going on and it excluded him. He jerked his chin.

"Want to tell me what happened back there? Who are you, doctor? And what the hell's going on?"

She pursed her lips, taking a moment to study him. He looked relaxed, if a bit irritated. He was utterly in his element, staring down at her, one arm looped comfortably around the panel that hung quiescently above her head.

When she didn't immediately answer, he stirred impatiently. "Look. I'm just a pilot, ma'am. I go where I'm sent, do what I'm told. Now, it seems my own military wants me dead—and I have no idea why."

Sam nodded, took in a breath, and then let it out before launching into the tale. "Harper's been assigned to deGrasse for the past year. She contacted us when she realized things weren't adding up and she began to suspect we have a traitor in the Alliance." She saw his eyebrows climb at her words.

"If I'm right," Harper chimed in, "then that someone is desperate to get their hands on what we've discovered here in Luyten's Star. Evidence suggests they'll kill to get their hands on it."

Sam saw his expression flicker at Harper's mention of killing. It briefly disrupted the skeptical gleam in his eyes. "Still trying to wrap my head around the part where there's an Alliance research station in Luyten's Star. If that's really where we are."

Harper's voice turned derisive. "It is and you know it. I heard you order the ship to head for the gate before you went all commando on me."

The man's face tightened at the word 'commando'. Sam could tell he didn't like it. His gaze moved from Harper to the cockpit and then back to Sam, distrust evident.

"Luyten's interdicted because it's a dangerous star system," he stated flatly. "Now you're telling me the Alliance has some sort of top-secret research facility, right in the middle of it?"

She nodded. "That's right."

He grunted, his body swaying as he shifted hands. "Lady, it's interdicted for a reason. We did a lot of damage to the fabric of spacetime in this part of the Milky Way when we arrived. A fleet of research drones with first-gen Scharnhorst drives saw to that."

"That's what they'd have you believe, yes. The truth is... somewhat different."

His eyes narrowed, and something flickered in their depths. Abruptly Sam recalled who this man was.

He knows something—something about this ship he's not telling, she thought.

"Different, how, exactly?" he asked, his tone neutral.

Sam thought about where to begin. She decided to let his odd reaction go for now, and focus instead on the situation they now found themselves in.

This was when things got a bit tricky. "What's the last thing you can remember, before today?"

He reared his head back, seeming surprised by the unexpected direction of her question. He pushed away from the holopanel, drifting in front of her, arms crossed and brow creased in thought.

"I... Well, I..." he said after a moment, and then lapsed into silence as he thought about it. Shaking his head, he said slowly, "I remember being called into a briefing by Colonel Valenti, about a mission—"

"Who?"

His eyes narrowed on her, his earlier suspicion returning. "You know, maybe you'd better tell me more about yourself. Mission briefs are need-to-know. Sorry, doc, but I'm not sure you qualify."

Sam cracked a smile. "Fair enough, under the circumstances." She glanced around at the ship she knew he considered his. She wondered briefly how he would feel once he discovered she'd been in here quite a few times over the past few days.

And that she had access to things aboard his ship that he didn't.

"You're right about the mission," she began. "It was to bring me here. My uncle commissioned it, three weeks ago."

"Your uncle." His tone was flat, laced with disbelief.

"Yeah, her uncle," Harper interjected. "You might've heard of the guy. He's the Director of National Security for the Alliance."

He blinked in surprise.

"Duncan Cutter?" His eyes tracked from Harper back to her, the question in them clear.

"Yes. He arranged an opening on the science teams, one I was qualified for and could fill." She blew out a breath. "I was just supposed to observe and report back to him on what I saw."

"But something happened," he guessed.

"You happened."

Sam ignored Harper's interruption, her eyes on the man in

front of her. "I've never heard of a Colonel Valenti, but I'm guessing that's your superior, the person who authorized you for this mission. It was just you and a Marine co-pilot, Jack Campbell. Not your usual crew." She hesitated. "You were sent to, ah"

Her voice drifted off uncomfortably. Another voice intervened.

{You were sent as undercover security, to keep her safe. Black op.}

Sam knew he heard the words as well, although not through any conventional means. They were being sent directly into the mind of the man before her. It was a completely different and utterly unexpected way to communicate, and one she was itching to investigate.

{Your cover was as a transport shuttle captain,} the voice continued. *{Wraith was in the cargo hold of the ship you were flying, masquerading as a vanilla Helios. You dropped Sam off and then reported to deGrasse's security squadron as a relief pilot, rotating in from Procyon. Admiral Toland was the only person on deGrasse who knew who you really were.}*

"Undercover? What the hell, Jack? Whose dumbass idea was that? A pair of pilots don't make good bodyguards."

There was a pause from the other end. The voice returned, a sharp urgency to it that hadn't been there a moment before.

{Hate to break up this little party, but we're going to need to be able to maneuver real soon.}

As a distraction, that worked. Even though she knew it was at best, a brief reprieve, Sam couldn't help but be thankful for the diversion.

* * *

At the voice's warning, Micah's attention snapped immediately back to the ship.

"Status?" he barked, motioning for the doctor to secure herself in the cradle.

They've figured out you're no longer on deGrasse, the voice in his head informed him.

Cursing softly, he grabbed Harper's arm and pushed her toward the gunner's station. She landed awkwardly with a soft *oompf,* but once there, began to efficiently lock-and-web.

I'm reading multiple Novastrike launches.

This was unsurprising; an installation the size of deGrasse usually had a unit of the smaller fighters.

"Copy that."

His glance flicked once more between the two women to confirm both passengers were secure and then he pushed off, arrowing for the cockpit once more.

Looks like they're mounting a search, standard grid pattern.

"Do they know what they're looking for?" he asked as he snapped his own restraints into place.

It took several long seconds for him to pull up the information on ship's scan. His neural interface would have provided it instantly.

The last time he'd had to access data manually like this was during basic training. He shoved the handicapped feeling away, recognizing that he still had full access to his strongest weapon—his brain.

They know Wraith *is missing,* the voice cut into his thoughts, *but they'll be scanning for the wrong ship. Her DAP capabilities were never revealed to anyone on station.*

"We can work with that," Micah murmured. The Helios fast-action spacecraft were the workhorses of the Alliance Navy, capable of carrying an entire squad of fully-kitted Marines. *Wraith* was one of the few Helios modified as a Direct Action Penetrator stealth unit.

All DAPs were assigned to the Geminate Alliance's Special Reconnaissance Unit, often referred to as SRU or simply, The Unit.

The teams that flew the DAPs were known as Shadow Recon. They deployed on classified missions, dropping elite Marine fireteams to destinations none spoke about.

Wraith could play hide and seek with a few Novastrikes without breaking a sweat.

At the moment, Micah was the weak link. Not only was he without both wire and lattice, the generic shipsuit he wore wasn't a Helios-issued uniform. It lacked the connections his usual flight suit had to his ship's helmet.

Despite that, he reached for the helmet recessed into the cradle's headrest. Its seal might not be a perfect match, but he'd take it over nothing. If the ship suffered a containment loss and vented atmosphere to space, it would hopefully buy him the time he needed to seal the leak.

More importantly, the helmet could also be used as a poor-man's HUD. The helmet's SyntheticVision mode could interface with ship's sensors, providing a low-res, full spherical view of nearspace.

A series of blinks provided crude manipulation of ship's data, projected as an overlay. It wasn't as intuitive as his wire, but it'd suffice.

He heard a noise and realized Harper had activated the gunner's station. He swiveled in his cradle and shot her a warning look.

"Don't worry," she said, lifting her hands, palms out. "I'm not firing anything. I just want to see what we're dealing with."

Micah grunted, then returned his attention to the display. Placing the helmet on, he swept his head around, up, and down, testing the unit's SV interface. The helmet tagged each of the small Navy fighters as they registered on scan. He saw that six had scrambled, each taking a quadrant of space.

Suddenly, minute specks appeared, populating the space around each Novastrike. He enlarged the display, rotating it to examine the specks more closely. "Are those—?"

"Novastrike Microdrones? Yep."

Micah was impressed. "Not even a Helios can pick those things up on scan. How'd you manage it?" He watched as a web of tiny dots spilled from each ship, each one serving as a sensor to widen the fighter's coverage.

"I'm with Mil-Int, remember?" Harper's voice sounded smug and self-assured. "I've backdoored us into the torus's combat net."

Micah whistled his appreciation. Now, there was a tactical advantage he could get used to.

He brought the readout for *Wraith*'s fusion reactor to the foreground. He didn't like the projections and ordered the cone-shaped dynamic fusors to lower their output by thirty percent.

Even with the best sensor-scattering tech the Alliance could produce, there would still be a faint heat bloom from *Wraith*'s drives when they came online.

Ordinarily, he'd be willing to risk it. With Novastrikes closing in on their location, all actively seeking *Wraith*, that wasn't such a good idea.

"Got anything in your bag of tricks that'd get them to look the other way while I bring our drives online? Be nice if we were a bit farther than seven hundred kilometers from that torus."

"Sorry, no. Except maybe" Her voice trailed off, and when Micah prompted her, she held up a hand.

"Not sure this'll get us any reactions, but I just gained access to that incinerator where you were held in the morgue. Did you know there are several volatiles in that area? Wouldn't be hard to make that thing go boom."

Micah couldn't suppress the grin that formed at her words. Given how he'd spent the last few days, he held no love for that place.

"Feel free, but try not to kill anyone—other than that asshole sergeant that was out to end me. Not sure it'll stop the Novastrikes though."

"It might, if they think you're still on-station," she countered.

There was a pause, and then Harper whooped and shot both arms straight up in the air. "Take that, sergeant asshole!"

Sam's voice cut in, and Micah heard the strain in it.

"Harper, were there people there?"

The analyst blew out a breath. "No. I just rigged the data to implicate him when they investigate. His token will be the only one they see when they look at who had access to the area last."

They waited another few minutes, but the Novastrikes remained on course.

"Dammit. Okay, then. How about more strafing runs, maybe on the other side?"

Micah heard the hopeful note Harper injected in her voice. He shook his head.

"All of the Banshees have been recalled," he reminded her. "Looks like we'll be doing this the hard way."

"What way's that?" Sam's voice joined the conversation.

Micah shrugged. "We lay low, and wait for them to give up the hunt."

He didn't tell the doctor that, with the number of microdrones each Novastrike released, the odds that one of the things might physically bump against *Wraith*'s stealthed hide were fairly high. He'd deal with that problem if it happened.

Countermeasures? the voice asked.

"Good idea," Micah muttered back. He gestured, and a constellation of microdrones flushed from several points along the Helios's hull. The tiny machines jetted outward into a protective sphere around the ship.

"What's that?" Harper asked.

"Just stacking the deck in our favor, in case anyone gets too close," he told her. "Those are some of *Wraith*'s active countermeasures."

"What do they do?" Sam joined the conversation, her voice curious.

"If it looks like any of those fighters' drones are taking a particular interest in our little corner of this star system, *Wraith* can hack their systems," he said. "They'll take over, blocking the drone's sensor return while sending a fake reading back to the search ship."

"Sweet!" Harper said. "So they're essentially a cross between system spyware and a rootkit program."

Sam sounded amused. "Careful, Captain. Harper's going to start thinking you're talking dirty to her if you keep that up."

Micah's mouth cocked up into a grin as Harper made a rude noise.

"Roger that, doc. Thanks for the warning."

He nudged the stealthed Helios out of the path of an oncoming vessel.

"Sit back and relax, ladies, while we play hide-and-seek with deGrasse's best. It's liable to last awhile."

EVACUATION

MEDICAL CENTER
DEGRASSE RESEARCH TORUS

GABE BRACED A hand against the clinic's reinforced bulkhead as a secondary explosion followed on the heels of the first. Dodging panicked people racing for the exit, he pinged his security team back.

{Mandatory lockdown's been initiated,} the voice on the other end announced before he had a chance to say anything. *{Where are you, sir?}*

Gabe grunted. Lock-down meant everyone was supposed to report to their assigned stellar event shelter-in-place location.

{I'm at the clinic,} he responded.

He looked around, spotted a medic standing guard at the entrance to the treatment area and angled in that direction.

{Things are nuts down here,} the voice continued. *{Fraley's scrambling Novastrikes, says the attack's coming from outside the torus.}*

{Did he mention anything about who's behind it?} he asked.

{No, except they don't appear to be targeting vital systems,} the officer responded. *{Attack's localized, too.}*

{Let me guess,} Gabe's tone was dry. *{Research.}*

{That vicinity, yeah.}

Gabe frowned. *{That last hit we just took didn't feel like it was on the torus's outer skin. It was too sharply defined. Came from inside, I'd wager good creds on it.}*

{Yeah,} the officer agreed. *{That's what Douglass said, too.}*

Douglass was their munitions expert. Her word was good enough for Gabe.

{What about our guests? Have the Marines dropped them off yet?}

{Guests?} The perplexed tone on the other end told Gabe they hadn't.

His eyes tracked to the icon Fraley had dropped onto his HUD, the one that gave him access to the Marines' combat net.

{Hang on a tick,} he told the man as he tapped into it. What he saw had him swearing silently.

Two of the Marines were down. Alive, but down. He could tell by their biometric data that they were out cold. The visor cams streaming from the other two indicated they had just arrived. One swept the area with her weapon while the other checked for injuries.

Micah Case and Samantha Travis were nowhere to be seen.

{Scratch that,} he told his officer. *{Negative on the guests.}* Before exiting the Marines' combat net, he ordered their visors' recordings sent to his wire's data cache.

{Uh, sir?} His subordinate cut in, sounded distracted. *{I just received a ping from Colonel Fraley. He's sending a squad of Marines down. We're to coordinate with them on an internal sweep for more bombs.}*

{Good.}

Gabe was relieved his people would be able to contribute to the fubar currently unraveling.

{Ask Douglass about team assignments. She's been cross-training some officers; it'd be smart to spread them between the three fireteams.}

The officer sent him a nod. *{Colonel also said to let you know* *they'll be issuing an evacuation order in five minutes. He said it was more of a precaution, while they checked containment. Consensus is that the attack was some sort of diversion, and that the explosions did minimal harm. Except for the one big boom that happened inside...}*

{Very good. I'll stay here until the evac's announced, and escort Doc Mason to the flight deck.}

Gabe straightened as he severed the connection and looked around. He'd come to a stop while finishing his conversation and was now facing the door that separated the clinic's waiting room from its medical treatment area.

A man was there, trying to argue his way past the medic guarding the entrance. From the cut and color of his coveralls, Gabe guessed he was one of the station's maintenance techs.

The medic was doing her best to calm the man, but he was having none of it. When the tech shoved his face into hers, his own red with anger, Gabe took that as indication he should intervene.

The man turned at his approach, and when he spied Gabe's security uniform, grabbed him by the arm.

"What in hell's going on?" The questions came rapid-fire. "Are we under attack? Why aren't you doing something about it?"

"Right now, you know as much as I do... Private," Gabe added as his wire automatically supplied the man's name and rank. "But if you're volunteering to help..."

He suppressed a smile as the man shoved away from him, muttering under his breath as he stormed off.

Crisis averted, Gabe turned back to the medic guarding the door. He shot her a questioning look.

"Going to give me the same trouble about getting past?"

The medic's annoyed expression had morphed into ill-concealed amusement at Gabe's handling of the man. She swept out a hand, stepping aside so that he could pass.

"Not at all, sir," she quipped, a grin playing about her face. "Go right on in."

Things were much the same on this side of the door, though as time passed without another explosion, he began to see the fear on faces retreating. That might change, once the evacuation orders were broadcast.

As if on cue, alert klaxons sounded, the automated system ordering people to move to their sector's designated exit.

He side-stepped, barely avoiding a nurse rounding a corner at a dead run. He turned down the hallway she'd just vacated, lined with rows of offices.

A quick glance at Addy's workspace told him she wasn't there. Her voice sounded behind him and he spun, craning his neck to see past swiftly-moving personnel as he sought the tall, dark-haired chief physician.

He pushed further into the heart of the trauma unit, forcing the people between them to part so that he could catch up to her. Her commanding tone cut through the chaos as she directed gurneys to the clinic's private lifts.

Gabe knew those lifts provided direct access to belowdecks levels, where medical personnel could quickly transit to the nearest escape craft. He also knew Addy saw her role as a critical one.

There was only one problem: a nagging suspicion had begun to form in the back of Gabe's investigator's mind. It told him the pieces of the puzzle weren't adding up correctly.

Addy wasn't going to like it, but in case Fraley was wrong, Gabe needed to get the doctor out of here—and he needed to do it now.

But he needed her to grab something first.

* * *

When the explosion first hit, Addy instinctively fell back upon her Navy training, the routine settling into place like a well-worn glove.

She assembled a triage net through her wire, pulling her staff into the connection and doling out roles. She couldn't help a swell of pride when she saw the smooth and efficient way they swung into action.

She was standing at the nexus, calling out reminders and confirming critical systems had been secured, when she felt a presence at her side.

"Doc," Gabe's hand wrapped around her forearm. "The forensic data your team took in the lab. Got it with you?"

She stared at him, surprised. "Is now really the time? We're in the middle of—"

"I need you to delegate this and go gather that evidence," he interrupted. She stared at him for a beat, wondering if he'd lost his mind, until he tugged on her arm, urging her back toward her office.

{Tamsin,} she sent over the triage net as he dragged her along, *{take over for me.}*

Not waiting for the resident's response, she pulled her arm from Gabe's hold but continued to keep pace with him.

"What's this about?"

Gabe's expression was shuttered.

"Just a feeling. If I'm right and this is a diversion, then I want to make sure that evidence is secured."

He shot her a quick glance. "Don't want to get back and find out it's been compromised, messed with, or gone missing, is all."

She stared at him in disbelief.

"You really think they'd go to all this trouble just to corrupt some data?"

He shrugged but didn't otherwise respond.

She shook her head as they entered her office and she slid into her chair.

"It'll take a few minutes," she warned him. "We're going to be, ah, late for the evacuation."

Gabe smiled at that.

"Well, I have it on good authority that the evac's more of a precaution." He held up a hand when she began to protest, "We're not ignoring it. Just grabbing some stuff before we head to the flight deck."

He looked back out into the corridor, his eyes flickering as he checked something on his HUD.

"I'm guessing we won't have time to swing by the morgue and retrieve the body—"

He stilled, an arrested look on his face.

Addy finished uploading the reports and unjacked from a data port. "What body? One of the pilots? I was told they were all cremated."

He nodded, seeming distracted.

Reaching for a portable holoprojector, she pocketed it, and then rose. "Okay, ready."

"Let's go, then." He turned and headed down the now-emptied corridor toward medical's lifts.

She followed. "So?" she prompted.

"So, what?"

"What just occurred to you?"

Gabe turned to her as they came to a stop in front of the lifts and he pressed the call button.

"I just realized that last explosion could very well have come from the morgue."

TACTICAL EXIT

CLINT JANUS'S OFFICE
DEGRASSE RESEARCH TORUS

THE MOMENT THE medical team had taken the body and Clint had been assured the research staff were all back at work, he'd excused himself from the Advanced Isolation Lab. With the assassin following silently at his back, Clint had ducked into Stinton's office, intending to make a final, cursory sweep for any overlooked or misplaced documents.

He couldn't have been more wrong. Stinton had been holding out on him. The inordinate amount of digital hard copies he'd found in Stinton's office proved that.

Clint hadn't expected to come across a cache of files that documented experiments Stinton had hidden, even from him. The potential edge this could gain Akkadia couldn't be ignored. The material was too valuable to leave for the Alliance Navy to find, so he'd hauled it all back to his office where he could dispose of it a bit more handily.

Stinton had always been a bit of an eccentric. He'd claimed the act of holding physical plas sheets in his hand when reviewing data helped him to think.

Right now, with alarm klaxons sounding in the corridor, all they were doing was causing Clint a massive headache.

He stared down at the dwindling pile and reached for the next document. Once his hand came into contact with the sheet, Stinton's hacked token—now connected to Clint's own biosignature—performed a handshake with the security nanofiber embedded in the page. Once its contents were transferred, Clint slid it into a slim case that held the already-scanned sheets.

One last document remained. He glanced over at the assassin, waving it in the air.

"This is the last of them. Damn fool set us back a good hour with his idiot ways."

The assassin shifted but remained otherwise silent. Clint grunted, piqued by her lack of response before he sealed the document case and ordered it to erase all data within.

"They're running for the exits," he reminded her as he set the case aside. "We'll have to wait until the research teams have returned after the evacuation to confirm the samples have been destroyed."

Clint looked over at her, one eyebrow raised. The woman's implacable gaze pierced him.

She shook her head, once. "We will not wait. I have contingencies in place. It will be handled."

Her words ran cold down his spine as it occurred to him that she might have a contingency plan for him, as well. It was not a comfortable thought.

The assassin stepped forward. "It is time. You have the research. The courier ship is waiting."

Clint gave her a quick nod. He turned to program the robotic drive unit attached to the biosphere sample case. Linking the drive to his own security token so that he could track its progress on his overlay, he sent it on its way to the flight deck ahead of them.

The rumble of another explosion sounded in the distance. Straightening, he turned back to the assassin.

"Do you have any idea what is behind these explosions?"

The assassin's face turned contemplative.

"This was not an attack so much as it is a distraction, I think. A diversion, set most likely by whomever helped your experiment escape the morgue. Effective, too. We must assume that he is lost to us."

She made a small gesture toward his office entrance.

"It is of little consequence. As I said before, I have contingencies in place. We go. Now."

* * *

The lift carrying Clint and the assassin to the flight deck came to a stop, and the doors parted. Instantly, they were assaulted by sound from all directions, drowning out the distant explosions they'd heard en route. He stopped, taking stock of their surroundings.

The great freespan bay that housed the torus's small fleet of Novastrikes was nearly empty of ships. Those that remained were hotbeds of activity; crews swarmed them, and stragglers hustled toward them, preparing to evacuate.

Clint's attention swerved to the bay doors when an alert sounded, warning bystanders to stay clear of the demarcation line. A flare of bright blue energy sprang into existence, framing an invisible wall. On this side of the line, the atmospheric shield maintained the flight deck's ambient air and pressure. On its other side, the bay was exposed to the vacuum of space.

As Clint watched, one ship departed while another taxied into position. His gaze swept the remaining ships, coming to light on the one parked beside his crate. It was a courier ship.

A hand wrapped around his arm and tugged.

"Quickly, before anyone notices our departure."

The assassin barely vocalized the words, urging him forward.

The ship was a sleek design, small yet capable of traversing distances that required a several day journey in relative comfort. The pilot standing next to it nodded as they neared, his face vaguely familiar.

A connection request appeared on his wire, and Clint accepted it, transferring the token for the crate over to the man. Without a word, the pilot took control of the robotic unit, steering it inside the tight confines of the courier ship's cargo area.

Clint shot the assassin a questioning look, his eyes cutting from her to the pilot and back. She gave a slight shake of her head.

So. Not an Akkadian, then. He repressed a sigh of annoyance. Buying the loyalty of Alliance traitors was wearisome. It prevented him from speaking freely, and forced him to present a façade he was tired of assuming.

At least the man would be silenced before he could betray those who had bought his loyalty. He took small comfort in that knowledge.

He didn't notice the two figures that burst hastily through the flight deck's doors. Had he seen them, he would have noticed Addy Mason halt midflight as she caught sight of him. He might have seen the assessing look in her eyes when she saw the crate being loaded into the courier ship.

But he didn't, and neither did the assassin. By the time either looked up, the doctor was halfway across the deck, Gabriel Alvarez's hand at her back as he steered her toward a waiting ship.

UNEXPECTED ANSWERS

GNS *WRAITH*
700 KM FROM DEGRASSE RESEARCH TORUS

AS THE SEARCH for *Wraith* continued, those inside the DAP Helios maintained an uneasy silence. Nothing disturbed it, save for the occasional warning ping that announced another one of the Novastrike drones had been intercepted and hacked.

Micah was used to the kind of hyper-focus required to remain vigilant for long periods, but he could tell it was wearing on his passengers. He blinked to relieve the strain, nudging the Helios off the projected heading of yet another fighter that had strayed too close while searching for them.

Just then, one of the Novastrikes flipped, its pilot turning to have a second look. Micah tensed as the vessel neared for another slow pass. "Move along," he murmured. "Nothing to see here."

"Hang on," Harper said, equally soft. "I just intercepted something. I think— Yes. They just called off the search."

The Novastrike casing the area continued its sweep for another few seconds. Micah waited, rubbing his palms against his flight suit, the material wicking away the slickness of sweat.

"C'mon buddy," he coaxed. "Just follow orders already."

A few seconds later, it turned, pointing its nose back toward deGrasse's flight deck.

Micah waited until the Novastrike was dozens of kilometers away before he let out a breath. When it was clear that none of the vessels remained a threat, he unsealed his helmet. Removing it, he racked it into a recess beside the pilot's cradle. After several hours of cat-and-mouse, the muscles in his neck were a roped, knotted mass and he gratefully released the cradle's restraints, rotating his head to work the kinks out.

"Everyone good back there?" he asked, swiveling his seat so that he could view the two crew stations. Sam nodded and Harper gave a thumbs-up before brushing dark bangs away from her forehead.

"Okay, then." One hand still working at the base of his neck, he turned back to the main holo. "Don't know about you, but I'd feel a helluva lot more comfortable if we had a bit more distance between us and that station. *Wraith*, spin up one of the drives, half power."

The SI sent a verbal affirmative.

He saw the doctor look up at him in alarm. "Won't they be able to see us if we do that?"

Micah shook his head, a tired grin playing about his face as he unwebbed and floated away from the pilot's cradle. "Not unless they're specifically looking for us. Now that the search has been called off, we should be fine."

He felt power thrumming deep within the ship's bulkhead, the Helios readying itself for flight. It resonated in his bones, familiar and bracing. His feet slowly settled to the floor as the drive came online and its thrust provided them with the sensation of gravity once more.

"Our fusion reactor's a newer, more compact design," he continued his explanation, "and it's buried behind layers of high-performance electromagnetic shielding. Our sensor return only shows a small fraction of our true emissions, thanks to the new smart metal."

Sam's face lit with fascination as she unwebbed and joined him. "So it's true, then? I'd heard they'd found a way to integrate some twisted graphene with the foam substrates. Those Dirac semimetals show some interesting time reversal and spatial inversion symmetry."

Micah's brow rose and he shrugged. "Don't have the slightest clue what that means, doc. Maybe it sounds familiar, maybe not." He tapped the side of his head. "The team doing the refit used a lot of big words this simple pilot's brain can't comprehend, so they dumbed it down for me. Told us the new hull was seriously badass and could take one hell of a pounding. Could shake off a direct hit from a small-yield tactical nuke like a dog coming in from the rain."

Sam nodded, her eyes getting a faraway look as she contemplated what he said. "I'd imagine so," she murmured with a slight smile. "The metal foam would absorb the strike, dispersing it across the external surface area."

Micah looked her over with a fresh intensity. "You know, you've never said. Exactly what kind of doctor are you, again?"

"The serious braniac kind of doctor," Harper said as she rose from the gunner's seat. "Radiation physicist *and* medical doc, all rolled into one."

Micah considered her words. He cocked his head, understanding flowing through him. He jerked a thumb toward the aft bulkhead. "So you're the reason why my cargo hold's now a medbay?"

Surprise crossed Sam's face. "You know what's back there?"

He folded his arms across his chest. "Cargo manifest. Anything brought onto this ship is automatically catalogued. Gear, supplies. People."

At that last, her expression changed, clouded by worry. "If we're safe now, I have a patient back there I need to check on."

He felt a flash of surprise, but merely nodded his head toward the cargo doors. "After you, doc." He stepped back to give Sam room. She paused at the entrance, eyeing him thoughtfully.

"And maybe it's time for some introductions, too." With that cryptic comment, she turned and lifted her palm to the control plate.

"Uh, doc, that's not keyed to your biosig" He felt a shock when the doors—doors that should only open for him and his crew—slid apart.

A chittering noise sounded. He looked down and saw a small paw wrap around the edge of the door. It was followed by a pair of bright, inquisitive eyes that quickly fastened themselves on him. The ferret chirruped again and scurried toward Micah.

"Whoa, there!" Sam laughed as she moved to intercept the small, furry bundle. "He can't hear you yet. We need to get him a working wire, remember?"

Micah's eyebrows rose. "He's enhanced?"

Harper groaned as she joined them. "Oh, yes. So are the others."

"The others?" He crooked an eyebrow at the analyst as she sauntered over to them and lifted the ferret from Sam's arms. "Since when did my ship become a menagerie?"

"Not a menagerie," the doctor corrected. "There are only two pairs of them. This is Snotface. The other ferret's Sneaky Pete."

Ignoring the introduction, he frowned, looking from one to the other. "Two pairs of what? And why are they on this ship?"

A loud chuffing sound reached his ears. His head whipped around as the hairs on the back of his neck stood on end. Pushing past the two women, he eased into the cargo bay, hand reaching for his weapon as his eyes swept the interior.

He froze at the sight of a large and deadly predator. The creature was easily a meter tall from shoulder to paws, and all black with subtle rosettes lining its flank. Jewel green eyes stared back at him, unblinking.

"What the hell? You brought a panther onto my ship?" The

words were directed at the two women though his eyes remained riveted to the animal in the cage. The panther looked lethal.

"That's Joule."

"Jewel?"

Harper's voice sounded amused. "Nope, Joule, like the physics guy."

Micah turned disbelieving eyes on the two women. "And there are *two* of them?"

"The other one's named Pascal." Harper offered, as if that would change his opinion. "Also a physics guy."

He didn't miss the mirth in her eyes at the healthy distance he maintained between himself and the crate as he moved further into the bay.

The big cat must have found humor in it too. She flashed her fangs, mouth dropping open in a yawn, her eyes slitting shut. Micah could sense the animal's amusement at his caution.

"Hey, you'd be careful, too, if you came across an apex predator you'd not met before," he glared at the cat.

Joule shook her head convulsively in response, stretching out and resting her head on her paws.

Micah reluctantly pulled his eyes away from the crate when he sensed the doctor was no longer beside him. A low, rhythmic beeping intruded upon his mind, and he realized he'd been hearing it ever since the bay doors had opened. It seemed to come from behind a stack of crates that had been maglocked to the bulkhead.

He stepped around them, Harper following in his wake. He was unsurprised to find the noise belonged to a portable surgical suite. But the patient inside—

Micah stopped cold as he realized who he was looking at.

"That's not Jack."

HIGH ALTITUDE TOUR

FLIGHT DECK
DEGRASSE RESEARCH TORUS

DEGRASSE'S FLIGHT DECK was shockingly empty, but that wasn't what had Addy grinding to a halt.

What is Clint Janus doing with a shipping crate in the middle of an evacuation? Her eyes narrowed in suspicion, and she jerked her head around to Gabe, but the warning in his eyes and the pressure of his hand between her shoulder blades told her to curb her response.

She wasn't sure what she would have done if Gabe hadn't encouraged her to keep moving.

Probably gone over and confronted the asshole, she thought. *And wouldn't that have been a dumb move.*

She didn't need Gabe's hand propelling her forward to figure out he didn't want her doing any such thing. She also didn't need his help to figure out their destination; the weathered tug was one of the few ships remaining on the flight deck. If that hadn't clued her in, the pilot's rolling hand motion urging them forward would have done it.

Still, Gabe's hand urged her toward the tug, as if he was

afraid of what she might do if he let loose of her. She felt a peer-to-peer connection snap into place inside her head.

{Don't look back at them or call attention to us. Just let it go,} he instructed. She shot him a sidelong glance and a brief nod as they pulled to a stop in front of the tug.

"Hello, sir. Doc," the pilot greeted them. Tall and rangy, the woman stood hipshot, hands jammed loosely against her waist. Her hair was cut so short it was little more than a cap of fuzz, and it was dyed a shocking blue.

"Cutting it a bit close, there, aren't you?"

The woman's grin turned the observation into a gentle jibe. She gestured them up the ramp.

"Harriet pinged to let me know you're the last of the stragglers. Sorry for the slim pickings, but when you wait until the very end to be evacuated, you get Ol' Betsy here, 'stead of a ride in a Novastrike." She slapped the side of the ship with affection.

Addy started up the ramp, Gabe's hand still at the small of her back. The pilot leapt after them, bypassing the ramp altogether, surprisingly graceful despite her gangly appearance.

She motioned them to two seats crammed behind the pilot's cradles. The co-pilot's position was already occupied— by a jowly, sad-eyed Basset hound.

Gabe's eyebrows climbed into his hairline when he saw the dog. A quick glance at the tug operator told Addy the other woman had seen his reaction as well.

The pilot, whose nametag identified her as Chief Warrant Katie Hyer, responded with a shrug and a sheepish look before turning to secure the hatch.

"I know he's not regulation, but I'd rather be prepared in case this 'not-a-drill' evac turns into something more. So, Fred goes where I go." The woman's firm tone told Addy this was non-negotiable.

Once she'd confirmed the hatch's seals read green, Hyer maneuvered past them, slipped into her seat, and began the ship's startup sequence.

"Batten down, folks. You know the drill," she called out as she secured her own webbing.

The ship began to move, taxiing into its hold-short position behind holographically-projected lines that indicated an active zone. Once cleared, the tug's thrusters would maneuver them into position, ready for Space Traffic Control to take over.

They were number two for departure, right behind the courier ship.

The courier ship

Addy shot Gabe a concerned look. "Did you get a look at their cargo? That's not an evac—"

A single shake of Gabe's head had her breaking off the rest of her comment, and she looked up in time to see Hyer's head tilted back to catch her words.

The pilot glanced back at them, a curious expression on her face. "If you're talking about the courier, you're right. They just filed a flight plan for the heliopause."

She did something to her forward screens and the projection of the flight deck just outside their ship was replaced by a diagram, populated by colorful icons with alphanumeric tags. The icons slowly advanced as the image refreshed, and Addy realized they represented the various ships outside the torus.

Hyer pointed to the lower right corner of the diagram, where the words 'deGrasse Space Traffic Control' were displayed.

"This is us," she said, pointing to one of two ship's icons, sitting inside a shaded area that Addy realized must represent the torus. Hyer's hand moved. "And that's them."

The pilot tapped on the icon representing the courier ship, and it opened up a flight plan. She enlarged it so they could see for themselves what it said:

GA16914, DEPT. DEGRASSE, 1435 LOCAL, DEST. LUYTEN C-Y GATE.

Gabe leaned forward to get a better look. "Need you to do

me a favor, Chief. Keep tabs on that ship, but don't do anything to draw attention to the fact. You get what I'm saying?"

"Five by five, sir."

She reached into the display and swiped, clearing the flight plan. With a pinching motion, she bracketed the icon displaying the courier ship's tail number and dropped a virtual pin on it.

Hyer reduced the STC feed, shunting the clutter of icons floating in nearspace to one of the tug's smaller displays, returning the forward screens to a projection of their surroundings. She reached over to check the webbing around her canine co-pilot, then straightened as her console beeped an alert.

"Here we go," she announced and Addy saw that the STC's holographic countdown, splashed across the flight deck's outer bulkhead, had moved the tug's ident from the number two position into the active slot.

Hyer brought the tug's thrusters online and Addy felt the craft lift into a hover. The pilot maneuvered the ship into the operational area, and then neatly pivoted, bringing their port side parallel to the flight deck's open maw. A slight bump told Addy that the torus's rail system had maglocked itself to their ship.

The next thing she knew, they were moving sideways, the rails pushing them across the bay's threshold and outside the torus. On the tug's forward screens, their view of the flight deck was replaced by the darkness of space, populated by dozens of small spacecraft.

Tiny sparks emitted by ships' thrusters twinkled across the visual canvas as the vessels maneuvered according to STC directives. All were within the wake-free zone mandated for Alliance nearspace. No ship within it was allowed to power up a fusion drive. To do so would not only strip a pilot of their license, it would be a death sentence for any vessel caught in its exhaust plume.

Addy shifted her gaze to the STC feed, her eyes seeking the

courier's icon. It was easy to spot. Its track cut between two stacks of tiered icons that moved in a coordinated, racetrack-like holding pattern.

She pointed it out to Hyer. "He's not wasting any time, is he," she murmured.

The pilot tossed another look over her shoulder. "He's in the corridor, that's for sure," she agreed. "At the rate he's going, he'll be able to bring his fusion drives online within the next hour or so. After that—"

Her voice cut off as the rails' maglocks released their hold.

"Hang on," Hyer announced. The ship seemed to shoot forward as it was cut loose from deGrasse's rotation. At the same time, Addy experienced the familiar weightlessness that occurred when parting from the torus.

Gabe waited until Hyer had engaged thrusters and entered into the pattern with the rest of the ships before he leaned forward. "ETA to the gate?" he asked, pointing to the courier ship still highlighted on the display.

Hyer reached a hand over and rubbed one of Fred's ears vigorously as she thought. The basset hound let out a low groan and somehow managed to flop over, exposing his belly, despite the low gravity the tug's thrusters imparted.

"Depends on how hard they boost," she said after a moment, her hand moving from Fred's ears to his stomach. "Twenty-eight days if they stick to one g. They could cut it in half if they do a hard burn. Be hell on the passengers, though, if they don't have pilot's augments."

"It'd get the attention of everyone in the system, too," Gabe mused, stroking his close-cropped beard. "Somehow I doubt they want to do that."

Hyer slapped Fred's belly lightly before straightening. "Well, whoever it is must be cleared for a gate transit. It's not like there's a customs station they can waltz into, what with Luyten being interdicted and all. Gotta be government-cleared," she repeated.

Addy shook her head at the mental picture Hyer's comment

evoked. When Gabe shot her a questioning look, she responded with a wry smile and a small shrug.

"I've never been that eager to approach a Calabi-Yau gate."

She could tell she'd surprised him. "But you're—"

"A captain in the Geminate Navy," she finished for him. "True. But I signed up for the free ride through medical school, plus the opportunity to serve and give back."

"Not a 'join the Navy, see the worlds' kind of person, eh?" Hyer interjected, tossing a smile over her shoulder.

Addy's mouth twisted in apology. "I just have this mental thing I can't get over, knowing my insides are being folded up when I go through that."

"Well, they're not literally doing that, you know," Gabe protested. "I'm not an astrophysicist, but the way I understand it, they punch a hole between dimensions to get from one location to another. There's no folding involved."

"Eh." Hyer wobbled her hand back and forth to let Gabe know his description wasn't quite tug-operator-approved. "Actually, the 'fold' part comes from how the gate is powered. It siphons dark matter out of a Ricci-flat manifold. That's a special curvature of space found in the Bulk."

"Voodoo and pixie dust, as far as I'm concerned, Chief." He crooked a grin at Hyer.

"Just one of the many layers in hyperspace, sir. The universe we live in is another one. A brane—a kind of an indentation—pokin' out of it."

Addy exchanged looks with Gabe. "Do you understand anything she just said?" she asked in a stage whisper, and Gabe chuckled.

He held up a hand, finger and thumb spread apart by about a centimeter. "Maybe that much," he admitted.

Hyer looked a bit sheepish. With a shrug, she explained, "Working a tug tends to give you a lot of down time, so I signed up for a few quantum engineering courses back home." Suddenly, she held up a hand. "Hang on a tick. STC's calling."

Hyer nodded at something they couldn't hear, then bent

toward the tug's flight controls to adjust their heading as she responded to the torus's tower. After a moment, she turned back to face them once more.

"Okay, now, where was I? Oh yeah, dark matter. Well, a Ricci-flat manifold lets us convert the dark matter into Casimir energy. Build up enough of that, and it kinda lets you bend all those compactified branes stacked up within the Bulk."

She held out her palm, flat, and then curled her fingers in until they touched her thumb. With her other hand, she mimed hopping over from the fingers to the thumb.

"Once that's done, we just pop on over to the other side."

Addy laughed. "You realize I have absolutely no idea what you just said."

Hyer winked and turned back to face the ship's forward screens. "That's okay, doc. I know just enough to be dangerous. Probably got it all wrong in the telling anyway." She shrugged. "Pretty much all I do is point the nose of the ship where the folks staffing the gate tell me to go, and they do the rest."

"I don't think you're making her feel any better, Chief." Gabe said, amusement coloring his tone.

Fred whoofed his agreement, which caused Hyer to frown at him in mock affront and accuse him of selling out.

"So, how long will it take for deGrasse to recall all these ships, once they give the all-clear?" Addy asked.

The pilot heaved a huge sigh, her expression so mournful, it reminded Addy of the woman's canine co-pilot. The same thing must have crossed Gabe's mind, if his stifled laugh was any indication.

"It could take a good two hours, maybe more." Her despair lasted for all of two seconds before she bounced in her seat and turned to them, a mischievous gleam in her eyes.

"Hey, want to take a turn around Vermilion while we wait? Not much else to do up here, and trust me, all of this—" one finger circled the air, mimicking the racetrack-like pattern they were flying, "—is going to get really old, really quick."

Gabe cocked his head, cupping one hand over his mouth to

hide an amused smile at the chief warrant's bubbly, irreverent attitude before giving a slow nod.

"You're the driver," he told her, sending a sidelong look Addy's way. "It's not like either one of us is certified to fly this boat."

Addy held up both hands. "Trust me, you wouldn't want me to try."

Hyer smothered a laugh, turning around to face her cockpit controls.

"One aerial tour, comin' up!"

CHEMISTRY LESSON

GNS *WRAITH*

THE MAN WHO thought of himself as Micah Case stood frozen, a look of stunned surprise on his face, as he took in the identity of Sam's patient.

"That's not Jack," he repeated. His voice sounded steady, calm.

Sam had anticipated the surprise. She hadn't expected him to handle the revelation with such equanimity.

"No," she said simply. "It's not."

He moved forward, eyes taking in every detail.

His hands clenched at his sides as he took in her patient's double amputation, both legs gone below the knee. His gaze traced the woven network of nanofiber surrounding the crushed left hand, a hand she was desperately trying to save.

And then his eyes tracked up to her patient's face. They fastened upon the lone visible blue eye, identical to his own, save for the pain bracketing it. The man standing in the cargo bay faced off against his mirror image in rigid silence for one long moment—and then his breath came shuddering out. "You're the voice in my head."

The words were low, yet they carried clearly to all in the room.

The injured man nodded faintly.

"How— What—" The other stumbled to a stop, sounding lost.

Sam inserted herself between the two, one hand coming to rest lightly on the bio-gel pack that encased her patient's injured arm.

"I have to put you under again," she gently told the man in the surgi-suite. She turned and laid a hand on the shoulder of the man standing over him, her eyes seeking his, willing him to understand.

"He insisted on remaining conscious until we got you to safety, but the strain is too much for him," she said softly.

The man in the surgi-suite made a gurgling noise, a wheezing protest. She turned a stern look on him.

"You two can talk later." Her words were firm now, doctor to patient. "Harper and I will fill him in on what he needs to know."

{S'okay, Navy. We'll figure it out.} The man's mental words were slurred, dulled by pain and exhaustion. {Ship's yours.}

"I have the ship," Sam heard his doppelganger murmur in response. Something about the exchange made her think that a ritual had just passed between the two.

{You can trust them,} her patient added. {Even Harper.}

Sam's friend made a choking sound from her position beside the stack of crates. "Idiot," she heard Harper mutter, and Sam saw the injured man's cheek twitch in the semblance of a smile.

The man standing beside her saw it, too. His grip tightened momentarily against the side of the surgi-suite before he nodded reluctantly and pushed back, giving Sam room to maneuver.

She made a few small adjustments to the surgical program then pressed a sequence to reengage the system.

"See you soon," she murmured, smiling down at him. His

eyelid fluttered and then drifted closed, the nanoparticles injected into his system rendering him unconscious. Taking a deep breath, Sam turned to confront the man standing at her back.

Shock and confusion chased across his face. His gaze sought Sam's. "That's me. Or I'm him. How—?"

She gripped his arm lightly. "It's a long story. Give me a second to check you over, then we can talk." Not waiting for his response, she stepped over to a smaller medical unit maglocked to the top of a crate and began manipulating a holoscreen. She shot him a look from over her shoulder. "Come on, Captain. Let's get you back online."

He stared down at the surgi-suite, rooted to the spot. She slipped a medical bracer onto her non-dominant hand and turned to face him. The unit encased her fingers like a glove, reaching up almost to her elbow. The bracer's controls blinked twice as they made the connection with her wire and the holographic readout along her forearm came online.

She waited, medical injector in her other hand. He ripped his gaze from his double and, with effort, focused first on the bracer and then on the injector. He cleared his throat and then asked, voice hoarse, "Medical nano?"

She tilted her head. "Nano click-assembly bots," she corrected, deliberately adopting a matter-of-fact tone. "You have no working neural lattice for a wire to interface with, and no store of medical nano. We need to remedy those things."

She suspected he was too stunned to process the true meaning behind her words. Click-assembly bots were used to build things. Things like neural interfaces inside the human brain. These interfaces, in turn, allowed humans to connect with the constellation of Starshot communication buoys seeded throughout this system.

They were also used to build the SmartCarbyne lattice of nanofloss, woven throughout soft tissues and organs, to protect against the stress of high-g maneuvers.

In truth, this man had no web of any sort, neural or

physical, woven throughout his body. This, despite memories insisting they were already there. Neither did he have a wire implanted inside his neocortex. He never did.

Stars, how am I ever going to explain that to him?

He stepped forward as she motioned, his expression dazed. She waved him to sit on a low crate she'd commandeered as a makeshift triage table. As he sat, she activated a sterile field.

He jumped, feeling the static wash as the field enveloped them.

"Doc?"

"Bend forward and let me see the back of your head. This'll only take a minute," she murmured, resting her hand against his shoulder until he complied. Brushing his hair away from the nape of his neck, she held the injector against his skin and activated it.

The load of nano being delivered into his body was extensive. If she had a second surgi-suite, she would have hooked him up to a central line to deliver the material. Instead, she had to do it manually—and that took time.

She popped an empty ampule out of the injector, grabbed a fresh one from the med unit, and inserted it. He stirred, the muscles in his neck cording with tension as he sensed she was doing something out of the ordinary.

"Doc," his voice held a warning edge.

"Hold still," she said, squeezing his shoulder. "We're almost done."

He took in a deep breath. "Want to tell me what you're doing back there? Sure as hell isn't a new batch of medical nano. Doesn't take this long."

Sam kept her voice calm and professional. "You're right. It doesn't. As I mentioned before, these are click-assembly bots, not medical nano. These take longer."

The injection complete, she patted his shoulder with one hand. "You can sit up now, but please remain seated. There's one more thing I need to do."

He straightened, adjusting the collar of his shipsuit. She

reached for the surgical tool that would allow her to make the minor cranial incision to install the implant in his neocortex. She then placed her hand atop his head, her thumb coming to rest against his skull, just above and behind his ear.

"I'm going to tilt your head to one side. You'll feel a cold sensation, and then a slight numbness," she quietly informed him as she lifted a surgical laser microdrill.

She inhaled swiftly as the man's hand shot up. She found her wrist encased in a hard grip.

"I don't think so," he said, voice like steel. Cold blue eyes bored into her, suspicion in their depths. His gaze shifted to the surgical tool she held, his hand tightening. Pain forced her to release the drill, and it landed beside the med unit with a small clatter.

The pressure around her wrist let up, but his expression remained unyielding, an unspoken demand for answers playing across his face.

"That is a surgical tool I plan to use, to embed a wire inside your head," she said, indicating the laser unit. She kept her tone even, matching his stare with her own. "You recall what it was like to have your wire implanted?"

His eyes flicked from the device to her face, his expression wary. "You're telling me the reason I can't access my wire is that they stripped it from my head?"

"You have no wire inside you, that is correct." She chose her words carefully. "No database, and no implant."

He stared at her for another beat, and then nodded. Releasing her wrist, he bent and turned his head to the side.

She picked up the scalpel once more, her other hand brushing his close-cropped hair from his nape. Her eyes on the med unit's display, she positioned the instrument, activating its biolock to sterilize the site and secure the small machine in place.

"Hold still," she murmured as she began the procedure.

Tied to the med unit, the machine projected a 3D rendering of its progress on her optical overlay as it bored a microscopic hole through his skull.

That step completed, she swapped the drill for a preloaded autosyringe.

Inside the vial was a fresh wire implant, plus biological nanomachines that would guide the unit into position. Once their job was complete, they would disassemble, the man's body eventually flushing it from his system.

After the injector released its payload, Sam applied sealant to the surgical site, stepped back, and disengaged the sterile field.

"All done."

She pointed to the holoscreen on the small medical unit, where the device she had just inserted began its slow march toward the base of his parieto-occipital sulcus, where temporal lobe met occipital.

"Your wire should be operational within a minute or two."

While they waited, Sam used her bracer to run a cursory exam on the man. She was relieved to see his vitals were all within range, considering who he truly was.

A quick glance back at the unit showed the implant had reached its destination. She caught his gaze.

"Ready to try it?"

He nodded, and she brought his newly-installed wire online.

{Can you hear me now?} she sent, and saw his eyes flicker.

{Yes,} he replied, voice curt and with an undercurrent of anger. She couldn't tell if it was directed at her or at the circumstances he found himself in. *{Are we done here?}*

"We are, Captain."

Sam shut off the small unit and stepped away, allowing him to rise. She exchanged a swift look with Harper, who had remained off to one side, quietly observing the procedure, two ferrets in her lap.

The analyst released the animals and stood.

"Guess it's time for that talk."

He stared straight ahead, jaw clenched.

"Damn straight. I'll be in the galley."

A derisive tone entered his voice. "Something tells me you already know where that is."

* * *

Micah stood inside *Wraith*'s tiny galley, palms braced against the small, fold-out prep counter. Head bowed, he pinched the bridge of his nose between two fingers as he fought to make sense of everything he'd just seen and experienced.

He'd been so certain the man inside his head was Jack. Despite his physical appearance, Micah knew the man could very well still *be* Jack. But he couldn't fathom why anyone would go to the trouble to surgically reconstruct someone to look like him.

Somehow, that had to tie into what the doctor, Samantha Travis, had said about traitors, classified discoveries, and their mission. If he'd been captured, brainwashed, he could understand his memory loss. But someone had gone to the trouble to remove his wire *and* disable his lattice.

What the hell is going on?

He lifted his head and stared speculatively at the nearest storage unit before popping it open. It was fully stocked. He considered what he'd seen in the cargo bay he'd just left. It, too, had been filled to overflowing—save for the part of the hold set up as a provisional hospital.

So the ship was configured for a long mission. When had this happened? More importantly, why?

The questions squirrel-caged in his mind, his hands fisting in frustration as he came up empty.

He turned as both women appeared at the galley's entrance. One of the ferrets scampered over to him and began to climb up the leg of his shipsuit.

{Micah too. Got food?}

He looked down to see a small paw clinging to the place

where his name would ordinarily be displayed, two bright eyes regarding him intently. Micah found his anger slipping away as the animal stared earnestly up at him.

That irritated him. He wanted to hang onto that anger for a bit longer. He looked over at the women from under lowered brows. "Uplifted and with evanescent comm access?" His tone was laced with sarcasm. "This little guy have a full wire implant, too?"

Harper shook her head, ignoring Micah's aggressive tone.

"Simple E-V circuitry, limited range. But enough to make a nuisance of himself." The smile on her face softened her words. "Want me to take him?"

"Which one is he?" he grudgingly asked, hand curling around the ferret to support him, oddly hesitant to give him up. The creature obligingly settled around his neck.

"Snotface," she said and Micah smothered a laugh at the name.

"He was born deaf," Sam added. "I think that might be why he's a bit more chatty than his— Than the other one, now that he has the ability to communicate better."

The ferret nuzzled him behind his ear. *{Snacks?}*

Micah shot a sharp look at the doctor, wondering what she had been about to say.

"He's an obligate carnivore," she said before he could voice his question aloud. "There's some jerky in the cabinet by your left knee; he can have a piece."

Micah slid her a jaded look before he bent and peered into the cabinet, unsealed the container, and offered the ferret the treat. "Looks like you've made yourselves at home here," was his caustic observation. "Want to tell me how, and why?"

Sam's expression turned resigned. Harper stepped deeper into the little galley and unfolded one of the benches built into the retractable bulkhead. Flopping down onto it, she waved to Sam. "All yours. You get to do the honors."

Sam made a face at Harper, but nodded. She reached overhead, opening a nearby storage compartment. She grabbed a few water bottles from within, handed one to Harper, and chucked another at him. The third one she kept for herself before settling onto the bench beside her friend.

Micah unfolded the bench across from them and the ferret immediately made himself at home. Sitting across from the two women put his knees a scant half-meter from theirs, close enough to feel like a threat should he choose.

Neither seemed bothered by that fact.

"Drink," Sam ordered, nodding at the bottle, and he frowned at her. "Your medical scan indicated you were dehydrated."

Micah barked a humorless laugh. "Guess they don't worry about things like that when you're in the morgue."

He popped the bottle open and took a long pull, then braced his elbows on his thighs, the bottle held between both hands.

Snotface took that as an invitation. The ferret wiggled under one arm and draped himself across his thigh with a contented sigh. *{Humans gonna talk. Time for a nap.}*

It broke the tension.

He huffed a laugh at the creature in his lap and sat back. "Okay, doc. Talk."

* * *

Sam unconsciously mimicked the actions of the man across from her, rolling her water bottle between her palms. She studied it for a long moment before giving her head a small shake.

She hated what this was going to do to him when he found out. Expelling the air in her lungs in a quick breath, she began.

"Tell me, captain. Have you ever heard of chirality?"

He frowned. "No. Should I?"

She shook her head.

"Prior to deGrasse, it's been something relegated to pharmaceutical companies and research grants. So, no. I would have been surprised if you'd said otherwise."

"So?" he prompted when she didn't continue. "What is it, then? And what does it have to do with why someone wants me dead?"

"I only have a basic understanding of it, myself, really," Sam admitted. "Radiation biology is my specialty, not biochemistry. Based on the fact that they were trying to detain me, too, maybe I didn't fake my way through this assignment as well as I thought I was."

Harper coughed. "If you think your understanding of it is basic, I'd hate to hear what you call my understanding of it."

Sam's gaze flickered to her friend. Her mouth kicked up in a half smile and she shook her head at the other woman before returning her attention to the man who thought of himself as Micah Case.

"Chirality refers to the way atoms are oriented when they're bonded together," she told him. "Depending on how the molecules are formed, they can have a 'handedness' to them."

The man who looked achingly similar to her patient blinked at her. "A 'handedness'," he repeated, sounding lost.

She raised both hands, palms facing out, and then placed one in front of the other and wiggled her thumbs.

"You can't superimpose one hand over the other and have them line up. Your thumbs mess up the symmetry there. But if you bring your palms together," her hands came together in a prayer position, "you *can* make them match—as mirror images of each other. That's what chiral means."

She dipped into her pocket and pulled out a small holoprojector she'd grabbed before joining him in the galley. Thumbing it on, she called up a diagram she figured he might recognize from a college chemistry class.

It was a model of a molecule. The black sphere in the center was a carbon atom.

Four spheres encircled the carbon atom. They were brightly colored—white, red, blue, yellow. She knew he wouldn't have the slightest idea what they were, but it really didn't matter *what* they were—the principle was what counted.

"This is a molecule, a connected grouping of atoms of different types. Building blocks of nature, right?"

He nodded. So far, so good.

She duplicated the molecule—and flipped it. The mirror images faced each other as they floated over the device, the atoms on the left now encircling the carbon atom in a reversed yellow, blue, red, white pattern.

"This is a chiral molecule. Each atom attached to the carbon atom in the center is assigned a priority. Going from the highest to the lowest, you'll travel around it in either a clockwise or counterclockwise direction. If you move clockwise, the molecule's right-handed. Counterclockwise, it's left-handed."

Sam's finger traced the paths along the two holographic figures as she spoke.

"Now, both of these molecules have the exact same physical properties—the same boiling and freezing points, the same densities, and so on. But they can react *very* differently with biologically active molecules."

She wiped the mirror molecules from the holo and replaced them with images of two plants. One was feathery and fernlike, the other had deep green oval leaves that looked almost furry.

She looked expectantly over at him, then after a moment, when it was clear he wasn't going to speak, she raised an eyebrow.

"What? Don't tell me you've never seen either of these plants before?"

The man who looked like Micah shook his head with a smile. "The one on the left looks like an herb. Dill, maybe?"

She nodded.

"The other one, though Sorry. Haven't the first clue," he confessed.

"Let me guess." Her tone turned dry. "You aren't the kind of guy who drinks the occasional mojito or mint julep."

He barked a laugh and shook his head. "Can't say that I do.

Rather have a beer than anything fancy."

His response had her smiling despite herself. Turning back to the holo with a shake of her head, she pointed to the two plants.

"Well, you're right. The one on the left is dill. The other one's mint. Both of these have a compound in them called carvone. The mint carvone has sweet notes to it and is right-handed. The dill one has savory notes and is left-handed. But other than that, their *physical* properties are identical."

He shot her a skeptical look. "You're telling me that just because they spiral one way and not the other, they taste different?"

She nodded. "That's exactly what I'm saying."

He looked puzzled. "But...what's the big deal, then? Why would scientific research be so interested in something that just changes the way something tastes?"

"Because, while that's a harmless example of the differences a mirror molecule can exhibit, some of the compounds created can be quite dangerous."

His eyes narrowed. "In what way?"

She waved a hand dismissively. "Oh, it's all well documented. A left-handed pharmaceutical that offers palliative effects has a mirror pair that causes deformities in human embryos. We learned centuries ago to be very careful with chiral direction."

The man stared at her for a long moment, scratching the sleeping ferret in his lap idly as he contemplated her words.

"So." He drew the word out. "What does this have to do with deGrasse and Luyten's Star? More importantly, what does it have to do with me?"

She looked down, rubbing the tops of her thighs and gathering her thoughts.

"Bear with me for another minute, and I'll get to that, I promise. All life we've found so far in the galaxy is decidedly left-handed. And, although we've been able to synthesize right-handed molecules in the lab, science has been pretty spectacularly *unable* to get it to live outside the lab."

She looked back up at him, her eyes traveling over his face, sweeping down to his hands. Hands that were very much alive, cradling the ferret.

"Until now."

He followed her gaze down at the animal in his hands. "Until now?"

"A probe discovered naturally-occurring chiral life on the planet deGrasse is orbiting. That's why the torus is here."

He blinked, processing the news. After a moment, he asked, "Okay. Why is that so important?"

She shrugged. "For some scientists, it's a sort of holy grail, I guess. They kept trying to find right-handed life that exists somewhere in nature, even knowing that if we did, it likely wouldn't be able to survive in our own ecosystems."

He looked up at that.

"Why not?"

"A chiral organism can only feed from its own kind," she explained. "Oh, it can digest a substance from its mirror-environment, but it gains no nutritional benefit from it. So right-handed life in a left-handed world would, in essence, starve."

Snotface began gnawing on Micah's thumb, interspersing it with small licks. He rearranged his hold on the ferret, but Snotface squirmed away, running up to his shoulder instead.

He stuck his nose in Micah's ear and snuffled. *{Sneaky Pete right-handed. So is Micah too.}*

* * *

The ferret's words seared their way through Micah's brain. The small creature couldn't have understood the implication of what he'd just said, could he? His head snapped up, his gaze seeking the doctor's.

"What did he mean by that?"

"He means we ended up with two problems on our hands,"

Harper interjected. The analyst glanced toward Sam.

"We weren't just dealing with a traitor, out to get their hands on our chiral research. It turned out the Navy's chief scientist was running an illegal series of side experiments."

"Side experiments," Micah repeated, his gut tightening.

The voice inside his head. They'd done that.

He caught and held Sam's gaze, a wary apprehension building inside him.

The truth. He needed it. Now.

Sam ran her hands up and down her thighs as if suddenly chilled.

"Once we got here," she said, her words slow and deliberate, "we realized he'd been creating chiral clones of complex, multicellular organisms. Mice, ferrets. Larger animals, like the panthers."

Her eyes met his. He read pain there, mixed with an inexplicable guilt.

"And then he began to experiment on humans."

She stood, reached past him, and opened a cabinet. He heard the rustling of a wrapper, and when she returned to her seat across from him, a candy was in her hands. She held the mint out to him.

"Go ahead, captain." Her voice was a mix of sadness and curiosity. "Taste it."

He reached for the mint, unwrapped it and popped it into his mouth. And immediately spat it back out.

"What the hell?"

Her eyes met his steadily. "It tasted like dill, didn't it."

The burst of flavor, sharp, savory, still clung to his tongue.

"This is some sort of sick joke—"

"Captain," she interrupted, one hand reaching out to land on his knee, "the person in your cargo hold"

He looked up sharply. "The one who looks like me."

"You have to understand, Captain." He was drowning in the guilt he saw in her eyes. "I took an oath. I couldn't let them kill you. And I couldn't let him die."

Dropping his hands to the bench, he gripped the edge tightly, until it cut into his palms, the pain grounding him in reality. "He's... the original, isn't he?"

She nodded, the guilt in her eyes morphing into a sympathetic pain.

"And what does that make me?"

Her hand tightened on his knee.

"Micah Case's chiral clone."

VERMILION

ALLIANCE NAVY TUG, GNS *BETSY*

THE TUG'S BLUE-HAIRED pilot turned out to be both a knowledgeable and competent tour guide.

The moment Gabe gave Hyer the green light, the chief had broken away from the holding pattern and pointed the *Betsy*'s nose toward the planet below.

The station's geosynchronous orbit above Vermilion's main outpost meant they had tens of thousands of kilometers to traverse before hitting atmosphere. The tug covered that in a matter of minutes.

Certified for both space and air maneuvers, the vessel's descent through Vermilion's thermosphere was unremarkable, though a bit bumpy.

"Sorry," Hyer called out, her voice not sounding the least bit apologetic. "The old girl's a workhorse, not a passenger ship."

Addy didn't care. Her eyes remained glued to the forward screens as Hyer sent them streaking across Vermilion's skies, treating them to a breathtaking view of the verdant world's surface.

Addy had put in for a tour of duty down on the scientific

outpost the moment she'd arrived, but she hadn't been on deGrasse long enough for her rotation to have been called.

This was the closest she'd ever come to being there, and she intended to make the most of it. She bent eagerly toward the forward screens, watching the terrain below as the tug approached the planet's terminator.

They flew in a companionable silence, the cloud cover parting to reveal the blues of a large ocean directly beneath them. The greens and browns of a continent began to grow in the distance as deGrasse slipped behind the planet's horizon.

"Hard to believe that this has been here for millennia, and we just now got around to investigating it," Addy murmured.

"Well, that whole interdiction fiction the defense department's using to hide us isn't completely a lie," Hyer said, glancing over at her with one brow raised. "They're still not entirely sure what's behind it, but the unusual spacetime anomalies in this system did quite a number on every unmanned probe we've sent here since the diaspora."

"So, you're saying it wasn't that we didn't try to get a closer look at Vermilion" Gabe prompted.

"Exactly. We just decided our credits were best spent looking elsewhere."

Hyer bobbed her head decisively, sending the blue fuzz of her hair shivering. "Especially once we developed the Scharnhorst drives, and managed to make it to Alpha Centauri, and then Sirius and Procyon, without the need for generation ships."

"Those drives didn't do us any favors in the long run," Addy commented. "Tearing into the fabric of dark matter like they do."

"Oh, they're not all bad," Hyer said cheerfully. "Sure, they're banned for in-system flight, but now that we know the effect they have on the interstellar medium, we use them sparingly. The good news is that we discovered the IM does repair itself, eventually."

She made a wry face, waggling her hand back and forth. "It

was kind of a damned-if-you-do situation. Without the drive's ability to generate a Casimir bubble, we couldn't have harnessed the Scharnhorst effect and tripled the speed of light. And without that advantage, we'd just now be setting foot on my homeworld in Sirius."

She shot them a pointed look, jabbing a finger in their direction for emphasis.

"It was our own ignorance of the drive's long-term effects on spacetime that was to blame. Once we dropped the idea of dedicated spacelanes, we stopped wearing ruts into the interstellar medium that eventually tore through it."

Addy made a strangled noise.

"Never thought I'd say it, but I think I'll stick to gate travel, thank you very much."

Gabe barked a laugh at that, and Addy decided it was time to change the subject.

"Okay, then, not that I don't appreciate the science lesson, but biology is more my wheelhouse," she said, leaning forward once more and peering intently at the image on the screen. "I'm particularly interested in the biology beneath us. Is that Cinnabar?"

"Nope, that's Garnet. Cinnabar is on the night side at the moment."

Hyer grinned suddenly. "Anyone ever hear why the GA was so literal about its naming conventions?"

She pointed to a smaller screen, one that held a view of the star and two close-in planets, to illustrate her point. "Rufus and Vermilion. Red dwarf, red names."

She glanced back at them. "Sirius suffered the same fate, you know. Blue-white stars, renamed Big and Little Blue. I have relatives on Beryl, which orbits Little Blue. Dad worked for Cobalt Mining. Their headquarters is based on Heliodor."

Gabe grinned and shook his head. "You figure that one out, you let me know."

The pilot passed the flat of her hand across the top of her hair. "Couldn't stand to look at anything blue when I left. Now, though"

Addy heard a wistful tone creep into Hyer's voice. "It kinda reminds me of home."

Addy smiled at the pilot. "It's human nature, I think." She nodded toward the continent they were flying over. "I grew up on a farm on Hawking, but it's been years since I've been back. Seeing those prairie grasses down there makes me want to land and wander through them."

A lush, fertile planet, Vermilion's topology included vast swathes of prairie land, found on both its continents. The super-earth was three times the size of Terra, orbiting just under a tenth of an AU—about fifteen million kilometers—away from its star.

Habitable zones around red dwarf stars were, by necessity, close in. That factor, combined with Vermilion's mass, gave the planet a 3:2 spin-orbital resonance. That translated to an eighteen-Terran-day year, but it took twelve of those days to see a new Vermilion sunrise.

"From what I understand, it's no small feat that life managed to take root here." Gabe's quiet comment pulled Addy's attention back inside the confines of the ship. "It helps that it has a sizable molten iron core that produces a decent magnetosphere."

"And that Luyten's is one of the most stable red dwarfs ever discovered," Hyer added. "Otherwise, it would've had a hard time hanging onto its atmosphere, even with a strong magnetic field."

Addy looked over as she felt Gabe's hand on her arm.

"As much as I enjoy talking planetary science," he began, and she nearly laughed at the polite fiction, "it occurs to me that we're in a unique position to discuss today's incident."

His eyes held hers for a beat, a question in them. When she nodded, he turned to the chief warrant. "Katie, I'm going to have to invoke the security clause in your naval contract. What you hear from this point on is classified. Other than me, Doctor Mason, or Admiral Toland herself, you're not to repeat what you hear to anyone. Am I clear?"

Hyer's casual demeanor dropped.

"Yes sir," she responded crisply, tone matching his. "You'll want to access the tug's flight recorders to encrypt them, too. Sending you my security token now."

Gabe's focus shifted into the near distance as his wire established a connection with the tug and he placed an imprint on it, sealing the ship's record.

His attention returned to Addy. "Now that's settled, I'd like to go over the data your medics gathered from the accident site, and compare it to what my security team collected."

He held up a hand. "Initial impressions only. I promise not to hold you to anything if further examination causes you to change your opinions."

She nodded. "The only thing I can say with certainty at this point is that Stinton's body was crushed under that prototype printer."

Gabe lifted one brow. "I like to think I'm a good judge of character. Based on how you acted in the lab, you think the accident was staged every bit as much as I do."

Addy nodded. "As we suspected, the total volume of blood, both what was found on site and what remained in Stinton's body, doesn't add up. The missing amount would have been enough to cause death by exsanguination."

"So he was killed elsewhere, and the accident staged to cover it up." That fit with Gabe's suspicions. "Anything else?"

Addy shook her head slowly.

"Nothing concrete. There wasn't much time between when we arrived in medical, and when we were forced to evacuate. I'd just completed a cursory scan when the alarms sounded."

She reached into the pocket of her scrubs and lifted a small data device with an ironic smile.

"And then someone showed up and demanded I make a copy of my records."

Gabe's lips twitched. "Guilty as charged." He gestured to the data chip in her hand. "May I?"

"Sure." She handed it over.

"Katie, you have any kind of portable projection—" He stopped when the pilot extended a hand, a small holoprojector in her palm. "You're a keeper, chief."

"That's what all the guys say, sir."

With a chuckle, Gabe connected the device to Addy's recorder and activated it.

"Talk me through what I'm seeing, doc," he instructed, settling the device between them.

"As you can see," Addy's fingers skimmed across the recording's timeline until she came to the right spot, "the gantry's impact crushed both the skull and ribcage. A cursory exam like this one won't be able to give us much in those areas. On the other hand"

She fast-forwarded to the point in the recording where the scanner hovered over the corpse's neck. Fanning her fingers, she enlarged the image. A quick, harsh inhale from Gabe told her he saw it, too.

"Someone got him in the carotid?"

She nodded. "With an injury like that, death due to exsanguination could occur in as little as five minutes."

"Yeah, but ordinary medical nano should have kept it from being life threatening, wouldn't it?" Hyer joined in, twisting to look at them.

Her eyes widened and she paled a bit when she caught sight of the projected image. Whipping around to face front again, she muttered, "Hoooookay, and that's why I dropped out of paramedic school."

A brief smile skated across Addy's face. "Sorry, Chief. But you're right. Medical nano would begin to repair the damage, as well as accelerate wound clotting."

Gabe's eyes narrowed and he sat back, regarding her with an expression that told Addy he knew where she was going with this.

"What did your scan tell you about the condition of his med nano?"

Addy's expression hardened. "There wasn't any."

Gabe cocked his head. "What could cause that?"

She gestured to the recording's image, frozen between them. "Any number of things. We use nanoagents during surgeries to essentially paralyze a patient's own medical nano so that it doesn't interfere with a procedure."

She held up a hand. "But they're created to disassemble when sent an autodestruct command, so that the patient's own nano can be brought back online."

"I don't suppose you found any in Stinton, did you?"

Addy grunted in annoyance.

"Would have been convenient if we had, but no."

After a moment, Gabe nodded.

"So, we're agreed. This is murder."

* * *

Gabe's words drew chills down Addy's spine. She shot a glance at the STC feed, relayed by Vermilion's orbital satellites. It showed the courier ship had cleared the wake-free zone. She pointed, and both Gabe and Hyer followed her gaze.

"My money's on Janus."

The speed at which the courier's icon advanced began to increase.

Hyer tapped the icon, enlarging it. The telemetry indicated the courier ship had jumped to an acceleration of one g.

"And away they go," the chief said.

"I would have thought they'd be going faster," Addy commented.

"What, and draw attention to them?"

Gabe grinned at her, his eyes lit with amusement. The action gave him a boyish look that momentarily erased his grim expression. Then he shook his head, the smile gone.

"No, he's acting exactly as I'd expect, if he's truly guilty. I don't disagree with you that the man's hiding something," he told her. "But a situation developed just as the evacuation began that suggests others may be involved."

Addy swiped the image closed and proffered the projector to Hyer with a nod of thanks.

"What kind of a situation?" she asked.

Gabe shifted his gaze from Addy to Hyer.

"I'll remind you, Chief, that this falls under the same confidentiality clause."

At her nod and "yessir," he drew in a breath, and turned back to Addy. He studied her intently, then shook his head.

"What is it, Gabe? You're acting as if I'm not going to like what you're about to say."

His brows drew down. "I don't think you are, Addy. You and Doctor Travis are friends—"

"Absolutely not." Addy cut him off, anger rising swiftly. "She's a doctor, for sun's sake! She's taken an oath to do no harm!"

Gabe's eyes held a hard glint, and then his expression blanked as he sat back.

"That third pilot. Tell me again what happened that night, everything you can recall, up to the time he was pronounced dead."

Addy narrowed her eyes at Gabe, wondering where he was going with the topic change.

"What does this have to do with Stinton's death?"

Gabe held up a hand. "Humor me."

She blew out a sharp breath.

"Okay. Okay."

She broke eye contact, turning to face forward once more as she gathered her thoughts.

"When the report came in that there was another crash, and we had injured on the way, I didn't even need to contact Sam," she began. "She must have set up some kind of filter to monitor the triage net. She ran into medical just after I did."

At Gabe's suspicious look, she snapped, "I set the same filter, Alvarez. It's a common thing to do, especially when you fear that more of the same might be coming your way."

"What made you think that?"

"Sam and I held some pretty long discussions over the past few weeks, following the deaths of those first two pilots," she explained in a calmer voice.

Then she ticked off each fact on her fingers as she recounted them, one by one.

"Jack Campbell should not have died. Clint Janus showing up in medical was out of character; that man doesn't have an altruistic bone in his body. He had no business escorting the body to the morgue. The fact he volunteered just made us even more suspicious."

"Suspicion's not going to buy you anything," Gabe reminded her.

She lowered her hand and nodded.

"I know. But you have to understand, it fueled our determination to make sure nothing like this ever happened again. The next victim—if there was one—was going to live."

"But he didn't." Gabe said.

As if she needed reminding.

"No. He didn't," she agreed.

Gabe nodded, his eyes never leaving hers. "Go on."

"We went over this already. Neither of us was surprised to see Janus pop into the medical clinic's emergency room the evening of the second accident. As I told you before, Sam refused to let him anywhere near Micah Case."

Addy hesitated, than added, "The animosity between the two of them was pretty intense. I got the impression it predates her arrival on deGrasse."

"So they have history, then," Gabe murmured thoughtfully.

Addy lifted a shoulder in a 'maybe' gesture.

"Sam never mentioned it. But she wouldn't have. She's too professional to bring up anything personal."

"Would you say Case's injuries were less severe than Ettinger's or Campbell's?"

"I wouldn't say that. Different? Yes. Less severe? Not necessarily."

Addy wondered where he was going with this line of questioning.

"We managed to stabilize him, but we had to amputate both legs. His hand was touch-and-go, and he lost an eye. Before I left that night, I looked up his service record and placed an order with the regen lab for them to be 3D printed. I planned to discuss the transplant schedule and post-op therapy with Sam the next day."

"But you never got the opportunity," Gabe said. "Case died overnight."

Addy answered with a tight nod. The news had hit her hard. She'd known his injuries had been extensive, but he'd been in guarded condition when her shift had ended.

"Sam told me first thing the next morning. She said Janus had paid another visit to medical in the middle of the night."

Gabe sent her a sharp look.

"She was there?"

"For all the good it did our patient. She said she locked Janus out of the triage net and had placed token-level access on the medical node servicing the intensive care unit."

Her hand tightened on the data chip. "Janus shouldn't have been able to do any harm, but shortly after he left, Case coded."

"Did Doctor Travis say why?"

Addy's troubled gaze met his, and she saw something she couldn't decipher in his expression, a kind of knowing expectation that vaguely disturbed her.

She shook her head, recalling Sam's incandescent anger. It was true that the details surrounding Micah Case's death had been a bit vague, but Sam's anger toward Janus had been bright and hard.

"I'm not sure what you think you have on Sam, but if you're implying she had something to do with his death, you're dead wrong."

Gabe laughed, but there was no humor in it. He turned away, one hand reaching up to cup the back of his neck— contemplating what, Addy didn't know. After a moment, he nodded to himself and straightened.

"I'm going to show you something, doc. But you'll be held to the same oath the chief is when you see it," he warned. "That information stays between you, me, Colonel Fraley, and Admiral Toland, am I clear?"

She nodded warily. Gabe reached forward and tapped Hyer on the shoulder. She slapped the holoprojector into his hand without a word.

He flipped it on and blinked at it, and Addy realized he was having it handshake with his wire. Whatever he was about to show her came from his own personal database, housed in his implant.

The holoprojector flared to life, the image one from the perspective of someone jogging through the torus's belowdecks passageways.

The view was an augmented, full-spectrum composite and she realized she was seeing someone's personal feed. Wherever they were was lit only by emergency lighting.

"Marine visor," supplied Gabe.

The Marine rounded a corner. Addy's eyes narrowed and her jaw tightened when she recognized one of the two figures that came into view. It was Sam.

Her fist clenched and she swore softly as the scene played out and the Marines fired on them. Whoever was with Sam at least had the decency to cover her when the pulsed energy beam fired.

"What in the hell—"

Gabe held up a hand. "Wait for it."

She didn't have long. The man shielding Sam grabbed her and sprinted toward the intersecting passageway, pulling his own pulsed weapon as he ran.

Just as he twisted to fire at the Marines pursuing them, Gabe froze the feed and pointed at the image.

"Can you identify that man for me, Addy?" he asked softly.

"That... impossible," she stated flatly. "That has to be an impostor."

"Biosignature says otherwise."

Addy shot him a cold stare. "He had to be spoofing it somehow."

"How?"

She blew out an exasperated breath, voice laced with sarcasm. "I don't know, Gabe. You tell me. You're the security expert."

She jabbed a finger at the image. "It's not medically possible for that man to be Micah Case. When his body left for the morgue, it was minus two legs, an eye, and a functioning hand."

She stared at him, daring him to contradict her.

Gabe raised a placating hand. "Okay, let's shelve the identity of our mysterious Micah Case lookalike for the moment. That still leaves Samantha Travis as a person of interest."

"How can you know that?" Addy asked. "Clearly she was there under duress."

Gabe didn't say anything else; he merely let the visor's recording play out until the two Marines fell unconscious. The angle of the fallen Marine's feed gave the recording an odd, canted appearance, but Addy could clearly see the man who looked like Micah Case come back into frame. He lifted Sam and carried her unconscious form back down the way he'd come.

Gabe reached for the holoprojector and shut it off. "I have to consider this man's actions as suspect. First, if it is Case, then he faked his own death. Second, he had to have help, and your friend certainly has the means by which to do it."

Addy drew in a breath but Gabe talked over her incipient protest.

"Putting aside for a moment that this effectively means he's AWOL, he's in a section of deGrasse he's not cleared to be in. Although Doctor Travis is."

"As is Clint Janus," she countered quickly.

They stared at each other a moment, in a silent battle of wills.

"Since when do Marines police this station?" Addy tried a new tactic. "You're the security chief. Shouldn't that have been your own people? Doesn't that strike you as odd?"

Gabe ran his hands through his hair and nodded, once. "Yes...and no," he admitted. "Just before I arrived at your clinic, I was contacted by Colonel Fraley."

"Admiral Toland's XO?"

"Yes. You're in the Navy," he reminded her. "You understand Joint Security Operations. He's deGrasse's JSO, and if he perceives a threat, he can order joint operations, combining my security forces with his own tactical teams."

Addy processed this information, realizing she'd been looking at deGrasse as a home assignment, rather than a deployment outside Alliance borders.

While technically true, Luyten's Star was interdicted, as well as being uninhabited. They were just as unprotected here as they would be at an embassy or foreign base in another star nation.

"So he thinks we've been infiltrated by an enemy? He activated a joint tactical team?"

Her eyes sought his for confirmation. He nodded.

"Does Fraley think the imposter had something to do with Stinton's death?"

"He added me to the Marines' combat net just before I arrived in medical. Once they secured the area, I pinged the fireteam and asked who had authorized their actions. She told me her sergeant had mentioned Janus, but when I requested a copy, there was no record of it."

"And you don't find that the least bit suspicious?" Addy demanded. "Janus has as much authority to order Marines around as I do—which is none!"

"Agreed. And if he tried, they'd ignore it. The order had to have come from someone within their own command structure. Although," he conceded, "it could have been based on information they received from Janus."

"But there's no record of it." Her tone was skeptical. "You

heard that recording; that Marine said Janus *was* in charge. And you don't find that the least bit suspect?"

"Don't get me wrong," he countered. "I think Janus is as crooked as they come, and he's in this up to his pointy little ass. But in order for me to make an arrest, I need proof. The only data point we have at the moment is your friend in the company of someone who looks suspiciously like a dead man."

Hyer interrupted them. "Sorry to bust in on your discussion but you have a data squirt coming in from the torus, sir."

Gabe thanked her and stared off into the distance as he accessed the information. A tightening around his eyes indicated the news wasn't welcome.

"What is it?" she asked.

He shook his head. "They've completed their search belowdecks. Your friend and Micah Case's lookalike appear to have escaped. Case's ship is reported missing, too. A search is underway now, in nearspace around the torus."

The eyes that met hers were understanding, yet firm. "It's possible she was under duress, but at this point, Addy, we have no choice. Fraley's sent out an order to capture and subdue both Doctor Travis and Micah Case, suspected in the death of Lee Stinton...and the bombing of deGrasse."

Addy's shocked gaze met his. "Bombing! What in stars—"

His eyes shifted. "I was under orders not to say, but given the circumstances" His voice trailed off, before his gaze refocused on hers. "DeGrasse didn't evacuate because of a systems' failure. Those explosions were an attack from space."

"Okayyyy" Addy drew the word out as she turned this over in her head. "I still don't see what that has to do with Sam."

"That Marine fireteam was dispatched to apprehend Doctor Travis and an accomplice, shortly after the attack began," Gabe told her. "The report I just received said that the bombings stopped immediately after they escaped. Looks like they were staged to cover their departure."

"She can't be involved," Addy protested yet again. "It makes no sense. Janus is the one with the questionable actions, not

Sam."

Gabe dipped his head in acknowledgement. "Necessity sometimes makes for strange bedfellows. Maybe he was blackmailing her to do it, then decided to frame her to take the fall. We won't know until we can apprehend them both, and bring them in for questioning."

Addy's lips compressed in anger at that, but she held her tongue.

Gabe's gaze softened, and she understood his next words for the olive branch that they were.

"I promise you that we'll get to the bottom of this as discreetly as we possibly can. If she's innocent, she has nothing to worry about. If she was coerced, we'll bring the ones responsible to justice."

CONTINGENCY PLANS

ALLIANCE COURIER SHIP

CLINT EXPELLED A sigh of relief when the courier ship began its one-g burn and his body began to feel grounded once more. A satisfied smile crept across his features when it came to him that his part of the mission was complete.

Heady with that knowledge, he unwebbed and stood. Anticipation unfurled as he turned to face the ship's aft cabins.

Courier ships were usually reserved for senior diplomats and high-ranking officials. Rather than standard crew cabins, they boasted staterooms worthy of a senator. Instead of standard shipboard fare, their galleys were stocked with true cuisine.

He'd flown in such a ship once before, several years ago. At the time, he'd been working for a biochemical firm on Hawking, the habitat orbiting Procyon's main star. When Parliament had asked him to testify on the benefits of chiral research, they'd sent a courier to ferry him back to the senate hearings on Ceriba.

That trip had taken almost five days, and had been the most lavish he'd ever spent aboard a ship. As far as Clint was concerned, this was his reward for completing his assignment. It was a luxury he intended to exploit, starting now.

The assassin's eyes followed him as he passed her seat, and Clint imagined he saw judgement in their depths. His lip curled, resentment rising inside him.

She had no right to judge; he'd done his duty to the empire. The crate sitting in the cargo hold was proof of that.

He heard a quiet snick and the hiss of her webbing retracting, and knew she followed silently in his wake. Acutely conscious of her presence at his back, his surroundings didn't immediately register when he stepped through into the stateroom.

Disappointment hit hard when he realized what was before him. The room had been stripped. What remained looked more like a prison cell than a stateroom, austere and cold.

Turning on her, he demanded, "What the hell?"

"Akkadians do not believe in a hell."

The assassin's dispassionate tone held a hard edge. It telegraphed a silent warning, had Clint bothered to notice. The pleasures denied him had Clint too disappointed to care.

"Neither do most Geminate citizens, but it doesn't stop them from using the word," he snapped.

One of her brows rose. "You are not Geminate."

"I was raised to act like them! It's my job!"

"You have assimilated too much of their culture. You have become soft. You have forgotten the one to whom you owe obeisance." The assassin began circling him slowly. "That will now be remedied."

His lizard brain, sensing the threat she posed, insisted he keep her in his sights at all times. Following her movements, he seethed, "I have done everything asked of me. *Everything.* If it weren't for me, we wouldn't have the damn samples!"

"If it weren't for you," she countered calmly, still circling, "Lee Stinton would still be alive. There would be no investigation into his death. A Navy pilot would not have disappeared, along with a prominent scientist with whom you seem to have a history."

Samantha Travis. His fists clenched, recalling another time, years ago, when she'd caught him doing things he shouldn't. But he'd salvaged that misstep, hadn't he? No one suspected—except perhaps Travis herself.

The assassin stopped circling and Janus shifted, the back of his knees coming into contact with a hard edge. A quick glance showed him she'd herded him against a simple table-and-chair unit, bolted to the ship's deck.

The assassin crowded him, forcing Clint to sit.

"You must rule your passions, Clint Janus. You do not let them rule you."

"What is this?" he said, dredging what little bravado he could muster. "Recruit training? I'm a scientist, not a soldier."

"You are an Akkadian, first and foremost. You appear to have forgotten that."

The assassin withdrew a karambit from its sheath at her waist, the rasp of the blade an audible threat.

Clint swallowed hard, hands raised. "I've... not forgotten. This assignment has been... stressful, is all."

"I have found pain to be a useful tool to focus the mind." The assassin's voice was distant, almost as if she spoke to herself.

Clint began shaking his head spasmodically. "Not really. It's a distraction, truly all you can think about at the time. Trust m—"

A quick snap of her wrist had the karambit embedded, hilt-deep, through the center of Clint's palm. She drove his hand back with a quick thrust, burying the blade's tip into the table.

Shock delayed the agony, but sensation quickly caught up as white-hot pain slashed through him. He gasped, agony causing his vision to gray at the edges until his medical nano could shut off the receptors in his hand.

Just as quickly, the assassin reversed her move, withdrawing the blade. Clint cradled his abused hand against his torso, eyes wild. "Are you *crazy*?"

Dark, emotionless eyes met his, then dismissed him to focus on the cleaning cloth she had retrieved. As she tended to her weapon, she spoke. "You misunderstand, Operative Janus. It is not the pain itself that is the focusing mechanism. It is the promise of pain should you fail." Her eyes rose once more, pinning him to his seat. "You would do well to heed my advice."

He jerked a wordless nod her way. She gestured with her blade, before sheathing it. "Avail yourself of the medical kit, then bring us food. If I were you, I would spend the rest of the day meditating on this discussion."

Clint stared at her. "Discussion?" he choked out disbelievingly.

She held the karambit up and studied it. "Indeed. I've found the edge of a blade can be quite persuasive."

* * *

Clint's fumbling investigation of their quarters revealed that the cabinet once dedicated to expensive liquors was now home to a well-stocked medical station. He shuddered to think what she had planned for him that might require such supplies.

He bandaged his wound as quickly as he could, then crossed to the cabin's private galley, carefully skirting the assassin.

The moment he'd risen from the table, she had entered into a graceful series of movements. Each pose in the kata flow was methodical, almost hypnotic, her toned body moving through the series with precision and strength.

He stole glances at her as he reached for one of the galley's cabinets. Her current pose was inverted, forearms supporting an arched body, toes hovering just above her head. It looked uncomfortable, yet she held it effortlessly.

He returned his attention to the open cabinet, displeasure coursing through him at the sight. Prepackaged Alliance Navy field rations lined the shelves. Rows and rows of MREs, enough to sustain both of them for the duration of their trip.

Sliding the cabinet closed, he searched through the rest, but found nothing else. The galley's small hydroponics bay was shut down, and the blast chiller was empty. Other than a supply of water to accompany the MREs, the galley was bare.

Lips pressed firmly together in distaste, Clint grabbed the two nearest MREs in his good hand and retraced his steps to the table. The assassin uncoiled her body in a graceful, controlled motion and stood. A light sheen of sweat covered her exposed skin as she took a seat across from him.

Clint shot her a black look as he slid one of the packets toward her. "MREs are going to get very old after three weeks."

"If you find it intolerable, please let me know and I will be happy to put you out of your misery."

Clint squeezed his eyes shut and clenched his good hand into a fist.

"Fine," he bit out, searching for a subject change that didn't include his death or dismemberment. "You mentioned a contingency plan back on deGrasse. Now would be a good time to share that, don't you think?"

Her face creased in a spare smile. Clint realized this was the first physical expression of emotion he'd seen the assassin display.

"I fail to understand why that is relevant, but since there is no longer a chance for you to alter it, I'll tell you."

She waved a hand at the stateroom's holodisplay, and it came alive. An image resolved before them, of a sea of ships, circling patiently around the research torus, awaiting recall. A blinking icon five thousand kilometers away from the station marked the courier ship's position.

His gaze was drawn abruptly back to the assassin when she resumed speaking.

"When the Geminate Parliament approved deGrasse's construction, they did so under one condition: that their Navy include an auto-destruct. It was a contingency plan, in the event Vermilion proved to be dangerous. Or that one of your experiments suffered a containment failure."

Clint's eyes bugged out at this news. "I... that's impossible. I would have known if something like that existed. They never said a word to us about such a thing."

The assassin tilted her head. "Be that as it may, it exists. I used Toland's security token to gain access to it. And now that we're safely outside the blast radius, it's time we took care of the loose ends you left behind."

He sucked in a harsh breath, his eyes following hers as she turned her attention to the torus at the center of the stateroom's holodisplay.

EXPLOSIVE DECOMPRESSION

DEGRASSE RESEARCH TORUS

THE AUTO DESTRUCT triggered a series of shaped explosives throughout the torus, generating fireballs that sped throughout deGrasse's ventilation shafts. Pushed by a massive pressure wave, the superheated cloud of vapor and dust traveled at an incredible speed, using the station's atmosphere as the oxidant needed to feed itself.

The combination of pressure, heat, and carefully-spaced accelerant boosted the energy of the explosion within the confined space. The compressive force caused a chain reaction that traveled to the torus's armory, allowing the conflagration to mix with the arsenal there. The subsequent bloom took out the series of small fusion plants at the torus's spoke—as intended.

Ships in the no wake zone were flung outward just as a raging inferno belched from the flight deck's open bay doors. The flash of intense heat carried by the expelled atmosphere reached the ships, incinerating them instantly.

A concussion wave propagated outward from deGrasse, but did little damage beyond the immediate vicinity. Its strength was dependent on the medium that carried it, and once the atmosphere was depleted, the wave dissipated.

The energy contained within the debris field, however, did not. Without atmospheric resistance, its velocity remained constant. When the debris cloud slammed into vessels farther out, it broke them apart like tinder smashed against the craggy rocks of a stormy shoreline.

It expanded outward in a perfect sphere, taking out many of the communication relays scattered from deGrasse all the way to Vermilion's low planetary orbit.

A lone orbital weapons platform disguised as a larger communications array was also caught in the backlash. The platform was on an air-gapped system, and functioned as a second stage for deGrasse's auto-destruct.

A simple programming error caused it to delay the execute command sent by the assassin. Just as it launched its warheads toward the remote outpost on the planet's surface, the debris field slammed into it, knocking the missiles' trajectories off course.

The tactical nukes weren't smart weapons. Rather than self-adjust, they simply followed the new heading imparted by the debris' impact and detonated at a prescribed time. This resulted in explosions several hundred kilometers above the planet's surface.

A complex electromagnetic multi-pulse ensued. This initial, very brief but intense electromagnetic field caused all the surviving communications relays in Vermilion's low planetary orbit to exceed their electrical breakdown voltages, destroying them instantly.

The flare of neutron radiation emitted by the collapsing fusion plants that powered deGrasse did much the same to the remaining communication relays and the lone Starshot Comm Buoy at geosynchronous orbit.

Those on the planet, and one lone tug orbiting on the

backside of Vermilion, were effectively cut off from the rest of Luyten's Star.

At least they were alive—for now.

DODGING DEBRIS

GNS *WRAITH*

{WARNING, DEBRIS FIELD inbound. Brace for impact, twelve seconds.}

Wraith's alert cut through the stunned haze that had settled over Micah at Sam's revelation. It galvanized him into action. He bolted to his feet, shoving the ferret into Sam's hands as Wraith repeated the collision warning.

"Batten down!" he snapped over his shoulder as he raced toward the cockpit. He lunged for the pilot's seat and strapped in with a single, practiced move.

He breathed a silent thanks to the doctor when his newly-implanted wire awoke, handshaking with the Helios's systems. His brain throbbed at the initial contact, and he recognized it as a sign that his neural net hadn't had time to fully adjust to the new implant. It probably wasn't wise to put his mind through much mental exertion quite yet.

That was too bad; it wasn't like he had a choice.

Quick as thought, the cockpit dissolved, his optics transmuting his view so that he seemed to be floating outside the ship. He ignored the searing pain tracing its way through his head. The connections working their way down the long, threadlike axons and dendrites that functioned as the two-way transmission lines for his nervous system weren't fully formed, he knew.

Many of the filaments remained unshielded. He swore he could feel them being built; the expanding web felt like fire was licking through his nerve endings as it grew.

He didn't have the luxury of time to discover if his actions would do him permanent harm. The oncoming debris field was coming at them too fast for any other option.

The leading fragments grew rapidly, filling his vision. Instinctively, he ducked, his body's motions translating themselves to the ship's thrusters as the vessel dodged the pieces of wreckage.

He continued to bob and weave like a fighter circling his opponent while he awaited the plot *Wraith*'s SI was busy calculating.

His teeth gritted against the acid flames that licked at his mind, his interface avoiding the oncoming strikes as best he could. Some he chose to take, the ones he knew were survivable. The ride might get a bit rough, but the ship would just shake them off, as he'd told the doctor earlier.

As for the rest

He brought weapons online, dropping a mental pin on the larger pieces. *Wraith*'s automatic weapons system plotted solutions for them, and presented a firing sequence that would help carve a hole in the debris field that the Helios could slip through.

Micah accepted the sequence, and his interface popped it up on his HUD so that he could monitor its progress.

And then *Wraith*'s SI signaled it had plotted the best path through the debris field. Micah turned control of the ship over to the SI. His job now was to ghost the system, overriding it with nuanced adjustments that provided the edge of human intuition a ship's Synthetic Intelligence lacked.

A warped piece of metal clipped a particularly large

fragment, causing it to career off its calculated path just as it came abeam the ship. The fragment slipped past, striking *Wraith*'s hull and detonating on impact.

Distantly, Micah was aware of Snotface chirping in fear, of the big cat's answering hiss. Harper's voice cut in, pitched to a soothing tone as she attempted to reassure the animals. Both barely registered, immersed as he was in the ship.

The initial, blindingly bright explosion stabbed like a hot poker, but quickly diffused to a coronal glow, thanks to the Helios's picofoam interlayer. It dispersed both kinetic and heat energy from the force of the impact across its wider structural area, with minimal effect to the craft.

Twice more, Micah dipped and twisted, taking *Wraith* through tight maneuvers to avoid unanticipated trajectory changes from larger fragments as they collided with each other. Thrusters fired in a mad and uncoordinated dance, sending the ship along a drunken path to evade the worst of the wreckage.

The time it took for the debris field to overtake them, and then pass beyond the ship, felt interminable. In reality, the event lasted less than fifteen minutes.

Micah began the process of disengaging from his deeply enmeshed state, and handing full control back to the ship. Surfacing from such an interface felt a bit like swimming to the surface from a deep, deep pool.

As he severed his interface with *Wraith*'s nav and weapons systems, a final ribbon of fire lanced through his skull.

He reached for the webbing that held him fast to the pilot's cradle. The action was usually second nature to him, but his hands felt thick and unwieldy, and refused to cooperate. It took two missed tries before he could free himself.

"All clear," he called out. "It's safe to get up."

He lifted a hand to rub wearily at his aching temples and fought to still its tremor. He pushed out of the cradle, and stood on unsteady feet, blinking his eyes to clear the strange double vision he seemed to be having.

He tried to move forward and staggered. Feet tangled over his first step, and he fell hard onto his knees. The last thing he saw was Samantha Travis's alarmed face as she rushed toward him.

* * *

In the tug above Vermilion, at about the same time *Wraith*'s alarm klaxons began to sound, Gabe's attention was wrested from the planet below by a brilliant flash of light. Horror hit him as the tug's sensors flashed a brief image of an expanding ball of orange gas. Immediately, the ship's forward screens went dark.

At the same time, Hyer pushed the tug's reverse thrusters to full throttle. Air was forced from Gabe's lungs as he found himself jerked forward, his body pressed hard against the seat's webbing.

"What the hell?" His shout was cut off by the chief warrant's next words.

"EMP, sir."

Warning sirens began to sound and Hyer silenced them one by one, hands racing across a darkened set of holoscreens.

"I thought that couldn't happen in space." Gabe's voice came out strained, pushed by the tug's acceleration.

"deGrasse is—was—" Hyer cursed under her breath, "at geo."

Geostationary orbit.

"Vermilion has just enough electrons up here to seed a decent-sized pulse?"

"Yes… and no, sir," Hyer said. "I think that was more than one blast. The big one was higher up, but something definitely hit the upper atmosphere, too."

"Are we…" Addy began, voice thready. She cleared her throat. "Are we going to crash?"

Gabe wished he could reassure the doctor but he was law enforcement, not an aviator. He had no idea what their situation entailed.

"No ma'am." Hyer's voice cut in, dispassionate yet confident. "The only thing that got hit was our forward sensors, mainly because I wasn't expecting anything, so they were unshielded and exposed to the pulse. Only reason I accelerated so hard was to get us out of the way, to avoid a possible debris strike."

Hyer eased up on the thrusters' pressure, allowing Gabe to take in a full breath for the first time in the past minute. He straightened in his seat.

"Okay, then." he said. "What's our status?"

"Good question." Hyer scrubbed at her blue fuzz, a distracted motion he noticed she adopted when deep in thought, while one hand worked her console. "We're safe now; planet's between us and whatever happened over there. And we're fully operational, except for those forward sensors. I've dispatched a pair of drones to give us a peek at what happened."

She twisted in her pilot's cradle, one hand coming to rest comfortingly on Fred's mournful head. Gabe rather suspected the one needing comfort was Katie, not the basset. Her worried eyes met his.

"I can't raise anyone on comms," she told him. "Not one single person. All of the relay units associated with deGrasse are offline, and I haven't received a pingback from the Starshot buoy stationed in orbit, either."

Beside him, Addy stirred. "That's not unexpected, though, is it? I mean, if the blast took out the buoy at the torus, we could still target the next one in line, couldn't we?"

Hyer compressed her lips and gave a little shrug. "Yeah, but not without some loss. The buoys have collimators built in to focus the signal. With the nearest one gone, the feed to the one an AU out is going to be weaker and more dispersed. Plus, we'll have eight minutes or so of lag."

Gabe nodded as he thought through what he recalled from his briefing prior to arriving in the system. Luyten's Star had more of a quick-and-dirty string of buoys, positioned at one-AU intervals, rather than the full-system spread that existed in the Alliance's two main population centers of Procyon and Sirius. Still, the Navy had done a fine job planting a solid corridor between Luyten's C-Y gate and the torus.

The buoys weren't connected to the gate in any way, but they did use it as an anchor point for the naval station located beside it. They tracked the gate as Vermilion swept around the star every eighteen days, automatically adjusting their paths so that the small naval station next to the gate remained in sight at all times.

This guaranteed that, no matter where you were along the flight path, communications lag between you and anywhere in the Geminate Alliance was, at worst, four minutes long. All you needed was access to a comm system, and secured credentials that the Ford-Svaiter node within the buoy would accept.

Hyer interrupted Gabe's reverie with a sharp exclamation. "You're gonna want to see this, sir." There was something odd in her tone.

She flicked her hand up and an image appeared on her main holo. It was a split-screen feed from the two drones. The image they showed sent a jolt through Gabe.

DeGrasse was... simply not there.

Stunned silence fell over the three of them. After a few long moments, Hyer turned and pinned him with a grave look.

"Orders, Captain Alvarez?" Her voice was quiet, and very formal.

Gabe blinked, Hyer's use of his cover's rank throwing him for a second. He blew out a breath and forced his mind to consider immediate next steps. There weren't many. Nodding to the cockpit screens, he asked, "Can you pull up a screen shot of the last real-time data you recorded?"

The chief warrant turned back around. "Coming up, sir."

The holoscreens flickered, then lit up with data. Gabe could see from the timestamp that they were about two minutes old. He leaned forward, studying them.

"Damn, that's a lot of ships," he commented as he watched the vessels that had been circling in the no wake zone. "We need to get over there and search for survivors."

"No can do, sir. Radiation in that area's too high right now for what this ship can take. The drones' sensors are telling me it's equivalent to the yield of five small fusion reactors losing containment." Pained eyes met his as she added softly. "DeGrasse was powered by five reactors."

His lips compressed and he gave Hyer a wordless nod of understanding, which she returned.

He turned to a holoscreen that displayed deGrasse STC's last deep-system scan of all space traffic. He spotted the courier ship, now more than five thousand kilometers closer to the heliopause. Another cluster of dots, hundreds of AU away, marked the Navy's picket, stationed at Luyten's C-Y gate. And then his eyes landed on a lone dot, much closer in.

"That ship, right there." He pointed it out to Hyer. "Who is it?"

Hyer tapped on the icon and the ship's ident opened up in a floating window. "It's the *Haversham*, sir. Patrol boat," she said. "About two AU away."

Gabe cocked his head at the pilot. "Far enough to not be harmed by debris, then."

Hyer waved a hand in dismissal. "Not a factor."

Gabe scratched the side of his chin, feeling stubble from where he'd neglected to shave that morning. "How much of a light lag?"

"Little under ten minutes."

"And what's our status? How long can the tug remain in flight?"

"Oh, indefinitely, sir. It's not the tug that's the limiting factor. It'll be our bladders." Hyer grimaced. "And the number of meal rats I have in storage."

He nodded. "Okay, then." He glanced over at Addy. "Looks like you're going to get your wish to see the planet sooner than you expected."

Addy's mouth compressed into a thin line and she shook her head. "This isn't how I envisioned it happening." She paused, an uneasy look in her eyes. "Gabriel This wasn't an accident, was it."

He heard Hyer suck in a sharp breath.

"Can't rule out foul play, no." Turning back to Hyer, he ordered, "Send a message to that patrol boat. Tell them we're headed down to the surface to rendezvous with the survivors at the outpost. Send them a data burst of all the information you have on the event, then request a secured comm once they're within range."

"Will do. And Captain" She twisted back around to face him. "The *Betsy* has a whole store of those microdrones. I could program them to scout the area, and send us a feed. At the very least, we'll have something to share with whoever the Navy sends to investigate."

Gabe's eyes hardened. *Hell, yes, they would.*

"Yes, someone should hold vigil for them," Addy's voice was soft, barely a whisper. "It's the only thing left to do."

"Do it," he instructed Hyer before turning to Addy. "Oh, we're going to do a hell of a lot more than hold vigil, doc. If there's evidence out there, I aim to find it."

BEDSIDE MANNERS

GNS *WRAITH*

AS *WRAITH* SLICED its way silently through the black toward Luyten Gate, Micah slowly regained consciousness. His head pounded, and his eyes refused to open. He tried to form words but they came out as a groan.

Moving proved to be a huge mistake. Fighting a wave of nausea, he reached up to try to keep his brains inside his skull—and discovered he only had use of one arm.

"Guhhhh," he muttered, swallowing convulsively. He forced himself to take slow, deep breaths until the sick feeling passed. Instinct had him reaching for his wire, but his mind felt like one big bruise, so he opted to wait.

Cracking one eye open on a low moan, he found his field of vision filled with a pointed, furry face. A wet nose pressed against his cheek as a voice boomed inside his head.

{Micah too's awake!}

Before he could protest the ferret's volume, it had scampered off his chest. It was then that he became aware of another, heavier weight. This one lay across his thighs, immobilizing one arm. Hot breath blew onto his exposed hand.

Micah's other eye flew open in alarm. Carefully tilting his head forward, he got an eyeful of midnight-hued cat. The panther lay across his torso, both paws pinning his arm against his chest, its muzzle resting between them. That put the cat's jaws far too close to his hand for his liking.

Micah jerked his arm away, or tried to. The motion caused pain to explode inside his head and he fell back with another moan. He heard footsteps approach and he risked another look, to find Sam's face hovering above his own.

"Good kitty," he whispered hoarsely. "Nice kitty. Go away, Joule. Shoo."

The doctor tried unsuccessfully to hide a smile. "That's Pascal," she corrected. "Harper brought him out. We needed his help to get you up onto the bunk after you passed out."

He must have shot her a skeptical look. Her expression turned wry. "You locked us out of the controls, Captain. We couldn't very well reduce speed and lower the gravity without access. And you're kind of heavy at one *g*."

"So, the cat...?"

{Don't worry. Was careful with fangs. Only tore your flight suit in two places.} The panther's mental voice held a distinctly amused flavor, as if he knew Micah was scared witless and was enjoying that fact.

"Uh" Micah said, the ability to form anything more coherent momentarily escaping him.

"Pascal won't hurt you. I told him to stand guard and let me know when you awakened so I could examine you," Sam said. "You're in bad shape, Captain. I need you to remain still and let some of the damage you sustained heal."

Micah tried to utter a protest, but she cut him off. "I only have the one surgi-suite, and it's occupied. You're suffering from several small brain bleeds. I had to do some fast work to repair it."

"But—" he began weakly. He felt a dip in the bunk's mattress and the panther's bulk shifted as Sam pushed Pascal over to make more room for herself. He felt a hand probing at the back of his skull, then the coolness of her bracer-clad fingers as they came to rest against his temple.

"In matters like this, I outrank you," she informed him, studying the bracer's readouts. She pulled her hand back and straightened, giving him a severe look. "Pascal is going to stand guard, to make sure you don't get up until I say you can. Understood?"

Micah grimaced. "Just so long as he doesn't get any ideas," he said. "I'm pretty sure I wouldn't taste very good."

Pascal's eyes glittered at him, mischief in their green depths. Bending his head, he licked Micah's hand, the tongue a warm, wet sandpaper against his skin. *{Mmmm. Needs salt.}*

Sam laughed and lightly slapped the back of the big cat's head. "Behave," she admonished, as the cat's jaw dropped in a feline grin.

Micah let his head fall back and squeezed his eyes shut. "I will. He can go now. Really."

"I was talking to the cat."

The cat just chuffed a laugh and settled his head back down onto Micah's chest.

* * *

Sam left Micah to Pascal's questionable humor and went to find Harper. The intelligence officer was seated in the co-pilot's cradle, deep in thought. One foot was tucked underneath her, the other foot pushed against the deck, swinging the chair idly back and forth. She looked up at Sam's approach.

"You realize that wasn't an accident." The analyst's eyes burned with intensity. Sam nodded wordlessly as she took a seat across from her friend.

They sat, silently staring at each other for a long moment. Finally, Harper spoke. "Whoever did this thinks they've destroyed all the Alliance's research, and the samples that were being studied, too." Her words were soft, quiet.

Sam shook her head. "Not all of it," she countered in an equally soft tone. "Just the data that hadn't already been archived and sent back. The material, however Yeah, we were careful to keep that isolated here, within this system."

Harper tilted her head to indicate the screen that took up most of *Wraith*'s main holo area. The image showed the position of every ship in the system known to deGrasse at the time of its destruction.

"I was monitoring the frequency the Novastrikes were on when they were searching for us. I had the STC feed up on another screen, so I could confirm all the fighters had docked after the order to stand down had been issued." Harper shrugged. "We kind of got sidetracked in the cargo bay, and I didn't bother turning anything off. The STC feed kept recording while I was away."

With a gesture, Harper narrowed the image's focus, and a small courier ship sprang into view. The analyst nodded at the vessel. "I went over the recordings while you were treating our friend back there. Three people boarded that ship, along with a large shipping crate. One of those people was Clint Janus."

Sam frowned. "You think Janus fled with both the research and the samples, don't you."

Harper shrugged. "It makes sense." She tilted her head, as if looking at the image from a different angle might gain her fresh insights. "The one thing I can't figure is who he's working for. Could be one of the big pharma conglomerates back in the Consortium. Could be Akkadia."

Sam sucked in a breath. "Those... could be two very different motivations."

Harper's smile held no mirth. "You're telling me. Greed—" She turned one palm up. "—or terrorism." The other palm rose to hover beside the first.

Sam suppressed a frisson of fear that slithered down her spine. "What Akkadia could do with what we discovered doesn't bear considering." She stood and began to pace. "I need to place a call to Duncan. *Now*, Harper."

The other woman looked up at her and nodded, but then immediately followed it with a shake of her head. "I agree, but I'm not quite sure how we can to do that and still play hide-and-seek with the Alliance Navy."

Sam came to a stop and clutched the back of the pilot's cradle. "We don't know that they're still trying to find us," she countered.

Harper's sigh was explosive. "The freaking research torus just blew the hell up, Sam! Given the fact that they had just called off the search for you and Micah when it happened, I'm pretty sure they'd consider us the most likely suspects."

Sam could hear the exasperation coloring her friend's tone and nodded reluctantly, ceding her the point. She glanced back at the man resting under the care of the black-furred, green-eyed panther, and sighed.

"Okay, I don't dare risk awakening our chiral friend until some of the inflammation has gone down in his cranium. The surgical procedure I set to run on the original Micah has another half hour left in its cycle. Once it's done, I'll awaken him and get him to alter course for us."

Harper cleared her throat, drawing Sam's attention away from the somnolent man.

"You know we're five hours behind Janus, right?" At her nod, Harper continued. "That's going to get a lot longer if we stop at a buoy long enough to talk to your uncle. Are you sure that's the best thing?"

Sam's mouth twisted in a humorless grin. "I'm pretty sure the Director of National Security has a lot more resources at his disposal to track Janus down than we do."

Harper sat back. "Point."

Sam sighed and stood. "Guess now would be a good time to check on the surgi-suite, then. We need at least one of those men awake so I can contact Duncan and give him an update."

She strode over to where Pascal and the unconscious pilot lay. The medical nano she'd recently injected into his system was slaved to her own wire so that she could monitor his progress. She checked it one last time, relieved to see the intracranial swelling she'd spotted after he'd navigated them safely through the debris field was beginning to recede.

In a few more hours, Micah Case's chiral clone should be as good as new.

Of course, considering how 'new' he truly is, I guess that's not saying much

SUPERBOLIDE

REMOTE RESEARCH OUTPOST
VERMILION

THE RESEARCH OUTPOST was in a state of hushed tension when
Addy, Hyer, and Gabe arrived.

They were met at the landing pad by a grim-faced Marine.
One glance at the woman's holopips told Gabe she was a
butterbar, a second lieutenant. A ping of her ident token told
him her name was Angell, newly-arrived at Luyten's Star.

Given Fraley's last orders uniting them into a joint task
force, Gabe's position as deGrasse's security chief put him at
the top of the command chain—and her current superior.

"Sir," she snapped him a crisp salute. "Glad to see someone
survived."

Gabe nodded, returning the salute. "Believe me, Lieutenant,
so are we."

He turned, scanning the compound in a fast visual
assessment.

People hovered in small clusters, talking in low tones, the
light of the artificial mini-sun that hung above the settlement
throwing long shadows behind them.

Their hands shielded their eyes from its glare as they cast quick glances up into the air, attempting to see past into the upper atmosphere.

Others rushed between the central hub and a cluster of smaller outbuildings, hands filled with equipment, their shoulders reflexively hunched as if waiting for the sky to fall.

"Status?" he asked as he turned back to the Marine.

"Everyone's pretty shaken, but the scientists are monitoring the atmosphere for any additional problems headed our direction. By the way," she added, "if they do find something, don't be surprised if power cuts out on you. The bucky ball's not strong enough to keep a plasma shield operational at all times."

"Oh?" Gabe turned his head to look at the small mini-sun overhead.

The meter-wide bucky ball that hung suspended a few hundred meters above them had a microfusion plant buried deep inside its radiation shadow shield. In addition to providing illumination, it was also the outpost's chief power source.

"Yessir. The thing's only got enough juice to light the compound—and run the heaters to keep the temperature from dipping too low for the civvies."

Her tone implied her Marines were too tough to be bothered with a little thing like extreme cold. Given Vermilion's night cycle was six standard days long, Gabe was pretty sure even the hardiest Marine would have a tough time fighting that kind of chill.

He decided not to point that out.

"So, if we have to generate a shield strong enough to repel a piece of shrapnel, we'll be doing it in the dark. Good to know."

Angell's crisp nod confirmed his assessment.

An alert flashed on his HUD, and he saw she'd pushed a data packet his way. It contained a brief synopsis of the impacts the outpost had sustained thus far.

Three fragments had made it through the crucible of

atmospheric friction above their heads. According to the report, they'd hit within minutes of each other.

"The science folks say the explosion shot out in a mostly spherical wave, so we only got hit by a few of the wreckage fragments. Hell of a scare, though."

Gabe gave a low whistle when he saw the vid feed she'd appended to the brief. The outpost's holocams had captured every dramatic detail.

He watched the brilliant flash of molten metal grow larger as it descended toward the camera's lens, and a thought crossed his mind.

Bet more than one of them needed to change their shorts after that

Angell lifted her chin to indicate something off to the right. Gabe's eyes tracked in that direction, and he saw columns of smoke rising lazily into the night air.

"Small brush fires. After the shield bounced them off us, the fragments landed in the grasses."

She clasped her hands loosely behind her and continued her debrief as they crossed over to the main building. Gabe punctuated her commentary with a few well-placed grunts here and there. Addy and Hyer trailed silently behind.

Inside, Marines staffed the outpost's communications station, while researchers monitored the few sensors that were still functioning.

Gabe angled a questioning look at the lieutenant. "Any indication of survivors so far?"

Angell shook her head. "None yet." She turned to face Hyer. "We patched your drones' feed into our system. Honestly, the radiation's still jacking up the connection a bit, but we anticipate that'll clear up within an hour."

Addy stepped forward, urgency in her tone. "If we find any, what are our chances of getting to them?"

Angell's expression grew bleak. "We only have the one shuttle, ma'am, and now the tug. Our other shuttle was up at the torus, resupplying when the evac order came."

Gabe met her eyes, his head dipping in a wordless show of sympathy for the woman's fellow Marines, now presumed lost. After a beat, he turned to the Marine seated at comms, who had looked up at Angell's words.

"We sent a sitrep to a patrol boat a few AU away," he told the man. "Have you heard back from them yet?"

"That's the *Haversham*, sir?"

At Gabe's nod, the Marine swiveled to face him. "Yessir, we're in contact. They just sent us a revised ETA, should be here in seventeen hours. That's oh-nine hundred, local, tomorrow morning."

Gabe acknowledged the man's words, and then his gaze swung around the command center.

"Anything we can do to help out?"

Angell shook her head. "Things are about as status quo as you can get around here, considering the news we just received."

Arms crossed, his fingers beat a silent tattoo against his sleeve as he thought a moment, considering next steps.

Tilting his head toward the closed doors that led deeper into the building, he asked, "Got somewhere private I can hang out for a bit? I need to write a report and send it on up the chain."

Angell's face took on a wry look as she shook her head. "Camp's pretty basic. You could use the break room for a while, though. We'll make sure no one disturbs you."

Beside him, Hyer stirred and hooked a thumb over her shoulder. "Hey, boss, I think I'll go back to ol' Betsy, and see if I can't repair her forward sensors, if that's all right with you."

He nodded. "Good idea, Chief."

His gaze slid to Addy. She looked... pensive.

"I don't imagine anyone here needs medical help, but I'll ask around anyway. Maybe they could use a hand packing up." She gave a small shrug. "After that, I might wander around a bit, I suppose."

He cracked a smile at her. "I know the circumstances aren't

ideal, but you did say you've always wanted to check this place out."

The look she shot him was humorless. "Not what I'd envisioned, Alvarez."

He tipped his head, acknowledging her point.

She and Hyer departed and he turned to follow the lieutenant to the command center's break room. She left him alone, as promised.

After filling a mug with stale, lukewarm coffee, Gabe sat down to try to compose a message to Admiral Toland—and to his boss, his *real* boss, at the NCIC.

No more than twenty minutes into the unpleasant task, he was jolted from his thoughts by a warning klaxon. The voice that came after it warned of an imminent blackout.

Gabe set his coffee aside and saved the report he'd been composing, in case more than just the lights winked out. In the next moment, his wire pinged him.

{Gabriel!}

The mental shout was Addy's; he'd set his wire to auto-accept any comm she sent. The tension in her voice had him shooting to his feet.

{Where are you?}

{South field, just beyond the cultivars,} came her terse reply.

As he raced down the hall that led to the central hub, everything went dark. He exited into a world of semi-darkness, of shadowy figures eerily lit by their consoles' holoscreens.

"Stray piece of debris," he heard a sensor tech announce to the room. "Looks like it collided with something else up there. That altered its trajectory and sent it our way."

He skirted his way around them, heading for the entrance. Once there, he paused, his gaze raking the settlement—but he saw no one.

The blue glow emanating from the bucky ball above his head told him the plasma shield was in place, but he seriously doubted it extended beyond the compound.

He queried the local net for the location of Addy's ID token, and an icon appeared on his overlay.

Eyeballing the distance to the perimeter of the small settlement, Gabe got a sick feeling in his gut. Addy's icon was outside that boundary.

*{Get under the shielding, **now**.}*

{On my way,} was her grim response.

As he stepped off the ceramacrete floor and onto packed Vermilion soil, he heard a second voice say with quiet authority, "Looks like a thirty-meter section of regolith from the torus's outer shell. Most of that'll vaporize when it hits atmosphere, but not all. There's a fifty-fifty chance that whatever survives entry will airburst overhead. They'll be smaller bolides, closer to two meters. But they're going to crater when they impact the surface."

Thirty meters. Shit, that's a damn seven-story building!

Gabe took off running in the direction of Addy's ID token, knowing he had a few minutes at most to get to her.

"Traveling at—" the sensor tech's voice faded as he moved further away from the entrance, "—mach sixty!"

Minutes? Gabe thought with rising panic as he broke into a sprint. *Who'm I kidding? We only have seconds.*

{Talk to me, Addy!}

Her mental voice sounded winded.

{I'm coming. Ground's a bit too rocky to run full-out without risk of a broken ankle.}

{No excuses, Moran.} He barked the command, fear lending a harsh edge to his mental tone. *{Do it!}*

He spied her just as the skies above him lit up with a brilliance that outshone the red dwarf. He put on a burst of speed, crashing into the tall grasses that lined the outpost's perimeter, using his optical implant's full spectrum to try to eke out any additional details from the terrain.

He reached Addy and hooked an arm around her waist, his greater strength and speed pushing her bodily forward. They were twenty meters from the perimeter when the superbolide exploded, and he urged Addy forward, knowing the blast wave would catch up to them soon after.

A secondary explosion, this one much closer to the ground, hit when they were within three meters of the clearing. At the same time, the blast wave from the first explosion caught up to them, flinging them to the ground and causing Vermilion to shiver under a small seismic quake.

Gabe looked up in time to see a two-meter round shape hurtling past them, a remnant of the larger piece of regolith. He had no time to react before the now-subsonic fragment struck the area Addy had recently vacated, and he felt the ground shudder beneath him once more.

Distantly, Gabe registered that the shield had winked out of existence, to be replaced with the bucky ball's return to artificial daylight. He groaned and rolled to his side to alleviate the pain from the sharp rock that was digging into his left kidney.

As he took in huge gulps of air and tried to get his thudding heart under control, he took stock of his various aches and pains. He turned his head to eye the woman lying prone beside him.

"You okay?" he asked.

Addy merely nodded, face obscured by a fall of blue-black hair. He could tell she was too busy trying to get her own breathing under control to voice a reply. She pushed to a crouch, her hands buried in the soft grasses. Her head remained down, her torso shaking in reaction.

Reaching over, he wrapped a hand around her arm and gave it a brief, reassuring squeeze.

"You scared the livin' shit outta me, there, doc," he managed on an exhale.

Rolling onto his back once again after carefully relocating the rock, he looked up at the sky, giving himself a few more breaths before pushing himself wearily to his feet. He turned and offered her a hand up, and she struggled to her feet with a wince, pushing her hair back from her face with a hand that still shook.

"Let's not repeat that any time soon, okay?"

She stared back at him for a beat before dipping her head in a quick, silent nod. They turned and walked back onto the outpost's grounds without another word spoken between them.

Several hours later, Gabe sat in the outpost's communication center nursing a hot cup of coffee as he watched Addy stand at the edge of the clearing that ringed the outpost. She was running a hand absently across the tops of the grass stalks growing tall at the clearing's edge as she stared out at a lazy spiral of smoke that rose from the spot where the bolide had impacted.

The doctor was made of stern stuff. She'd handled the shock of deGrasse's destruction better than he would have expected, and she'd come through the near brush with the torus fragment just fine, too.

I suppose she's used to functioning under stressful conditions in the ER, he mused. Taking one last sip of his coffee, he forced his thoughts away from the doctor and back to the task of composing his report to his superior.

He'd become increasingly convinced Toland's request for an undercover NCIC agent had been warranted when the pilots, and then Stinton, turned up dead. But the demise of nearly twenty *thousand* souls aboard deGrasse? That removed all doubt.

Gabe sealed the report with his military token and used the outpost's signal booster to push the data packet to the patrol boat. From there, it would be routed through the nearest Starshot buoy to the offices of the NCIC in Procyon.

With a weary sigh, Gabe pushed away from the comm console. He knew a response would take a number of hours to arrive.

He rose to refill his coffee, snagged a ration bar from the cabinet above the beverage dispenser, and then sat back down to wait.

AFTERMATH

Remote Research Outpost
Vermilion

After their near brush with death, Addy walked the compound, too wired by adrenaline to stay in one place. She hated the fact there was nothing she could do to make the situation any better. She'd checked in with the research team when they'd arrived, but none had needed the services of a trauma surgeon.

The kind of trauma they were experiencing was more in line with the needs only a psychologist could provide, and it made her feel damn useless.

So she'd wandered. Her path dumped her out of the outpost's main working space into a climate-regulated nursery. Inside were dozens of seedling beds, spaced evenly beneath computer-controlled misters. The lines of beds stretched dozens of meters outward until they reached a large hangar-like door that opened out into a meticulously groomed garden area.

This was filled with neat rows of native plants, monitored by robotic crop-tenders. Beyond that stretched the compound perimeter.

Addy wandered the outpost alone, eschewing the offer of an escort. She knew those living down here were still processing what had happened, just as she was. But she'd had the benefit of an hour-long flight and an opportunity to view the tug's data, first hand.

The people on the planet's surface were still sifting through it all. One of the first things Hyer had done was to link the *Betsy* to the outpost's main node so they could download all the information the tug had gathered. That's where those planetside were, poring over the data, trying to make sense of everything.

Addy looked up, realizing suddenly that she'd gravitated once more to the outpost's southern edge. A scattering of bioluminescent plants in the distance cast the landscape outside the circle of light in an ethereal glow.

Closer in, the trail of smoke from the fallen fragment could still be seen. She stared out at it, unable to stop thinking about what that small, smoking fragment represented.

The numbness that had initially overtaken her as the disaster unfolded was beginning to wear off and she mentally ticked off the names of those friends and colleagues she would never see again.

She looked up, shading her eyes against the warm, golden light from the bucky ball. It mimicked the sunlight that would strike Garnet when the continent was on its day-side rotation, five standard days from now.

"You doing okay?" Gabe's voice broke into the quiet that surrounded her. She turned, and he offered up a steaming cup of coffee as he came to a stop beside her, staring out at the smoldering piece of metal. After a moment, he shifted.

"It's natural to feel survivor's guilt, you know," he reminded her quietly, with a glance up at the sky.

"Guilt," she repeated the word. She cringed at the bitter tone she heard in her own voice, cradling the warm mug between her hands. Giving herself a mental shake, she turned to him and forced a smile. "So. Any news?"

He tilted his head, sympathy in his eyes. Shoving his free hand into a pants pocket, he nodded. "I spoke with the commander of the patrol boat."

He gazed off into the distance, eyes roaming over the bioluminescent foliage as he lifted his mug and took a sip.

"They're hauling ass to get here, pulling five gs. Should arrive first thing tomorrow morning."

Addy nodded as she considered the number of people who'd made the outpost's prefabricated buildings their temporary home.

"That's good. The supplies down here will last for a good month, maybe longer. But I'm worried about the strain that'll put on the camp." She waved a hand to indicate the foreign landscape, then nodded at the tidy rows of experimental plants being cultivated within the settlement's borders. "That chiral stuff's edible, but utterly useless for sustaining human life."

Gabe snorted a laugh. "Water, water everywhere, and not a drop to drink?"

That brought a reluctant smile to her face. "Something like that, yes."

"Well, they only have to rough it until tomorrow morning, then the patrol boat can begin airlifting them out of here and heading to the gate. Speaking of which…" He turned serious eyes on her. "I spoke to the patrol boat's captain, and told her I have an important lead that needs to be pursued. They have a fast pinnace that can get me to the naval station ahead of that courier ship. I'd like to take any analysis you have on Stinton's death with me when I go."

Addy eyed him curiously. "Do you really think there's a connection between the deaths and…"

Her voice trailed off and she looked up toward where deGrasse used to be.

"I can't rule out that possibility at this time, no."

The way he said that made her look at him more closely.

"Isn't this a bit out of your wheelhouse as chief of security?"

she asked.

Something shifted behind his eyes. She moved toward him, stepping into his space.

"Hold on, here. What is it you're not telling me, Alvarez?" she demanded, jabbing a finger against his shoulder.

Gabe tilted his head, one eyebrow lifted, and considered her silently for a moment. Nodding to himself, he seemed to come to an internal decision.

"I guess it won't hurt to tell you. I'm not Navy Security, Addy. I'm with NCIC. Toland requested an agent on deGrasse. Based on the past few weeks' events, I think we can conclude she had a legitimate reason to believe someone was making a play for the chiral research." He jerked his chin skyward. "What happened up there could be an accident, but—"

She nodded her understanding.

"But your gut is screaming at you. I get it. Mine is, too." She hesitated, then crossed her arms. "You didn't mention your suspicions about Sam to your superiors, did you?"

When he remained silent, she dropped her arms and glared at him.

"You did. That's just wrong, Gabe. Don't tarnish her reputation posthumously like that."

He shook his head. "Sorry, Addy. I had no choice. It's my duty to report all suspicious activity, especially since we don't know for certain she died in the explosion. I told you they were searching nearspace for Case's Helios when the evacuation was ordered. Just because they didn't find anything doesn't mean that ship wasn't lying doggo, right under their noses."

Addy pivoted to face the field of crops as she considered his words. If Sam had slipped away from deGrasse, Addy knew there was a very good reason behind that action. She just wasn't sure how she'd convince Gabe of that.

Her eyes rose to his once more. "Have you considered she might've felt she couldn't trust the people in authority on the station? That she had somehow been compromised and they wouldn't be able to keep her safe?"

Gabe tilted his head to one side, studying her from narrowed eyes. He nodded slowly. "It's possible. She'll be free to present her case to the authorities after I bring her—and whoever is with her—in for questioning."

Addy's mouth firmed. "Then I'm coming with you."

Gabe shook his head impatiently and turned away. He blew out a sharp breath, hooking a hand around the back of his neck as he stared down at the grass beneath his feet. After a moment, he turned back to face her.

"Look, doc. This won't be a pleasure cruise," he said in a tired tone. "We're going to be pushing five *g*s all the way in."

"Okay."

He shook his head, crossing his arms. "Come on, Addy, let's be realistic here. There's no reason for you to—"

"I can handle it. I did my first deployment on a combat search and rescue hospital ship. CSAR medical personnel embedded with the Helios crews when they went into a hot zone, to rescue downed personnel. We sometimes pulled as many as thirty *g*s on a mission like that," she reminded him. "I have the same Smart Carbyne lattice Navy pilots do."

"But why would you voluntarily subject yourself to something like this when it's not necessary? Don't you trust me to do the right thing?"

She stared steadily back at him, hesitating.

"I do," she admitted finally. "I'm just concerned you might not be willing to consider all possibilities, and I have this terrible feeling that time is of the essence with whatever's going on."

At some point during their conversation, the bucky ball had transitioned through an artificial sunset. She looked up now, past the rounded structure and out into the night sky. "Don't you feel it? Somehow, the search for Sam and that Navy pilot they were trying to apprehend is connected to whatever Clint Janus is up to."

She turned back to Gabe, her eyes shining with a determined light. "And whatever it is, I'll be damned if I let him get away with it."

WEIGHING OPTIONS

GNS *WRAITH*

WHEN MICAH AWOKE a few hours later, he felt relatively human again. He wasn't back to full capacity, but at least his brain no longer felt like it was going to leak out his ears.

A quick glance told him that his feline caretaker has slipped away. He breathed a bit easier at that. The big cat was going to take some getting used to. His tendency to amuse himself at Micah's expense was... unsettling, to say the least.

He stood and looked around. The cabin was empty, but the cargo bay doors were open, so he headed in that direction in search of his passengers. Murmured voices reached his ears the moment he passed through the bay doors. Rounding the stack of crates, the surgi-suite came into view.

His other self was conscious once again, and for some reason, that surprised him. The mental connection they shared had been silent since he'd awakened; perhaps that was why.

He slowed his approach, not wanting to interrupt, but then the man looked over, and the doctor turned to follow his eye-line.

"Sorry, I didn't mean..." Micah began to step away, but Sam

beckoned him forward.

"How are you feeling?" she asked as he came to a stop beside the surgi-suite.

He jerked his head to one side, in one of those brief, wordless motions that could mean anything. The man in the bed coughed a laugh.

Guess that means you're feeling better.

Micah started.

I thought this thing between us might have gone away, he sent tentatively. *You haven't said anything in a while.*

The voice inside his head made an amused sound.

Didn't want to fry your gray matter. Doc said to let your brain heal before trying it again. But it's not causing you any pain.

That last thought was stated with a confidence that told Micah his counterpart wasn't asking a question; rather, he was stating a fact.

Dark brows winged up as Micah shot his mirror image a questioning look.

He felt a mental shrug in return. *Don't ask me how I can tell; I just can.*

"So, what's up with this special connection we seem to have, doc?" Micah asked, his eyes never leaving the single bright blue one of his doppelganger.

*I guess **I'm** the doppelganger, though...* he thought.

The thought hurt.

Sam's eyes shifted thoughtfully from him to his mirror-twin and back.

"If I had to guess," she said slowly, "I'd chalk it up to quantum entanglement."

Micah quirked an eyebrow at her and tapped the side of his head. "Simple pilot's brain, doc. Remember?"

Sam shook her head and quirked a half-smile. "Try selling that fiction somewhere else, Captain; I'm not buying. But okay, I'll give it a shot."

She paused as if to gather her thoughts, and then lifted her hands, bringing her index fingers together, side by side. "Entanglement is what happens when two particles interact. The interaction forces a kind of interdependence upon them both."

She pulled her fingers apart. "Once separated, that interdependence remains. If you looked closely at one of them and saw it spinning in one direction," she sent one finger circling in a clockwise motion, "then you'd instantly know the other's spin."

The other finger moved, counterclockwise. "It's as if they're twins, separated at birth, but they still look the same and have the same traits."

"So we're entangled?"

She nodded. "I think so, yes. You two are literally the same person, except for molecular spin."

"Yeah," Micah muttered. "Except I was 3D printed. He came out the usual way."

Sam cocked her head, pinning him with a look.

"Not so different, really. He was just 3D printed *in vitro,* is all. Isn't that what childbirth is, in essence?" She smiled. "All that really matters is that you're alive. I know we're in completely uncharted territory here. We'll just make up the rules as we go along. Deal?"

Micah glanced at his counterpart and nodded reluctantly.

"Okay, then. Enough science for now." The doctor studied him, her eyes intent. "Let's talk about your recovery. How does it feel to use your wire?"

He sent his mind down the mental pathway that allowed him to connect with the ship, and turned sharply to face his twin. "You altered our course?"

"It was at my request," Sam quickly interposed. "We're on our way to the nearest Starshot buoy so I can report in."

"We don't need to dead-eye the buoy to send a message," he protested. "We can just squirt a comm packet to it as we pass by. I think getting back to Procyon with the news about the shit this Janus guy was experimenting with on deGrasse should be our priority right now. Plus, we're the only real torus survivors. We're going to need to report on that as soon as possible."

Sam shook her head at him. "I hear what you're saying, but I need to talk to my uncle, and to do that, I need a real-time, encrypted link."

Micah's eyes narrowed at her words.

I already told her that slowing to rendezvous with a Starshot was going to increase transit time by two days, his mirror-twin warned.

Micah looked up as Harper joined them. The words she led with had him rocking back on his heels.

"Janus survived the explosion," she informed him. "He's headed for the gate."

Micah arrowed an angry stare back at Sam.

"Another reason we shouldn't stop," he snapped. "We should be hauling ass to catch up to him."

Harper shook her head. "This calls for a bit more subtlety than that. If I'm right, then Janus is much more than a murderer. He's our traitor. Sam's work inside the labs suggests that someone's been siphoning material from the samples brought up from Vermilion."

Sam nodded, expression tight. "Harper found STC footage of Janus leaving the torus. The ship he was on loaded a large shipping crate into its hold before it departed. We think Janus has the research on him. The samples, too."

Micah opened his mouth once again to protest the detour, but his mirror-self beat him to it.

A DAP Helios has far more under the hood than that courier. We can beat Janus to the gate without breaking a sweat.

"Only if we're willing to reveal that we survived deGrasse," Sam countered, "and I'm not so sure that's a good idea."

"Listen," Harper said, exasperation creeping into her tone. "Before the torus went up, someone used Toland's token to issue an order for your arrest, and then erased all record of where it originated. It's only because of my MilInt access and my training as an analyst that I could see where Toland's token had been used and then written over."

"But...why?" Micah asked.

"Know who Lee Stinton is?" Harper crossed her arms and shot him a questioning look.

Micah's brow furrowed as he considered the apparent non-sequitur. His mirror-self supplied the answer.

Stinton? The Navy's Chief Scientist?

Harper waggled her finger between the two men and the doctor. "Well, you're all wanted for questioning for his murder."

"What? That's... I didn't do it!" Micah protested.

Harper nodded. "You know it, and I know it, but the Navy doesn't. The problem we now face is that the torus pushed the warrant system-wide, when they thought you might've managed to escape in a stealthed ship."

She uncrossed her arms and planted them at her waist, shooting them a knowing look. "So you tell me: what's the first thing you think the Navy's going to do if we break cover? You think they'll listen when we tell them to detain that ship, or do you think they'll arrest first, and ask questions later?"

"She's right," Sam said quietly. Micah saw worry shadowing her eyes. "Fugitives wanted for the murder of Lee Stinton aren't going to be believed when they accuse the torus's lone surviving scientist of collusion with a foreign power. At least, not at first."

Micah crossed his arms and blew out a breath. "Well, geez, when you put it that way," he muttered, eliciting an amused laugh from his twin.

"There's something else to consider, and I'm not quite sure what this means. Harper intercepted an encrypted communications packet a few hours ago that she couldn't crack."

Micah cocked a brow at her. "Why is that suspicious?"

Harper shot him a look. "It wouldn't be, not to anyone else. But I happen to have access to the highest levels of Alliance encryption through the NSA. If I can't read it, then something's up."

Micah whistled through his teeth. "Another alphabet agency, maybe? Or are you suggesting it was sent by an enemy star nation?"

Harper lifted one shoulder in a half-shrug. "All I can tell you is it was followed by a comm packet I *could* read. That one ordered the patrol boat that's on its way to Vermilion to reassign a pinnace to deliver someone to the gate. My guess is they're going to try to intercept someone before they transit. What I don't know is who they're gunning for: us or that courier ship."

"That's why we need to let the NSA know," Sam added. "They have a better chance of stopping Clint Janus than we do. I want to relay the message as quickly as we can, to give my uncle as much time as possible to pull an operation together from his end."

Micah shot Sam a look. "They're going stop that ship regardless, you know. They're going to want to question them about what they saw."

"Yes, but stopping them and *detaining* them are two very different things," Harper cautioned. "And if they have the muscle to destroy deGrasse, then they can't be working alone. We can't know they don't have accomplices working to grease their way through the picket on that end."

Micah nodded reluctantly. "I get it." He tossed them a hard look. "You do realize that nothing happens very fast when you're inside a star system, right? At best cruising speed, it'll still take that courier ship another twenty-seven days to get to the gate. If they're truly trying to sneak out, I doubt they'll push to a higher acceleration. That'd draw unwanted attention."

Speaking of unwanted attention… Since we're wanted criminals now, that means we have the same problem, his twin said.

Rotating his head on the hospital bed pillow, he shifted his one-eyed gaze from Micah to Sam.

You going to talk that uncle of yours into calling the heat off?
Sam nodded.

Silence descended between them. After a beat, Sam shot a look at Harper and tilted her head. They stepped away, giving the two men a brief bit of privacy.

Micah stood awkwardly for a moment, facing his double. He realized suddenly that the other man's mental voice no longer sounded exhausted like it had when they'd last spoken. He forced himself to examine... himself... more closely. The man's color was better, his single eye clear of pain. The tension bracketing his mouth earlier was now gone.

"You, ah..." Micah cleared his throat as he drew closer to the medical bed. "You're looking better. You doing okay, there?"

The other Micah nodded. "As well as can be expected. Bit of phantom pain from my legs, but the doc's working on blocking that."

This was the first time his doppelganger had spoken aloud; the man's voice sounded rough and scratchy. He grimaced, the gel-pack adhered to his face crinkling with the movement.

"Guess I'll have to get used to being half a man until we get back to Humbolt," he rasped.

Micah winced in sympathy, but nodded at his alter ego's mention of the Navy's main base of operations.

Humbolt Base sat in geostationary orbit above Procyon's capitol world of Ceriba. It made sense that they'd head there once this mission ended.

"About that. How do you think they're going to handle—"

Micah broke off, waving a finger between the two of them.

"I've been doing some thinking while you were getting your beauty sleep," the other man said, voice growing slightly stronger now with use. "For now, you're the only operational Micah Case. I think you should keep the name."

Micah began to protest, but his twin held up his one good hand.

"For convenience—" his gaze shifted to Sam, who had

stepped up to the bed once more, "—let's call me by my first name, Jonathan."

Micah scowled. "We've always hated that name."

The original wheezed a laugh. "Yeah, well. It's expedient. Until this whole thing gets sorted out, it'll do."

Micah nodded to the man. *Jonathan*. He reminded himself to start thinking of him by that name.

He groped for the right words to say to his mirror image. To someone who hadn't done a thing to deserve what had happened to him.

"I know who I am," he told the other man haltingly. "I know you're the... original... and I don't want you to think I'm going to try to steal your life or anything..."

He stabbed his hands through his hair as he stared up at the overhead, his emotions a confused jumble.

"Fuck, this is harder that I thought it was going to be," he muttered, eliciting another laugh from his counterpart.

"Shit, man, you can say that again." The words were little more than a whisper.

"Well, you're not alone, either of you," Sam said. "You have me and Harper in your corner. As soon as I contact Duncan, you'll have the National Security Agency behind you, too."

He swallowed hard, nodding his wordless appreciation.

She nodded back.

"We'll work this out. In the meantime, until we reach that buoy, you both have a bit more healing to do." She squared off with him, wrapped a hand around his upper arm, and then tugged lightly.

"You and I need to talk. You have a few special dietary requirements now that you never had before."

Micah shot her a wary look.

"Permanent ones?"

At her nod, he asked, "Do they have anything to do with why that mint you slipped me tasted like dill?"

"Dude." His twin in the bed, Jonathan, made a face. "Maybe I don't envy you that much, after all. That's disgusting."

Micah's mouth twitched. Somehow, he knew Jonathan had said that only to lessen his tension, and he felt a surge of gratitude toward his other self.

Sam smothered a short laugh.

"In a manner of speaking, yes. You'd better hear this too… Jonathan," she stumbled over the unfamiliar name. "The captain—Micah, here—can ingest any food you or I can, but it won't provide him with the nutrition he needs to survive."

Micah looked at her questioningly and dipped his head, eyes glued to hers, in an invitation to continue.

She took in a deep breath.

"Remember what I said earlier, that chiral organisms needed to feed from their own kind? No food, grown on any planet other than here in Luyten's Star, will adequately fuel your body," she clarified.

"No food, anywhere?" He heard the disbelieving tone in his own voice.

She shook her head. "Not without intervention, no."

Micah swallowed as the implications dawned on him. "Well, then. I guess that answers that. I'm either stuck on Vermilion for the rest of my life, or I die of starvation."

He saw a fierce determination cross the doctor's features.

"Not on my watch, you won't." She pointed to a DBC unit attached to a nearby bulkhead. Beside it sat a familiar-looking shape. "You remember that duffel I forced you to go back and get, when they were shooting at us?"

He looked closer at the shape, recognizing it. "I do."

"The molecular bricks inside are chirally polarized. I can use them to create the necessary supplements you need to survive. Better yet, I can use them to replicate themselves, and create additional formation material. With those supplements, there's no reason you can't live a normal life."

She sighed. "It's not a perfect solution, but it beats the heck out of the alternative at the moment."

Hell of a weight-loss program you got going, there, dude. Jonathan's voice sounded inside his head. *Just think, you now have a license to eat as much of mom's homemade lasagna as you want without having to worry about any added weight ruining either your PT or running scores back at the base.*

Micah shot his twin a dirty look. *Yeah, but how'm I gonna explain to her that she now has to cook her famous garlic-dill potatoes with **mint** now, huh, genius?*

Jonathan grinned. *That's your problem, bro, not mine.*

Unaware of the mental exchange, Sam continued.

"In a way, it's no different than some of the diseases we faced, pre-Diaspora. Type I Diabetes, Grave's disease, the mutagenic Weber strain of viral meningitis that appeared in the late twenty-one hundreds." She waved a hand. "All of those were easily managed by daily medication, just like this will be for you."

The concerned expression on her face caused Micah to want to reassure her, even though he knew she was the one trying to do the same for him.

"I get it, doc. And I appreciate it. I literally owe you my life."

"We both do," Jonathan said.

Micah turned to look back at his mirror image.

"We both do," he agreed.

"Here." Sam held out her hand. In it were two capsules.

"Sorry about the delivery system; it's a bit clumsy at the moment. When we get back to Procyon, I'll fit you with an internal nano pump so you're not burdened with anything as archaic as pills. For now, it'll do."

She dropped the capsules into Micah's palm. "Go get something in your stomach, and take these with a full glass of water."

Micah cocked an eyebrow her way.

"Take two and call you in the morning?"

Sam shot him a perplexed look. "What?"

Jonathan coughed a brief laugh.

"Sorry doc. Long story, and it involves an uncle who was a pre-Diaspora history buff."

A bemused expression crossed her face before she

straightened.

"Well, then," she said briskly. "I'll just set up the next round of therapy for Jonathan on the surgi-suite, and let you gentlemen be about your business." She shook her head and stepped past Micah.

"Hey, bro," he turned to Jonathan. "About *Wraith*..."

His voice trailed off, uncertain exactly what it was he was trying to convey.

"She's *ours.*" Jonathan leaned on the word for emphasis. "Yours, as much as she is mine. She responds to us both equally, and we're not changing that."

He tilted his head to one side.

About the Starshot buoy, he sent along their private connection.

Micah frowned, and then reached out to the ship's SI through his wire for an ETA. Before he could, Jonathan provided the answer.

Little more than a day before we get there.

Micah nodded, and then shot a quick look the doctor's way.

You realize we'll be tipping our hand, he warned his twin.

The look in Jonathan's single eye told him the man did, indeed, know. Streaming a signal for any length of time would alert the buoy's monitoring system to the presence of a ship nearby, a fact it would automatically report.

When its sensor sweep came up negative, someone in communications at the Navy picket was bound to make the connection that a stealthed ship had come calling.

Can't be helped, Jonathan pointed out. *We get too far away, the whisker will lose its coherency.*

"Yeah," Micah echoed, stroking his jaw thoughtfully. The whisker his twin mentioned was a tightly-focused, directed laser beam connection, so named because its diameter was so small.

"Narrow as a whisker," someone had once said, and the moniker had stuck.

The beam's narrow cross-section meant a ship would have

to physically cut across its path to detect it. The problem was that, in order to keep the beam from spreading wide, they needed to be within a thousand kilometers of the buoy to do it.

Under normal circumstances, a whisker was only used to send information in a quick data squirt. The Helios could do a close pass and then be gone before the buoy had time for a positive ident.

Guess we'll need to be ready to play hide-and-seek again, until her uncle gets the heat off our backs.

Micah gave his mirror-twin a resigned nod, then opened his palm to look at the two capsules the doctor had given him.

"Okay, then," he told them both, stepping away from the medical bed. "Guess I'll be in the galley, if you need me."

A cold nose touching the back of his hand had Micah nearly jumping out of his skin.

{I take my steaks raw.}

Micah looked down to see Pascal. The big cat lolled his head to one side, grinning up at Micah. He didn't have to look far; the panther's head reached the top of his thigh.

Micah glowered down at him.

"Who said I was making you dinner, fuzz-brain?"

{Call it payment for services rendered.}

"Services rendered?"

Micah shifted his skeptical gaze from Pascal over to the doctor, who was unsuccessfully hiding a smile. "What the hell kind of services did you render, you mangy piece of—"

{For watching you while you slept.}

Sam laughed and shook her head, eyes twinkling.

"Don't even try to argue with cat logic. Trust me, you'll lose, every time."

STATE SECRETS

MINISTRY OF STATE SECURITY
CENTRAL PREFECTURE, ERIDU
AKKADIAN EMPIRE

FOR THE SECOND time in a week, Citizen General Che Josza found himself facing the Minister of State Security. The report from Luyten's Star had come in two hours ago. After reviewing it, he'd brought it to her attention personally.

"And there is no way that the explosion can be traced back to Akkadia?"

Rin Zhou's question hung between them as she stared at the feed's final image, the debris field that was once deGrasse frozen in midair.

He shook his head. "Impossible to completely rule that out, but our agent believes it'll take some time before the Alliance will be able to mount any sort of investigation into it."

Rin Zhou nodded thoughtfully. "That same agent is on her way back to us, with the samples?"

"And with Janus, as well. They departed for the gate just prior to the evacuation."

Rin Zhou tapped her stylus lightly against her desk. "Janus."

She drew the word out, tone contemplative.

"One of our Geminate-born and -raised assets. A biochemist. We arranged matters so that he would be selected for the deGrasse team early on." Che allowed distaste to cross his features. "Our agent reports Janus is slipping his leash."

"How so?"

Che really wished he did not have to tell her this. But it would not go well for him if others brought this to her attention. No, he needed to own up to this.

"He killed without authorization," he said, "and in a manner that could have garnered unwanted attention, had our agent not cleaned up after him."

Rin Zhou shot him a sharp glance. "He was trained with the Junxun, was he not?" Her words held an edge to them.

Che inclined his head. "Janus was born on Ceriba, in Procyon. As with all of our sleeper agents embedded within Geminate space, we had to limit his visit to months and not years, lest we raise suspicions. He came here for training at an early age, and returned for periodic reconditioning under the guise of visiting relatives."

"His conditioning is failing."

Che dipped his head lower, accepting the rebuke.

"Janus is a true sociopath. He requires stringent controls to keep his… proclivities in check." Che straightened, meeting her gaze once more. "We assigned one of the assassins to him as a control."

"We do not suffer ineptitude. Get rid of him." Rin Zhou's voice was implacable.

"With respect, minister, we cannot. He is our only asset in Alliance space who understands what the scientists in Luyten's Star have found."

He lifted his gaze once more, spreading his hands in a gesture of supplication. "We need him, if not to bring our own scientists up to speed, then to continue to interface with Alliance experts and bring us more intelligence on what they have discovered."

Rin Zhou stared at Che for a long moment, saying nothing. He resisted the urge to shift uncomfortably under her regard.

"Very well," she said finally. "Tell our agent that he is to be reminded of his place and to whom he owes his allegiance."

Che bowed yet again. "It will be done, Minister."

PART FOUR: THE CHASE

UNWITTING PAWN

REMOTE RESEARCH OUTPOST
VERMILION

"CONTACT!"

The shouted word, followed by pounding footsteps, heralded the appearance of the Marine sensor tech. The man clung to the frame of the command center's open door as he shouted, "They've found survivors!"

Gabe tossed a box of ammo aside and stepped away from the makeshift table he'd set up under the building's awning earlier that morning.

"Where?" he demanded, his voice cutting through the chorus of voices clamoring the same thing.

The tech shook his head. "Chief Warrant Hyer just sent the news. She's up there with the *Betsy*, helping the patrol boat haul a dragnet through the debris. Came across one of the torus's shuttles. She's picking up life signs. Seven, I think." The tech's expression tightened. "Although two of them are pretty faint."

The sound of rapid feet approaching was followed by Addy's voice. "Lieutenant, I need a ride," she ordered the shuttle pilot.

Her words were clipped. She held an emergency kit in one hand, and wore a medical bracer on the other, encasing it from fingers to forearm.

The pilot raced to comply and Gabe followed, stopping Addy just before she boarded.

"I'll talk to the captain of the patrol boat, smooth the way for you," he told her, and she nodded her thanks. Reaching out to touch her shoulder, he initiated a secured connection.

Before he could speak, her voice sounded inside his head.

{That ship has better medical facilities than anything I can provide from down here, plus a small medical staff to assist me.}

He felt her hesitation, before she added, *{You know this means I won't be going with you to catch Janus. Or to be there when you try to arrest Sam.}*

{You have my word I'll be fair,} he reminded her. *{You know that, Addy.}*

She sent a mental nod, and the impression of a stern look. *{You'd better, or I'm coming after you, Alvarez.}*

That earned her a mental chuckle.

{Stay in touch, and let me know what you find.}

She nodded once more, and then broke away. Their connection flickered as it automatically cycled from their closed, peer-to-peer link to an open one on the outpost's small research net. That would last only as long as the shuttle remained in range.

{Ping me once you're aboard,} he suggested, and she sent an affirmative.

The hatch closed and those around him stepped away to give the pilot room to maneuver. He hurried to join them as the shuttle's thrusters came online.

He set a reminder on his wire to contact her before the day was up. By then, hopefully she'd have the survivors stabilized.

As soon as Addy determined they were medically fit and would allow it, he wanted them questioned about deGrasse. It was always possible they'd seen something, either on the torus or out in space, that might make a difference in solving this case.

In the meantime, he had a flight of his own to catch.

He turned and retraced his steps back to the supply of ammunition he'd been pillaging as he mentally worked through his plans for pursuit. Despite what Gabe had told Addy, he had no intention of pushing the patrol boat's pinnace to an acceleration of five *g*s. That would telegraph his intentions to those in the courier ship as surely as if he'd announced them himself.

*A slightly higher than usual one-point-five-*g* push could be explained by the fallout from the deGrasse incident,* he reasoned as he sorted through the crate of ammunition he'd snagged from the outpost's meager armory. *Especially if we made it a point to broadcast status updates over standard military frequencies along the way.*

Transit time would be twenty-three days. At that rate, they'd overtake the courier ship at the twenty-nine-AU mark. That would more than make up for the two-day head start the courier had on them, and give him three days to set his snare on the other end.

Far better to let them continue to think they're hiding in plain sight, he thought, *rather than risk them going dark.*

He flipped the CUSP pulse pistol in his hand, adding it to the growing pile he planned to take with him, before sealing the outpost's ammo crate once more.

A notification appeared on his HUD, an incoming message from the patrol boat's comm officer. He accepted it and found himself looking at the avatar of a battlebot in full charge.

Kids these days, he thought, feeling suddenly older than his thirty-eight years.

{What can I do for you, Lieutenant?} he asked as he accepted the connection.

{Sir, the pinnace is on its way down to you now. ETA, thirty mikes.}

That was his ride.

{Got it. Thanks for the heads-up.}

His eye flicked to the chrono on his HUD as the comm officer signed off. If he hustled, he'd have just enough time to grab a bite and rummage through that second crate of ammo in the outpost's tiny armory. He sealed the crate he'd just finished pillaging and hoisted it off the ground before heading back inside.

Half an hour later, Gabe stood, frowning at the clearing where the patrol boat's small fleet of shuttles were being loaded, as he turned the matter over in his head.

"You look like you're thinking hard about something, sir."

He looked up to see the chief warrant approaching. Hyer stopped just in front of the table where he'd parked himself, the awning of the main building sheltering him from the fine mist that had begun to fall from the skies.

Nodding to the crate of ammunition in front of him, she added, "Looks like you're planning on taking on an army, too."

He flashed her a quick smile as he set the CUSP aside. "No, just a renegade biochemist."

The lanky tug operator leaned against one of the shelter's support posts and eyed him thoughtfully. "You know they'll have a weapons cache on the pinnace. Afraid they won't let you liberate anything?"

Gabe's mouth twisted into a wry grin as he nodded to the pistol. "Bird in the hand, Chief."

Her mouth twitched. She stuffed her hands into her pockets as she leaned against the awning's support beam.

"Think you'll have any trouble catching up to the courier ship?"

"It's not the catching up part I'm worried about."

"Oh?" Hyer's brows rose.

"If Janus is spooked, he'll find a way to turn off the courier ship's IFF."

Hyer nodded her understanding. The transponder that identified them as friend and not foe wasn't supposed to be something a Navy ship messed with, unless they were in the middle of a clandestine operation, like entering hostile, enemy-held space.

"Yep. If that happens, they'll be hard, if not impossible, to find," she agreed, as he reached for a spare battery to power the CUSP pistol he'd appropriated.

The search for Case's Helios proved his point easily enough, although he held his counsel on that, for now.

The courier didn't have a Helios's stealth, but Gabe knew it didn't really matter. Space was vast, and if the courier ship cut all emissions, it could become a difficult target to locate.

"Well, you could always hang out at the gate and wait for them there," she suggested. "They'll have to show up at some point, if they plan to leave the system."

Gabe shook his head as he looked up from the backpack he was filling.

"That ship doesn't necessarily have to use the C-Y gate to get to Procyon, if they're willing to break interstellar law. You're a Navy pilot, you know that," he reminded her.

Hyer's eyes widened at the implication. "Shit—ah, pardon the language, sir—I hadn't thought about that."

Despite the seriousness of their conversation, Gabe's lips twitched in amusement at the chief warrant's apology.

Most civilians weren't aware of it since they'd been banned commercially, but almost all Navy ships still had working Scharnhorst drives. It would be all sorts of illegal to spool up that drive, for no military ship was allowed to do so without an Executive Order.

"That courier pilot wouldn't do that, sir." Hyer hesitated. "Would he?"

"He could, if he's in on it. Or if they force him to. You think a little thing like legalities would stop someone like Janus? I'm not about to rule it out."

He saw understanding cross Hyer's face as she processed his words.

The plain truth was that the courier ship could bug out of Luyten's Star at any time. They could deviate from the gate's flight path, fire up the Scharnhorst, and propel themselves through the interstellar medium at three times the speed of light, leaving behind nothing but an energy signature to indicate the ship's point of origin. If they did that, they'd make it to Procyon in a little over three months.

If they ran for Procyon, Gabe knew he had little to no chance of finding them. Searching for them would be like finding a specific grain of sand on the ocean floor. Space, even in an inhabited system, was just too vast.

Hyer nodded thoughtfully.

"Fuel wouldn't be a problem," she mused. "Their hull will be able to feed its fusion drive a constant supply of hydrogen from the IM out there."

The courier ship was surfaced just like all Alliance Navy ships, with an MXene membrane. Gabe didn't know much about MXene, other than that it was a 2D molybdenum carbide material that functioned as an ultrafast sieve.

He knew it pulled $H(0)$, the ultra-dense hydrogen that dark matter was made of, from the interstellar medium. The hydrogen was then stored in CNT-reinforced receptacles lining the ship's hull.

Unfortunately for them, interstellar space between Luyten's Star and Procyon was currently passing through a nice little region of local fluff. It was rich with the stuff.

Yeah, they won't be hurting for fuel, he thought bitterly, as he tossed the battery he held inside his backpack.

"Although you'd think someone in Supply woulda noticed if they'd stocked the ship with enough food for that length of a trip before leaving the torus."

"You have a point there, Chief."

Gabe looked down, grabbed a few canisters of breach nano and tossed them into his backpack, next to the CUSP's spare batteries. "Let's just hope they didn't."

He finished packing and hefted the backpack on one shoulder and nodded toward the pinnace.

"I'd best get going. That ride's not going to wait on me

forever."

She sent him a cocky salute and a sly grin before walking back toward the ships in the clearing. "See you around, sir."

He grunted, hiding a smile at her cavalier attitude and shaking his head at her departing figure.

As he hauled the second crate back to the armory, he reviewed the instructions that had arrived moments before Hyer appeared. Now that he was no longer hiding his status as an NCIC agent, he figured a data packet might show up from the home office in Procyon.

He'd been right.

What he hadn't expected was for it to originate from someone other than his direct superior. The whole thing was highly irregular. He hadn't decided yet what he was going to do about it.

Gabe hoisted the crate back into the shelf where he'd found it, and then sealed the door using the outpost's master security token. Hand still on the lock, he stood there a moment, considering the instructions he'd received from the NCIC's deputy director.

Proceed to gate, the dispatch had read. *Target will be apprehended from this end. Monitor and report progress, but do not engage.*

He turned and walked slowly through the compound, his thoughts a light-year away. The news that he was being denied a part in Janus's arrest didn't sit well with him, but it didn't cause the unease that churned in his gut when he considered the rest of the missive.

Send future reports directly to this secured token. This case is now restricted, Director-Level Only.

Gabe trusted his immediate superior implicitly. It bothered him that he was being ordered to keep Rhea out of the loop. He could think of no good reason why the deputy director would do such a thing, and plenty of bad ones. What if the corruption that had found its way onto deGrasse had infiltrated his own organization?

I'll let matters ride for now, he decided as he strode up the pinnace's ramp and nodded a greeting to its pilot. For the moment, the instructions didn't directly conflict with his own goals.

Always honest with himself, he admitted privately that he was holding his options open. Only time would tell if he would continue to comply with the deputy director's orders.

Time, and whatever future developments might unfold.

REPORTING IN

GNS *WRAITH*
STARSHOT BUOY
ONE AU FROM DEGRASSE REMAINS

WRAITH HAD FLIPPED and begun its deceleration four million kilometers sunward of their current position. Sam spent most of that time in the gunner's seat, going over her notes.

She didn't really need to be in the cockpit, but Harper and Jonathan had been exchanging verbal barbs with one another for the past hour, and she needed a reprieve. She wasn't sure what sparked the antagonism between the two, but it seemed to magnify whenever they worked together.

After Joule had chuffed and then told them to {*get a room,*} Sam opted for a hasty exit. Especially after receiving dirty looks from both parties when she'd been unable to stifle a surprised laugh.

"It's giving me a rash to be this close," she heard Micah mutter under his breath as they came to a stop relative to the buoy. "We're well within the detection cone of the buoy's sensor suite, in case anyone was wondering."

{*Tell me something I don't know, Navy.*} Jonathan's sardonic comment told her he'd been monitoring from the cargo bay.

She stifled a smile at the derisive look Micah shot toward the back of the ship. "Dumbass," he said under his breath.

She cocked her head. "That's kind of like calling yourself one, isn't it?"

"Don't remind me."

She heard Jonathan's mental laughter filtering in over her wire, as Micah unwebbed. "Okay, *Wraith*'s holding station and her rangefinder's locked onto the buoy," he said. "You're safe to unweb now, doc."

They reconvened around the surgi-suite, where Harper had rigged one of the field comm units to project the whiskerbeam transmission. Out of habit, Sam had her wire connect with the medical unit as she neared it.

Jonathan looked a bit piratical at the moment. She'd removed the gel-regen pack blanketing half his face, and replaced it with a black patch to cover his missing eye. His hand was still encased in a wireframe bandage that continuously fed nano repair bots to rebuild bone and sinew, but overall he was much improved.

She anchored herself on one side of the surgi-suite, Harper on the other, while Micah remained out of range of the holotransmitter until she signaled him to join in.

"You ready?" she asked, and felt the weight of Micah's glance before he nodded.

"As I'll ever be," Jonathan agreed, angling his good eye so that he could see her. "Comm's all yours, doc."

She smiled her thanks, then used her wire to interface with *Wraith*'s communications station. A moment later, the holoscreen at the foot of the surgi-suite flared to life.

She let out a breath in silent relief when she saw the familiar golden seal of the Alliance's National Security Agency rotating slowly against a sea of black stars.

Thirty seconds passed agonizingly slowly. And then—

*{Sam? My **god**! **Sam**!}* Though the seal remained the same, the welcome sensation of Duncan's presence flooded into her

mind. His voice cracked as he said her name, and she could feel the swell of emotion that underlaid his words.

Grief. A terrible guilt that she had perished, under his orders. And then a staggering relief at the sight of her personal token, when it popped up onto his HUD.

{My god, you're alive!} he repeated.

{I am,} she responded, unable to stop herself from smiling. *{We're in Micah Case's Helios, and we're stealthed. Are you in a position to talk securely over holo? There's something I think you should see. I'd send you an info burst, but I think it's best if we had this conversation face to face.}*

There was a pause at the other end.

{Okay, now I'm intrigued. I can be at a secured location in about five minutes,} Duncan replied. *{Stealthed, you say. Should I be concerned? Do you need backup?}*

It was Sam's turn to hesitate.

{I think that would be a good idea,} she admitted after a beat. *{But be careful; Harper thinks there's a leak somewhere high up in the Navy, someone who knows about the Vermilion Project back in Procyon. You might want to be selective with who you bring in on this.}*

Sam knew her words were cryptic. If Duncan didn't implicitly trust her, that might be cause for concern.

Her uncle didn't hesitate.

{Got it. Consider it done. Whoever I send, their loyalty will be to me, and me alone. Are you headed back here, to Ceriba?}

She sent him a mental head shake.

{No. You sent me here to find out if our chiral research is being stolen. You were right; it is. Records have been altered to show smaller volumes of samples than what were actually harvested. Someone's siphoned off a rather large selection of material from Vermilion. The person we think is responsible is headed for Luyten Gate.}

*{**Think** is responsible?}*

Sam made a mental face.

{All circumstantial evidence. Harper says he's good. Nothing

within the torus's encrypted network indicates tampering. That's another reason we think there's a leak higher up. We think he had help. Someone gave him access to a secured token—Admiral Toland's, actually. With that, the entire torus would have been an open book to him.}

She felt a flicker of dismay from her uncle before he shut the emotion down.

{Who is it? Stinton?}

She sent a negative.

{No. Clint Janus. The vessel he's on is carrying a large shipping crate. I need a look inside to confirm, but I think we both know what I'll find.}

She heard her uncle sigh.

{Well, the good news is that he'll be forced to jump to Procyon. There's no other place he can go. Luyten Gate is locked down.}

{We kind of figured that. He'll also have to go through customs at Leavitt Station,} she reminded him.

{We have to assume he's not operating alone. I'll have reinforcements waiting for you at Leavitt,} he replied. *{Okay, I'm at a secure spot, now, and ready for your visual. Do I need to brace myself?}*

There was a trace of gallows humor in his voice that had Sam's lips twitching.

She switched the connection over to the holoprojector. "Yeah, you probably should," she said aloud as his visage resolved onto the holoscreen in *Wraith*'s cargo bay.

A slight widening of Duncan's eyes was the only indication of his surprise, and she waited while he studied the scene before him. He remained silent for several seconds, taking in the cargo bay, medical bed—and Jonathan's physical condition.

"Sir." Her patient broke the silence with a nod.

"Captain Case," Duncan responded. He took in a deep breath. "It would seem you didn't come through the destruction of deGrasse unscathed. I'm truly sorry for that,

Captain."

"Actually," Sam interjected, bringing a hand to rest on Jonathan's shoulder, "the captain sustained these injuries several days ago. We suspect the ship he was piloting at the time was tampered with, and that's what caused the accident that injured him."

Jonathan nodded. "I was out on a routine maintenance flight, a check of the torus's fusion generators. I'd just vectored in from the inner side of the ring when my ship experienced explosive decompression."

"There was a fire," Harper spoke up. "He ejected just as the ship disintegrated around him. I downloaded the initial report on the wreckage they recovered. The person who wrote it up suggested metal fatigue, but—"

"That's bullshit, sir," Jonathan cut in. "The Navy maintains their Novastrikes better than that, and the report itself—"

"Was suspiciously light on detail," Harper finished.

Sam could see the muscles in her uncle's cheek twitch as his jaw tightened at the news.

"You think someone found out you were there to investigate?" His words fell between them, hard and flat. His eyes cut from Jonathan to her.

Sam slanted a sideways look over to where chiral Micah floated just out of sight.

"No, actually. I think we ended up stumbling upon an entirely different situation that no one back in Procyon had a clue was happening. Something our enemies would kill to get their hands on."

* * *

Micah saw Sam glance his way, and he took that as his cue to move forward. Pushing off, he floated over to the medical unit and bumped gently against the bed beside Harper.

Micah's mouth quirked in a half smile at the white-knuckled death grip the analyst had on his twin. It faded the moment he turned and saw the disgust playing across the National Security Director's face.

Don't worry, bro. We've got your back.

Micah looked down to meet Jonathan's steady gaze. His lone good eye held a steely look. Micah gave him a sharp nod of thanks before returning his attention back to the holo.

He saw Cutter's fists curl, the man's head shaking as if he would deny what his own eyes were showing him.

"Cloning a human is illegal. Have you run the biometrics on him, Sam? Maybe he's just been gen-modded to appear like Case."

Sam shook her head, the movement causing her short blonde hair to halo around her.

"He's not a clone, Duncan. Although what was done to him was just as illegal."

She sighed, her voice taking on a weary tone as she raked her fingernails through her short strands. "Stinton was running a little side experiment. The man you see here is Micah Case's chiral twin."

The NSA director's mouth twisted into an angry snarl. His hand made a sharp *crack!* as he slammed it down onto the desk in front of him.

"God*dammit.* That's immoral! An abomination—"

He cut off his words just as abruptly as the angry outburst had begun. It was clear Cutter was fighting to contain his reaction. What Micah couldn't tell was whether or not the man considered *him* to be the abomination.

For the first time since this disaster had unfolded, the thought crossed Micah's mind that the Alliance might not recognize him as a human being. A sentient, with freedoms and rights of his own. Apprehension began to curl deep in his gut at the thought.

PUPPET MASTER

ALLIANCE COURIER SHIP
4.5 AU FROM DEGRASSE'S REMAINS

TUCKED AWAY INSIDE the passenger cabin of the courier ship, Clint Janus sat quietly against an outer bulkhead. The cushion beneath him was comprised of nothing more than a thin, reed-like mat. It was the sole comfort the assassin had allowed him so far on this journey.

His world had shrunk to an avid awareness of her location at all times, and a prey's attempt to remain motionless in the hope that the predator would forget his presence. He startled when she moved suddenly, an action that was unusual for the woman.

The assassin had, for the past several hours, been working through her daily exercise regimen. His wary gaze tracked her as she gracefully extricated herself from another inverted position. She reached for a towel and slung it around her neck as she rose, wiping her face with it.

"We have news," she said.

Clint returned her look with a guarded one of his own as he waited for her to continue.

"The clone you allowed to escape, and the physicist who aided him, have surfaced."

Clint shook his head, holding his hands as if to ward away an incipient attack. "I had no way of knowing Case's chiral clone would survive. None of the rest did—"

"Regardless," she cut him off. "We know where they are now. Even better, we know where they will be."

Her tone suggested that perhaps, this time, a punishment would not be meted out. Clint straightened cautiously.

"Where did this information come from?"

The assassin didn't smile, yet he received the impression his question amused her.

"Another sleeper agent, positioned where critical information might be acquired." She took a step toward him and he had to work hard to suppress the urge to flinch.

"They are following us to the gate. They made a stop at a buoy to send a secured message, which increased our distance by another three AU."

She fell silent. Clint turned her words over in his head, frantically casting about for something to say that might appease her, or at least not set her on him again.

"It's too bad we don't have a Marine fireteam to set on their trail, like on deGrasse," he said without thinking. When he recalled how that operation had failed, he flinched internally.

She tilted her head, birdlike, looking at him from those inscrutable eyes. One minute passed, then two. Finally, she nodded.

"An excellent idea, doctor," she told him.

"It was?"

"Indeed. In fact, it will solve two problems at once." She nodded to herself as she paced slowly before him.

"Two problems?" he asked haltingly. "What would the second one be?"

Her eyes landed on him once more.

"It would seem that the torus's security chief was also not who he appeared. He is an NCIC agent, placed on deGrasse at

Admiral Toland's request. It is our misfortune that he happened to have been away from the torus when it was destroyed. He survived."

Her pacing stopped and she took another deliberate step toward him.

"It also appears he has reason to suspect your actions. Fortunately, the deputy director of the NCIC is one of ours. She is working on a way to divert his attention away from us without raising suspicion."

"That's," Clint's voice broke. He swallowed hard, then tried again. "That's good. Right?"

"Your comment about the Marine fireteam suggests a course of action that has merit as a red herring. Agent Alvarez will soon have a different quarry in his sights."

She smiled, her dark eyes as still and cold as the frozen void.

"Micah Case's Helios."

SURVIVORS

THE *HAVERSHAM*'S MED bay was far too small to accommodate seven gravely injured Marines, but it was a fair sight better than the first-aid center the research outpost housed on Vermilion.

Makes sense, I suppose, Addy thought. *The outpost always knew medical help was just an hour or two away, in orbit above them. This patrol boat could be weeks—and dozens of AU— away from the nearest human.*

She waved over the next maglev cart that had been pressed into service as a gurney, and did a quick assessment. The Marine on the cart was in rough shape, just as the last three she'd seen.

This one was in light armor, but missing an arm from the elbow down. The suit had triggered a foam sealant that prevented the woman from bleeding out.

It had also administered pain meds that would have worn off half a day earlier. A piece of shrapnel still pierced the suit's left thigh; again, foam sealant had done its job and maintained suit integrity.

Addy placed a finger along the inside of the woman's arm and sent a command to her medical bracer. It administered a dose of local anti-inflammatory nano and repair bots to begin the job of cleaning up the Marine's shredded elbow, and additional pain medication to make the woman more comfortable.

Once the metal shard was removed and the bleeding stopped, she stepped back and waved to the ensign pushing the cart.

"She's stable for now. Get her settled somewhere and send me her location," she instructed.

The ensign maneuvered the cart down the passageway, likely headed toward a crew cabin someone had vacated for the wounded.

Addy rotated her head from side to side to relieve the stress, blinked away the fatigue, and turned to meet her next patient.

The survivors all came from the same shuttle. Chance had dictated that the shrapnel impaling the vessel had done so in a manner that left portions of it intact.

The co-pilot had survived, her suit automatically sealing when atmospheric integrity had been compromised. The pilot had not; neither had those in the main cabin, unprotected from exposure to the vacuum of space.

Oddly enough, a fireteam of Marines in heavy armor had been loaded into the ship's cargo bay. These, plus two additional Marines, who had also been in cargo but kitted out in light armor, were the only ones to survive.

One of the patrol boat's midshipmen had told her they'd found a Marine's lifeless corpse, maglocked to the outside of the sealed cargo section as it spun silently through space. From the looks of it, those inside owed that man their lives.

Ship's logs, which had survived the shrapnel intact, showed the man shoving someone through the open cargo doors before slapping the controls shut and ordering his heavy armor to fasten itself to the side of the shuttle.

It appeared he'd intended to ride the maelstrom out while hanging onto the exterior of the ship. The plan was a solid one; his heavy armor would have provided enough life support to have kept him alive until their rescue, had not another wave of shrapnel torn into his legs and back.

The sound of another approaching makeshift gurney had Addy shaking her head to force the mental image from her mind.

I need to focus on those I can save, not those beyond my help, she reminded herself.

As the cart drew near, she could tell this patient was in a semi-conscious state. Contusions marred the left side of the sergeant's face. The rest was caked with dried blood.

Her gloved hand turned his face gently as she sought the source of the injury, and the man moaned, slurring something unintelligible.

The wound wasn't hard to find. She didn't need the data streaming from the bracer onto her HUD to see that the entire right side of the sergeant's face was a mess. The man's eye had been pulverized, the maxilla and zygomatic bones beneath it shattered. His skin flapped loosely, all the way to his missing right ear.

The Marine shifted beneath her hands and began to rock his head back and forth, words rapidly spilling from his mouth.

She could understand one out of every three of them, and none of them made sense. The man was delirious from the pain.

"Shit-shit-shit-shit-shit," the man chanted, followed by a string of something that she couldn't parse, then, "hurts like hell."

She stilled his frantic head movements, injecting him with a dose of pain medication. His head movements slowed, but the incoherent words kept tumbling out.

"We've got you, sergeant," Addy assured him as she followed the pain meds with additional clotting nano. A quick scan of the rest of his body showed more contusions but no additional perforations.

Looking up at the midshipman who was standing beside the cart, his face averted, she said softly, "He's in shock. His mind is telling him he's still in pain, but he's not."

She looked down once more at her patient when she caught the word 'morgue' in another string of mumbled words. She gripped the man's uninjured arm and squeezed softly.

"You're not dying, soldier. You're going to be fine."

The man jerked his head to one side in response.

"Don' have nine lives, doc," she heard him whisper, "not like that damn pilot, fuckin' case wouldn't die…"

Addy froze, her hand tightening on her patient's arm.

What did he just say?

"No one's dying," she responded, then, leaning closer to catch the man's fevered words, she played a hunch. "Case won't die either."

The Marine sergeant made an ugly sound.

"Janus owes me for that…" The words were barely there, but Clint's name was unmistakable.

Addy jerked her hand back, letting go of the man's arm as if it were a hot poker. Straightening, she eyed the midshipman as she tried to judge what, if anything he had heard.

She needn't have worried. The young Navy cadet was too busy holding in his lunch, if Addy was any judge.

"Okay, then," she said briskly, and the midshipman's eyes swerved back to meet hers. "We're going to need to get him cleaned up before we can begin repairs, but otherwise, he's stable. Go ahead and get him settled; I'll send one of my nurses to you as soon as I can."

The midshipman swallowed convulsively and nodded. The poor kid looked green.

Addy dialed in a drug that would help the young Navy man control his queasiness. Before he could protest, she pressed her fingers to the side of his neck, the bracer injecting the antiemetic into his system.

Smiling at him, she stepped back.

"Can't have you getting sick all over the patients," she explained.

The man shot her a sheepish look, but nodded his appreciation.

Another gurney came to a stop in front of her, but Addy couldn't break her gaze away from the departing form of the Marine sergeant.

Okay, Alvarez, what am I supposed to do now? she thought to herself as the cadet pushing the sergeant's gurney turned a corner and the injured man's form floated out of sight.

RULES OF ENGAGEMENT

ALLIANCE NAVY PINNACE, GNS *YORK*
0.5 AU FROM VERMILION

THE PINNACE HAD been underway for a full day, and Gabe could not get the message from the NCIC's deputy director out of his head. He supposed there were any number of reasons why his own superior had been cut out of the loop. But his gut was telling him something more was going on than met the eye.

He wasn't entirely sure it was aboveboard.

A ping from the cockpit had him straightening. He looked down at the plas sheet he'd been taking notes on, and pushed it aside. A look at his chrono told him he'd been sitting alone with his thoughts for more than an hour.

{Yes?} he asked, standing and stretching as he opened the connection.

{Incoming message for you. It's Doctor Moran on the Haversham,*}* the pilot told him. *{At our distance, there's a four-minute delay, so it was sent as a packet, not a livestream.}*

{Thanks,} Gabe replied, as the pilot initiated the transfer of the data.

He stood, hands resting on top of the back of the chair he'd just vacated, and waited for the packet to finish downloading. When he saw Addy's face materialize on his HUD, he could tell something was bothering her.

{Gabe,} she began, *{one of the patients I just triaged was a bit incoherent. He said a few things in his delirium that, well...}*

She shook her head and paused briefly, as if gathering her thoughts. Gabe mentally urged her to get on with it.

{He begged me not to send him to the morgue, said he didn't have nine lives, not like—and I quote—'that damn pilot, case,' who wouldn't die.}

Gabe's attention sharpened, but he could hear by the way she'd said it that she was using the word 'case,' and not the name 'Case.'

{I wasn't entirely sure how he meant the words, so I took a chance. I told him he wasn't going to die and neither would Captain Case.}

She paused, this time a deliberate one, as she dropped her next bombshell. *{His reaction wasn't...pleasant. And then he said that Janus owed him for that.}*

Gabe blinked as he assimilated what she'd just told him. She wasn't done.

{I figure you're going to want to interrogate him once he's well enough for it, but I'm not sure how to go about it—or who on this ship can be trusted, given the circumstances.}

She cocked her head, eyebrows raised. *{What do you want me to do, Alvarez? This is your territory, not mine.}*

Her image froze as the recording came to an end.

Drumming his fingers along the top of the chair, he thought for a moment about how to proceed. In the end, he went with his gut.

He recorded a quick missive to his superior, asking her to run a security check on *Haversham*'s crew.

I won't share any details, he told himself, *but it can't hurt to let her know something's not right out here in Luyten's Star.*

Promising to follow up with more information soon, he sealed it with an NCIC priority token, and then pinged *York*'s pilot. The man promised to move the message to the top of the queue.

That done, Gabe palmed the plas sheet he'd been scribbling on and left to go find a change of scenery. The entrance to the Action Information Center drew him to a stop. He stood there a moment, considering the implications of the deputy director's instructions that he monitor but not pursue.

The AIC was currently not in use, so he stepped inside. The tactical table before him was dark; he placed a hand on its surface, using his NCIC token to gain access. Pulling up a holo of the star system, he narrowed it to the distance between deGrasse's remains and the gate.

A string of new icons dotted the area near the Navy's picket, representing ships that had been sent through the gate to assess the deGrasse incident, and help with cleanup. He tapped one of them, noting its acceleration and projected course.

His finger traced a line between the ship and the patrol boat, where recovery efforts were underway. The table obligingly supplied the information: a twelve-day trip at five *g*s.

It emphasized a truth that seemed to remain unchanged throughout all of military history: hurry up and wait. Waiting to arrive at your destination, waiting on a crisis to react to, waiting for orders. Often in his case, waiting for permission to pursue a suspect.

The canvas of his career had been laid upon this foundation, just as it had for everyone else in the Alliance Navy. Moments of intense action served as the accents to military life, the occasional exclamation point at the end of a long sentence.

Even instantaneous communication wasn't immune. Here he stood, as testament to that fact. Trapped, waiting for a response.

Monitoring from this distance isn't going to do anything but give me an ulcer, was his first sardonic thought.

But on its heels, he considered his secondary quarry. Since

the Helios was operating under stealth, it might be much closer to the pinnace than the courier ship.

He narrowed the table's field of view, condensing it to the sector of space just ahead of the pinnace. He had no way of knowing if Case was keeping the Helios to one g, but if he were a betting man, that's where he'd put his credits.

Samantha Travis was a civilian, with no military augmentation. Gabe knew she'd be able to withstand higher accelerations, especially if Case kept her in a crash couch. To do that for almost two weeks, however, would place an unnecessary strain on the physicist.

He swiped his hand through the holo and the image flattened, painting the surface of the tactical table in front of him. Bracing his hands on the table's edge, he let his eyes roam the pinnace's cramped AIC as he considered the variables.

No, they're somewhere between us and the courier ship, he decided, his gaze returning to study the glow of symbols now shining up from the table's surface.

Icons called out the topographical features in the immediate vicinity. Two caught his eye: an airless rock that still bore the ancient designation GJ 273d, less than half an AU away; beyond it was a Starshot buoy, holding station at the system's 2-AU mark.

A noise at the AIC's entrance pulled at Gabe's attention. He looked up in time to see the chief warrant's tall frame fill the doorway.

It hadn't really surprised him that Hyer had volunteered as crew for the pinnace. With so many needing evacuation from the outpost and the limited number of vessels available, it made little sense for Gabe to insist the pinnace be reserved for his exclusive use.

In truth, he was glad to have her along. Aside from him, she and Addy were the closest thing to an eyewitness to deGrasse's destruction that the Alliance was going to get—at least until Addy's patients revived.

Hyer shouldered her way through the AIC's hatch, dipping

her head to clear its frame. She stopped at the 2D rendering, staring down at it. Hooking a thumb at the map, she shot him a questioning look.

"Anything nearby you wanted to stop and take a gander at, boss?"

He blew out a short laugh and shook his head.

"Classified, Hyer."

Hyer tugged at a pierced earlobe, drawing his attention to the blue gem that adorned it. Her gaze was contemplative.

"You know, boss, you talked pretty freely in ol' Betsy. If this," she gestured to the tactical table, "has anything to do with that, then I'm already on record as being sworn to secrecy and stuff."

Gabe studied her for a long moment. The chief warrant had a point.

Nodding at the entrance behind her, he said, "Shut the door." As she moved to comply, he shifted over to make room for her beside him.

"If you were piloting a Helios and you wanted to stay hidden, what would you do?"

Hyer didn't look down at the table. Instead, she studied him from behind inscrutable eyes. After a moment, she spoke.

"You're hunting Micah Case."

He nodded. There was another pause as she came to some sort of internal decision.

"Permission to speak freely, boss?"

"Always."

She gave him a perfunctory nod.

"Okay, then. Here's the deal. I didn't say anything when we were back in the *Betsy*. It just didn't feel like the right time, plus then there was the big explosion and all."

Her chin jutted out and her eyes lit with certainty. "I know Case. I knew Campbell, too. Campbell was good people. So is Case. They're the real deal, sir, if you get my meaning."

Gabe opened his mouth to protest, but she held up her hand.

"Hang on, lemme finish." She turned to face him, leaning a hip against the table. "People like Case and Campbell don't get transferred to a place like deGrasse. They sure's heck don't get slotted into rotation for basic patrol duty."

Gabe cocked his head, unsure what the chief warrant was trying to tell him.

Suddenly a sly smile spread across Hyer's face and she crossed her arms.

"I'm thinkin' you're more than just a run-of-the-mill security officer for the governor-general's Navy, am I right?"

Amused at the chief warrant's astute observation and a bit curious about her sudden change of topic, Gabe felt an unwilling smile tease at his lips.

"Got me dead to rights, Hyer," he admitted. "No, I'm not with Naval Security."

"I *knew* it!" she crowed, slapping a hand on her thigh. "You're with The Unit or some such shit, just like Campbell was, aren't you?"

He shook his head at her mention of the Special Reconnaissance Unit, though he made a mental note to follow up on Campbell's prior military history. It sounded as if some critical items might have been scrubbed from the record, and he wanted to know why.

"I'm NCIC," he clarified for her after a moment.

His smile widened at her crestfallen expression. "So sorry to disappoint," he murmured in a dry tone.

She shrugged. "Guess we can't always make it to the elite teams," she said, and the twinkle in her eye belied her harsh words.

"I'm wounded, Chief. Crushed you'd say such a thing."

Hyer waved away his words.

"At any rate, you understand covert ops. You were on one at deGrasse."

She paused expectantly, but Gabe refused to confirm. There was another quick shrug and she continued.

"Well, you see, a few years back, Captain Case and his Helios ferried a team of Unit boys and girls out to Sirius. One of the Unit boys was Campbell. They... well, they saved my life. Mine, Fred's, heck, they saved an entire mining platform."

At Gabe's raised brow, she explained. "Remember that crazy goon that protested the Alliance's mining of Molly-B around Big Blue?"

It took him a minute to parse her words, until he recalled that "Molly-B" was miner's slang for molybdenum, the transition metal used to create MXene. He nodded.

"Well, that guy decided the best way to get what he wanted was to go into politics. Sort of. Ever heard of the SS? The Secede Sirius gang? They were harmless loons until he took over their leadership. They ended up taking a Cobalt Mining platform hostage." She tilted her head. "Case and Campbell were part of the team that freed us."

Gabe thought a moment about what her words implied.

"I remember that incident," he said. "About seven years ago, wasn't it?"

She nodded.

"Seven years is a long time, Chief," he reminded her. "Somewhere in that time, Case could have fallen out of favor, or maybe he did something to get his ass booted from the SRU."

Hyer looked skeptical. "Well, technically, he's not SRU, he's Shadow Recon."

"Same difference, Hyer."

She snorted her derision. "That, right there, tells me you're not a grunt, and definitely not spec-ops, either. SRU's the boots on the ground, boss. The teamguys."

She jabbed a finger at him to emphasize her point.

"Shadow Recon are the pilots, the ones that insert them wherever we need 'em to go. We call them night stalkers. They rule the black. What they can do with a spaceship is pure magic. Shadow Recon can slip an SRU team in, and then bring them back out again right under your nose purty as you please, and you'd never know they were there."

Gabe looked back down at the map, considering her words. Stars, he hoped she was wrong.

"So, maybe Case decided he wanted something less high-octane. Or maybe he's lost his edge."

"My guess is he was sent in, just like you were," Hyer said. "And if he doesn't want to be found, you're not going to find him."

"Well, we're sure as hell going to try."

Hyer began to shake her head but he forestalled her with a raised hand.

Gently, he said, "Just accept it, Chief. If Case is innocent, he has nothing to worry about. There's no harm in stopping him and questioning him. We're doing it, and that's nonnegotiable, understood?"

ABOMINATION

GNS *WRAITH*
STARSHOT BUOY, ONE AU FROM DEGRASSE REMAINS

IMMORAL! AN ABOMINATION!

The words ricocheted through Micah like a fragmentation bullet. He could hardly miss the fury in Duncan Cutter's voice when the NSA director had uttered them.

"This man is not an abomination!" Harper's denial, hot and angry, cut through Micah's shock. "He's the victim here, sir! Both of them are."

Micah saw Cutter's anger turn to surprise and then to chagrin as Harper spoke. The man raised placating hands toward her.

"I assure you, Miss Kinsley, everything I said was directed at the late Doctor Stinton, not at... ah, Micah."

His stumble was noticeable, and to the man's credit, he didn't try to gloss over it. Instead, he leaned forward and shot Micah a direct look.

"How should I address you, son?"

It was his other self who answered. "My given name is Jonathan Micah Case, sir. For now, I'll go by Jonathan." He tilted his head. "And he'll be Micah."

Twin furrows appeared on Cutter's forehead. "Exactly how similar are you two?"

"Identical, from what we can tell, sir." Micah exchanged a look with Jonathan. "Even down to our memories."

"How is this possible?" Cutter leaned forward. His eyes narrowed, intent upon his niece. "I'm a simple man, Sam. I need simple words. The fewer syllables, the better."

Sam nodded. "Okay, then. Let's start with this: While the rest of deGrasse was busy studying the plant life on Vermilion, Stinton managed to successfully clone it. Then he developed a way to replicate life from our planet, only in chiral form."

"Despite how dangerous that could turn out to be," muttered Harper.

Sam shrugged. "Yes, but that's what deGrasse was built to do—investigate chirality in a controlled environment to mitigate the risk. To figure out how it developed naturally in this system, and to try to replicate it. What he did wasn't technically illegal... until he began experimenting on humans."

Cutter nodded slowly. "We knew they'd succeeded in cloning the local samples; Miss Kinsley's last report said as much. That's why we issued the directive to shut the project down and seal the records."

Sam looked surprised. "I never saw that. When was the directive issued?"

Cutter's expression grew grim. "The morning the torus was destroyed."

Micah exchanged a look with his other half. They were both thinking the same thing; the timing could not be coincidental.

"How did Stinton progress so quickly?" asked Cutter. Gesturing between Jonathan and Micah, he added, "Even illegal cloning operations can't recreate thoughts and memories."

"Stinton developed a prototype digital-to-biological converter unit that added a polarized spin to the molecules before the copy was 3D printed," Sam told him. "But it didn't work."

Harper shot Sam a dark glance. "Until you figured it out for him," she muttered.

Shock washed over Micah at those words; he saw the same mirrored in Cutter's eyes. The man reared his head back.

"*You* did this, Sam?"

A squeak sounded from deeper in the cargo bay, bringing the doctor a brief reprieve. Micah turned just in time to see a small furry projectile—Snotface, or Sneaky Pete, he couldn't tell which—crash into Harper. The impulse sent the analyst careening away with a small shriek.

Micah heard Duncan's startled exclamation as he launched himself after Harper to retrieve her. "What in the heck was that?" the man shouted.

Micah maneuvered Harper and the ferret back to the surgi-suite, the animal chirping cheerfully as Harper scolded him. "How did you get out of your cage? Don't you know that's dangerous in zero-g?"

The ferret wriggled a paw at the analyst. *{Thumbs!}* he chirruped. *{No lock. Was bored. Say hello to new guy!}*

He scrambled out of Harper's grasp and onto the bed, latching onto one of the straps that held Jonathan in place. Turning his nose toward the holoprojector, he bent his whiskers forward and peered curiously up at Sam's uncle.

Sam moved to intercept just as the creature launched himself straight at Duncan's image. At the last second, she managed to snatch the ferret out of midair.

"Stop it," she scolded. "He's not really here. He's just a projection. Besides, he can't hear you anyway. You're not in on the conversation."

{Rude, rude, ruuude!} The ferret pushed against her hold, his outrage at being left out obvious, even to the one person not privy to what the ferret was saying.

"You're talking to it?" Cutter asked. "It's enhanced?"

{Not an 'it',} the ferret grumbled while Sam pushed him into Jonathan's waiting hands.

"Yep. Meet Sneaky Pete," she told her uncle. "He's one of the chiral copies. One of the few successful ones," she amended.

"Thankfully, Stinton never found out why it was successful," observed Harper.

At that, a look of confusion crossed Duncan's face. "How is it possible that you knew and he didn't? When I asked you to go to deGrasse, you protested, and said you'd stick out because this wasn't your field."

"It's not, and you're right," she confirmed. "Most of the researchers on deGrasse specialized in various forms of biology or chemistry, like mycology, bacteriology, or genetics. There were no physicists. Specifically none who knew anything about quantum states."

"Small words, Sam," the man on the holo reminded her.

The doctor held up a hand. "Stinton successfully printed chiral versions of various small mammals, but he couldn't keep them alive," she told them. "Not long after the animals were created, they perished. Every single one of them. It wasn't until Harper hacked into Stinton's isolation lab and I was able to study his invention that I began to suspect what was going on."

She reached for Sneaky Pete, who obligingly scrambled up her arm and onto her shoulder. He buried his hands in her hair, sneezing as the strands shifted in the weightless environment, tickling his nose.

"I was able to align the timestamps across several research labs and compare the chiral animals' progress against that of the donors. The process Stinton set up required that samples from the donor animal be harvested prior to the creation of the chiral one."

She seemed to avoid Micah's stare as she added, "In each instance, the donor was no longer alive when its chiral counterpoint was created."

"But—" Harper protested, a perplexed look on her face, "we have originals here. A ferret and a panther."

"That's because I asked to swap with one of the researchers during each of those experiments," explained Sam. "Instead of euthanizing the originals, I sedated them while harvesting the samples needed for replication. Then I hid the 'corpses' and falsified the records."

"How'd you figure out the original needed to remain alive in order for the chiral version to be viable?" asked Duncan, bringing Sam's attention back to the holo.

She shrugged. "I knew Stinton's prototype forced a polarized spin onto the molecules he used to form each chiral creature. The artificial polarization introduced a residual quantum effect that no one else seemed to have picked up on. It created a state of quantum entanglement at the cellular level, between the original and the chiral copy."

"And that means...?" Micah's voice was steady but he saw an anxious light in Jonathan's lone eye that he knew must be reflected in his own.

"Well, if the original wasn't still alive when he printed the chiral version, Stinton was never going to get one of his chiral creatures to live."

Micah heard Cutter draw in a swift breath.

"And if, after the chiral pair is formed, the original were to die?"

ENTANGLED

GNS WRAITH
STARSHOT BUOY, ONE AU FROM DEGRASSE REMAINS

DUNCAN CUTTER'S QUESTION had Micah reeling as if from a physical blow. He locked eyes with his other self as he reached down their shared mental pathway.

Is he suggesting my existence is tied to yours? If you die, I die?

Jonathan's expression shuttered. *Not going there, bro. The doc might be a friggin' braniac, but she'd be the first to tell you this is uncharted territory. Let's not borrow trouble.*

His attention snapped back to Sam when she spoke.

"We don't really have an answer to that," she said carefully. "It's possible that, after a set period of time, the chiral twin has established a more stable mental neural 'stamp,' for lack of a better term, and it wouldn't be an issue."

"But you can't know that for certain," Cutter said.

Sam shook her head, a look of deep regret crossing her features as she shot a quick glance at Micah and his twin. "No, we can't."

She straightened. "At any rate, it was shortly after the success with the animals that we began to see a sudden uptick in accidental deaths on deGrasse."

Cutter's gaze sharpened. "You mean the mid-flight collision," he stated flatly. "Your last report on the incident that killed those two pilots over a month ago said you suspected foul play. Is this still the case?"

"Yes," the doctor said. "Captain Case went over the investigation himself after Harper acquired it. We think it was sabotage."

Harper nodded. "I did a bit of poking around and found a few private messages that connect the incident investigator with Clint Janus. It's circumstantial, I know, but it does fit with the bigger picture we're piecing together."

"And that is?"

"That Janus was providing Stinton with fresh cadavers to experiment on." Harper's words were harsh, angry.

Silence fell as the NSA director processed everything they'd told him. After a moment, the doctor cleared her throat. Micah looked over at her, wondering what new thing she was going to drop on her uncle.

"Duncan...." Sam shot Micah a glance. "I'm not sure what was transmitted from deGrasse before it went up, but there might be a warrant out on me and Captain Case. After losing Jack Campbell, I was afraid to leave the captain alone in medical for Janus to find, so I faked his death."

"Yeah, I kind of doubt the reason they sent a Marine fireteam after us with live ammo is because I went AWOL," muttered Micah.

Cutter's brows rose. "Live ammo?"

Micah nodded. "Yes, sir, and apparently under Janus's orders, too."

Cutter's eyebrows climbed once more. "I'll have someone look very carefully into Janus from this end. It's sounding more and more like there's an Akkadian connection."

"I'll append some records to the end of this transmission," Harper added. "They'll bring you up to date on everything we know, and will include all the data we've gathered up to this point."

Sam shot her uncle a pointed look. "If we hadn't hatched our own plan to escape, all the research we're about to send you would have been lost. Nothing from deGrasse would remain."

Cutter straightened. "Message received. Give me a few days on this end to get things in motion. Let's connect at the second buoy, and we'll discuss next steps."

SLEEPER AGENT

MINISTRY OF STATE SECURITY
CENTRAL PREFECTURE, ERIDU
AKKADIAN EMPIRE

CHE JOSZA FOUND himself sharing ritual coffee with Rin Zhou a bit sooner than expected. Nodding politely in response to the barista's silent query, he extended his cup to the man. The barista bowed, taking the cup, and began the careful, ritual pour.

Rin Zhou looked over her steepled hands at Che as the attendant completed the ritual, the rich aroma of coffee rising to fill the air around them. That wasn't all that hung between them, Che could tell. He sensed an air of dissatisfaction emanating from her that had him treading very carefully.

She nodded a dismissal as the servant bowed his way out of the office. Che waited politely until the minister had lifted her cup before retrieving his own.

Rin Zhou waved her hand over her brew, inhaling the aroma on a slow, deep breath.

"Your earlier report did not indicate there were survivors," she commented.

Che tilted his head, acknowledging the point. "My apologies for the omission. The Alliance has always kept a small enclave on the planet. Our agent had hoped to be able to eliminate those as well, but could not do so without raising suspicion. It was a small cadre of researchers who rotate in to observe and take samples."

"What of this Alvarez she mentioned?"

Che stifled a sigh, lowering his cup. "That was an unfortunate bit of circumstance no one could have predicted. Alvarez should have been killed along with the rest who evacuated. Why his ship was on the other side of the planet at the time of the explosion is unknown."

"Time and chance happen to us all," Rin Zhou acknowledged with a rare and dry smile. It vanished in the next instant. "His true identity, however, should have been known. Will he pose a problem for us?"

Che nodded. "We suspect that was Admiral Toland's doing. She kept his identity as an NCIC agent a closely guarded secret."

"Will he pose a problem for us?" Rin Zhou repeated, placing more emphasis on the question this second time.

"No," Che was quick to assert. "The NCIC's deputy director is one of ours. She intercepted the report Alvarez submitted and is handling it herself."

QUESTIONING ORDERS

ALLIANCE NAVY PINNACE, GNS *YORK*
0.7 AU FROM VERMILION

GABE AND THE chief warrant spent a few hours hashing out a plan for locating Case's stealthed ship, and then Hyer left to try to wheedle a few favors from the ship's engineer. Gabe hit up the ship's captain for a few hours of dedicated sensor time to hunt for the Helios, and then headed back to his assigned cabin.

He'd learned earlier in the day that the pinnace had a simulated shooting range programmed into its small rec room. He decided he'd treat himself to an hour's worth of practice and signed up for a slot later in the day, after he finished his workout.

Weight work while under an acceleration of one and a half *g*s had his body crying foul, but Gabe persevered, reminding himself that criminals didn't play fair, either. Muscles burning with fatigue, he carefully lowered the resistance bar as he finished his final set of lat pulldowns.

The heavy bar clanked against the unit when he released his grip, and then retracted back into the bulkhead when he signaled the system he was done with the weight machine configuration.

He grabbed a towel and checked his chrono. If he hustled, he'd have just enough time for a quick wash before his hour-long reservation in the rec room began.

It occurred to him that the fall of hot water in his shower was going to feel a lot more like a high-pressure water massage at the pinnace's current one-point-five *g*s. Anticipation had him increasing his pace.

He was just dressing when he received a ping from the cockpit.

{You're a popular guy, sir,} the pilot's mental voice drawled. *{Another message just came in for you, from Procyon. Sending it to your queue now.}*

Gabe thanked the man. Tapping on the icon, the seal of the NCIC appeared, followed by the deputy director's token. The message was brief, and text-only, just like the last one.

We have news on the whereabouts of Micah Case, it read. *His ship is headed to the Starshot buoy two AU from Vermilion. The vessel's last known location, and the time it departed, are appended.*

Our informant has indicated the ship will get close enough to initiate a real-time whiskerbeam transmission. This will be your best opportunity to apprehend the subject.

Gabe suppressed a flash of irritation as he read the next paragraph.

The monitoring and pursuit of Clint Janus has been handed over to another NCIC operative. Your primary objective now is to detain Case for questioning. He is to be considered armed and may have an accomplice.

The message ended abruptly. Data on the Helios's location streamed into his wire's database immediately after.

Gabe chewed on the inside of his cheek, not liking that he'd been removed from Janus's case entirely. The feeling that something was off continued to eat at him.

The new orders didn't completely divert him from his

investigation. His gut told him Case was involved in the deGrasse situation in a significant way. But he could no longer ignore his instincts where the deputy director was concerned.

I'll capture Case, he decided, *and then to hell with the DD's gag order.*

He'd send the complete file to his superior and see if she could find out exactly what the deputy director was up to. He hadn't come this far to see Janus slip through their fingers over some bureaucratic cock-up with a field assignment.

That decided, he took a quick shower, canceled his time in the rec room with real regret, and pinged the pinnace's Synthetic Intelligence for Katie Hyer's whereabouts.

The SI pushed a map of the pinnace onto his HUD, then dropped a flashing icon over the engineering department. Gabe dismissed the map, then headed out in search of the chief warrant.

A stream of curses greeted him as the doors parted to admit him into Engineering. The colorful words weren't from Katie, and Gabe didn't immediately see evidence of human occupation.

For a moment, he contemplated the thought that someone aboard the pinnace had programmed the SI to cuss like a sailor. The thought amused him.

As he rounded the corner, he realized the voice was all too human. Someone's head was buried inside a column that held a multitude of fiber strands, and he was busy calling out readings to his unnamed partner.

"Forty-seven... forty-eight... c'mon, you piece of shit-for-brains bucket of—"

"Found it!" Katie Hyer's voice interrupted, and Gabe saw the man sag in relief.

"About time," he heard the man mutter under his breath as he began to extract himself from the column.

Gabe looked in the direction the chief warrant's voice had emanated, but didn't immediately spot Hyer. Stepping past both man and column, he bent down to look under the engineer's control console when a flash of blue caught his eye.

She was lying on her back beneath it, some sort of tool clamped between her teeth and her arms extended up into the unit's guts as she tied off a series of connections. She stuffed them back up into the console, sealed the access panel, and then shimmied her way out from under it.

Gabe extended a hand. She grabbed it with surprising strength and nodded her thanks as she popped upright.

"What's up, boss? Hear anything new?"

Gabe frowned and shook his head slightly, darting a glance at the engineer, who was striding over, a smile creasing his face. He waited until the man had thanked her for her help before indicating with the jerk of his head that she should follow him out into the passageway.

"Got a minute?" he asked when she joined him.

"Minutes, hours, days," she shrugged. "Not a lot to do between here and the gate. I'm all yours."

He sent her a curt nod. "Good. Let's head back to the AIC. I want another look at that map."

He'd pinged the pinnace's captain on his way to engineering, asking permission to use the Action Information Center for NCIC business. Gabe sealed the doors once they were inside the AIC, and brought up the tactical table once more.

Narrowing the system map to a two-AU radius, he tapped on the Starshot buoy where the deputy director said Case was headed. Looking over at Hyer, he asked, "How close do you need to be to one of these things to establish a real-time stream?"

The confused look on Hyer's face told her she had no idea what he was up to, but she answered his question anyway.

"A thousand klicks. Closer's better."

He nodded, then transferred the deputy director's data on Case's Helios to the map in front of them. A ship's icon appeared beside a Starshot buoy, one the pinnace had passed almost half an AU back. Beside the icon was a timestamp indicating when the vessel had been spotted.

Hyer huffed out a breath. "Is that who I think it is?"

Recalling her earlier comments, Gabe kept his response brief and his inflection noncommittal. "Yup."

He glanced over at her, giving her a moment to absorb the spatial awareness of their position and that of the Helios in relation to Luyten's near-space objects.

"I just received information that says Captain Case is headed toward the next buoy in line," he said, pointing to the one at the two-AU mark. "We need to get there before he does."

He turned back to the map, noting the distance between the two ships. He started to ask his implant to do the math for him, but the tug pilot beat him to it.

"If we assume his accel is one g," she said, staring intently at the map, "then depending where and when we choose to flip for our decel burn, we could beat him there by a day and a half."

Gabe watched her closely as she studied the layout.

"And if we don't want them knowing we're coming after them?"

Hyer rolled her eyes at him and gestured to the map.

"Not a helluva lot of stuff out there to hide a big-ass fusion burn behind, boss, in case you hadn't noticed. Except..."

Her voice trailed off and she leaned in to study the map more closely, a finger tapping her lower lip thoughtfully.

Gabe gave her a moment, but impatience won out. He sent her a verbal nudge.

"Except...?" he repeated, leaning a hip against the table in an unconscious mimic of her earlier pose.

"Except for that, there," she murmured, pointing to the rocky planet. "It'll take some finagling, and you're going to have to convince the pinnace's pilot to do it—and good luck with that, by the way."

He ignored her sardonic commentary and folded his arms, wordlessly ordering her to get on with it.

"Okay," she played her hands across the table, generating a dotted-line track that indicated the pinnace. "If we set our flip point *here*, and we burned hard for about five minutes—and I do mean hard..."

Her look told him that the burn she referenced wouldn't be anyone's idea of fun.

She continued. "Then you should be able to go dark and coast the rest of the way in, using the asteroids scattered nearby to mask the thrusters you'd need for course adjustment. Bit of fancy flying for a few hours, but it can be done."

He clapped her on the shoulder.

"Good job, Chief. Now tell me how we're going to find them once we get there."

She looked at him and shrugged.

"Not a whole lot you can do except look for a hole in space as they pass by."

He shook his head, realizing he'd left out a crucial bit of information. "They're stopping at the buoy to have a little chat."

Hyer's face lightened in comprehension.

"Ah, I get it. *They're* the ones needing the whiskerbeam. Thought you meant us. Well, then, that's easy enough."

She frowned and shot him a wary look. "Hope you don't expect some next-level Shadow Recon type move to pull it off, because I can tell you right now, I don't have one."

She nodded to the map. "But if you can get me to the buoy with a few hours to spare, I can unleash a cloud of microdrones that'll be able to intercept a whiskerbeam, slick as you please."

"And once you've found that?"

"Easy," she grinned. "Just follow the beam back along its reciprocal, and bang, you've got yourself a Helios."

ADAM'S RIB

GNS WRAITH
EN ROUTE TO STARSHOT BUOY AT TWO-AU MARK

SAM HAD JUST finished feeding the animals and was on her way to find Harper when she heard voices in the galley. She paused just before its entrance, listening.

"Well, hell," complained Micah. "Oranges, too?"

"No, shit?" came Jonathan's voice. "What does it taste like?"

Micah made a gagging noise. "Like a pinecone got together with a citrus fruit and had a baby."

"Oh, man. That's gotta suck."

Sam winced as she realized what the two men were doing: testing the chiral differences of various foods.

Yeah, oranges aren't going to taste anything like they used to, she thought wryly.

Sam leaned her back against the bulkhead outside the galley and pinched the bridge of her nose in thought.

There was truly nothing she could do about Micah's taste receptors, and she felt bad for him, but if mints that tasted like dill and fruits that tasted like pine oil were the worst of his problems, then she'd count him very lucky, indeed.

With a mental sigh, she pushed away from the bulkhead. Squaring her shoulders, she plastered a smile on her face and stepped forward into the opening that separated the small galley from the ship's main cabin.

"Comparing notes, guys?" she asked, and received a grimace from Micah in return.

"Dang, doc, if Stinton weren't already dead, I might have to murder him myself, just on principle," muttered the man. "I really like oranges."

Jonathan, seated on the makeshift maglev chair they'd cobbled together from a cargo lifter, grinned. With two days' stubble and a black patch covering his ruined eye, the effect was rakish.

"Guess you'll have to just settle for chugging some of that shit the autowashers use to swab the decks with to get your fix. That's pine scented isn't it?"

Micah threw the half-eaten fruit at his twin's head. The man picked it out of the air with an effortlessness Sam found gratifying, considering the condition he'd been in just forty-eight hours previously.

She settled onto the bench where Micah sat and braced her arms on the table.

"As bloodthirsty as it might make me sound, if you found a way to bring Stinton back to life just so you could commit a capital crime, I just might hold him down for you," she murmured with a wry twist of her lips.

Sitting back, she glanced between the two. "Now that you've had some time to digest what we discussed, do you have any questions I can answer?"

Micah turned to face her. "Yeah, doc. You said the only reason I survived was because you faked Jonathan's death, right?"

Sam nodded.

"If that's true, why did I wake up in the morgue? I would have thought they'd want to keep their success around a bit longer. Study me, or something."

Sam looked down, hoping he couldn't read the guilt on her face. "I... may have inadvertently been responsible for that," she admitted.

Micah remained silent, and she turned from him to Jonathan, who'd stopped peeling the orange and was staring intently at her. Her glance flicked up to Harper, who'd come to stand in the galley's entrance, before settling once more on her patient.

"After I faked your death," she told Jonathan, "I put you into medical stasis, so if they did attempt a chiral cloning, it would fail," she said quietly.

"And I would never be born." Micah's mouth twisted. "And yet here I am."

Sam gave him a crooked smile. "It seems my timing was slightly off."

"But if I was a success, then why did they..." Micah swallowed hard, "discard me?"

She spread her fingers flat on the cool surface of the table. "There was a moment when Jonathan coded," she admitted. "I managed to stabilize him, but I had to put him into stasis again briefly, in order to do it. In the midst of all that, you must have died, too. Janus and Stinton would have assumed another failure, and given you over to the morgue."

Micah stared at her, expression unreadable, as he processed what she was saying.

Regret roughened her voice. "I'm deeply sorry for my part in all this."

He shook his head. "You weren't the one running the experiments, doc. And you certainly weren't the one trying to incinerate me in the morgue. According to what I overheard, that's on Janus, too."

Jonathan waggled his brows at Harper as she slid past him to take a seat.

"Good thing we had someone to hack the morgue's incinerators then, wasn't it?" he said.

Sam realized he was trying to lighten Micah's mood. It

worked, somewhat.

Micah cracked a brief smile.

"Yeah, thanks for that," he responded, giving Harper a small chin lift before his serious gaze landed back on Sam.

"You know, between waking up in the morgue, getting shot at by Marines, dodging exploding space stations, and finding out I'm some sort of mirror-me—" Micah shrugged, "—there hasn't been much time to fill in the blanks. For some reason, my memories end at about the time we arrived in Luyten's Star."

"I suspect the reason your memories are incomplete has something to do with what Jonathan experienced in the accident," Sam said. "Trauma has long been associated with short term memory loss, with patients reporting that they are unable to recall events leading up to an accident. The triage team imaged a brain scan right after the crash. Stinton had to have used it to create you; he had no access otherwise."

"Wait," Micah held out his hand. "Doc, you said Stinton required tissue samples from the donor animal in order to create its chiral clone. If he never had access to Jonathan, then how..."

Sam winced at the question Micah left hanging in the air between them. She'd really hoped no one would ask, at least not in front of Jonathan.

"Well," she said slowly, shooting an apologetic look at the man in the floating chair, "hospital procedure when we amputate is to send the failed limb as biomatter to the morgue for incineration. My guess is that Janus—"

"Oh man, that's just gross," Micah interrupted, his face twisted in distaste as he turned to Jonathan. "I was made from your *legs?*"

Harper grinned at that. "Shades of Adam's rib, huh?"

Micah shot her a look that promised retribution, but then his expression turned somber and his eyes landed back on Sam. "About Jack, doc..."

Sympathy welled in her and she shook her head. "I'm truly

sorry I couldn't save him."

"What—" Micah cleared his throat and tried again. "What happened?" he asked.

Sam saw his gaze track from Jonathan to Harper before finally settling on her.

This was more Harper's bailiwick than hers. Sam turned to her friend and lifted an eyebrow in wordless encouragement.

"When you and Jack arrived," Harper said, "your cover was as relief pilots for the deGrasse Novastrike unit, so you were put into rotation with the rest of the torus's pilots. Jack was on patrol the night the two Novastrikes collided."

Micah leaned forward, his eyes narrowing. "But that kind of accident—"

"Shouldn't have been possible, not with the Synthetic Intelligence built into those ships' systems." Jonathan interrupted, raking his uninjured hand through his hair. Sam saw Micah nod his agreement.

"Unless you're being deliberately sabotaged," agreed Harper. "And they were. Both systems were hacked. SIs were offline. Worse, the data fed to the two ships plotted a course that had them driving directly into each other."

"So..." Micah drew the word out. "Stinton tried to clone him, too?"

Sam nodded slowly.

"Did he succeed?"

She shook her head.

Jonathan's single eye squeezed tight, a look of pain crossing his features as Micah asked his final question.

"So he's dead, then."

"I'm sorry, Captain," she said softly. "He's dead."

Emotion welled in Micah's eyes. He cupped his mouth with a hand, his gaze tracking up to the overhead for a moment before seeking her out again.

"How did it happen?"

She nodded. "He was in serious but stable condition when I left that night. Janus stopped by early the next morning. He was there when your friend coded. He was the one who reported the death."

Micah's voice held a hard edge. "We're going to nail that bastard's ass to the wall."

"You bet we are," Sam said, her jaw clenching as she considered the implications of the missing chiral samples.

"If he's in possession of material from Vermilion, then he's either doing it for personal gain, or he's working for an enemy of the state. Either way, he has to be stopped."

AN UNORTHODOX APPROACH

Alliance Navy pinnace, GNS *York*
INTERCEPTING BUOY

In order to comply with the deputy director's orders to apprehend Case, Gabe had been forced to reveal his identity as an NCIC agent to the *York*'s captain.

It was impossible not to notice the look of incredulity that crossed the woman's face when he'd followed his NCIC credentials with his plan for her ship and crew. He knew what he was asking of her ship was next to impossible.

A pinnace was a rank amateur compared to the Helios's heavyweight champ. But he had orders to follow, and he had to at least *try* to bring Case in.

His newly-revealed identity earned him a front-row seat during the pinnace's close pass of the rocky planet, GJ 273d, otherwise known as Luyten D. Their braking burn had been every bit as hard as Hyer had predicted it would be, but now they were coasting to a gentle stop, a full three hours ahead of the Helios's predicted arrival time.

The pinnace's crew had almost two full days to figure out a plan of attack. During that time, several ideas had been tossed about. In the end, the chief warrant's strategy had been the winner.

Hyer had potential. If they managed to survive this crazy situation, Gabe had plans for her talents. She'd be a great addition to NCIC.

The easiest part of the plan entailed positioning a ring of microdrones around the buoy's surface. As Hyer had explained to Gabe before, the drones would be tasked with detecting the whisker the Helios would soon initiate. Once they intercepted the laser beam, Micah Case's location could be extrapolated.

That was when the *York* would enact the second and more complex part of the plan. The first step involved a bit of misdirection that required some critical timing, and had to be enacted just as the ship cleared Luyten D's shadow.

The chief warrant helped the engineering team alter a drone so that it mimicked the pinnace's emissions signature. While the ship coasted its way to a rendezvous with the buoy, the drone would continue along a trajectory that would intersect with the gate.

This wouldn't fool anyone for long if the drone came under close scrutiny, as its mass was obviously nothing near that of the pinnace. But if Case had his SI set to monitoring surrounding space for any anomalous changes in velocity within an AU of their position, this shell-game maneuver should suffice to spoof it.

Hyer's solution for how to actually *capture* Case was a bit more unorthodox and she'd nearly come to blows with *York*'s captain over it. In the end, none from the pinnace could come up with anything that offered the vessel a better chance, both for success and survival. Interestingly enough, it was based in no small part on her experience piloting a tug for the Geminate Navy.

It turned out that pushing ships and hauling loads involved

more of a comprehensive understanding of spacecraft than Gabe had initially thought. Whereas the pinnace's crew thought in terms of what their ship's armament and capabilities were as opposed to that of the Helios, Hyer came at it from a much more basic approach: tonnage, inertia, vectors.

She was also far more well-versed in jury-rigging her way through a problem than those on the *York*. Gabe suspected she had more experience than most in the creative art of repurposing a minimal set of tools for maximum efficiency to get a job done.

Hyer's plan relied upon the use of the ship's magnetic sweepers. A combination ES/magnetic field, the sweepers preceded the vessel a kilometer ahead of its anticipated track. They cleared a path in front of the ship, deflecting small objects much like cowcatchers did with ancient, land-based trains.

The *York*'s sweepers were modified so that, rather than deflecting the material, they captured it instead. After two days' work, the ship had collected a sizeable amount of detritus, enough to scatter randomly around the circumference of the buoy. The resulting clutter produced enough sensor noise to easily disguise the asteroid-buster mines Hyer had liberated from ship's stores.

The mines would work to get Case's attention, the equivalent of a warning shot across the bow. Gabe planned to set one off right before he ordered the man to surrender—but not before the pinnace had maneuvered behind the Helios.

Woefully outgunned, Gabe knew the *York* had but one chance to take down the kind of attack craft Case commanded. This depended on two things: the element of surprise, and the ability to deliver a point-blank, up-the-kilt shot right through the Helios's engines.

He'd instructed the pinnace's captain to pull their punches. He didn't want the Helios destroyed, just disabled. She'd argued against this, pointing out that, should they fail to disable the vessel's drive and Case were to power it up, everyone in the pinnace would be killed by its exhaust emission.

The captain wasn't wrong. Yet Gabe's gut told him that Case wasn't the kind of man to commit premeditated murder. Whatever had happened back on deGrasse, and to whatever degree Case was involved with Janus, he'd bet a month's credits the man was in over his head.

His actions so far had been those of a man running scared, not of a cold-blooded killer. Gabe had studied everything he could find on Micah Case. Hyer had been right; the man was a decorated pilot with a distinguished service record.

No, Gabe was convinced that, if things went balls-up, Case would find a way out that didn't involve the obliteration of the *York*. He just hoped to hell it didn't come to that.

Their trap set, Gabe had nothing to do but sit back and wait for his quarry to show up.

RENDEZVOUS

GNS *WRAITH*
STARSHOT BUOY, TWO AU FROM VERMILION

MICAH FELT JONATHAN'S physical presence behind him as the Starshot buoy grew larger on the Helios's main holo. He looked up to see the makeshift maglev chair hovering between the two crew stations.

You ready for this, bro? he asked his other self, and the man nodded. Micah stood carefully, bouncing in the almost-nonexistent gravity, and lifted the equally-light Jonathan into the co-pilot's cradle.

A look behind him showed both women already webbed, with Harper seated at the gunner's station, and Sam in the flight engineer's chair.

"Everyone ready?" he asked. Harper gave him a thumbs-up and Sam nodded solemnly.

Micah returned the nod, and then settled into the pilot's seat. Interfacing with *Wraith*'s nav systems once more, he made a few last-minute course adjustments to the Helios and then brought it to a complete stop before the Starshot buoy.

He heard Jonathan shift in his seat, and in the next moment

Micah felt his mirror-twin handshake with *Wraith* as well. The two men met in the mental space reserved for the symbiotic relationship every Helios pilot had with its SI system.

It felt different, weirdly like a mental echo. He shot Jonathan a quick look.

You feeling this, man?

Through their spooky, quantum connection, he felt Jonathan's mental confirmation. He started to say something more, but just then Harper initiated the whiskerbeam connection and the main holoscreen sprang into life with the National Security Agency's seal.

Duncan Cutter's image resolved, and Micah noticed the security adviser's location had changed. He'd only seen a room like this once before. It was a SCIF, he was sure of it.

A SCIF was a sensitive, compartmentalized information facility. Fully sandboxed and air gapped. He was certain that whatever term people used to describe that room couldn't begin to cover all the secured measures it employed.

Unlike the last time they spoke, Cutter wasn't alone. Beside him sat Colonel Tala Valenti.

Of its own volition, Micah's spine straightened into a modified parade rest when he caught sight of the colonel. He saw Jonathan's unconscious attempt to do the same from the co-pilot's cradle.

Colonel Valenti led the Special Reconnaissance Unit. All Shadow Recon teams, Micah's included, reported up to her. The last time he'd seen Valenti was the day Major Snell, their team lead, had briefed him for this mission.

"Sam," Cutter greeted. "Jonathan, you're looking better than the last time I saw you."

"Can't say I'm a big fan of being stuck in a maglev chair, sir," replied Jonathan, "but it's a fair sight better than the alternative, and I have Doctor Travis here to thank for that."

Cutter nodded, and then the smile dropped from his face.

"I believe you gentlemen know Colonel Valenti."

"Ma'am," Micah said. Jonathan echoed the same.

The woman nodded back at them, then braced her arms on the desk and leaned forward, hands clasped.

"Captains. The security director told me you've already received reassurances from him, but I'll add my voice to it. The Unit has your back. Both of you."

Micah nodded wordlessly, thankful for the show of support.

Cutter cleared his throat, his expression serious. "We think we've figured out Janus's agenda. It's not greed. We believe he's an Akkadian sleeper agent."

"You had an Akkadian assassin with you on deGrasse," the colonel added bluntly. "The SI program we had reviewing the data you sent flagged it."

"What?" Harper's voice rose so high, it was dangerously close to reaching a pitch only dogs and augmented humans could hear.

"We think she was there as Clint's handler," the colonel told them. "It also explains how Janus was able to get certain things accomplished that might, on the surface, appear to have been beyond his skill set."

"How did this get past us?" Harper asked, and Micah gave her props for recovering so quickly. "I ran everyone on the torus past our database of suspects, and everyone checked out."

Cutter nodded his understanding.

"A recent exchange of intel with our counterparts in the Coalition included dossiers on several Akkadian operatives. Known to them, but new to us. The SI cross-referenced your data feed against the new intel, and came up with this."

The holoimage of the SCIF was replaced by a woman's likeness. She was a study in browns, from her dusky complexion, to her hair—hair that looked like it had beads woven through it, pulled back into a tight braid.

Micah glanced around at the others inside *Wraith*. The expressions on their faces held no recognition. They, like him, had never seen the assassin before.

"Don't be surprised if she doesn't look familiar to you,"

Cutter remarked as he and Valenti returned to the screen. "They're notorious for their ability to be utterly forgettable."

"Given what we know, we have to assume Janus and his accomplice will pass both the research and the samples to a contact on Leavitt," added Valenti.

If possible, her expression turned even more severe. "We're operating on the assumption that the deGrasse military was compromised. The picket at the gate may be, as well. I'm sending a Marine from one of the SRU teams over to escort you through to Procyon. He'll be landing on the carrier this afternoon and will run interference for you."

"Anyone we know, ma'am?" asked Micah.

"I think you'll recognize him. I'm sending his token over now," she informed them.

Micah looked at Harper, whose fingers flew through the co-pilot's holopanel.

"Got it," she said. She tapped on a floating icon, and brought up a secondary window that displayed the agent's identity.

"Severance," murmured Jonathan as a familiar ebony face appeared.

Thaddaeus Severance was one of the captains assigned to Valenti's Special Reconnaissance Team Five. A heavy-worlder, the man was built like a tank, and fought like a mean sonofabitch.

Micah knew, because he'd seen the man in action, many times.

"Captain Severance has been read into this mission, so you can speak freely around him," the colonel told them. "He'll get you back through the gate and onto Leavitt, and will stay to help apprehend Janus and recover any stolen material."

"To that end," Cutter took control of the conversation once more, "we've authorized the use of your Helios's Scharnhorst drive. Severance knows to look for your signature… here."

His visage was replaced by a holo of the immediate area surrounding the Luyten gate. The image then shrank, the holo's mapkey helpfully providing tick marks that informed everyone they were now seeing the gate from a distance of five AUs.

A sphere at the one-AU mark shaded in red appeared next, with the gate at its center. The picket materialized several hundred thousand kilometers from the gate's event horizon. A flashing icon denoting the carrier appeared at its center.

"You're cleared to jump from your current location, but remember," continued Cutter in a warning tone, "those drives don't play well with Calabi-Yau gates."

Micah gave a terse nod and felt Jonathan do the same. An echo along their shared pathway told him the other man was thinking of the same memory he'd just pulled up from their training days.

Gate safety had been something drilled mercilessly into him during flight school, and at every flight review since. The destructive energy unleashed when a drive's Casimir bubble came into contact with a gate's field was the stuff of nightmares and something no pilot ever forgot.

The holo blinked, and he saw a new icon pop up just outside the sphere, this one with *Wraith*'s designation attached to it.

"Here's your exit point," Cutter told them. "Severance has this information and will be monitoring. If you'd like, you can give us a departure time and the colonel will forward it onto Thad for you."

"Got it, sir," Jonathan told the security director as Micah shunted the data to *Wraith*'s SI, locking in their destination. In the next instant, the map dissolved and Cutter and Valenti reappeared.

"Wait. That's it?" asked Harper, her tone one of disbelief as she looked from Micah to the holo. "No offense, Colonel, but you're sending *one* Marine? You said to assume the military's compromised. What if Janus does have an accomplice embedded somewhere in the picket? Couldn't that person countermand Captain Severance's orders? He could order them to board us, or worse, shoot us out of the black."

Micah shook his head.

"It doesn't work that way. Severance is with the Special Reconnaissance Unit. He'll make sure we get through unharmed. Besides, we won't be broadcasting an ident."

"And when they see a Scharnhorst signature this deep inside Luyten space, they'll assume we're headed out of the system altogether," added Jonathan. "With the amount of gate energy at the picket line, it's unlikely they'll be able to separate our arrival energy from the background noise."

A smile teased at Cutter's lips at the skeptical look still on Harper's face.

"Sometimes a smaller, more surgical approach is called for, rather than a show of force. That is doubly true in this situation, considering what we just learned." Cutter sobered and then pinned them with a look. "I don't have to tell you how dangerous this situation is. Akkadian assassins are highly trained and lethal."

The director's words triggered a burst of frustration from Jonathan that Micah felt across their mental link.

"I'm sure as hell of no use to anyone," he muttered, slapping the side of the co-pilot's chair that he was strapped into with a low growl.

Harper shot Jonathan an annoyed glare that said she'd had it with the man.

"Look," she snapped, "I'm not of any use to them outside the ship, either. I'm an analyst, not a field agent. But get me a secured connection inside Leavitt's main node and I'll cause all sorts of mayhem."

She turned back to the screen and jerked a thumb in Jonathan's direction. "He'll help."

Micah wisely kept his expression neutral and did what he could to curb the amusement he felt. The look Jonathan shot him told him how utterly he'd failed at that last part.

He turned back to the holo when he heard Cutter's sigh. "I fear it's going to take the concerted efforts of all five of you to ensure the research doesn't fall into their hands. I don't have to tell you what it could mean for us, if they ended up with actual chiral samples."

Cutter pinned his niece with a stare. His voice held an undercurrent that set off warning bells inside Micah's head and had him turning in his seat to stare at the doctor.

Sam gave a slow nod.

"With the destruction of deGrasse, Janus thinks he's now the sole person in possession of deGrasse's chiral research," she said. "Although we know that's not true; *Wraith* has it, as well. Once he finds out we're still in play, he'll do anything he can to destroy us."

Micah looked from Sam back to her uncle.

"I feel like I'm missing some context here," he began. "Is there something we should know?"

Sam shot Cutter a questioning look and the man straightened, his expression taut.

"Tell them," he ordered.

Sam's gaze met Micah's.

"Remember what I said about how a chiral organism can only feed from its own kind? That it can digest a substance from its mirror-environment, but it gains no nutritional benefit from it?"

Micah barked a harsh laugh.

"Yeah, doc. I don't think I'm likely to forget that." He saw her flinch slightly, but then she nodded, a silent acknowledgement of the bitterness he must feel.

"Well, what I told you isn't technically true. Or at least," she corrected, "it's not *always* true that right-handed life in a left-handed world would starve."

She hesitated, appearing suddenly uncomfortable.

Micah shot her a 'get to the point' look.

"Okay. You know what photosynthesis is. How plants absorb energy from light to grow?" When he nodded, she continued. "Well, so do cyanobacterias. These microorganisms form the foundation of a planet's food chain. They produce the oxygen on every planet we've ever terraformed. They're the algae in every ocean. And they replicate through photosynthesis."

She fell silent and Micah processed what she'd just said.

*Oh **crap**.*

Jonathan's mental voice ripped through his head, alarm pulsing through their connection as though it had been electrified.

Micah's eyes had never left Sam's. They widened in realization as he came to the same conclusion his mirror-twin had.

'Oh crap' is right. If she's going where I think she is with this...

Sam nodded at his reaction.

"If they were able to introduce a chiral cyanobacteria into one of the oceans on any of our populated worlds, it would have no natural enemies," she said. "Left-handed pathogens would have no impact on it. It could, theoretically, multiply very quickly. If that happened, it would eventually choke out the foundation of all left-handed life. With the collapse of our food chain..." Her voice trailed off.

A harsh curse was ripped from his lips as he studied her intently. Micah drew in a ragged breath as he prepared to put voice to their fears.

"Shit, doc. It'd be the ultimate WMD."

WARNING SHOT

GNS *WRAITH*
STARSHOT BUOY, TWO AU FROM VERMILION

THE SILENCE THAT descended after Micah's declaration was pierced by the wailing shriek of a proximity alarm. Micah's head jerked up as *Wraith*'s feed tagged a sensor ghost, portside, aft. In the next moment, the Helios bucked as an explosion from somewhere just off its nose shook the ship.

Micah's world shrank into a realm of sensor returns and instrument panels, control surfaces and weapons arrays, as he and Jonathan re-linked with the ship at the same time.

He instantly noticed their connection was different than the previous time. It was at once the same and yet infinitely deeper than their 'spooky action at a distance.' It felt more complete, a melding of their two consciousnesses into one.

The fidelity was such that their enhanced senses immediately intuited the presence of the *York* crowding the Helios's engines, although sensors gave no indication a ship was there and no synthetic intelligence in existence would have posited its presence.

In the same instant and without conscious thought, the

Micah/Jonathan merge side-slipped the ship, protecting her vulnerable flank. It was a move no human could have replicated, and it happened just in time.

Wraith shuddered under a barrage of laser fire from the pinnace, its shielding dispersing what would have been a disabling shot had they not pivoted at that exact moment.

The startled voices of Harper and Sam registered as if at a distance. The Jonathan/Micah merge had *Wraith* create a combat net, the thought of vocalizing his/his thoughts at the moment too burdensome to consider.

{{We have company,}} the Micah part sent to the women. Distantly, he realized the words held an odd, resonant echo, and his delivery seemed more rapid than usual, but he shelved it as unimportant. *{{Have your cradles configure for battle maneuvers.}}*

After an almost interminable pause, he heard Sam react, giving both Cutter and the colonel an update. Harper passed along the attacking ship's ident, as well as a signal from the *York*.

The Naval Criminal Investigation Command logo appeared, followed by a male voice, speaking in commanding tones:

{Heave to, and prepare to be boarded.} The message repeated until Micah/Jonathan muted it.

You take nav, I'll handle weapons.

Micah wasn't sure where the thought originated from, him or Jonathan. At the moment, he didn't really care. The merged man sank more deeply into the connection, the cockpit fading away as *Wraith*'s defenses came fully online.

With it came an awareness that the dust cloud around the buoy was an artificial construct, there to hide... something. Mines, perhaps?

Yes, the merge agreed. He/he studied the situation, considering and then discarding possible actions and their various outcomes in a fraction of the time it usually took.

The *York* had lost its best weapon—surprise. It had no hope of subduing a ship with the speed and agility of a DAP Helios, if those in the pinnace even knew of *Wraith*'s special pedigree.

Unlikely, the merge concluded. Their mind turned next to the problem of leaving the area safely without loss of life.

We need to have at least a fifty kilometers between us and them before we activate the drive, the Micah portion of the merge sent.

The part that was Jonathan brought up the image of the pinnace, rotating it and then tagging it, port side, aft.

Eight ball, corner pocket, the Jonathan merge responded.

Micah saw immediately what his other-self meant.

He had no idea if they were communicating in a way the two women could follow, though he suspected it was happening so fast neither would comprehend it.

Harper's belated "Pool? You've got to be kidding me!" suggested she might have gleaned enough to understand the Jonathan merge reference.

They ignored it. They had to. They didn't have time for explanations.

We need to be here—the Micah part of the merge highlighted a location in space—*for the two mines to line up perfectly.*

An image of the pinnace rotated before the merge.

Tap the first one, right there, the Jonathan part thought, highlighting the spot. *Push it into the other one at this speed. Both will reach the ship within seconds of each other, and should detonate on contact.*

The Micah part agreed. *It'll cost them their port maneuvering thrusters. Pain in the ass, but easily repairable.*

The Jonathan merge nodded. *One of* Wraith*'s tungsten rounds ought to do it.*

He reached out to the map, tracing a reciprocal from the mine on *Wraith*'s screen back to where the Helios would be positioned.

Time slowed, resumed its normal march as Micah surfaced partially from the merge.

"Ought to do what?" he heard Harper demand.

* * *

The Jonathan/Micah mental merge held a beat-frequency resonance to it that Sam was certain originated in the unique chiral connection they shared. The physicist in Sam itched to study it, but now was hardly the time.

Neither man seemed willing to speak, choosing instead to use *Wraith*'s combat net to communicate.

{{*We're going to use their own mines against them,*}} the twinned voice sent. {{*Line them up, use a tungsten round as the cue ball. The bullet's impact will push the first one toward the* York. *The mine will accelerate faster than they can maneuver. It'll shove them out of our way so they don't take damage when we spin up the drive.*}}

"By shooting at them," Sam stated flatly, doubt coloring her voice.

{{*By setting off a directed charge,*}} the voice corrected. {{*Although from their point of view, they might think we're shooting at them.*}}

"Nice of you to acknowledge that, guys," Harper muttered under her breath.

Sam could tell her friend was shaken, but whether it was from the danger the other ship presented to them, or the unexpected gestalt the two men seated in front of them had entered into, she couldn't tell.

{{*Pass these coordinates to Cutter and have him tell Severance that we'll be exiting Scharnhorst space in—*}} The pause in the twinned voice was so brief as to hardly be noticeable, and then it was back.

{{*—exactly thirty-seven minutes from the time we engage the drive. We'll give him a countdown, but honestly,*}} the merge chuckled, {{*he'll know it the minute we lose contact. Communications don't work in Scharnhorst space.*}}

In a blink, the voice was gone from her wire.

She felt *Wraith* pivot, sensed the ship's weapons firing, and then the vessel leapt forward, pressing her into the cradle. She heard Harper send a data burst, and then the connection was cut as they leapt into the Casimir bubble the drive created.

CHAOS

ALLIANCE NAVY PINNACE, GNS *YORK*

THE WORLD AROUND Gabe went crazy as the pinnace slammed into an uncontrolled spin. Lights dimmed, red alert klaxons sounded, and Gabe fought vertigo as the vessel corkscrewed drunkenly about its axis.

"Dammit, Alvarez! Now look what you've done!" The captain's furious voice cut across damage reports being read from various stations on the pinnace's command center.

"Looks like you called it, boss," Hyer drawled from her position behind him, as she clutched the back of his seat. "That sure ain't no killin' blow. That was a precision strike."

Gabe would have sworn there was admiration in the chief warrant's voice.

"Yup," she said after a moment, and Gabe realized she was studying a display.

He turned to face her, and she grinned back at him. "Took out our port thrusters, pretty as you please. And with one of our own mines, too. If I don't miss my guess, that was a move straight off a billiards' table."

"Scharnhorst signature!" The cry came from one of the

pinnace's crew, and Gabe whipped his head around in time to see the Helios's icon wink out on *York*'s main screens. He banged his fist against his seat in frustration.

"Day-um, boss." A low whistle accompanied Hyer's drawn-out exclamation as she continued to study something on her screen. "I can only hope to be that good someday."

Her words cut through Gabe's angry mental self-recrimination for not accurately judging how Case might act when cornered.

Of course, I **thought** *we'd been covert enough to get off that first disabling shot, which would have made the 'cornered' issue a moot point...*

An apology to the ship's captain was on the tip of his tongue when Hyer interrupted him.

"Hey boss, thought you might like to know. The damage I'm reading is something this boat should be able to repair in under a day," she informed him in a low voice. "I could do it in my sleep. Heck, Fred could probably do it."

He ignored her, returning his attention to the frantic exchange going on between *York*'s crew, but the chief refused to be so easily dismissed.

"Huh. Would you look at that." Hyer drew out her third comment in a way that told Gabe she was baiting him with it.

He sighed and gave in. "All right, Chief, I'll bite. What is it?"

Hyer's face creased into a grin as she showed him her display. On it was the Helios's last known position before it jumped. Her display read the distance at fifty-point-one kilometers.

"Know what's the minimum safe distance to engage a Scharnhorst drive, boss?" Her knowing look clued him in. "Exactly fifty kilometers."

Gabe ignored the rapid-fire exchange as *York*'s crew worked to get the ship back under control and focused on Hyer's words.

"So, you're saying..."

"I'm saying they went to extraordinary lengths, not only to

make sure that we were at a safe distance, but that we were also temporarily disabled, so we couldn't endanger ourselves by closing on them while they transitioned."

Hyer speared him with a knowing look. "Now, does that sound to you like the act of a criminal?"

MASON VS. MARINE

ALLIANCE NAVY PATROL BOAT, GNS *HAVERSHAM*

ADDY AND *HAVERSHAM'S* team of medics had been kept busy. After their initial success in finding the wreckage that housed the Marine survivors, the crew had redoubled their search efforts. Broadened search parameters had them sweeping wider swaths that led away from the debris field in the hope they would find more survivors.

Seven more ships had been discovered, in various states of wreckage. Some were little more than broken shells while others held small pockets of atmosphere which had sustained life. More bodies were recovered, as well as thirteen survivors, scattered across three different wreckages.

Addy worked *Haversham*'s small team of medical corpsmen around the clock to get those patients stabilized. Some they'd lost; still more were in critical condition. The majority were stable and were steadily improving.

They'd nearly finished today's rounds. Addy had just one patient left to visit: the Marine who had mentioned both Janus and Micah Case.

"One more, doc, and then you can call it a night," her

assistant told her. "It's that sergeant, bunked down in that mess hall up ahead."

She accepted the plas sheet he handed her, and studied the Marine's vitals. Momentary doubt hit her.

Am I crazy to think I can do this on my own? she wondered, but knew it didn't really matter. This was an opportune time to question the man, and they needed answers.

Gabe hasn't responded, and that can only mean he hasn't heard back from his people.

She resisted the urge to reach out to him again, asking if he'd heard back yet. He would have told her if he had.

*We have no way of knowing who we can trust on this ship. Which means I have to do it myself. I can do this. I **have** to do this.*

She'd thought long and hard over the past few days about proceeding on her own. The man had given no indication that he recalled his fevered exchange, although she'd yet to be alone in a room with him.

She'd question him under sedation; it was the only way she could safely do so. She'd never be able to hold her own against an augmented Marine, otherwise.

She brought her mental debate to a halt and turned to the medic who had accompanied her on her rounds.

"I've got this one," she assured him. "You're way past due for a break. Check back with me in half an hour, okay?"

The relief on the medic's tired face was clear, and he left with more energy than he'd shown all shift.

Addy reached out to *Haversham*'s communications officer one last time.

{Have I received any messages from the York*?}* she asked, not holding out much hope. Surely if Gabe had sent her a message, they would have contacted her to let her know.

The lieutenant's avatar shook his head. *{No, ma'am. But if you need to reach them, you can do it real-time, now. We have a buoy back in service here.}*

Addy was surprised. *{How did we manage that?}*

He shrugged. {Haversham *performs routine maintenance on the Starshot birds while we're on patrol. We had one we'd taken out of service in our hold, so the engineers got it up and running.*}

{*Well that's good news. Thank you.*}

As she entered the mess hall, she caved and tried to reach Gabe one final time, but the ship didn't answer. She dropped a request into the queue for him to ping her back, and then walked toward the area partitioned off for her patient in the back.

The man looked like he was sleeping, though his hand was fisted, fingers working around some object he held.

Face it, she admonished herself. *You're on your own. Just get it done.*

Stepping toward the Marine, she activated her bracer, dialing in a dose of medication that would have him drowsy and compliant yet alert enough to respond to questioning. Bending over him, she placed her bracer against his neck and injected the serum into him.

"All right, sergeant. Let's see what you can remember about what happened back on deGrasse, shall we?" she whispered under her breath, and then, while she waited for the medication to take effect, turned the man's head to inspect his wounds.

Before she had time to react, she felt him kick one of her legs out from under her. She tried to right herself, but felt his hand wrap around her wrist while the other hooked behind her elbow. In an explosive move, he yanked her forward. Suddenly, she found herself face down on the gurney with the Marine on top of her.

Whatever he'd held in his hand was slapped against her neck and she found herself cut off from the shipnet, unable to call for help. In the next instant, he snaked his arm around her neck.

She jammed her bracer-clad hand back against the Marine's thigh, injecting him with more of the serum.

He cursed. "Shouldn't have done that, doc."

He released the hand at her back and replaced it with his knee. The action torqued her spine painfully. "I was going to let you live. Now, I'm not feeling so charitable anymore."

She pushed against the deck as she tried to get her feet under her, and he dug his knee into her back harder in response. The arm about her neck tightened and her vision began to tunnel.

Both her hands flew up and wrapped around his arm, and she ordered her bracer to deliver a strong sedative, then pumped it into the Marine's forearm.

How he wasn't passed out, she didn't know. He had to be blocking it somehow.

"Dammit!" Along with his curse came the sound of a weapon being unholstered, and the arm around her neck loosened minutely. She blinked the spots from her vision just as the cold barrel of a pistol settled under her chin.

"You have two seconds to reverse the effect of the drugs you injected me with, or I'm going to shoot you. Do you know what a pulse weapon like a CUSP will do to your brain at point-blank range?"

The words were barely a whisper, the Marine's mouth beside her ear.

Addy believed him. She reached mentally for the bracer and had it send instructions to the nano inside the Marine's body, neutralizing the drugs.

Her hand, still wrapped around his arm, sent a stimulant to counteract the ones that had already released into his bloodstream.

After a moment, he eased the pistol away, though the pressure of his arm around her neck remained steady, just shy of triggering ischemia.

"Okay, start talking." The Marine's voice remained low and threatening. "Who else knows about my connection to Janus?"

"I don't know what you're—"

The weapon's barrel stroked her neck, tapped lightly

against it. "You didn't think I was coherent enough to see your reaction when I mentioned his name that first day? Or to hear you mention that bastard Case's name?"

He laughed. "Well, you're right about that. My implant recorded your tender ministrations, doc. Since then, I've had plenty of time to get caught up. Tell me what I want to know, and I might let you live."

Addy fought past the panic and tried to focus.

Stall him, she told herself sternly. *Think! You have a medic coming back to check on you in half an hour. Just keep him occupied.*

The arm around her neck tightened and she felt herself losing consciousness.

"Talk!" the man hissed, easing up on the arm around her neck once more.

"Everyone knows about Janus," she rasped. "He's on the courier ship, headed to the gate."

"Not what I asked you, doc."

The gun's barrel pressed hard into the soft tissue under her jaw, forcing her head back.

"Try again. Who knows about *me?* You aren't getting another chance."

"Janus left you to die, along with the rest of us," she forced the words out. "He's long gone. Why do you care?"

A soft laugh. "My bank account sure as hell doesn't, as long as I remove all evidence that I was involved in anything he did. Time's up, doc. Tick-tock."

A sound came from the mess hall's entrance and she heard the Marine utter another low curse. His arm clamped around her carotid arteries like a vise. Her vision grayed.

"Sorry, doc. Time's up."

Distantly, she felt the gun's barrel move lower. Her body jolted, and she felt as if someone had just punched her in the chest.

There was a fiery sensation—and her world went dark.

HARBINGER

ALLIANCE NAVY PINNACE, GNS *YORK*

THE ATMOSPHERE ON *York*'s bridge was one of intense focus, interspersed with hostile glares shot Gabe's way. It was obvious he was no longer welcome there. Hyer's attempts to paint Micah Case in a good light hadn't endeared him to any of them.

"Criminal or not, that pilot just broke my ship." The captain glowered at Hyer before turning her gaze to Gabe. "I'm holding you personally responsible for this, Alvarez. Don't you have somewhere else you two need to be? We have work to do."

Gabe looked at Hyer and tilted his head toward the hatch. She nodded, unbuckled, and headed for the exit. He followed right behind.

"AIC," he murmured, and she nodded again to let him know she'd heard.

They'd just made it to the AIC's hatch when *York*'s pilot contacted him. The man's voice was noticeably cooler than the last time they'd spoken.

{Excuse me, sir. You received an automated request from Doctor Moran on the Haversham. *She asked you to ping her*

when you had a moment.}

{Thanks.} Gabe waved Hyer through and then followed her inside while he connected to the shipnet. It routed him through to the buoy that floated just forward of the pinnace's bow.

He grew concerned after waiting several long seconds for Addy's token to respond to his ping, and contacted *Haversham's* comm officer instead.

{Lieutenant,} he asked, *{do you know why Doctor Moran's not answering?}*

There was an awkward pause.

{Sir,} the officer said, and he heard the wary tone in the sailor's voice, *{you haven't heard?}*

{Heard what?} Gabe's mental tone sharpened.

{Sorry to be the one to tell you, sir, but the doctor… she's dead.}

Gabe grasped the edge of the AIC's tactical table in a grip so hard it was painful. *{When? How did it happen?}*

{One of the Marines she was treating, we suspect. He tried to escape in a small cutter. They have him surrounded in the shuttle bay now, but he's refusing to surrender.}

That last caught Gabe's attention.

{They're apprehending him right now?}

{As we speak, sir.}

{Then this just happened?} He imbued his voice with urgency as his mind fixed on a single memory from an earlier conversation with Addy.

The officer on the other end sounded confused. *{Well, he's not in custody yet—}*

{No, dammit! How long ago did you find her?} he demanded.

{Fifteen minutes, half an hour, maybe? They took her to medical so they could begin the autopsy—}

Tension coiled in Gabe's gut. *{Belay that! Get her into stasis, **now**.}*

{Sir—}

{We don't have much time. Do it!} Gabe tossed the

conversation to Hyer without explanation, and then used his NCIC credentials to contact *Haversham*'s med bay directly.

*{NCIC! Get Doctor Moran into stasis, **now!**}*

He roared the mental command, and was gratified to hear startled shouts from the other end. *{This is a direct order from NCIC headquarters! **Do** it!}*

Hyer's concerned face swam into view. As he became aware of his surroundings, he realized he was bent over the tactical table, head bowed between fisted hands.

"Sir?" she began, and he held up a hand for her to hold as he awaited confirmation that those on the *Haversham* had done his bidding.

A voice came onto the connection, the security token on the other end identifying it as Medic First Class Wilson.

{Sir?} The voice was strained. *{She's in stasis, but—}*

{Report,} he snapped, cutting the man off. Straightening, he nodded to Hyer, then brought her into the conversation with Wilson.

{Doc Moran was with one of the injured Marines when a corpsman stopped by to see if she needed help,} the medic explained. *{The medic heard someone running away as he approached, and then he found her—}*

Gabe heard the medic's mental voice falter, and felt a flare of remorse for the harsh way he'd been riding the corpsman.

{Go on,} he said, pitching his tone to be more gentle.

{She'd been shot,} the voice on the other end made a sound that was a cross between a sob and a sigh. *{He tried to triage, but it was a torso shot, point-blank. We'd lost her.}*

{Exactly how long ago was this, Wilson?} he asked as gently as he knew how. *{Think. It's important.}*

He got the sense the man was checking his internal chronometer. *{Sometime between ten and fifteen minutes, sir,}* the medic told him.

Gabe cradled his head in his hands and realized they were trembling. He took a deep breath, and felt Hyer squeeze his shoulder.

{Doctor Moran told me that she can usually resuscitate a patient if she can get to them within ten minutes after brain activity stopped.} Gabe paused a beat, considering his words carefully.

The medic's avatar nodded. *{Yes, as a general rule, that's true.}*

{And did you?}

{I don't know sir. The weapon the Marine used on her, it did a lot of internal damage. None of us on Haversham *have the skills to treat this level of trauma. To be honest, sir, it was just me on shift. Everyone else was scattered throughout the ship, treating patients.}*

Hyer's hand tightened on his shoulder.

{Wilson, let's keep the possibility that Doctor Moran might be revived between us for now, okay? No need to get anyone's hopes up, and besides,} Gabe's eyes met Hyer's *{it's possible that Marine could have an accomplice. You get what I'm saying?}*

He heard a gulp on the other end. *{Perfectly, sir.}*

{And for now,} Gabe grimaced as he added this last, *{continue to refer to the doctor as a … corpse.}* Even as the thought formed, his mind rejected it. *{I'll order a guard placed on the stasis unit just in case, and say it's to protect the evidence of the Marine's guilt.}*

(Understood, sir.} Wilson's mental tone was barely more than a whisper.

{Good man. Carry on.}

Gabe dissolved the connection and pushed himself upright once more.

"You okay, boss?" Hyer's words were quiet, her face drained of its usual color, the news of Addy's attack hitting her hard, as well.

"No, Chief, I'm not. This entire situation is one huge cluster. Why do I keep feeling as if we're either being played, or we're one step behind the bad guys, and they know our every move?"

MACHINATIONS

CENTRAL PREFECTURE
ERIDU
AKKADIAN EMPIRE

RIN ZHOU HAD invited Che to an exclusive club for dinner. The restaurant was run by those in the service to State Security, and its private dining room was both sandboxed and secure. The meal had been superb, the service impeccable.

Rin Zhou studied him over the rim of her after-dinner drink. "This man. Micah Case. The one our asset is using to derail Alvarez. This man is resourceful, yes?"

Che exhaled. "More so than we would like, apparently. Either that, or Alvarez is an incompetent fool."

"But the deputy director reports Alvarez is one of the NCIC's best agents."

Che made a sound of agreement, swirling the wine in his glass. "The deputy director set Alvarez a difficult task. Pitting a pinnace against a Helios is hardly a fair battle," he pointed out.

Silence fell between the two as Rin Zhou contemplated his words.

"Janus initially acquired Case for Stinton's

experimentation," Rin Zhou broke the quiet, her voice thoughtful. "Yet preliminary reports said Stinton failed and the man had died. Clearly, this is not so. Shall we assume, then, that Case is of value to us?"

"Unknown," Che admitted, bringing the wine to his lips for a slow, thoughtful sip. "But he was experimented on, and Janus appeared to think him worth acquiring. When he discovered Case was alive, he used our assets on deGrasse to try to recapture him."

"I see," Rin Zhou murmured. Her eyes narrowed in contemplation. "We should think on this. Perhaps, once Alvarez manages to capture him, we should find a way to acquire him. You say Alvarez believes him to be a person of interest in the deGrasse incident?"

"Yes," Che replied, "with possible ties to Stinton's murder."

Rin Zhou looked up sharply at that. "I was given to understand that the murder had been staged to look like an accident."

Che set his drink down carefully, using the action to gather his thoughts. "The assassin did the best she could, given the circumstances. Janus has already been disciplined for his actions."

Rin Zhou's lips tightened in displeasure. "Not enough if he ends up being the reason this operation fails."

Che thought a moment. "We have another asset in Procyon we can activate, someone high up who can manufacture evidence to further implicate Case, if we wish to use him."

Rin Zhou's eyes narrowed. "He is very well-placed. I thought you were holding him for an operation worthy of the effort it took to embed him."

"True," admitted Che. "But if played correctly, we may be able to activate him without tipping our hand." He straightened. "I will travel to Ceriba and oversee this myself."

Rin Zhou lifted her glass to the light and contemplated its amber depths. Setting it down once more, she nodded. "Very well, then. So it shall be."

A thought suddenly occurred to Che. With great deliberation, he brought his wineglass to his lips and took a sip. He rolled the wine around in his mouth as he turned the idea over in his mind, savoring the concept in much the same way he did the notes of melon, citrus, and jasmine that landed on his tongue.

Nodding to himself, Che set the glass down and looked Rin Zhou in the eye. He allowed a slow smile to spread across his face.

"This could work in our favor, you know," he murmured after a moment.

Rin Zhou looked intrigued, and Che's smile widened. He leaned forward, resting his forearms on the low table between them and pushing his wineglass to one side.

"If you recall, we've determined that Janus cannot be eliminated due to his special knowledge of the unique biology found in Luyten's Star," he said. "But his actions are already suspect. He has placed us in a tenuous position."

"Yes, yes, we know all that," Rin Zhou said brusquely. "Go on."

If possible, Che's grin grew even wider. "Patience, minister. This will be worth it, I swear."

He spread his hands. "What if we were to stage Janus's discipline as if he had been held captive and tortured by Akkadia? Not only would it exonerate him from suspicion, but as a victim, he would become a sympathetic figure. An unsung hero, if you will. One of the few survivors of the deGrasse Incident."

"And serve to cement him even deeper into the Alliance's scientific community, no doubt." Rin Zhou's eyes glimmered with a mixture of approval and sardonic amusement. "Do it. Tell the assassin to make it look convincing."

Che's eyes turned dark. "Oh, she will, minister. She is one of the guild's finest. It will be a work of art; I guarantee it."

DAMAGE CONTROL

IN A STAR system a light-year away, on a courier ship headed for its gate, a chime sounded.

Clint Janus's eyes followed the assassin as she rose gracefully from her mat and glided on silent feet to the cabin's entrance. The door slid open, bringing with it the heady aroma of greasy food. Clint inhaled deeply, his stomach cramping from the ascetic diet that had been forced upon him.

"Packet for Doctor Janus," the pilot said, handing a data chip over and glancing his way. The routine, set from day one, remained unchanged. Missives were always sent to Clint's attention, and the assassin always intercepted and read them.

The assassin lifted the chip from the man's hand and palmed the door closed without a word.

It had been days. Several long, interminable days filled with fear, hunger, exhaustion. The savory smells teasing his nostrils were more than he could take.

Clint decided he'd had enough.

He waited until the assassin returned to her mat, folded into a lotus position, and stared calmly into the near distance.

As always.

He stood and, refusing to look in her direction or to show any outward appearance of fear, strode out the cabin's door. When it slid shut behind him and he realized there was no knife protruding from his back, he let out a shaky breath.

He'd been more scared than he'd been willing to admit, even to himself.

What was the old saying? In for a gram, in for a kilo?

Clint smiled at the first blush of his success and decided to follow his nose. It led him to the courier ship's small common galley, where the pilot looked up at him in surprise.

"Never thought I'd see the likes of you outside that cabin, mate. Hungry?" The man pushed a basket of fish and chips toward him.

Clint thought he'd never seen anything more appealing in his entire life.

"Thanks," he said, with a quick jerk of his head. Sliding onto the bench opposite the man, he reached across the table, retrieved a crispy, batter-encrusted fillet and sank his teeth into it. The flavors exploding in his mouth made him want to whimper in relief.

The pilot lifted a bottle of beer, brows raised in silent question. Clint nodded, and the man sent the bottle scooting across the table in his direction. Clint lifted it, tilted his head back, and took a healthy swallow. When the cool, hoppy flavor hit the back of his throat, he actually did let out a small moan.

"Yeah, mate." The pilot sent him a knowing look. "Figured you two were in training or sommat, back 'ere. You can only do so much before you need a wee bit of a break, know what I mean?"

Clint set the beer down onto the table and began to draw circles onto its surface with the bottle's condensation. "You don't know the half of it, my friend. Not even close."

He sat for an hour, maybe more, conversing little and

drinking more, relaxing for the first time in more than a week.

I should have stood up for myself earlier, he thought, pleased with the evening's outcome. He looked up with a smile as a sound alerted him to a presence at the galley's entrance.

The assassin's expression remained unchanged, and yet somehow, he knew he had been judged and found wanting. When she spoke, her words confirmed his fears.

"You have had your reprieve. Come. We have work to do."

She disappeared as silently as she had arrived.

Clint briefly considered the idea of staying in the galley for another beer, to drive home the point that he did not report to her. But his sense of self-preservation took that moment to awaken from its temporary slumber, providing a vivid mental image of her deadly skills.

He rose and, with a last regretful look at the galley, followed her back to their shared cabin.

The assassin was once more in a lotus position on her mat. Unaccountably relieved, he lowered himself to the mat she'd assigned him. When he looked up, her eyes were trained on him, expressionless and cold.

"So," he asked, "what was the message this time?"

"You may regret asking that question," she murmured, her voice without inflection. "Your actions on deGrasse have garnered additional attention."

Clint tensed at her words, wishing he could take back his query.

The assassin continued to hold his gaze. "The chip held two bits of information. There was a data transfer from Case's ship to the National Security Director's office. It contained evidence connecting you to Stinton's cloning project."

Clint opened his mouth to protest, but no sound came. She continued.

"You owe your continued existence to the fact we have an agent in the NSA's office. He is at work now, manufacturing evidence to implicate someone else in the deaths you orchestrated on Stinton's behalf. Fortunately for you, the evidence they have gathered was mostly circumstantial, and linked to your security token. You will play the unwitting victim."

"I... that is fortunate." Clint swallowed. "And the second thing? What else was on the chip?"

"Apparently, our NCIC agent has a mind of his own. He was explicitly instructed not to share details of the investigation with anyone other than the deputy director, and yet he did."

She frowned in disapproval, the most emotion Clint had ever seen her express. "The Geminate Navy lacks discipline in general. This man's actions are a prime example. This would never have been tolerated in Akkadia."

"What happened?" Clint's words were low, barely audible.

"He became suspicious of his orders. He shared the details of his investigation with his immediate superior. The deputy director's loyalty has been cast in doubt, and her use to us as an agent may have reached its end."

Her cold gaze swept the room, then returned to land on him. "Your actions may cost Akkadia years' worth of careful effort and strategic placement. I deeply regret that you are still necessary to the cause, but Citizen General Josza informs me that you are the only biochemist in a position to understand what to do with the research we have appropriated from Luyten's Star."

Intense relief suffused Clint when he heard this. Moments later, he realized how premature, how fleeting, that feeling had been.

"You have become an embarrassment to our people, and to our way of life. I have been instructed to remedy that. Do you recall your first lesson when you arrived for training on Akkadia as a youth?"

Her gaze drilled into him, and he froze, prey caught in the crosshairs of a hunter's reticle.

Punish the body, harness the mind.

The words reverberated through him as memories from the worst six months of his life resurfaced. Junxun was a brutal school, its intent to break a person utterly, before building him or her back up into the image of the ideal Akkadian soldier.

"Ah, yes," the sibilant words slipped softly across the assassin's lips. "I see from your expression that you do. This is good."

She nodded, then, in one fluid motion, stood and began to approach him.

"Your mind requires harnessing, Clint Janus. We have twenty-three days in which to accomplish what would usually require months." She tilted her head, studying him from those black eyes. "Such rigorous instruction is not without consequence. It will take its toll, I am afraid. Your body will bear the marks for some time."

Clint recoiled at the coldness of her smile.

"Ah, but I am remiss. I forgot to mention the final bit of information that was contained on that chip. Your cover, Doctor Janus, will be that you were held prisoner on deGrasse. You were subject to weeks of torture at the hands of an Akkadian assassin, until you submitted to the demands of the motherland."

His previous fear of the assassin was nothing compared to the abject terror he now felt. Had he been any less narcissistic, Clint would have considered suicide, just to put himself out of his own misery.

ACTIVATION

HOME OF THE NSA ASSISTANT DIRECTOR OF OPERATIONS
ST. CLAIR TOWNSHIP, CERIBA
GEMINATE ALLIANCE

THE ASSISTANT DIRECTOR of operations for the National Security Agency backed into his condo after a long day of work, arms laden with Chinese takeout, his nightly folio of plasfilm briefings, and a bag of dog food.

He failed to notice the man seated on the tufted chair in a shadowed corner of his living room.

"Clancy!" the man called out, and when there was no canine 'woof' in response, no clattering of nails against the kitchen tile, he paused and very slowly set his burdens onto the foyer table.

As he turned to shut the door, he slipped his hand inside his suit jacket, his fingers wrapping around the grip of his pulse pistol, seated in its holster under his arm.

"No need to draw your weapon." The voice came from out of the darkness, causing the ADO to freeze. He lowered his hand and pivoted slowly on his heel. He kept his body turned sideways, presenting a smaller target as he turned his head in the direction the voice had originated.

"And you are...?" he challenged, sidestepping slowly to where he kept a holdout gun.

A glint of light played off an item that dangled from the hand of his visitor. His holdout.

"If you're hoping to get your hands on this, then I'm afraid I will have to disappoint you, Director Sullivan."

The stranger rose, stepped out of the shadows and into a shaft of light spilling in from the street lamp outside. "Or should I say, *Citizen* Director Sullivan?"

The noise Sullivan made sounded as if air had been pushed forcibly from his lungs. Realization crashed over him that his neatly ordered life had just been shattered. He was being activated, and by none other than the head of the Junxun himself.

"Citizen General Josza. To what do I owe this honor?"

The citizen general strode forward on silent feet. "I understand Duncan Cutter recently received a data packet from Luyten's Star. We need you to alter it."

DEEPFAKE

ALLIANCE NAVY PINNACE, GNS *YORK*
APPROACHING LUYTEN GATE
HELIOPAUSE, LUYTEN'S STAR

GABE HAD DUTIFULLY submitted an after-action report on the *York*'s encounter with the Helios. The deputy director's response was as predictable as it was unwelcome. Unsurprisingly, she blamed him for fumbling the assignment.

What Gabe hadn't foreseen was the woman ordering the *York* to drive to the gate, ahead of the courier ship.

Let me be clear, the missive—still text only—read. *Your assignment remains Micah Case, not Clint Janus. We believe Case will try to connect with the courier ship on Leavitt Station. Your job is to prevent that, at all costs.*

Make no mistake, the director emphasized, *Micah Case **will** try to hinder the NCIC's handling of the Janus situation. Do not allow him to do so.*

The resulting high-accel push to the gate had been anything but pleasant. It brought to mind one of his last conversations with Addy—the one where he'd tried to convince her to stay behind. He wished... he wished she was here with him, now.

Safe.

Instead, the doctor's body, still in stasis, was on its way back to Procyon under the watchful eye of a guard Gabe had personally vetted. It was all he could do for her, now.

After the attack, Gabe had asked *Haversham*'s captain to search for every recording she had made, anything that could shed some light on the assault. The search had yielded no results.

The Marine who'd attacked her had committed suicide that same night, in *Haversham*'s brig. This was no coincidence, Gabe was certain. Someone had gotten to the man before he could be questioned, but no one could provide evidence to substantiate his suspicions.

Unable to do anything else for Addy, Gabe spent the rest of the trip to the gate reviewing what he had on Micah Case. He asked Hyer to help him review their skirmish with the Helios, hoping it might give him better insight into the man.

Despite the many hours they spent poring over the records, they never could figure out what they'd done to tip Case off.

The pinnace made it to Luyten's heliopause mere hours before the courier ship arrived. Freed from his crash couch for the first time in days, Gabe was in his quarters when a final packet came through from the deputy director.

Once again, the message was text only. This time, however, it held an attachment: a security feed, from deGrasse's flight deck. When he accessed it, Gabe saw that the file had an NSA watermark overlaid in one corner.

The designation told Gabe the feed had been analyzed and remastered by the agency's crack team of data techs. The fact it had been sent to *him* meant the information they managed to salvage must hold evidence pertinent to his case.

Interestingly, the time stamp indicated he was looking at something that predated the fatal Novastrike collision. The footage showed a lone figure approaching one of the fighters. An overlay popped up, identifying the vessel as one of the two doomed ships flown by Ettinger and Campbell.

As he watched the feed, the figure rounded the tail of the craft, ducking inside its cockpit. It appeared at first as if a scrambling device had been employed to baffle any sensors. He was unable to make out who the individual inside the vessel might be.

Then, for a brief moment, the sensor feed cleared, and Gabe realized he was looking at the part of the feed the NSA's techs had processed.

I'll owe them one, if their clean-up gets us a read on who the bastard was, and what he was doing.

Moments later, Gabe got his wish as a military token appeared, superimposed over the image of the man inside the craft. The ID belonged to Micah Case.

The muscles in Gabe's jaw bunched as he watched the figure on the feed secure the cockpit. He watched as Case cautiously peered around the nose of the ship. The man jerked back, flattening himself against the cowling until an automated security drone flew past.

Case waited a few long seconds, then went to the next craft, his actions mimicking what he had done to the first vessel.

That murdering sonofa— Gabe's hand clenched. *I'd like to get my hands on whoever paid him to betray his fellow pilots like that.*

The evidence before him dispelled every doubt he'd entertained over the past ten days about the deputy director's motives. It drove away the suspicion he'd begun to harbor that someone was framing Case.

The feeling of being misled while the true culprit escaped faded in the face of overwhelming evidence from an unimpeachable source within the Alliance.

His doubts were replaced by a grim determination. He knew what he needed to do. And he didn't need the deputy director's reprimand to jostle his elbow and galvanize him into action.

Appended to the attachment were three simple sentences.

"Your orders remain unchanged. Case intends to rendezvous

with the courier ship at Leavitt. Use any means necessary to subdue and apprehend."

SEVERANCE

APPROACHING ALLIANCE CARRIER GNS *RAPPA*
LUYTEN GATE
HELIOPAUSE, LUYTEN'S STAR

SCHARNHORST SPACE WAS… odd.

Sam knew that, with *Wraith* encased in a Casimir bubble, there should be no physical sensation of motion. Studies had shown the atmosphere inside retained the same characteristics as normal space. Yet she would have sworn that the air had a different quality to it. Not all of it could be attributed to the tension, now palpable, that hung between the pilots and their passengers.

The animals felt it, too. Sam heard mental grumbling coming from both pairs, the restlessness they telegraphed through their evanescent connection.

She cleared her throat. "Okay if I unweb and reassure our friends in the back?" She felt the men send their assent and she rose, Harper following her.

Sam didn't like the wary look she saw in Micah's eyes. It was echoed on Jonathan's face. She suspected it was there as a result of the strange merge they had all just witnessed. It was

proof that both men, not just Micah, were now something...
other.

"That was weird," her friend whispered, and Sam shot her a
stern look.

Grasping the analyst's hand, she sent privately, *{Not now.
They have enough on their plates. Just let it ride.}*

Turning to the animals' secured crates, she bent to release
the panthers while Harper did the same for Snotface and
Sneaky Pete. Joule extended her paws in a long stretch,
wickedly sharp claws sinking into the special padding lining
her bed, while Pascal padded past, his nose seeking Sam's
hand.

{The Micahs feel different,} the big cat sent. He sniffed the
air. *{Smell different, too.}*

Joule joined them, mouth open and head raised as she
tasted the air. *{Scents layered on top of each other now,}* she
agreed, then her ears rotated forward. *{Is that going to happen
to us?}*

Pascal shot her a look of disgust. *{Don't even think that.}*

His expression was so comical, it forced a laugh out of Sam,
and she felt the tension flowing from her. Rubbing the fur right
behind the big cat's ear, she shook her head.

"I doubt it," she said. "Sometime, during times of great
stress, humans can rise to the task in pretty amazing ways. I
think this is an example of that."

Harper straightened from where she'd been crouching
beside Sneaky Pete, one ferret in her arms, the other draped
around her shoulders. "Think it's safe to leave them out for the
rest of the trip?"

{{Should be,}} the merge sounded inside Sam's head,
confirming what she had suspected—they were monitoring.

She smiled and said with a cheerfulness she didn't quite
feel, "Well, okay then. Anyone hungry?"

Thirty-seven minutes later, the ship emerged from
Scharnhorst space. They were a bit more than an AU beyond
the gate and the small Navy picket holding station a hundred

kilometers sunward. Past the system's bowshock, even, which put them officially in interstellar space—somewhere Sam could honestly say she'd never been.

The merge had suggested they remain seated for the transition, but there'd been hardly a ripple. By unspoken agreement, she and Harper waited for the two men in the galley. Several long minutes later, Micah appeared, pushing Jonathan's chair in front of him, expression guarded.

* * *

The merge faded when Micah pulled out of *Wraith*'s systems and came back to himself. He stared straight ahead for a moment, mentally poking at his mind, wondering if his thoughts were now his own.

They are.

Micah sliced a look at Jonathan. *Dude, you just proved that wrong.*

Nah. I figured you were thinking the same thing I was. Jonathan's tone turned tentative. *That was a real trip, bro. Not sure what happened back there, but it's seemed to have made our connection stronger.*

Yeah. Feels like there are more... points of contact, maybe? In the connection itself, he clarified.

Glancing over his shoulder at the empty cradles and the shadows he could just make out in the galley, he sighed.

Guess we'd better go face the music.

Minutes later, he was staring warily back at Sam as the doctor stood at the threshold between the galley and the crew cabin.

"Want to tell me what happened?" Sam looked between Micah and Jonathan, her expression unreadable.

She's pissed, Jonathan thought. *I think we scared her.*

Actually, Micah tilted his head to one side, *I think she's scared **for** us. And she seems both pissed and a bit intrigued. Can't you just see the wheels in her head turning?*

You mean, like she wants to put me in a petri dish and examine me under a nanoscope? Yeah.

For some reason, Micah wasn't yet comfortable with speaking aloud. He hesitated long enough that it was Jonathan who answered Sam, using *Wraith*'s shipnet.

His mirror-twin shrugged. {*We both linked to* Wraith*'s SI at the same time,*} he told her. {*And when we did, something just seemed to snap into place.*}

Sam's eyes narrowed at Jonathan's use of the net. She extended a hand, the one with her medical bracer wrapped around it. Slowly, she reached for Jonathan's head, her glove-encased fingers running lightly through his hair. Her hand came to rest at the base of his skull as she looked intently into his one good eye.

"Everything's nominal," she murmured softly, then turned and repeated the process on Micah.

It felt oddly like a caress, and he blinked at the sudden thought, pushing it hastily away lest Jonathan catch it.

A shaft of amusement passed through him and he realized he'd failed when Jonathan's voice entered his mind.

Huh. Didn't feel like that to me. Anything I should know about, o twin 'o' mine? Something going on between you two?

Micah mentally flipped the man off. *Maybe I should ask you the same thing about Harper.*

That earned him the same gesture.

He returned his attention to the woman in front of him. Her eyes met and held his for a long moment as she studied him intently. From where he was standing, he could see the filaments in her eye reflecting off *Wraith*'s lighting, and he knew her medical optics were online.

{*Are we going to live, doc?*} he sent jokingly, and his words brought a faint smile to her lips.

She stepped back, lowering her hand and breaking their connection.

"Well, I can't find anything medically wrong with you. At least not without a deeper scan with better equipment." She frowned, "or a better doctor to look you over. This isn't exactly my specialty."

{You'll get no complaints from me,} Jonathan quipped.

Micah saw the curious light reappear in Sam's eyes.

"Any reason you two are using your wires to speak instead of two sets of perfectly functioning vocal cords?"

He shifted, uncomfortable with the probing question. *{Maybe… it takes time for what happened to wear off?}*

She tucked her free hand under her bracer. Tilting her head to one side, her voice grew soft.

"Can you tell me more about what you both experienced? Did you feel any different when you were connected to such a degree?"

Micah thought back to the merge. He lifted a shoulder in a half-shrug.

{Might have been a bit faster at some things.}

{Oh, we were.} Jonathan sounded positive. *{Faster, more aware of our surroundings. We shouldn't have been able to sense that ship, at least not so quickly. And there's no reason for us to have suspected that they had hidden mines in a cloud of space dust. And yet we **knew**. On both counts.}*

Micah considered that a moment. *{Yeahhh,}* he drew the word out. *{It was like… some kind of intuition. We were hyper-aware of minor things, like the fact the concentration of space dust around the buoy was unnaturally high. Stuff like that was what tipped us off, I think.}*

Sam nodded. "Sounds like you entered into a gestalt with the ship's SI. By the way, that's something the Alliance is going to want to study when we get back."

Her words sounded like a warning. She moved back into the galley. Micah followed, pushing Jonathan's chair.

"I agree with your assessment about the intuition, too," she tossed back at them from over her shoulder. "It fits the definition. The subconscious brain is constantly cataloguing things, observations we don't even realize we've made. Microexpressions, and other tiny details that the waking mind isn't even aware of. This can result in some astonishing leaps of logic."

A look, almost of envy, crossed her face.

"At any rate, I expect that your merge will fade a bit with time. It already has, to a degree, hasn't it?" She halted and pinned Micah with a shrewd gaze.

He looked down at Jonathan and his gaze clashed with the man's lone eye. He turned back to her and she nodded as if they had confirmed her suspicions.

She resumed her walk.

"Just...let me know, once things feel like they've stabilized, if anything is different from when we left deGrasse. I know I've said it before, but we're in uncharted territory here."

* * *

Three and a half days later, *Wraith* was vectored into the flight deck of the Alliance carrier, GNS *Rappa*. After crossing the threshold, the Helios was directed to a cradle some distance from the vessels assigned to the massive carrier.

Sam sat in anxious silence as Micah set the Helios down and put the ship into standby mode. He kept the external sensor feed running on the main holo, which allowed them to see the small force of armed guards approaching the ship. Sam exchanged a concerned look with Harper, but she refrained from commenting as Micah unwebbed and exited the cockpit.

The faith both Micah and Jonathan had in this Marine of Colonel Valenti's seemed unshakeable. Seeing the firepower held in the hands of the soldiers moving to surround the Helios, she fervently hoped it wasn't misplaced.

Micah moved to stand beside the hatch, and Jonathan retreated into the galley. Harper took up a position at its entrance, blocking Jonathan's chair from sight. Sam stayed put in the flight engineer's cradle.

She felt Micah's gaze pass over her in a quick assessment before he turned and cycled the hatch open. Immediately, a figure shouldered its way through the guards to greet them.

"Severance." It was the first word Sam had heard Micah verbalize, since his gestalt with Jonathan.

In response to his greeting, the beefy, barrel-chested man strode up the ramp, enveloping Micah's outstretched hand in a firm grip. Ducking inside, he gave the soldiers a wave and they nodded respectfully and dispersed, setting up a defensive perimeter.

"Better shut that hatch, *ami*." The brief statement, uttered in a deep Cajun drawl, was delivered with the slap of a meaty hand onto Micah's shoulder. He straightened and Sam found herself the object of his regard. The intensity of it was an almost physical thing.

Thaddeus Severance was a mountain of a man with ebony skin, short, curly hair, and a square jaw that looked like it was made of granite. The man's easy-going nature overlaid a restrained energy that seemed to suck up all the remaining space in *Wraith*'s cabin.

"You must be Doc Travis," he said with a flash of white teeth, then nodded at Harper, who stood just inside the galley's entrance. "And you're that NSA analyst Cutter's been raving about. Nice to meet you."

"They have dossiers on you, too," Micah said in a dry tone, and the big man laughed, a sound that seemed to ring off the bulkheads.

"You'd best be worried about your own damn dossier, hoss," the Marine drawled. "My record's as lily-white as they come."

He slouched casually against the far bulkhead, and Sam thought she might not have ever encountered a man as comfortable in his own skin as this one. "Where's the other one?"

"Right here." Jonathan's voice came from behind Harper, and she stepped aside so that Severance could see.

The Marine shook his head, his glance bouncing between Micah and Jonathan. "Damndest thing I've ever seen," he murmured, rubbing a calloused hand along his clean-shaven jawline. "How'd you manage to go and get yourself cloned?"

"Long story, man," Jonathan said.

One eyebrow rose. "Which one are you, the original?" Jonathan nodded, and Severance opened his mouth to speak. Micah didn't give him a chance.

"And I'm *not* a clone," he said, baring his teeth at the Marine.

Thad laughed at that, then pointedly looked Jonathan up and down.

"The way I see it, you got yourself a bit of a high mileage problem, there, *mon ami*." He jabbed a thumb in Micah's direction. "Might need an upgrade to come up to 2.0 specs, here."

"Can it, Severance." Jonathan uttered the words with a growl, which only made the big man's grin grow wider.

Severance let out a snort, which turned into a silent chuckle, shoulders quaking in amusement. He shook his head, his eyes shifting between the two men. That lasted all of three seconds before the man began howling with laughter.

"Severance," Jonathan drew the man's name out in a warning tone.

The Marine held up a hand to forestall him. "Hold on, now, hoss. Just allow me a moment to savor this." He straightened, humor still dancing in his eyes.

At length, he reached into a pocket, withdrew something, and chucked it at Micah.

"Least he's got two working hands," the Marine remarked, which earned him another dark scowl from Jonathan.

Micah flipped the item over in his hand, and then held it up between finger and thumb.

"That, my friends, is an encoded communications chip from your uncle," Severance pointed at Sam, "that explains what to do with a big-ass crate that's waiting outside to be loaded onto this tin can."

Samantha gestured to the communications chip in Micah's

hand. "May I?"

Micah held the chip out to her. When the chip made contact with her wire, it accepted her ID and pushed its contents onto her HUD.

As she skimmed the information, she heard Severance explain to Jonathan, "It's got your marching orders on it, my man. Yours, too, 2.0."

Sam caught Harper's confused look. She shrugged, and shifted her gaze to see matching looks of confusion on Micah and Jonathan, as well.

Ignoring all of them, Severance pivoted and strode toward the cargo bay doors. "Someone want to open up the aft hatch for me?"

Harper sprang into motion, following the big Marine. "I'll secure the animals," she tossed over her shoulder. Bemused, Sam continued to scan the data.

A wave of astonishment crashed over her as she realized what was in the case Severance was loading into the Helios.

"Wow," she murmured, then looked up and realized two sets of eyes were staring back at her expectantly.

"Well?" Micah demanded. "Are you going to share?"

Sam turned to Jonathan and felt doubt creeping in as she considered what his reaction might be to her uncle's and Valenti's plans for him. She had a feeling he wasn't going to like this one bit.

"Well..."

"Just spit it out, doc. Can't be any worse than what we've already been through." Jonathan's words caused her to raise an eyebrow and shoot him her best 'you want to bet?' look.

Her eyes cut to Micah before settling back on Jonathan once again. "I think you'd better hear this straight from them."

Turning, she accessed the console at the flight engineer's cradle and fed the chip's data stream into it. An image morphed into existence, of Valenti and her uncle.

"Information has come to light that suggests we may have a mole somewhere within the NSA." Duncan said, his expression

grave.

"For now, we're limiting this operation to you four, plus Severance. I don't have to tell you how critical and time-sensitive this mission is. To that end, I've authorized a temporary solution that will get Jonathan operational once again."

Sam heard Jonathan stir, and when she glanced at him, she saw an expectant, almost impatient look on his face.

Oh, but wait until the other shoe drops, she thought, knowing what was about to come. *I'm not so sure you'll feel the same way after you hear what they have planned...*

Colonel Valenti took up the explanation.

"We're sending along one of the infantry's field cybernetics systems as a short-term fix, until you're back on Ceriba and we can grow you a set of replacement limbs."

Sam darted another glance at Jonathan. He was nodding in agreement. He caught her stare and sent her a reassuring smile.

"Not a problem, doc. I'm tired of feeling helpless, and I want to be a part of the action. As long as cyber limbs don't mess me up for regen, we're cool. I'll do anything to nail these bastards."

The recording continued. If possible, Cutter's expression turned even more serious.

"In order for you and Micah both to move freely about Leavitt, we've created a new, temporary identity for you, Jonathan. The data chip in Doctor Travis's possession contains a program for your surgical suite that will implant Jack Campbell's secure token and overwrite your own biosignature with a signal transmitted from your new limbs."

"What? No!" Jonathan shouted, followed by Micah's "Oh *hell* no." As one they turned to her.

"I won't do it, doc," Jonathan said, jaw clenched. "I'm not impersonating a dead man—"

"I told them you'd say that," Severance said from the cargo bay entrance. He crossed his arms and shook his head. "I had the same reaction. At first. But they convinced me this was about expedience."

He stepped into the main cabin, an intense expression on his face.

"We don't have the time to get a clean cover built and inserted into the system before this shit goes down. Jack was registered as your co-pilot when you arrived in Luyten's Star. And with the destruction of deGrasse, along with all its records, Jack's death hasn't been made official."

He locked eyes with Jonathan's angry one, and Sam wondered which of the two would fold first.

Severance spoke again, quietly.

"Jack would have wanted his pound of flesh for what those sonsabitches did to him. That cyber program's going to put you back in play, man. And you can do it in Jack's name, and in his honor."

The Marine's voice dropped to a menacing whisper. He leaned forward, the tendons in his forearms bunching as his fists clenched.

"And wouldn't it just be a nice little slice of revenge if Janus ended up facing the man he killed in cold blood? Think about it, *ami*." He paused, straightened, and then added a quiet, "Ooh-rah?"

A tense moment passed between the two as their eyes remained locked, and then Sam saw the tension flow from Jonathan's shoulders as he replied with a "Hooyah."

Unaccountably, that made Severance break into a big grin.

"Get it right, Navy. Campbell was a *Marine,* not a pussy-ass flyboy."

Jonathan just grunted, and then turned back to Sam.

"Guess I have a date with that damn surgi-suite again, doc. And just when I thought I'd seen the last of it for a while, too."

* * *

Micah watched as Sam worked the flight engineer's station to extract the cybernetic program from the data chip.

His eyes shifted from Jonathan to Severance. "So, what *is*

the plan, anyway?"

"We split up. Word is that there's a warrant out for you and the lady doc, so you two will transfer to my ship here on *Rappa*, and lay low. The three of us will keep eyes on that courier ship, make sure it doesn't do anything unexpected."

Then he nodded to Harper and grinned down at Jonathan. "The lady spook and ol' 1.0 here, posing as Jack, will take your bird on in to Leavitt, but she'll be sporting a different tail number and squawking a fake ident—the *Katana*."

That was a vanilla Helios Micah knew was stationed back on Humbolt. "No one will question it?"

Severance shook his head. "The real *Katana*'s in for maintenance at the moment, but we've doctored the paperwork to make it look like it's in service and was tasked to escort the ships sent to sift through the deGrasse remains."

He flashed another grin. "You know the governor-general's navy; ships get shuffled around all the time. *Katana*'s new orders are to proceed to Leavitt and await rendezvous with the light cruiser *Exemplar.* And don't it just figure that your schedules are two weeks out of sync." Severance made a *tsk*ing sound, which brought an involuntary laugh to Micah's lips.

"Get a feel for anything suspicious," the Marine continued. "See what you can find out about any shipments being planned for Akkadia, but most important, make sure you're seen. It'd be nice if Campbell's ID token prods Janus into showing himself."

Jonathan nodded. "We can do that."

Sometime during Severance's explanation, Sam had finished with the flight engineer's station and Harper had taken her place. She cleared her throat, drawing the attention of all three men.

"You guys might be interested in the rest of this information," she pointed to a written addendum that had been attached to the chip. "It says here that the other reason they're splitting us up is so we can test the connection you guys share."

Micah saw Severance roll his eyes. "Oh yeah, they tried to

sell me some shit about you guys not needing a wire to talk. Straight up mental telepathy?" He shook his head and made a disbelieving sound. "Didn't figure you for one of those woo-woo types. Pull the other one, hoss."

Jonathan grunted. "You think that's strange? Try it from this side of the looking-glass."

Harper shook her head. "It's real. According to our resident expert in the back, it's grounded in some sort of quantum field theory."

Micah caught a glint of apology in her expression as she shifted her attention to him.

"Looks like they want to see if it's limited by distance, or if it's possible your connection could actually span the light-years between the gates."

"So now we're guinea pigs for the NSA." Jonathan's comment was acidic. There was an underlying apprehension only Micah could sense. It echoed his own fears.

"Not what I signed up for when I joined the Navy." Micah said aloud. "If this is what Cutter's offering with the NSA, then no thanks. I'm a pilot, not a test subject."

Severance shook his head, clapping Micah on the shoulder. "Nah, you're too valuable to be stuck inside a lab. Then again, what'd you expect when you joined the wrong branch, eh, *amis*?" The Marine shook his head in mock sorrow.

Micah gave him a small shove.

"Rather be a space jockey over a jarhead any day, dude," he shot back. "Remember, you're just as stuck on this side of the gate as I am. What's worse than being a guinea pig? Pulling baby-sitter duty for some damn courier ship."

Thad's brows drew together. He lowered his chin and frowned. "Don't remind me," the Marine rumbled in a warning tone.

Harper smirked at them both.

"Well, I, for one, am happy to do my patriotic duty," she said, then nudged Jonathan's chair. "Especially if it means wandering through malls while space jock here gets used to his new metal legs. Leavitt's duty-free stores kick ass. When do we leave?"

"Geez, you're all heart, Kinsley." Jonathan shot her a black look. Then his expression hardened and he straightened in his seat. "I'm tired of being chair-bound. Let's do it."

PART FIVE: SHOWDOWN

LEAVITT STATION

LEAVITT STATION
PROCYON GATE
PROCYON HELIOPAUSE

Two weeks later....

{THEY'RE COMING THROUGH now.} The voice in Harper's head was Jonathan's but the figure striding beside her as she exited the shop looked nothing like the man she'd begun falling for, back in Luyten's Star.

His strange link with his chiral twin had seemed to return to normal after they'd passed through the gate.

Or for what passes as normal, in this situation, I suppose, she thought. *The whole thing's beyond strange. Sam's predictions were right, too. Distance seems to have no effect on it.*

She realized belatedly that she hadn't responded to Jonathan's comment.

{Guess we'd better get back to the ship, then} she sent, keeping her eyes pinned to the storefronts they were passing.

{No real hurry,} Jonathan replied. *{They're in the queue on the Luyten side. It'll still be an hour or two.}*

His hand at her elbow brought her to a halt in front of a display case featuring Centauri blown glass figurines from An-Yang. Pointing to them, he said, "Hey, don't you collect those things?" *{You have to stop avoiding me, Kinsley. We're supposed to be a team.}*

She took a deep breath and turned to face him. Green eyes, one real but with altered pigment and one fake, stared back at her. She smiled and shook her head. "No, those are Venusian glass bowls I collect. Nice try, though."

She resumed walking and felt a hand at the small of her back. *{Better. See? It didn't kill you to look at me.}*

{I looked at Jack, not you.}

She felt him stiffen beside her, and she shot him a quick, apologetic look.

He returned it with a wry smile. "Let's grab a bite. I'm starved."

"You're always hungry," she retorted, chancing another glance at him.

Jack had been shorter than Micah by ten centimeters, and Jonathan's cybernetic limbs had been modified accordingly. Just one more thing she had to adjust to, along with the curly, auburn hair and a more rounded face, courtesy of a few strategically-placed prosthetics.

The hand at the small of her back increased its pressure, propelling her forward.

"I'm from Larimar, cupcake," he drawled, staying in character for any who might be eavesdropping. "We Sirians need more fuel than you puny Procyons do."

{I don't think our tail's going to show today,} she told him. *{Maybe we should just head back to the ship.}*

{It's early yet,} Jonathan countered. *{Let's give them a bit more time to find us. I want to see if yesterday was a fluke. The more info we can gather on him, the easier it'll be for you to trace him using Leavitt's sensors, right?}*

She made a skeptical sound.

{I'm right and you know it.}

{You're just hoping for a confrontation,} she countered.

{Not gonna lie. If that guy tries to corner us, I'm not passing up the chance to learn why he's so interested in a man who's supposed to be dead.}

Jonathan's mental voice was as hard and sharp as a carbyne-tipped blade.

Harper subsided, sensing the anger that seethed just beneath the surface of the man walking by her side.

They exited into one of the station's atriums. Pristine white colonnades made of clearsteel and coated in a bioplas polymer rimmed the area. Lit from within, they cast a soft, diffuse glow. She gestured to a restaurant on the other side, partially obscured by a leafy tree.

"Europan Thai food sound good to you?" she asked, chancing another look at Jack's face.

"Lead on," he said with a smile. *{Good job. We'll make a field agent of you yet.}*

She sent him a mental eyeroll. *{You can't convince me you're enjoying this. I'll bet you're counting the days until you get to look like you again.}*

{You mean like Micah?} There was an uncharacteristic bite to his voice, and she leveled a sharp glance at him.

{You're not—}

{Angry with him?} He cut in. *{No, just at what they did to him. Me. Us.}*

{Are you going to take back the name? It would be completely justified, you know.}

She paused at the entrance of the restaurant, submitting a request for two under Jack's name to the SI-run kiosk.

{Nah. I've gotten used to being Jonathan,} he replied, his hand moving to curl around her waist. *{And maybe even to a certain analyst being a pain in my ass about rehab.}*

She bent his fingers back when his hand tightened and he began to pull her into him. He yelped and stepped back, an accusing look on his face. "What the hell, Harper?"

She smiled at the green-eyed, red-headed man. "Keep your

hands to yourself, Marine. I'm partial to sailors, Jack Campbell, or didn't you know that?"

Jack's face grinned back at her, eyes dancing. "Oh, yeah?"

"Yeah." She bumped shoulders with him. *{And someone standing under that tree is extremely interested in the fact I just called you Jack.}*

{Oh, really.} He moved to lean his back against the maître d's kiosk, facing her. The position would also allow his optics to scan the atrium behind her. *{Got him. Forwarding on to Micah. He'll get it to Cutter's people for analysis.}*

Their table offered a good view of the diners while offering privacy screening that allowed them to freely talk. They settled in and Jonathan tapped the table to pull up the menu.

"They've transitioned and are inbound," he announced as he passed a finger through one of the projected menu items to select it.

She looked up from the menu.

"More spooky connection stuff, eh?" she asked with a smile.

When he nodded, she stared at him curiously.

"And there's really no noticeable difference between him being here, and him being in Luyten's Star?"

Jonathan shook his head. "Nope. The only difference is that I can tell he's closer. Much closer. But it's not a signal-strength thing; it's kind of a compass thing."

He swung his head around and pointed a finger above and behind her. "He's that-a-way."

Harper shook her head. "That's...remarkable."

Jonathan's—Jack's—mouth twisted.

"Weird is more like it. But it's come in handy," he admitted.

They finished their meal and left to return to their ship's berth, appearing outwardly oblivious to the tail they'd picked up just outside the restaurant. The sensors Harper had installed in the bag slung over her shoulder provided them both with a feed of their surroundings. They saw the moment their tail was joined by a second man.

{Think my cover's solid enough?} Jonathan asked, his hand

once more at the small of her back. *{I know we timed Jack's emergence with the researchers' arrival from Vermilion, so it's believable we'd be on Leavitt right now, but what if this biosig's not holding?}*

{Nothing we can do about that now.} She sent him a mental shrug. *{They've taken the bait, though, and that's promising. Notice how they're hanging back? This is reconnaissance, nothing more.}*

Jonathan ducked into a passageway that would take them to *Wraith,* masquerading as *Katana.*

{Then let's lead them back to our fake bird.}

JUNXUN

WAREHOUSE DISTRICT
LEAVITT STATION

THE TRANSPORT THAT pulled up beside the Leavitt warehouse was nondescript, as Citizen General Che Josza had ordered. He waited for his security detail to confirm the station's pubnet and sensor feed was actively being jammed before triggering the release on the transport's door.

The ostovar, an Akkadian rank equal to that of corporal, hopped out of the vehicle and moved quickly to guard his Citizen General's exit. Che waved off the soldier's proffered hand, schooling his expression to its usual stern and forbidding mask.

Inwardly, he smiled, pleased at the young noncom's scrupulous attention to his duties, despite the fact the attention was unwanted.

He took note of the deserted street littered with empty pallets, battered recycling bins, and parked lorries. The logos of various corporations were splashed across each warehouse, advertising the leaseholder's identity.

He didn't know if it was just plain luck that no shipments

were scheduled to arrive or depart from these storehouses on this day, or if his people had ensured that this would be the case.

In the end, it didn't matter, only that it had been made to happen.

He turned to the Akkadian commander exiting the vehicle. "Good work. You've ensured the feed will remain out of service for as long as it takes to complete this transaction?"

The commander gave a slight nod. "Exactly so, Citizen General."

The man turned, eyeing the soldiers that flanked them. A sharp flick of his wrist had the pair snapping to attention.

"Clear the warehouse."

The two ostovars nodded, then moved to secure the facility.

They had arrived early. A message from the assassin earlier in the day announced the courier ship would soon transit the gate. Not one to leave anything to chance—and knowing how the Minister of State Security was counting on this mission's success—Che had chosen to oversee this exchange himself.

If Clint Janus was to be believed, the crate contained a bargaining chip potent enough to hold the entire Geminate star nation captive.

Che hoped Janus's assessment was correct. Akkadia had risked many operatives on this venture, including one of Che's personal protégés.

He'd named the assassin *Dacina Zian*, "Fierce Dagger" in the Old Tongue. She remained one of his favorite students, despite the fact that it had been decades since she had left his tutelage to enter into the assassin's guild. Dacina would never fail him.

The ostovars appeared at the smaller entrance just to the left of the large bay doors, crisp nods indicating the way was clear. As Che strode through the entrance, his optics automatically adjusted for the dimmer atmosphere.

This particular warehouse was between shipments, which afforded them more space to move about than usual. An observation alcove had been set up against the far wall. It was tucked into the front corner, opposite where he'd just entered.

Light was directed in such a way as to draw the eye further into the center of the space. Containers strategically scattered about encouraged the same.

The observation area itself was in deep shadow, purposely so, that Che might observe without being seen.

Che knew this was nothing more than stagecraft, something an experienced soldier would see through. Should they have unwelcome guests, the way in which they entered would tell him much about their abilities. Would they conduct a quick sweep, slicing the pie to identify the location of any possible adversaries? Would they launch microdrone surveillance, thus giving away their own location to anyone with the tech to trace a localized EM signal back to its source?

Che found himself intrigued by the possibilities, anticipating the afternoon's events more than any exercise in a long time. He almost hoped an adversary would show up. Almost.

Che knew, better than most, that keeping an operation covert was the only certain way to ensure that a plan was executed flawlessly. No battle strategy ever survived contact with an enemy—at least, not fully intact.

He settled into the shadows with the patience borne from long years running operations such as this, and considered the arrival of his assassin.

Che regretted that he wouldn't be able to look Clint Janus in the eye to gauge the man's mettle for himself. Dacina would have stamped out the vein of impurity within the biochemist, of this he had no doubt. Janus would be molded once more into a useful tool, worthy of the Premier's army.

As he waited, he called up the most recent reports from the assets they had stationed here on Leavitt, to see if anything new had cropped up.

Che had familiarized himself with Akkadia's on-station resources prior to his arrival, as any good soldier would do. Although he had people to tell him of news filtering in from those sources, he'd always prided himself on keeping his finger on the pulse of any active situation in which he found himself.

He was surprised to see an update flagged as urgent, and even more surprised to see the subject matter. Tapping a finger thoughtfully against his lips, he sent a ping to the assassin. His wire automatically filtered the call, adding the necessary anti-surveillance layers to secure the connection from prying eyes and ears.

He smiled when Dacina's likeness appeared on his HUD. *{Dacina-cheh.}* He only added the diminutive on those occasions when they would not be overheard, as was the case now. *{Tell me things.}*

A dry amusement flowed through the connection and into his mind. *{Of what things shall I speak? The grind of coffee? The pour?}*

The back-and-forth was comfortable, like that of an old friend. It was a code-word exchange they'd set up years before, a way to ensure both were free to converse.

{Tell me what you know of Jack Campbell. Why would this particular Alliance soldier be flagged?} He pushed the highlighted report to her through his wire, then waited while she read the notification that the pilot had been spotted nearby.

{Hold one moment.} Her avatar froze, and he felt the sensation of dead air that came from a transmission line that was still open, yet devoid of data.

She returned within a matter of seconds, her avatar shaking its head. *{This is unexpected. Campbell's name was added to the watch list in case the Alliance issued an inquiry into his death.}*

{His death?} Che asked, mental tone sharp.

{Yes. Janus tells me this was one of the pilots he arranged to have killed. Campbell's body was one of the ones he sourced for Stinton. According to the doctor, the results were unsuccessful. The clone was not viable.}

{Curious,} he replied, *{because according to this report, the*

man is very much alive.}

{Hold once more,} Dacina held up a hand, the image freezing, this time for a much shorter duration. *{Janus assures me the original Campbell is quite dead. Somehow, this must be the clone.}*

Che thought for a moment. *{That makes two clones who seem to have mysteriously survived.}*

{It would seem so,} she agreed. There was another brief pause. *{Janus suggests there might have been other non-Geminate entities undercover on deGrasse. If they discovered the experiment Stinton was conducting, they may have managed to divert the clones for their own purposes. A competitor star nation, perhaps. Or one of the biotech companies.}*

{Hmm,} Che mused. *{That would mean they managed to falsify the results back on deGrasse, hiding them from both Stinton and Janus.}*

{Yes, although Janus has no idea how they did it.}
{Of course he wouldn't.}

Che's mental voice was dry. He crossed one leg, running a hand down the crease of his pants as he considered the ramifications.

{If this is true, we shouldn't ignore this. Campbell may turn out to be easier to acquire than Case, if our NCIC puppet fails to apprehend him for us.}

The assassin remained silent, her avatar politely watchful as he mulled this over.

{Very well, then. I'll have our people on this end handle it. What is the situation with the samples... and our wayward student?}

His star assassin followed the subject change effortlessly.

{Both are well in hand. We are in the queue to transit the gate, and scheduled to arrive within the next three hours.}

{Very good.} Che responded. *{Brower Biologics has personnel on-site. They will adjust their schedules to match yours. They understand Janus is to return to their employ, and will resume his status as an inactivated asset within Procyon.}*

Dacina's avatar nodded. *{I have said as much to him. The doctor will comply.}*

Che allowed himself a grim, satisfied smile, and forwarded Brower's contact token. *{They're holding the ship for departure and will rendezvous with him at your discretion.}*

Her avatar bowed. *{It will be done.}*

Curious, he asked, *{What of his physical condition? Will the story hold up?}*

A thread of satisfaction momentarily colored Dacina's mental voice. *{I did nothing to erase the marks of discipline, Citizen General. As you know, his conditioning was accelerated, which will only serve to enhance his cover story. The scars will attest he was a scientist under coercion. Janus will have no trouble playing his role.}*

Che sat back, pleased. *{Excellent. Let us hope he retains this lesson, at least until he is no longer needed and can be eliminated.}*

Dacina's avatar dipped her head in agreement, then made the traditional gesture of farewell, student-to-teacher.

{We will be there soon.}

SHOWTIME

PROCYON GATE
APPROACHING LEAVITT STATION

THE VESSEL COLONEL Valenti had loaned Severance for this mission didn't have nearly the sex appeal *Wraith* had, but it got the job done. The small cutter exited the gate in a scintillating flair of light, and immediately began moving toward the space station a hundred thousand kilometers away. Micah was on sensors immediately after, scanning the station's records for a Helios named *Katana*.

"I've got them," he told Severance. "Their berth's on level seventeen, section A42. There's a slip next to them, but it's occupied." He turned and looked at Sam. "Think your uncle could make whoever's sitting in that cradle disappear?"

Sam's expression made Micah realize his words could have been taken differently. "Not permanently, if that's what you're asking," she responded tartly.

Severance favored first Sam and then him with an amused look. "You think we don't have these things covered, *mon ami*? That ship's owned by a Navy contractor, manufactures those fancy railguns you like to use for target practice. When the colonel asked them to hang around for a bit, they were happy to oblige."

He nodded to the holo. "Right about now, I suspect that ship's requesting clearance to depart the station, inbound for Hawking."

Micah grunted. "Thought of everything, have you?"

The Marine shook his head. "I'm not your damn Navy, 2.0. We Marines know how to get shit done."

That elicited a cough out of Sam that sounded suspiciously like a smothered laugh. Micah sent her a glare that promised retribution.

"Yeah," he told Thad, "but how're you going to guarantee we're assigned *that* berth?"

"Oh ye of little faith," Thad *tsk*ed as he made a minor adjustment to the cutter's approach vector.

Micah rolled his eyes and had his wire connect him with Leavitt STC. Seconds later, he sat back, scrubbing the stubble on his jaw with a resigned sigh.

"Okay," he admitted, "I'm impressed. They came back with that exact slip assignment. ETA, forty minutes."

* * *

Three levels down and half a dozen slips spinward, the pinnace *York* had just settled into its assigned berth. Gabe was up and grabbing his go-bag before the all-clear sounded. He knew the clock had started, could feel it ticking away like a metronome in the back of his brain, spurring him onward.

He'd done a lot of thinking en route to the Procyon system, trying to put all the pieces together—starting all the way back to the day he'd stood in Addy's office, reviewing the medical charts on the three dead pilots.

The one data point that seemed out of place was the deGrasse fireteam's admission to Samantha Travis that Janus had sent them after Case.

Perhaps they'd had a falling-out over what was in that crate aboard the courier ship. If so, then perhaps the deputy director was correct and Case would try to reacquire it.

That crate was the other thing Gabe had spent a lot of time considering on the flight here.

If he'd learned two things in his career, the first was that there was truly no honor among thieves. The second was that things could just as easily go missing on a military base as they could in the civilian world.

He'd bet good credits that the crate aboard that ship was one of them. It would never pass through customs' doors, he was sure of it.

Then there was the fact Leavitt was a joint-use spaceport. He was pretty sure the crate wasn't going to end up on the military side of the station, either, but he couldn't rule it out.

Bottom line, he needed to find a way to tag that crate before it slipped through his fingers and disappeared. In order to do that, he needed to be around when they unloaded.

The courier ship was scheduled to dock within the next three hours. He intended to be there when it did.

Pausing in front of the cabin assigned to Hyer, he sent her a quick ping.

{Whassup, sir?}

His mouth twitched at her lazy humor.

{Ready to go, Chief? I'm outside your cabin.}

A thread of mirth came across his wire.

{Gotcha beat, sir. I'm at the hatch already.}

{I should have known.} Pivoting, he skirted a few ratings and headed for the ship's main hatch. *{Be there in five.}*

The moment their feet hit the dock, he motioned for her to follow. His NCIC credentials had given him access to the SI that ran the base's traffic control.

He knew where the courier ship would be berthed, and had inserted an unobtrusive bit of monitoring code into the system that would alert him if the ship's berth assignment changed.

As they walked, he launched a countersurveillance cloud that would allow him and Hyer to talk freely as they traversed the station. The cloud of microdrone jammers and scramblers would require a Level Ten clearance to countermand.

No one on Leavitt, save for its base commander, had the authority to do that, and the man was currently away.

Gabe knew; he'd checked.

"Did you get it?" He slanted a look her way as they rounded the bend and stepped into a lift that would take them down three levels.

Instead of answering, she reached into the bag that hung, cross-body, at her side.

"You know these things are illegal." She pulled out the tagger and handed it to him.

The small tool was shaped like a pistol. He turned it over in his hand, thumbing it on and checking its load. Satisfied, he tucked it inside a utility pocket on the outside of his pants leg, where he could quickly access it.

"Illegal? Not if you're NCIC, Chief," he said, then amended, "Well, not if it's Navy issued. I take it this isn't?"

"Off the books, just like the special agent ordered, sir."

Her grin was cocky, irrepressible.

"Good. All Navy-issued tags are registered in a database. If we're dealing with a mole inside the military, this could tip our hand. And it wouldn't do us much good," he shot her a look, "if we tag it, only to have it conveniently disappear on us."

Her lips firmed and she gave him a sharp nod.

"Copy that, boss."

The lift opened, and he led her down a passageway that spilled into a long, utilitarian dock. Berths lined the left-hand side, most of them occupied. Stacks of crates, assorted mag-lev lifters, and sundry other pieces of equipment littered the bulkhead on their right.

Nice to know Leavitt hasn't tidied itself up any since I was last here, he thought with some relief. *Shouldn't be too hard to find a place to hole up until they dock.*

Luck was with them. The space across from the courier ship's assigned berth had a jumble of crates stacked loosely against its bulkhead. They were arranged in a haphazard fashion, with gaps big enough to accommodate both himself and Hyer.

She clambered atop a short stack, then turned, grinning down at him.

"It'll be just like shooting swamp rats back home, sir."

He cocked a brow at her. "You do that a lot?"

"Nope, never have." Her grin widened and she lifted one shoulder in a half shrug. "Heard the phrase from a buddy of mine. Sounded good, so I kinda appropriated it, if you know what I mean."

Shaking his head, he hoisted himself up beside her. One look at his chrono told him they still had another two hours and some change left. He settled in for the wait.

"Hyer." She looked over at him but didn't respond as he slid onto the crate next to her. "Got anything in that kit of yours that will make a Crowbar?"

His question had surprised her, he could tell.

"Sir? Those are illegal, too." Her tone was cautious, almost polite.

She was right; they were. A Crowbar was a brute-force lock-picking program that borrowed click-assembly techniques used in chemistry to rapidly alter the properties of existing nanolocks.

Pre-loaded common codes, or 'bricks', gave the Crowbar a jump-start, pushing a cascade failure into the lock that cracked it wide open. In the process, it rendered the lock useless.

"I have a few LockPik programs I can install in a nano packet, if you'd like," she offered instead.

He shook his head. "Damn things are too courteous for my needs. By the time it sends its pretty-please request for access, the people I'm hunting will have ordered whatever's inside to self-destruct." He settled back against the bulkhead and speared her with a look.

"Don't tell me you never tried your hand at programming a Crowbar, somewhere along the line. Every mechanic worth his weight in creds experimented with one, somewhere along the line in their misspent youth. You really going to tell me you don't have a Crowbar story in your past?"

The chief warrant's eyes narrowed.

"Captain, sir, I'm gonna pretend I never heard you say that."

Gabe stretched his legs out in front of him and crossed one ankle over the other. He studied his boots for a long moment, then lifted the tagger and made a show of polishing its surface.

"I know something that might make you change your mind," he said casually, still polishing the tagger.

She looked over at him, skepticism in her eyes. He extended one hand, palm up. She looked down at it, then back up at him.

"What now? You gonna tell me to shake paws, like Fred?"

He cracked a grin at her mention of her pet, keeping his hand extended. He knew she missed the creature.

She'd left the basset hound in the care of the research team, back on Vermilion. They'd assured her they'd care for the animal until the two could be reunited.

After a moment, she gave in, placing her hand in his. The nano in his palm activated on contact, dropping a file into her wire's cache. A very high-level, Parliamentary-sealed, classified file. He knew she'd accessed it when she slid her hand free and gave a low whistle.

"NCIC priority override? Well hot damn, why didn't you say so, sir?" A grin split her face. "Hooo-eeee. License to break Alliance law. Now ain't that something."

He managed, just barely, to hide his amusement at Hyer's enthusiasm.

She interlaced her fingers and then cracked her knuckles, a move that made him wince. She reached for the bag at her side but then arrested the movement, a wary look on her face.

"Let me get this straight. You don't care about hiding the fact you're planning to snatch that crate? Because I gotta tell you, a Crowbar's not exactly a subtle hack."

One brow crept up.

"Thus the name," he said in a dry tone, and then shook his

head. "Hyer, if I need to use it, I'm going in guns blazing. I'm not looking to sneak in the back door, and I sure as hell am not going to knock politely and ask if they'd let me take a peek inside whatever crates they might be hauling."

He leaned forward, using the muzzle of the tagger to emphasize his point.

"I don't plan on giving them time to scuttle the evidence. I intend to kick in the front door, shoot first and ask questions later, and I need a blunt force tool like a Crowbar to do it. Now, do you have the chops to program one for me, or is being a tug operator all you ever really wanted out of your career in this Governor-General's fine Navy?"

"Well, gee, sir, when you put it that way..."

They sat in silence for a while, Hyer humming absently to herself while she worked. She shuffled around inside her kit, even slid past him and disappeared for half an hour with a murmured, "back in a jif, sir."

While he awaited her return, he accessed the base's STC to check up on the ships coming in on final. The courier's berth hadn't changed.

While he was in the system, he scrolled through recent arrivals, trying to get a feel once more for the ship Case would be on. Out of habit, he scanned for any Helios arrivals, but nothing pending showed up. Other than the Helios-class ships based at Leavitt, there were only a handful of that type berthed on base.

None held the tail number he was looking for, or the designation of *Wraith.* Not that he expected it to be that easy. Case might be a saboteur, but he wasn't stupid.

Gabe's eye caught on a berth that had opened up beside one of the Helios spaceships that had been on-station for days. A Navy cutter was assigned to it, scheduled to arrive shortly before the courier.

Curious, he reached for the ship's flight plan. The cutter's home base had been scrubbed. Even Gabe's class-ten access wouldn't gain him any information.

"Oh, you shouldn't have done that if you wanted to avoid prying eyes," he murmured to himself. While the cutter's identity was hidden, there was no real way to hide the ship's trajectory, especially from STC sensors.

He ran the base's traffic feed backward, noting the ship's arrival time at the gate and cross-referencing it against the gate's cycle.

"Bingo," he said softly, ignoring Hyer's curious look as she scrambled back up onto the crate beside him.

The ship had originated in Luyten's Star.

His gaze landed once more on the berth the cutter had been assigned, then shifted to its neighbor. The Helios named *Katana* had been berthed on Leavitt going on two weeks. Unusual for a ship of its type, although a quick search revealed the fact it had been reassigned to the light cruiser *Exemplar*, which wasn't scheduled to arrive for another few days.

On a hunch, he ran the calculations for the time it would have taken Case's Helios to arrive at Luyten Gate. He'd searched the Alliance database for regulations on operating Scharnhorst drives near Calabi-Yau gates and knew where Case's ship had most likely transitioned back into realspace, once *Wraith* disengaged its drive.

As he suspected, *Katana*'s arrival on Leavitt fit within the parameters. Had it arrived any earlier, it would have eliminated the vessel from suspicion. As things stood…

"Chief, do me a favor, will you?" He turned to Hyer. "Once you're done with the Crowbar, I have a feed I need you to take a look at."

"Oh, I'm done now, sir. Just didn't want to disturb you."

She held out a small cylinder, and he took it. She'd keyed the unit to his token, and it automatically placed an icon on his HUD.

He nodded in satisfaction. "Nice work."

She shrugged diffidently, but he could tell she was pleased.

He held up a hand, lifting one brow as he shot her a challenging look.

"You know what they say about how the Navy rewards good work? Got another job for you," he told her, flipping the feed's net address her way and dropping a pin on *Katana*. "Scrub through the station's records on that ship and see what you can find. If anything interesting pops up, flag it."

"Sure thing."

He ordered the base to grant her ID temporary NCIC-level access and she settled in to review the recordings, back slouched against the bulkhead, arm dangling across one knee. He could tell by how her eyes darted back and forth that she'd immersed herself fully into the assignment.

He turned his attention back to the dock just in time for the holographic sign above the slip that held the courier's cradle to switch on, warning people not to cross the demarcation line. As he watched, the blue telltales of an atmospheric shield snapping into place flared, and the bay doors for that slip began to slide open.

"Show time," he murmured to no one in particular as the ship floated in and settled onto the cradle. He lifted the tagger and rested it against the crate in front of him when the shield snapped off and the hatch began to cycle open.

His finger itched to press the trigger when he saw Janus disembarking, though he knew that would be the wrong move. Even innocent civilians had personal security programs that would warn of the presence of such tracking devices.

Janus was anything but innocent. Gabe suspected the scientist's security would be set to a high sensitivity level.

His finger relaxed against the trigger, and he tracked the man through its reticle as the biochemist walked past, heading toward the baggage claim area.

The pilot came next, followed by a nondescript female dressed in an engineer's shipsuit. They grabbed a maglev lifter from its position against the bulkhead a dozen meters to his left, then disappeared once more into the ship. Several minutes later, they reappeared with their load.

Gabe carefully sighted on the crate, waited for a clear shot, then spiked the carton with a tag. The spiked container would send out an electronic breadcrumb trail that he could follow, using a special app.

Since each spike had a unique geometric signature contained in the tagger's database, the app would have no trouble pinpointing its location while it remained on Leavitt.

He followed the crate until it disappeared from sight, then returned the tagger to his pants pocket.

"All right, Chief. Time to roll." He stopped when he caught the expression on her face. "What is it, Hyer? You look like you just saw a ghost."

Her eyes refocused on him, and she nodded slowly.

"Sir, I... think I just did, sir."

Gabe pulled back with a frown. "Come again?"

Hyer straightened from her slouch. She took a deep breath. "Base's feed identifies the *Katana*'s pilot as Jack Campbell."

Gabe just stared back at her.

"That's impossible," he said flatly. "The man's dead."

"You know it, and I know it," she agreed solemnly, eyes shifting to stare in the *Katana*'s direction.

"But I don't think anyone told him, sir."

MANHUNT

GNS *WRAITH*
LEAVITT STATION

MICAH, THAD, AND Sam remained inside the cutter, waiting for dock traffic to clear before heading over to the ship they were parked beside.

Wraith's hatch cycled open when they neared, and he motioned Sam through, only to stop dead in his tracks at the sight of his other self.

Thad shoved him from behind. "Make a hole! What's the holdup, two-point—ohhhh."

The Marine drew out that last as he caught sight of Jonathan. "Man, that'll really mess with your head, seeing you like that."

Jonathan ran fingers through curly hair, the cybernetic gauntlet that protected his still-healing hand glinting in the overhead's light. He blew out a breath. "You're not the one looking at a dead man's face every time you look into a mirror."

Thaddaeus raised a hand. "Point."

Micah's gaze skated away from his mirror-twin, as he

moved to the open weapons locker and began kitting up. He felt a flash of annoyance filter from Jonathan's mind as he shrugged into a holster and then redonned his vest.

C'mon, man. Not you, too. Took me almost a full week before I could get Harper to maintain eye contact, with me looking like this.

Micah's hand hovered between a second CUSP pistol and a pair of spare batteries. He looked up, meeting his counterpart's accusing stare with an apologetic one of his own.

Sorry. It's... unsettling. Hearing you inside my head, knowing it's you, and then my eyes telling me it's not...

Micah shrugged it off, choosing a second blade over the pistol and pocketing the spare batteries. *You're right. We have work to do.*

Turning back to Harper, he asked, "Have they docked yet?"

She nodded. "They're about to. Slip's one level down and six over from us." She pulled up a schematic of their surroundings. "There's a shaft right across from our berth that'll take you down."

"So if I needed to, I could be there in about thirty, forty-five seconds," he guessed, and she nodded again, flipping the visual back to the empty slip.

Thad leaned forward. "Here they come."

Harper split the view so they could see the ship coming in on final from various angles. Thad looked down at the seated analyst. "You anticipate any problems following them?"

Harper shook her head. "Not with the director of the NSA clearing the way," she said, slanting a look at Sam. "It's good to have friends in high places."

"That it is," agreed the Marine, slapping the back of Harper's chair. He straightened, and in the next moment, Micah saw an invitation to join a combat net appear on his HUD.

He accepted it and an overlay fell into place, showing avatars for each teammate. In the next instant, a fresh avatar joined them. This one was of a panther.

He cocked an eyebrow at Thad, the mission commander. "You going jungle on us, Severance?"

"It was my idea," Harper told them. Before Thad could protest, she nodded toward the map of Leavitt's industrial sector.

"There's a dead spot in one corner of the warehouse district. It appeared this morning, a system 'glitch'—" she air-quoted the word, "—that's broadcasting an out of service message."

Micah studied the map. The section she highlighted spanned about half a kilometer in a four-block area, down one of the lesser-used passageways.

"You think this is where that crate's going to end up."

She tilted her head. "There are at least seven buildings within that section that have leased space to out-system companies."

"Let me guess," Sam said, stepping forward to eye the map. "Those companies are Akkadian."

Harper shrugged. "Some could be legitimate businesses. Others are on the list of organizations suspected as fronts for their Ministry of State Security."

Thaddaeus scraped a hand across the stubble on his jaw.

"The Junxun operates under that ministry," he observed.

"Junxun?" Sam asked.

"Junxun Tèzhŏng, to be specific. Their version of special forces," offered Micah, "but with the added extra benefits of brainwashing and a 'the only way out is in a coffin' mentality."

He saw Sam's jaw tighten at that, but she bit back whatever comment she seemed ready to make.

He turned, his gaze tracking between Harper and Jonathan. "So, what is it about this dead coverage area that made you add a cat to the combat net?"

{Cat has a name.} Pascal's annoyed chuff preceded the panther's arrival. He padded in from the galley, eyes slitted and laser-focused on Micah. *{You still owe me that steak.}*

Thad cracked a grin. "Damn, hoss, haven't you learned by

now? Never owe a cat anything. Give 'em a centimeter, and they'll extort the crap outta you."

Pascal shot the Marine a baleful look out of jewel-green eyes. *{For you, I charge double.}*

Thad shouted a laugh and slapped his thigh. "I like your attitude, cat."

"Good, because you're partnering with Pascal," Harper announced.

"Wait, whoa, slow down here." Thad frowned at her, arms crossed. "I'm running this op, agency girl, not you. Let ol' 1.0 take the cat."

*{Name's **Pascal**.}*

Thad lowered one eyelid in a squint. "It can be Starkiller Deathstroke for all I care. You're not coming with me."

Harper merely smiled.

"We need *Jack*," she emphasized the name, "to confront Janus, for obvious reasons. We need to shake him up, catch him off guard. Coming face to face with someone he killed is the best way to do that, remember?"

"True, but—"

"Pascal's presence could dilute that effect. And before you say it, Micah and Sam are out, too. Pascal would bring them too much attention. The APB issued on deGrasse is still active, so it'd be too risky."

Micah felt Sam's gaze on him and he met the concern in her eyes with a look of assurance, despite the misgivings he had about exposing the civilian doctor to an active mission.

She'd already been shot at once. Twice, if he counted the warning shot from *York*.

The odds were high that it would happen here again, today.

"We weren't planning to split up," Micah reminded Harper. "Sam and I are with Thad."

"Not anymore you're not," Harper corrected, dropping two pins within the four-block area shaded in a transparent red. "These are the two most likely destinations for our crate. You'll need to split up if you're going to cover them both."

Jonathan stepped in, waving the vest he held in his hand. It looked like it was made from the same mottled gray material as the space battle uniform, or SBU, Thad currently wore.

"C'mon, soldier-boy," Jonathan said. "It'll be fun. You guys'll be twins. Pascal, posing as a working cat, patrolling Leavitt with his Marine handler. What could go wrong?"

Micah heard Sam smother a laugh at that, earning her a scowl from the big Marine.

Thad turned his scowl on Jonathan. "Now you've done it, Navy. You just had to go and say that last, didn't you. You've jinxed us now."

{Stupid humans.} The black panther blew a breath through his nose. A massive paw batted at the material in Jonathan's hand. *{Don't get ideas. Vest not active.}*

Micah tapped his fist against his mouth to hide a grin at Thad's thunderstruck expression.

"You're shitting me, right?"

An active vest was standard issue for working dogs and the occasional working cat. When paired with a control held by the animal's human partner, the vest could tether the creature within a certain radius of its handler, using magnetic fields to restrict its movement.

"It was the only way to get him to agree to wear it. But, *but*," Harper continued, raising a hand at Thad's protesting sound, "he's promised to follow your instructions while in the field. Yes?"

She leveled a pointed look at Pascal as Jonathan wrapped the vest around the big cat's torso.

Pascal slitted his eyes and yawned, flashing sharp incisors at them. He snapped his jaw shut and blew out a breath.

"Yes-s-s-s," he verbalized on a hiss. *{Agree. Will do what you say. Even if stupid.}*

Thad grunted and glared back at the cat. "Damn straight, you will."

"We have movement!" Harper called out suddenly, her eyes darting back and forth as she worked the station's feeds. She pulled up a visual of the courier ship and sent it to *Wraith*'s main screen.

As they watched, the ship's hatch opened, and the crate unloaded. Harper switched angles and leaned forward, gaze intent upon the metadata associated with the feed.

"Well now, that's interesting."

"What is?" Sam asked, leaning forward to peer over her shoulder and Harper jerked as if unaware she'd spoken aloud.

"Sorry." The analyst spared them an apologetic look, then pointed at the crate. "Look. Someone's spiked it."

That *was* interesting. Micah exchanged looks with Thad and his mirror-twin.

"Spiked?" Sam repeated. She turned to Micah for an explanation.

"It's a special operations tag, works as an electronic breadcrumb trail," he explained, knowing the mechanics of the tracker would intrigue the scientist. "Each spike has a unique geometric signature that makes it easy to follow."

"We have a search app that'll track the negative space that particular spike makes," Jonathan added, "*if* we can get a good lock on the spike in the first place."

"But why would they spike their own crate?" Sam asked, turning a searching look toward him.

Micah shrugged. "I could see them doing it as a fail-safe, in case they got separated from it, for some reason."

Thad nodded. "Makes sense. Harper, send us the null signature code if you can pin down that spike. Micah, you and Sam take the first warehouse, I'll take the one the next row over. I'll give you a minute head start, and will follow. Jonathan, you're up last."

He pointed to the floating crate. "Kinsley, don't lose that thing, you got me?"

"Yes, sir."

"Move out, people. And cat."

Thad's jaundiced look caused Pascal to drop his jaw in a feline grin but the animal obligingly rose and trotted after the

Marine.

Micah followed Thad to the hatch, turned and caught Jonathan's eye.

"Good hunting, brother."

And to you, too, the voice inside his head replied.

Something tells me we're going to need it.

CLOSING IN

Gabe and Hyer had split up. He was trailing the crate at a discreet distance, while monitoring the tagging program on the off chance he lost visual. Hyer was on her way to a nearby empty office he'd managed to obtain.

{You there yet, Chief?} He queried her location once more over their secured connection. A map appeared on his HUD, her icon merging with a nearby office address he'd lucked into.

{Patience, sir!} she huffed, her mental voice sounding a bit winded. A moment later, she added, *{Okay, I'm here.}*

There was a brief pause, followed by a mental whistle.

{Aw, sir, you shouldn't have. What a sweet setup!}

He stifled a smile.

{Don't get used to it. Station master's an old buddy of mine. He owed me one.}

He paused at an intersection, eyes scanning the crowd for any indication he'd been made. Satisfied he was keeping a safe distance from his objective, he continued his pursuit.

{All right. Lay it on me one more time. What, exactly, did you

see on that feed?}

Hyer sent an image of the cutter and the Helios, parked side-by-side. *{You've probably already guessed, but that cutter came from Luyten's Star. That's not the most interesting part, though. Take a look.}*

She let the station's recording play. Gabe saw three figures exit the cutter, headed for the Helios. The chief highlighted the figures, and a standard interrogation popped up, cross-referencing them against an Alliance database. All three refused to resolve.

{Well now, isn't that interesting.}

Hyer's avatar shot him a knowing look.

{Ain't it just? Guess we'll just have to do it the old-fashioned way. Check this out.}

On his HUD, the image zoomed as Hyer manipulated it. Two of the three faces were scrambled, the signature indicative of active military countersurveillance.

The man on the left was a hulk of a man, dressed in Marine SDUs. The other man's build suggested he could be Micah Case.

Someone had slipped up, though. The person in the middle was clearly identifiable. It was Samantha Travis.

He stopped in his tracks.

*{**Good** work, Chief. That's what I needed to see. A hundred credits that ship is Case's* Wraith.*}*

He spared a last, longing look at the tagged crate, debating the best sequence of actions. His instructions were clear: apprehend Micah Case.

Pulling up the station map once more, he made a quick mental calculation. He was fairly certain the crate was headed to the warehouse district, and would likely be moved inside one of the storage facilities, awaiting transfer to an Akkadian ship.

He was much closer to the Helios than he was to the warehouse sector; if he played his cards right, he could take Case into custody and still have time to do a bit of reconnaissance.

Decision made, he turned and began to retrace his steps to the dock.

{Copy that,} he told Hyer. *{I'm heading for the Helios now.}*

{Hold, sir,} she cautioned, and he slowed his pace. *{That visual's five minutes old.}*

He waited as she forwarded the feed.

Damn. I knew it was too good to be true, he thought, as he watched the same unidentified man and Samantha Travis leave the Helios. A minute later, the brawny, dark-skinned Marine departed, gesturing to an animal in an SDU service vest.

Gabe smiled as the database finally returned an ID on the man:

CAPTAIN THADDEUS SEVERANCE, SPECIAL RECONNAISSANCE UNIT, GA NAVY.

That wiped the smile right off Gabe's face. *How the hell did Thad become involved in all this? Just what in the ever loving stars is going on here?*

He and Thad had gone through Basic together. They'd been in the same platoon, had frequently sparred during close combat drills. The two had parted ways when their career paths diverged, but Gabe counted Thad as a brother and a friend.

A sliver of unease crawled up his spine, doubt creeping in as he questioned once more who was on the side of right and who was wrong in this crazy, mixed-up situation.

Not that it mattered; he was going to bring Case in for questioning, regardless. He'd have to trust those higher up to sort everything out.

Though Severance followed Case and Travis at a discreet distance, it was clear that all three were headed in the direction of the station's warehouse district.

In some respects, this made his job much simpler. Case, Travis, and the crate seemed to be converging in one location. The problem Gabe now faced was Thad.

He'd felt confident he'd be able to subdue both Case and

Travis without an assist. With Thad added into the mix, he knew there was no way he'd be able to get a drop on them. It looked like he'd soon be the one owing the station master a favor. He began to mentally compose his request for backup.

{Keep monitoring that Helios,} he instructed Hyer. *{I'm following those three.}*

{Want me to head for the cutter?} she asked, *{I could breach while they're away. Search for clues.}*

Gabe sent her a head-shake. *{Sorry, but you're not trained for this kind of work. I can't in good conscience ask you to do something that risky when Campbell could show up at any moment.}*

Hyer's avatar shot him a cheeky grin. *{Oh, I'm good at not getting caught, sir.}*

Gabe stopped at an intersection to let a large trolley trundle past, laden with boxes. He rolled his eyes, though he kept that expression to himself.

{Don't want to know about your escapades, Chief. Not right now.}

He started up again, only to stop abruptly as the feed showed Campbell exiting.

{Heads up, sir!}

{I see him.} Gabe was surprised to see the man turn in the other direction, toward baggage claim and the station proper.

Now that's odd. His thoughts raced as he wracked his brain for the reason behind the man's choice of direction. *Is it possible he's following Janus?*

{What about the woman they left behind?} Hyer's question cut into his speculations. *{Harper Kinsley. She's Agency. NSA. Has a good record, too. Wonder how she got mixed up in all this.}*

Gabe admitted the chief warrant made a good point. He approached the lift, absently thanking the soldier who held it open for him.

He leaned against the back wall, arms crossed and head down. Unseeing eyes traced the patterned metal beneath his feet as he turned the puzzle pieces over in his mind, seeking the right fit.

Gabe straightened, pushing away from the back of the lift.

{Okay, Chief. I've changed my mind. As long as you can keep a feed up that'll trace Campbell's progress, I'll clear you to approach the Helios. See what you can get out of Kinsley.}

He sent her a warning look. *{If Campbell looks like he's returning, you leave. Got it?}*

{Sir, yes, sir.} Hyer's avatar snapped a smart salute.

"Smart-ass," he said under his breath, a reluctant smile teasing the corner of his mouth as she closed the connection.

He hoped turning Hyer loose on Kinsley was the right call. Kinsley was no spook, and Hyer was still a trained soldier. He had to think the chief could hold her own against a desk analyst.

Shaking off his concerns, he exited the lift and resumed his trek to the warehouse district. The spike's coordinates were now well within that area.

A quick check on Case and Travis confirmed they, too, were on track to converge with the crate. He picked up the pace, wanting to arrive before they did, so that he was in a position to observe before closing in on them.

Two minutes later, he was staring down a long row of storage buildings. Conveniently, the entire four-block area was showing up as 'out of service' on the station's pubnet map. The security feeds were offline. Pulling up an archived copy of the area he'd downloaded while waiting for the courier to dock, he studied his options.

Two Akkadian import companies held back-to-back space at the epicenter of the blackout area. Tossing a mental coin, he turned down the alleyway leading to the nearest building, just missing the sleek vehicle that emerged from the street one row over.

WAREHOUSE DISTRICT

LEAVITT STATION
PROCYON GATE

THERE WERE NO real boundaries designating they'd crossed over into the warehouse district, at least not that Sam could see. The only indication was the gradual switch from buildings with storefronts, to ones that clearly housed offices, and then to stark and utilitarian facades covered in metal sheeting.

She came to a stop when Thaddaeus' voice sounded inside her head.

{Listen up, amis,} the Marine announced. *{Peer-to-peer communication from this point on, until those samples are destroyed and you exfil the area. You got it?}*

Micah's avatar nodded just before the combat net winked out. His hand grasped her elbow.

{That doesn't mean we can't still talk. Just means we need to make direct contact to do it.}

{I'm aware,} she replied. *{Direct-link won't send out an EM signature that can be traced back to us by the bad guys. Physicist, remember?}*

She tapped the side of her head, shooting him an

exasperated look.

Micah had the grace to look abashed. *{Sorry.}*

He glanced down the street in one direction and then the other, frustration in his eyes.

{Too bad Harper couldn't nail down that spike signature. Would have made this a lot easier.}

She shrugged, saying nothing. He took one more look around, and then motioned for her to follow him around the corner of a building. After ensuring no one was nearby, he nudged her into the shadow of a dumpster.

Giving her elbow a squeeze, he handed her a pair of gloves and a balaclava.

{Put these on,} he instructed, before breaking contact to do the same with his own set.

Sam turned them over in her hands. They looked like they were made from the same material as the Drakeskin stealth suits Thaddaeus had given them to wear.

The suits were made of a synthsilk material. A nanoweave embedded into the topmost layer was tunable, providing visible-spectrum stealth.

After slipping the gloves and hood on, she tugged on his arm, miming a question. He grinned, reaching up to tuck a stray strand of blonde hair back inside her hood.

He used the contact to reconnect and explain.

{Toggle the IFF token, and the app's predictive systems will paint an outline of my location on your overlay.}

She nodded. He stepped back with a questioning look and she gave him a thumbs-up. With a grin, he vanished.

She blinked at the accuracy of the illusion. She cycled her optics through all EM bands, and saw nothing.

Except—there. A slight ripple, along the far infrared, just as she felt his hand wrap around her arm. The movement was almost indistinguishable, but it was there.

{I know what you're going to say, and yeah, it's not perfect. But if they're not expecting company, no one will ever see us.}

She gave a shaky laugh. *{Then let's be quick about it, before I* *lose my nerve.}*

{A woman of action. My kind of girl.}

Accessing the token he'd given her back on *Wraith*, she found a new icon had been added to her HUD. When she launched it, Micah's form appeared before her, limned in a green glow.

He tugged at her hand, urging her forward, and she followed his shrouded form. She nearly bumped into his back when he stopped abruptly.

{This is it, just ahead.}

She took in a slow, deep breath. *{So, what now? Do we just walk up, pick the lock, and let ourselves in?}*

He sent her a negative. *{Let's backtrack to the end of the block. The building there has a maintenance ladder welded to its outside wall. I want to see if these structures have roof access. I'd prefer to enter from above if we can.}*

Sam followed, looking up at the structures with a jaundiced eye. They weren't multi-story buildings, but the warehouses made up for that by having tall, cavernous interiors. She had no clue how Micah expected her to scale such a thing.

As if he knew what she was thinking, she felt his hand tighten on hers.

{No worries, doc. We'll rappel in. I'll talk you through it; you'll be fine.}

Luck was with them. The maintenance ladder proved easy to scale, and while not all the buildings adjoined each other, they were close enough to leap across. Micah approached their target building with care, releasing a pair of microdrones to scout for tripwires or other traps the Akkadians might have set.

{Clear,} he told her, then kept hold of her hand as they spanned the meter-wide gulf between the roof they were on and the Akkadian warehouse.

She expected Micah to set off for the ventilation shaft that shoved its way through the center of the warehouse roof but he didn't.

{Too obvious,} his amused voice filtered into her mind. *{Besides, ductwork is both flimsy and notoriously loud. Real covert ops doesn't work like tri-D vids.}*

{I didn't think they did,} she retorted. *{But you make a good point. So now, where?}*

He showed her the feed from one of the microdrones.

{There's a row of transom windows along the other side. We'll breach from there.}

* * *

Thad had come to much the same conclusion Micah had, but he was damned if he was going to carry a fifty-kilo animal up a maintenance ladder. And he was sure's hell not going to let the cat ride on his back, not with the wicked, three-centimeter-long claws the animal sported.

Instead, he opted to breach the building across the street, one whose ownership was known and had been dismissed as not a factor. With the knowledge that he needn't worry about enemy combatants awaiting him behind closed doors, he made short work of the lock, and nudged Pascal's flank to get him to move inside.

{That makes five steaks you owe me,} the big cat's voice rumbled inside his head as he brushed past Thad, causing him to smile.

{Put it on my tab.}

Thad looked around for a way to reach the transom windows running along the front of the building and found a maglev lift off to one side. He took a moment to consider the possibility that someone might pick up on his use of the equipment, but deemed it an acceptable risk.

The unit came to life almost silently, and he steered it and its load of crates under one of the windows. Clambering atop the pile, he slid the window open, and then reached into his harness vest for the grappling hook and sturdy, carbyne-jacketed line stashed inside.

With a pneumatic puff, the grapple shot across, its unique hook-and-nano catch embedding itself just above the transom on the target building.

He pulled a pair of traverser hand grips and connected them to the line. Similar to ascenders climbers used, it gripped the line when locked, but slid freely when open. A direct-link connection to his wire allowed him to switch the mechanism's open and closed states.

He motioned Pascal up, and the cat gained the vertical distance in one giant leap. He looped a length of the carbyne line through a special reinforced channel that ran along the spine of the vest the cat wore, and then hoisted the cat through the window.

*{**Twenty**-five steaks,}* Pascal growled, clearly uncomfortable dangling eight meters above street level. Thad reached around the animal to grip the traversers and swung himself free of the building.

{Don't get any ideas,} he warned the cat. *{Claws into the **vest**, not the human.}*

Hot breath hit the back of his neck as Pascal chuffed. *{**Fifty** steaks, and we not leave the way we came.}*

{You keep those claws to yourself, hoss, and you've got a deal.}

*{**Not** a horse.}*

Thad chuckled softly as he began the repetitive release-and-slide motion that would pull them across. The time it took to cross the line was the longest five minutes Thad had experienced in a while.

The constant mental threats of evisceration hadn't helped any, but not because he held any real concern about them. They were funny as hell, but distracting.

He was fast learning that panthers didn't care much about operational security. In the end it proved completely unnecessary. The warehouse was empty; the crate wasn't there.

CORRECTING MISCONCEPTIONS

GNS *WRAITH*
LEAVITT STATION

HARPER WHIPPED HER head around as a noise from behind signaled she was no longer alone. She stared in shock at the stranger approaching from the rear, pistol aimed at her head.

Her gaze bounced around the Helios's cabin and she cursed mentally when she realized the nearest firearm was tucked neatly away in the weapons locker, three meters away. *But who the hell would have thought I'd need one on our own ship?*

"Hands up where I can see them," the stranger said, and Harper complied.

"How did you get in here?" she demanded, rising from the engineer's cradle and taking a step toward the locker. The pulse pistol in the other woman's hand jerked, arresting her movement.

Unaccountably, the woman grinned.

"LockPik," she announced with an air of pride, and Harper

realized the tall, gangly woman had actually answered her question.

Well, someone came prepared, Harper thought sardonically as the woman waved her back to her seat. *Too prepared*, she mentally added as she realized there was a localized jamming field preventing her from calling for help.

The woman's mention of the Navy's breaching app brought a flare of quick anger.

"Those are for military use only. Using one to interfere with a federal investigation is illegal," she snapped, then waved a hand at the air around them. "So is jamming a security agent's comm frequency."

The other woman's expression grew cynical.

"Not too original, Kinsley. Thought you might try for something a bit more creative than that, at least." She sauntered toward Harper.

Harper folded her arms and cocked her head. "Sorry, I'm a bit busy right now. Feel free to show yourself out, and don't let the hatch hit you in the ass on your way." She turned back to the console with a bravado she didn't feel.

{Joule? Can you hear me?} Harper's only hope was that the jamming field had been activated outside the ship, and wasn't on the intruder's person.

The only response was a snort that came from the stranger. "Can't tell who you're trying to reach, but I caught that EM pulse your wire just tried to send out."

She shook her head. If possible, her grin widened as she circled a finger over her head. "Jammer I'm using's pretty flashbang, too. Not something you're going to be able to get past anytime soon."

Harper shoved the cradle back and glared at the invader.

"Who gave you the right to break into this ship?" she demanded.

"NCIC," came the unexpected response.

"Excuse me?" Harper straightened, startled, just as a dark shadow launched itself at the lanky woman. She went down in a tangle of arms, legs, and black fur, her pulse weapon skittering across the deck.

"Wait! Joule, don't hurt her!" Harper yelled, jumping to her feet. Racing for the discarded pistol, she lifted it, only to drop it again with a yelp when contact with its grip gave her a jolt.

"Pistol's keyed to my biosig. Won't work for you," the muffled voice of the woman told her. "Get *off* me, you mangy mutt!"

{Not a mutt,} huffed Joule as she rose to all fours. A well-placed paw brought the full fifty-kilo mass of the big cat onto a tender portion of the woman's anatomy—purposely, Harper was sure.

She winced in sympathy, as the other woman jackknifed up and shoved the cat off her. "Mangy *cat*," she snarled, scooting across the deck to put a good meter between herself and Joule.

The panther sniffed and began cleaning her face with her paw, giving the intruder her back. Harper snickered.

"Oh you're in trouble now. You're being snubbed."

{Smells like dog.} Joule shot the woman a baleful look. *{**Mangy** dog.}*

The woman bristled. "Fred is not mang—" She cut herself off. "What in stars am I doing, arguing with a cat at a time like this?"

Harper tilted her head and fixed her with a narrow-eyed look. "Good question. Let's start with your NCIC claim. Who sent you, and what's the NCIC doing, crashing an NSA investigation?"

SEEING GHOSTS

LEAVITT STATION CUSTOMS
PROCYON GATE

CLINT JANUS STOOD on the outskirts of the baggage claim area, where he and the assassin had parted ways. She had gone to ensure their inside man deflected the crate from the prying eyes of the customs inspectors.

As for him... He knew his orders. He was to rendezvous with Brower Biologic's corporate cruiser, and resume his place as a biochemist in the private sector. He would do so, without complaint.

After he took a moment to just breathe.

His gaze roamed the station, allowing the crush of bodies and the noise of the crowd to wash over him as he took his first unguarded breath in more than three weeks.

Clint's hand shook and he clenched it by his side in an attempt to still the betraying tremor. A newly-formed ridge of flesh at the center of his palm pulled uncomfortably at the motion. He could feel it all the way through to the back of his hand.

The scarred line of tissue was courtesy of his most recent

round of reconditioning with the assassin, her karambit, and the special tebori needles she employed to ensure the wound would never truly heal. Each time he flexed it, made a fist, wrapped it around a tool, the roughened tissue would make itself known to him.

A gift, the assassin had told him, a permanent reminder that his life was not his own. He belonged to Akkadia.

As if the raised welts crisscrossing his back weren't reminder enough. The shipsuit he wore scraped against the tender, still-healing wounds, evidence of his 'torture' at the hands of Akkadian nationals.

He pressed the thumb of his unscarred hand into the center of his palm as he looked around at the passing throng. He envied them their carefree lives, yet at the same time, he despised them for the freedoms they took for granted.

His gaze lifted, taking in the arched colonnades that rose five stories to the station's clearsteel roof. The buildings that ringed the perimeter of each level glowed, alternating white and polished chrome façades gleaming in the discreet, indirect lighting.

Prosperity everywhere. Mere weeks ago, he'd luxuriated in it. Now, it made him ill.

The station's transparent canopy provided an unimpeded view of local traffic making its way to and from the gate. Tiny pinpricks of light moved in sweeping arcs, all meticulously choreographed by Leavitt's space traffic control.

Holographic feeds were projected at regular intervals across the canopy, providing an up-close view of each transit. He watched in a sort of sick fascination as the gate flared and swallowed yet another ship, bound for destinations unknown.

The extradimensonal lights dancing in the center of its maw were a vivid reminder of the disparity between the Geminate Alliance's affluence and the poverty of his native Akkadia.

This key tenet had been drilled into Clint relentlessly over the past twenty-three days, his long-dormant awareness of the inequality between the two star nations newly awakened.

The assassin, whose name he'd still not been given, had reminded him of the economic imbalance between the two star nations. It formed a gulf so wide, it could only be spanned by force.

The Premier had decided the Geminate people must give up their stranglehold on gate travel if Akkadia was to survive. He had a role to play in this mission, and he'd allowed his passions to cloud his awareness of that. No longer.

His attention jerked back to his immediate surroundings when he sensed someone approaching. His eyes widened in disbelief when he saw who it was.

* * *

Jonathan spied Janus at the edge of a crowded concourse. The scientist shifted as if he were uncomfortable. He held himself stiffly, cradling one hand in the palm of the other. He seemed disoriented and dazed.

Jonathan's brow creased. Something felt off, but what it was, he couldn't tell. He continued to work his way toward the man, careful to keep layers of people between him and his objective.

It wouldn't do for Janus to see him coming. He didn't want to lose the element of surprise.

Jonathan slowed as the crowd ahead of him cleared, quickly ducking behind a young family fussing over their luggage. He trailed behind them until they passed a kiosk three meters from his objective.

He pretended to study the selection of imported Martian candies as he scanned the area for accomplices. Janus appeared to be alone.

Jonathan used a thick knot of businessmen traveling in a tight circle as cover to shift to the next kiosk. A quick look around assured him the situation remained unchanged. He took a moment to study Janus more closely before stepping out and making his move.

The expressions playing across the man's face as he stared out at the crowds seemed to range from distaste to anguish and despair. He saw the man's eyes lift and he followed his gaze where a gate transit could clearly be seen. Turning back to the man, he caught a flash of anger in the man's eyes, quickly masked.

Something wasn't adding up, but Jonathan could see no reason not to continue with the mission.

{Starting approach now,} he informed Harper, the only person on the combat net, since the others had passed into the warehouse's red area.

{Copy,} she replied.

A quick scan confirmed his immediate surroundings were satisfyingly bare. He waited until Clint's attention was directed away from the kiosk, then he made his move. Stepping out from behind the small, automated shop, he began a slow, deliberate approach.

Janus stiffened and turned, some sense of self-preservation warning him he was being stalked. When his eyes landed on Jonathan's Jack Campbell visage, they widened, shock and disbelief chasing over his features.

In that moment, every bit of guilt and discomfort Jonathan felt in appropriating his dead friend's identity seemed justified. He experienced a fierce surge of satisfaction at the fear he read on Janus's face.

He stepped closer, his attention wholly focused on the other man.

"Surprised to see me, doctor?" he asked. "Or is it that you're surprised to see me alive after what you did to me?"

So intent was he on Clint's reaction that he lost his situational awareness. He failed to notice the two men approaching from the rear. He didn't see the signals passed between the men and the nondescript woman easing up behind Janus.

The last might have been excused by the simple fact that the assassin knew better than anyone how to hide in plain sight. She could see quite well the fiery anger consuming the Navy pilot. She took advantage of it, using Janus's own body to mask her movements as she drew a special nano-coated knife from its sheath.

She waited until the two men signaled they were in position, and then she drew her arm back.

In that last moment, Janus broke eye contact with Jonathan, his eyes shifting, first left and then right. The fear on his face melted away, replaced by a crafty expression.

Wary, Jonathan began to turn, but it was too late. The assassin had loosed her blade.

TRANSOM WINDOWS

Searing pain shot through Micah's chest and he stumbled back, taking a knee as he reached for the invisible blade that he felt buried, hilt-deep, just above his heart. His hand met empty space.

In an instant, he realized what had happened and he lurched to his feet, reaching out to his other self.

Hang on, brother! I'm on my w—

He reeled, unable to complete the thought, as his connection with his mirror-twin crackled, stretched, and then broke with an almost audible snap.

It was such a powerful surge, Micah was certain Sam must have heard it. His vision blacked and he crashed to his knees once more.

He shoved the balaclava back as he grabbed at his head, willing the effects to clear.

Sam appeared in front of him, her hands covering his.

{What is it?}

{Jonathan. He's been stabbed. I've lost our connection.}

Sam gripped his hands, hard.

*{Show me where, Micah. On your own body. **Exactly** where.}*

He tuned the nanoparticles in his suit back to the visible spectrum and pointed. She palpated the area gently.

{Here?} she asked.

He nodded.

{He can't be dead, right? I'm still alive. That means he's either alive or... or if he's dying, then I might not have long.}

She pulled back, stopping him.

{Hang on. That wasn't even a theory, it was just a WAG. There's no way to know, either way. We've discussed this.}

He stared at her, his need to help his chiral twin clawing at him on a visceral level, a desperate grasp for survival so strong he felt like he was fighting for his own life.

{WAG?}

She smiled. *{Wild-assed guess.}*

He gave her what he knew must look like a weak smile. He straightened, turned away, dragging her toward the transom window.

{We need to get to that crate. Now, while I still can.}

* * *

Gabe grunted in irritation at the view the microdrone was sending him. The warehouse was filled, but with rows upon rows of long, flat containers marked 'pashmina.' Nothing that remotely resembled the crate he was tracking.

The tracking app placed the spike against the far back wall of the warehouse, but clearly, it wasn't there. He sent a recall command to the drone, letting his head fall back against the dumpster he was using to shield himself from curious passersby.

The warehouse had a wide façade, spanning a full block. Streets ran along either side of it, with no rear access. In a way, he was relieved the crate wasn't there; he'd not relished a frontal assault of the building, though he would have done so if necessary.

Gabe stepped back into the street, his gaze traveling its length as he paced and thought. He refreshed the tracking app, pinging the spike on the crate once more, and saw its location shift slightly before settling.

Eyes narrowing in speculation, Gabe strode several meters to his left. He watched the display carefully, saw the spike wobble and rotate, the icon indicating its location jumping from one spot to the next and then back again, as if the program couldn't decide exactly where its target was.

He palmed his face, scrubbing at it in frustration. It made sense now.

The black market tagger Hyer had given him didn't have the same precision as one issued by the Alliance Navy. That meant the crate could be in one of the adjoining warehouses behind the one he'd just searched.

But which one?

Just pick a street, Alvarez, he thought, *and do it fast. Time's running out.*

Swearing to himself, he turned and began to jog toward the street on his left. He slowed to a sedate pace as he rounded the building, his eyes taking in the area without appearing to do so.

He released the microdrone once more, sending it winging toward the warehouse's roof as he studied the building for possible access points.

Motion caught his eye, from a row of transom windows that ran along the roofline. He kept his pace even, not giving away what he'd seen, while he directed the drone to get him a better view.

One of the windows was being eased open. He smiled in grim satisfaction when he caught a flash of blonde hair as Samantha Travis's balaclava snagged on the window's frame and pulled free of her face. In the next instant, she'd snatched it back down, but the damage had been done.

Gabe knew where the crate was now. Better yet, he knew

where to find Micah Case.

* * *

Thaddaeus slapped the stealth shroud back down over Pascal's face for the fourth time in as many minutes.

{Can't see,} the big cat grumbled, and Thad cuffed him lightly.

{Can too, soldier. Now pay attention. We're about to go into a hot zone.}

They'd seen a utility vehicle pull into the street that housed the building Micah and Sam were entering just as they made it to the corner. Thankfully, a stack of haphazardly-piled pallets sat between them and the truck, which was where they now stood, waiting to see where it would land and who it would disgorge.

He peered through the slats and watched as it came to a stop in front of the target warehouse and two thugs dragged a bloodied body from the back, hoisted it between them, and carried it inside.

His hand fisted in Pascal's vest at the same time the cat emitted a low, almost soundless growl.

{Jonathan,} the panther sent, and Thad's jaw worked as he fought to contain his anger.

{I saw,} he responded, looking down at the cat after he'd wrested his rage under control. *{How do you take your Akkadian steak?}*

Green eyes flashed in an ebony face. *{Bloody and rare.}*

"My kind of cat," he murmured softly. *{Come on, let's go hunting.}*

* * *

Sam kept her eyes fixed on the cable spooling between Micah's hands rather than the fifteen-meter drop to the hard ceramacrete surface below. With his hands sheathed in stealth gloves, the ascender grips he held would have seemed to be moving magically under their own power, except for her suit's predictive overlay.

Release, slide, lock. Release, slide, lock.

The routine was mesmerizing: one grip would move, and then the other, the line playing out above them as they slowly descended. She startled when her feet touched the floor.

Micah disengaged the grips, and they disappeared somewhere inside his vest, as she coiled the excess rope. He took it from her hands and tucked it into the shadows against the wall.

He caught her by the elbow, pulling her deeper into the warehouse.

{Let's split up. You take this row; I'll take the next one. Wait for me at the end.}

She squeezed his hand once in acknowledgement, then began to work her way down the row. Neither one met with success.

Micah nudged her toward the next row to begin the process again, but she pulled on his hand to stop him.

{Wait. Let's try closer to the front, first,} she suggested. *{They're going to want to move this thing quickly. Maybe they didn't take the time to conceal it.}*

Micah paused, then sent her a nod, leading the way on silent feet. He drew to a stop when they reached an area that had been cleared of boxes.

A low whistle sounded inside her head and he made room for her, so that she could see what he saw.

{Good call, doc.}

She stepped up beside him.

{Looks like that's our crate,} she agreed. *{They kept it on a maglev, too, so it's ready to move at a moment's notice.}*

He stopped her when she would have moved toward it.

{All I need you to do is confirm,} he cautioned. *{I'll do the rest. Got it?}*

She nodded.

{Okay, then. I'm going to do a quick sweep, make sure we're the only ones here, while you crack that thing open.}

When she got to within two meters of the crate, she felt a resistance, as if she had passed through a strong electrostatic barrier. She looked down and realized the field had reset her suit's stealth nano.

She was visible once more.

Micah's voice sounded inside her head, breaking radio silence. *{It's a trap! Run!}*

BEST LAID PLANS

AKKADIAN WAREHOUSE
LEAVITT STATION

THE MINUTE SAM'S Drakeskin suit failed, Micah sprinted toward her. She wheeled and bolted—thankfully in his direction. He grabbed her by the arm and urged her back into the shadow of the crates while he ran a diagnostic of her suit.

{You're fine. It didn't fry the nano, just reset it. Stay low while I take care of whoever set that trap.}

He wasted no time heading for a nearby pile of crates, activating his SmartCarbyne lattice as he ran.

Few outside the Navy knew the nanofloss woven throughout a pilot's body had a handy side-effect outside the cockpit: they enhanced muscle performance.

Artificial receptors embedded along the axons and dendrites of his neural circuitry did much the same for his reflexes. They functioned as supplemental nodes and signal boosters, enhancing his reaction time—both mental and physical—far beyond the human norm.

He used both to his advantage, pushing off a nearby crate and using the momentum to launch himself into the air in a quickly calculated trajectory much higher than an unaugmented human could attain.

He landed at the top of the stack, pausing to retrieve a small noisemaker from his weapons' stash before pushing off again. He tossed it toward the back of the warehouse, wanting to draw some of the heat away from Sam and the crate.

The small flash-bang effectively covered the slap his hand made as it came into contact with the steel truss that had been his next objective.

Piking himself onto its narrow ledge, he crouched in the shadow of a cross-brace as he took stock of the situation. He counted four figures. Two were roaming the warehouse, weapons drawn. A third was positioned to shield the fourth.

That told Micah this fourth man was the one calling the shots.

Seeing no other threats, Micah's glance returned to the two soldiers who were actively hunting them. He cycled his optics to maximum magnification and took a moment to study his targets.

Both held P-SCARS, pulsed short combat assault rifles, attached to tactical slings. Both looked well-trained in their use.

He waited until his two targets had chosen the row they would search next before releasing a small cloud of colloid audio chaff and dropping to the nearest stack of crates. The tiny noise-cancelling machines floated in the still air, masking his landing.

Hoping to keep his location a secret for a bit longer, he toggled his suit's magnetic field generator, drawing the colloid cloud tightly to him and minimizing its cross-sectional area. He crept along, sliding between cartons until he came abreast of the soldier nearest him.

Palming one of the Ziptie nano packages Thad had given him, he approached the man from the rear, wrapping his neck in a blood choke. The man's hand gripped his forearm reflexively, and Micah slapped the Ziptie onto the exposed flesh.

The nano app immediately unpacked itself, blocking the man's wire from transmitting a call for help, and rendering the victim temporarily immobile. Within seconds, the man was down.

Micah knew he was now on a tight clock. At any moment, the unconscious soldier's counterpart would realize the man was no longer active on their combat net, and would alert the others to the fact Sam was not here alone.

He rose from the downed man just as his partner rounded the corner. Micah bolted in the other direction, jinking wildly when the man caught sight of the slumped figure and opened fire.

The muted zip of projectiles whinged past, impacting the surface of nearby crates with dull *thwocks*. Micah dropped into a slide as the bullets traced their way across the cartons' surfaces, leaving dimples in their plas hides from the slugs the P-SCAR unloaded into them.

Their cover blown, Micah realized maintaining comm silence no longer provided an advantage.

{Sam! Where are you now?} he called out as he raced around a stack of empty pallets.

{Trying really hard to make myself as small a target as I can and avoid flying bullets,} she retorted.

Micah felt relief at her words.

{Stay away from the front of the warehouse. There are two others in here with us besides the asshole trying to kill me.}

She sent a mental nod, and he refocused on the man in pursuit. Hooking an arm around a nearby pole as he ran past, he used momentum to slingshot himself to a higher elevation once more.

The rapid mental calculations that allowed him to know exactly where to place his foot and how much force was required to achieve his goal felt different today than it ever had before. Smoother, much more rapid and precise. Instinctively, he knew it came from the inexplicable connection he and Jonathan shared.

That reminder caused a deep anger to unfurl within Micah. *I've had enough. Time to shut this down.*

Sliding his CUSP pistol from its holster, he waited for the enemy combatant to round the stack of crates and pass beneath him. Then he leapt, using the augmented strength from his SmartCarbyne enhancements to knock the man off his feet.

He brought the CUSP to the base of the man's neck and pulled the trigger, the directed energy beam shattering his medulla oblongata and instantly stopping the transfer of motor and sensory neurons to the man's body.

Not even Samantha Travis could have brought him back from that.

* * *

As the sounds of fighting erupted around her, Sam mentally reviewed her impression of the electrostatic field she'd passed through. The control for it must be somewhere near the crate. If she could just locate it...

She crept closer to the container once more, eyeing the area around it critically. Tilting her head sideways, she spotted an object lying beneath the pallet it rested on.

Bingo, she thought, then cast around for a way to remove it. *I know Micah said to lay low, but we're running out of time, and we need to see inside that crate.*

Her eyes landed on a long, narrow pole with a hook on the end. It looked like some sort of simple grappling tool, likely used to adjust crates on top of a tall stack. Seeing no one around, she pulled it from its hook and slid it along the warehouse floor, careful to make no noise.

With the flick of her wrist, the unit went skittering across the floor. She froze, waiting for the noise to elicit some response, but there was none.

Emboldened, she resumed her careful approach to the

crate, stopping at the two-meter mark and reaching a tentative hand out, seeking the electrostatic field.

There was nothing. She'd held some doubt that the small unit beneath the crate had, indeed, been the field generator. This confirmation caused the breath to whoosh from her lungs in a sigh of silent relief.

She resumed her approach to the crate once more, this time confident in her invisibility.

Ripping the glove off her right hand, she peeled back the protective cover of the breaching film adhered to her right palm and pressed her hand against the crate's locking mechanism.

"Come on, come on, come on," she chanted under her breath as she heard the chatter of a high-powered pistol, followed by the sound of flesh pounding on flesh. The lock fell to the floor with a soft clatter and she threw the hinged cover back so that she could see inside.

An Alliance logo was splashed across the casing of a biological sample case, its biohazard warning seal broken. She pulled off her left glove, freeing the bracer that encased her hand. Using the unit to crack the seal on the sample case, she sucked in a hard breath when she saw its contents.

That's no sample case, she thought. *The damn fool has four fully sustainable environments in here!*

Hovering her bracer over the one nearest her, she activated it and began to take bioreadings. The moment she confirmed the presence of chiral material, she slammed the lid back down, heart racing as she considered the ramifications.

Movement from the corner of her eye caused her to jump. She whipped around, dodging the arm that tried to wrap around her.

"Oh, hell, no," she growled, dancing back to put some distance between her and the figure who was clearly some sort of military man. She spun on her heel and ran.

Recalling the training Thad had given her during the time they'd been holed up on his ship awaiting Janus's arrival, she began to randomly change directions. At the last second, she angled for the far wall rather than a convenient stack of crates that might provide shelter nearby.

That action proved to be her salvation. A quick glance over her shoulder showed another man stepping out from around the crates, arms sweeping wide as if hoping to catch her. She allowed herself a small, smug smile as she slowed her pace and crept quietly into the shadows.

* * *

{Crate's confirmed. It's chiral.}

Micah had taken to the rafters once more to locate the remaining two men. He'd been readying himself for a final assault, but Sam's announcement gave him pause.

{How'd you do that?} he asked as he levered himself to the ground.

{Found the thing that decloaked the suits and got rid of it.}

Her tone was smug. She had a right to be. That could make things much simpler for them.

{Are you back against the wall again?} he asked after a moment.

{Yes.} She fed him a visual of her location.

Micah flexed the fingers of his stealthed hand, the one not holding the CUSP, as he thought. Coming to a decision, he reached for the explosive charges that would destroy the chiral samples.

{Okay, then. Let me set the charges. Then we can detonate the crate and leave. Stay there; I'll come get you.}

He skirted the warehouse, keeping pallets between himself and the two remaining Akkadians. He was halfway to the crate when a voice rang out.

"Captain Case."

He stilled, cocked his head in the direction of the voice.

"Captain. We have your man. Shall we make a trade?"

HOSTAGE

AKKADIAN WAREHOUSE
LEAVITT STATION

{Sir.} THE AKKADIAN commander stepped in front of his General, blocking him from following after Doctor Travis as she made her escape. *{We need to leave. It is not safe here.}*

Che stifled a flare of annoyance. He was not some doddering old crone who needed her hand held.

{Patience, Commander,} he sent in a sharp tone, then paused as a report came in. Smiling, he lifted a hand. *{All is well. I've received word; reinforcements have arrived.}*

The commander's head jerked back. *{How many?}*

{Two. And some leverage that will close the deal in our favor.}

The confusion in the commander's eyes would have been comical under less serious circumstances. As it was, Che merely nodded toward the warehouse door as it opened and two Akkadian agents entered, a man's body slung between them.

{Dead or alive?} the commander asked.

{Alive, just. He is one of the experimental samples, and is to

remain alive until our scientists can study and dissect him.}

Che didn't wait for the commander's response. He strolled out into the open, ignoring the man's aborted attempt to lay a restraining hand on him.

The fighting had ceased, his two ostovars dead, thanks to a man who, by all reports, could not possibly be alive.

"Captain Case," he called out, motioning the two agents to bring the body and set it beside the crate. "I have your man."

Silence was his only answer, but it was nothing more than Che expected.

"Captain. I thought you Geminate soldiers lived by a credo. What will Jack Campbell say when he hears you left him behind?"

He heard a muted gasp, but nothing else. He waited several long moment, then nodded to one of the agents.

"Very well, then. If your comrade means nothing to you, then he is no longer of any use to me..."

The agent raised his weapon and aimed it at the bloodied form of the man, slumped on the warehouse floor.

A deep-throated growl sounded behind Che. It was the last thing he heard before his world erupted in blood and chaos.

* * *

Micah let out a hoarse yell. He broke into a run, cursing, knowing he was too far away, and had no clean shot.

"Stop!" he roared, but his voice was drowned out by the ripping snarl of a panther in full attack.

Micah skidded to a halt as Pascal launched himself at the Akkadian holding the gun. At the same time, the head of the man next to him exploded in a spray of blood and brain matter.

He barely registered Thad's face looming behind the headless man as his body folded to the ground.

His attention was on the man and his bodyguard. He fired his CUSP as the man guarding the leader yanked him to one side.

His shot went wild, but it had given away his location. He dodged left as the man returned fire, and felt a sizzling sensation course through his body. He looked down, saw a small puck-like device at his feet, and realized he'd run into the same field generator that had disabled Sam's suit.

The whine of another shot cracked past his ear and he dove for a nearby stack of crates, shooting his CUSP without aiming, as covering fire to prevent the Akkadians from getting off another shot.

He caught a glimpse of Thad pulling Jonathan away from the battle just as the air stirred beside his ear, followed by a *crack*.

"NCIC!" a voice behind him called out. "Hands in the air, Case. That was a warning shot. The next one won't miss."

"You're making a mistake," Micah ground out. "I'm one of the good guys."

"Do it! Or I put a bullet in you."

The Akkadian cleared his throat. "I'd do what he says, Captain." The expression on the man's face held the look of someone who'd just called check and mate. He tilted his head and slid a meaningful glance to one side before meeting Micah's gaze once more.

Micah ripped his eyes from the Akkadian to where the man had indicated.

Sam stood frozen, her balaclava in the hand of a woman he'd seen somewhere before but couldn't place. A woman who held a knife to the doctor's neck.

Slowly, he lifted his hands.

"Toss the weapon to me, nice and easy," the voice behind him instructed. He did, and he heard footsteps approach, kicking the weapon further out of his reach.

Micah looked back at Sam and saw the woman easing her toward the back of the warehouse, toward a secret exit he'd already surmised must somehow be there.

He shot a desperate look toward where he last spotted Thad, but the Marine and Pascal were nowhere to be seen.

He glanced over at the two Akkadians, but they had disappeared.

"Dammit, they're getting away!" He started to turn, but a warning sound from the man behind him had him halting the movement.

"Look, whoever you are," he tried again, imbuing his voice with as much urgency as he could muster. "I'm working for Duncan Cutter. Check with the NSA office. He'll vouch for me."

"He's right, Agent Alvarez!"

Micah's head shot up as two women burst through the warehouse door, followed by a phalanx of Marines who began to systematically spread out. He realized with a start that the person who had spoken was Harper.

"We've been played, boss." The lanky woman beside the analyst said. "The deputy director's being taken into custody. We have a direct link to the NSA's office; they're standing by to speak with you to confirm Captain Case's innocence."

Micah heard the man beside him sigh.

"We good?" he asked the stranger behind him cautiously.

"Yeah, we're—"

Micah didn't wait for the man to finish.

"Private! With me!" he barked to the nearest Marine, and raced for the back of the warehouse.

He was met with a solid wall, but that didn't stop him.

"Start scanning," he ordered. "There's a door here, and we need to find it."

He turned as three more Marines joined them.

"I need you to get to the other side of this warehouse. One of the Akkadians took Doctor Samantha Travis hostage. We're getting her back, understood?"

"Sir, yes, sir!"

The Marines saluted crisply, then set off at a dead run.

"Got it, Captain!"

Micah turned at the exclamation, only to see an expression of frustration cross the Marine's face.

"Dammit," the private said. "It's not responding..."

A man Micah had never seen before stepped up beside the Marine.

"Here, let me," he said, holding up a small cylinder.

Micah recognized the voice; it was the man who had held him at gunpoint.

The Marine looked to Micah for direction. He nodded and the private stepped aside.

The man wasted no time; he slammed the cylinder against the seam and within seconds, a section of the wall slid free and Sam came tumbling through.

The stranger reached for her but Micah was faster.

"You okay?" he asked as he began a search for any obvious wounds.

She nodded, and pushed his hands away.

"I'm fine, just a little shaken."

She was staring at him oddly, her face drained of all color.

He pulled her closer, shielding her from the NCIC agent's sight. "You sure about that, doc?" he said quietly, and she nodded.

"That was the Akkadian assassin, wasn't it."

Her voice sounded strained. "She gave me a message for you."

Micah's head reared back. "What was it?"

Sam's eyes clouded with concern.

"She said to tell you, 'You're a hard man to kill, Captain Case.'"

SCIFS AND STONES

ST. CLAIR MILITARY HOSPITAL
HUMBOLT BASE, CERIBA
GEMINATE ALLIANCE (PROCYON B)

IT TOOK TWO days for things on Leavitt to be sorted out so the team could head home.

Jonathan was moved to the station's hospital, and that's where Sam ended up spending most of her time. She'd been the one to ask for the two-day delay, preferring Leavitt's medical facilities over *Wraith*'s portable surgi-suite. Jonathan hadn't protested.

Harper identified the woman who'd pulled the knife on Sam as the assassin Valenti had told them about. The news sent a jolt of anger and adrenaline through Micah that was so strong, it caused sympathetic reactions in his mirror-twin.

Unfortunately, that had occurred in the middle of a medical procedure. The spike in Jonathan's vitals had the surgical team confounded until Sam figured it out.

Micah would have been amused by how well Sam could channel a pissed-off drill instructor, had he not been the subject of her ire.

Neither the assassin nor the man Micah privately labeled the Mastermind had been found, despite the security sweeps ordered by Leavitt's stationmaster. No one was surprised by this; the station was simply too big, and their quarry too skilled, for any other outcome.

Harper had sent the feed from Micah's wire to Cutter and Valenti, and the colonel recognized her Akkadian counterpart instantly. The presence of such a high-ranking officer on Leavitt had been cause for some concern, resulting in an increase in station security at all gates, across inhabited space.

Cutter authorized one more Scharnhorst jump to bring *Wraith* to Ceriba. Upon their arrival, the Helios had been diverted to an unmarked hangar inside Humbolt Base and everyone aboard escorted to a secured wing at the base's military hospital.

Jonathan had been in and out of regen surgery, while Micah and the rest of the team had been kept busy writing after-action reports and answering questions.

After several days of this routine, it was finally coming to an end.

It's about time, too, Micah thought as he turned down the corridor that led to his other self's hospital room. *We're all one step away from going batshit crazy, cooped up like this.*

He came to a stop outside Jonathan's door, Joule padding quietly beside him. It was open, so he tapped lightly on its frame. His mirror-self was sitting up in bed, flexing a newly-attached arm.

Jonathan looked up at the sound and waved Micah in.

"Never thought I'd be happy to see someone else wearing my face," Micah joked, "but it's good to have you back."

He stepped into the room as he tapped his temple and added silently, *In here, too.*

Jonathan's mouth twisted into a half smile.

Since it usually means that one of us has been seriously injured or is in trouble, yeah, I'm down with not losing the connection again, he agreed.

He flipped the covers off and swung his new legs over the side of the bed. "You here to break me out of this joint? Glad you brought backup. Military nurses are sheer hell with the PT, bro."

Micah cracked a laugh and Joule padded over and snuffed lightly into Jonathan's palm.

{New hand?} the cat asked. *{Smells same as old one.}*

"It better smell the same. It's my DNA." Jonathan rubbed the panther behind one ear and she closed green eyes in momentary bliss.

He shot Micah a glance and spun a finger in the air with his free hand. "Hope they didn't mess up the spin-a-ma-business when they 3D printed it. I'd hate for it to wither away because it can't feed on regular molecules."

Micah grinned and dug into his pants pocket. "I have pills for that, if you want some."

"Nah, they'd just make me do PT for that, too, I'm sure," Jonathan grumbled, rising from the bed.

Outwardly, he knew the man had borne it in stoic silence. Inwardly, however...

Micah had caught an earful, a complete mental diatribe actually, as Jonathan raged against his tormentors during their morning sessions.

From what he'd been able to tell, it had been rough; the medical staff had put his mirror-twin's new limbs through their paces, and they'd ruthlessly forbidden him to cheat by using his lattice's augmented strength.

Micah studied his other self for any sign of weakness or fatigue, and was relieved he appeared to have none.

"Okay, brother. Get dressed. Cutter's ordered us in for a debrief."

While Jonathan shucked his hospital scrubs and donned a fresh pair of SDUs, Micah stepped back and reached into the corridor to snag the maglev chair he'd brought, just to tweak his other self.

As expected, Jonathan scowled.

"Oh *hell* no." He pointed to the chair. "Get that thing out of my sight."

"Doctor's orders." Micah tried to keep a straight face, but saw the moment his prank failed. He smirked and dodged the wadded-up scrubs Jonathan pitched in his direction.

Asshole.

Dumbass.

They stood there, grinning at each other for a minute before Jonathan slapped Micah on the shoulder and stepped past him into the hallway.

"C'mon, let's get out of here."

Getting out wasn't as easy as it seemed. This wing of St. Clair Med Center was locked down, high-level security access only.

He and Jonathan had been given strict orders not to be seen together outside of classified areas. That meant a two-seater tram with windows that had been obscured was awaiting them beside a freight lift.

If they were lucky, the thing would reach a whopping eight kilometers per hour.

Jonathan shook his head. "Welcome to the glamorous world of shadow ops territory, bro. Hang on; it's gonna be a wild ride."

* * *

This wasn't the first time Sam had been to NSA headquarters, but it was her first time inside a sensitive, compartmentalized information facility. It looked just like any other conference room she'd ever seen, save for the people inside.

She thanked the lieutenant who had escorted her, then turned as the door slid silently shut behind her. Harper was there, as were Severance and Colonel Valenti.

She hadn't expected to see the man who had hunted them across an entire star system, but Gabriel Alvarez was seated there, too.

"Agent," she greeted as she took the seat Harper had saved for her. She turned questioning eyes on the colonel, who held up a hand.

"The security director and Captains Case are on their way here," she said. "As is the chief warrant that assisted Agent Alvarez. We'll wait and do this just once."

As if summoned, the door slid open to admit Micah, Jonathan, and Joule.

Her hand itched for a bracer so that she could assess Jonathan's condition for herself. She stifled the unnecessary urge; she'd been following the medical reports and knew the grafts of the new limbs had gone without incident.

Chief Warrant Katie Hyer stepped in behind them, looking lost and a bit intimidated by her surroundings. Sam saw Alvarez wave her over, and the woman moved to sit beside him, relief on her features.

They sat in awkward silence, Harper tapping a stylus nervously against a plas sheet in front of her, before the door opened a final time.

"Thank you all for coming," Duncan Cutter said as he entered and took a seat across from Sam.

He shot her a quick smile before his gaze swept the faces of those assembled.

"You did a good job on Leavitt, all of you. You recovered the samples and kept them out of Akkadia's hands. Your two teams ended up finding each other and working together," one side of his mouth kicked up in an ironic half-smile as he gave Gabe and Hyer a nod, "despite the fact that an enemy agent purposely pitted you against one another. Well done. Well done, indeed."

Sam leaned forward. "What about the research? Did we stop them from getting it, too?"

Valenti shook her head. "We don't know."

Jonathan's brows drawing down in a frown. "We don't know? Didn't Janus talk?"

Valenti's mouth twisted in distaste. "He claims he destroyed every bit of research, just as the directive ordered."

"And you believe him?" Sam heard the incredulity in Harper's voice. "You told us yourself that Parliament never ordered the samples destroyed!"

"We have no choice," Duncan interposed. "Janus claims the order he received said otherwise. And Geminate law states you're innocent until proven guilty." He shot the analyst a pointed look.

"That's bullshit," Micah said, bracing his hands on the conference table. "I heard the sergeant in the morgue. Janus was the one who ordered me killed."

"And the one who sent the Marine fireteam after us," Sam added in a heated tone. "You know he's guilty, Duncan. We all do."

Alvarez stirred. "I think you'll find everyone at this table agrees with you, doctor. But we don't have enough on him to convict him."

He held up a hand as she began to protest.

"I'm a Navy criminal investigator; this is my job. Believe me when I say I want to nail his scrawny ass as much as you do. Addy Moran's still in recovery after that same sergeant who tried to kill Micah almost succeeded with her."

The man's expression looked murderous, and his jaw tightened before he forced the admission out. "But we can't."

Valenti pulled up a medical report. The images on the holo were graphic, showing evidence of Janus's torture.

"This, right here, is enough for a judge to throw the case out, if we tried to indict him. Even if we had direct evidence, any lawyer would argue that he was coerced. Janus is back in the civilian sector now, working with Brower Biologics. They've assigned their best corporate attorney to his case. And that attorney is very, very good."

Hyer waved to the holo, her eyes skittering away from the images. "Those could have been faked."

"It's not. But it also wasn't torture." Valenti nodded to the images in the holotank. "That was Junxun reconditioning."

"Reconditioning?" asked Jonathan, his brow creasing.

Valenti nodded at Alvarez, whose expression had just cleared as if the last piece of the puzzle had clicked into place.

"Janus went off the reservation on deGrasse," he said slowly, nodding to himself. "He wasn't supposed to kill Lee Stinton. That's what bothered me about the murder scene, and why Addy—Doctor Moran—said the evidence wasn't adding up."

Valenti nodded again. "Sociopathic behavior, from an asset who had slipped his leash."

She waved a hand through the holotank, the photo of the raised welts on Janus's back distorting as she did.

"He nearly got himself caught, too. We suspect that's why the Junxun sent an assassin along as his handler, to keep him in line."

"The same one who told me Micah was a hard man to kill," Sam realized with a jolt.

They sat, digesting this information for a moment before Hyer broke the silence.

"So, what now, ma'am, sirs?" she asked, her gaze roaming the table.

"You were all in Luyten's Star." Duncan took over the conversation, nodding to the colonel, who shut the holo and resumed her seat.

"It goes without saying that what you saw, what you experienced, is classified. Sensitive, compartmentalized, code-word classified."

"And that means…?" asked Sam.

"That, aside from the people in this room, you don't speak of this to anyone, ever," her uncle told her. "Not unless one of us tells you otherwise, using the correct code word that you, and only you, will know."

"And what about us?" Micah asked into the silence that fell after the colonel's announcement. His hand landed on the top of Joule's head. "And the animals who were experimented on?"

Cutter shot a quick, inscrutable look at Valenti.

"You present an interesting opportunity," he said, gaze moving between Micah and Jonathan. "All of the chiral pairs do."

* * *

Here it comes.

Micah didn't need Jonathan's warning to figure that out. He sat back, fixing Cutter with a stare.

"What kind of an opportunity?"

The NSA director chuckled at his jaundiced tone.

"You already know your unique ability to communicate gives you a significant tactical advantage. Consider the advantages your awareness of each other's location gives you. There's no need for stellar coordinate tracking. With one of you here and the other in the field, we'd know exactly where our asset is, at all times."

Micah exchanged a look with his twin.

"That... might have occurred to us, yeah."

"You wouldn't have to worry about signals getting jammed," Jonathan admitted. "It's basically a connection that's unhackable, untraceable, and completely secure."

Micah shot his counterpart a hard look. "At least until one of us loses consciousness and gets himself injured to the point of near death."

Cutter smiled. "You knew the risks when you joined the Navy," he said in a mild tone.

Sam held up a cautioning hand, shooting her uncle a glare.

"Tell me you're not thinking of doing this to anyone else. It's completely not worth it. Just think about what Stinton has done here, Duncan. Jonathan Micah Case was violated at the most basic, fundamental level—and without his permission."

Cutter shook his head. "I understand, and I stand by my statement that what was done here is an abomination. It will *not* be repeated, you have my word on that. But I'd like you to consider working for me." He turned from Micah and Jonathan, letting his gaze sweep the table. "All of you."

The chief warrant straightened in her seat. "*All* of us?"

Cutter leaned forward, making eye contact with each one in succession.

"Thanks to you, the research conducted on deGrasse was preserved. You provided key evidence we needed to prove the torus was destroyed by enemy hands."

He paused and tapped his forefinger on the table for emphasis. "That takes skill and initiative. I need that. The Alliance needs that."

Gabe shifted in his seat. "What are you proposing?"

Valenti leaned forward, her eyes intense. "We're putting together a new team. It will be part of the Special Reconnaissance Unit and will report to me. The captains will share the role of commander of the Shadow Recon transport. Captain Severance," she nodded to Thad, "will command a small Unit task force that will include the animals as needed."

Thad's mouth opened, to object, Micah was certain. Valenti's hand shot up to stay his protest.

"It won't start out as full time, at least not yet. You'll still have your existing jobs as your cover, with the exception of the captains, who will rotate in and out monthly as *Wraith*'s pilot."

It was Micah's turn to protest, but Jonathan beat him to it.

"What'll we be doing on our month off?"

"You'll be here on base, in a restricted area. Training, running surveillance at a distance, helping to organize the next operation." Cutter's eyes bored into him. "As far as the universe at large is concerned, there is only one Jonathan Micah Case. So when one of you is out there, the other one—"

"Is trapped in here, yeah, I got it," Micah said in disgust. "I feel caged already."

"Hold on, there, hoss."

Thad took that moment to finally break his silence. "We do essentially the same on any given day. You know the Navy's unspoken motto; it's the same as the Marines'. Hurry up and wait."

Thad turned and speared his superior with a look. "Beggin' your pardon, colonel, but are you intending to take *Wraith* out of operational rotation when these super-double-top-secret missions surface?"

A trace of amusement skated across Valenti's features. "No," she said. "We're commissioning a new ship. Her call sign is *Mirage*."

"*Wraith, Mirage.* I'm sensing a theme here," Thad muttered, eliciting a snort of amusement from Hyer. That earned her Valenti's attention.

"Chief, the report submitted by Agent Alvarez shows you've proven yourself to be a resourceful person. I could use someone like that." She nodded to Thad. "You're assigned to *Mirage* as her flight engineer. We'll work on filling out the roster as we begin functioning as a team and figure out the holes that need filling."

"You'll be assigned to sensitive and very special operations." Cutter nodded to Alvarez, Harper, and his niece. "You three will be on call, to help out as needed. I'm depending on you all. Something tells me the situation in Luyten's Star is far from settled."

* * *

Sam watched as the lift doors closed behind the rest of the newly-formed team before turning to face her uncle. They were the only ones left in the SCIF.

"You think Janus gave Akkadia the research, don't you," she said quietly, and he nodded.

"I can't afford not to think that way, and to prepare for the worst." His gaze intensified. "I know biochemistry's not your specialty, Sam, but I need you for this. You saved their lives; in essence, you cracked this case for us, back on deGrasse. Will you help?"

She tilted her head, staring back at him for a long,

considering moment, and then smiled. "Well, when you put it that way…"

Cutter smiled back, clapping his hand on her shoulder. "Thanks, Sam."

* * *

Sam kept turning the meeting over in her mind as she transited from Humbolt Base's orbiting platform back down the elevator to the planet's surface.

The weather in Ceriba's capitol city was warm and temperate, the breeze mild. The campus was less than two kilometers away from the spaceport, so she decided to walk. She exited onto St. Clair's sunny streets and turned in the direction of her offices at the university's Planck Center for Physics.

She'd taken only a handful of steps, her gaze on the seagulls spinning lazy arcs over the nearby wharf when someone suddenly rammed into her from the other direction. Apology on the tip of her tongue, she turned, just as hand gripped her roughly and a voice she recognized stopped her dead in her tracks.

"Careful where you're going, doctor."

The hand around her arm tightened cruelly and she jerked her gaze up, her eyes colliding with Clint Janus's icy green ones. His face creased into a cold, hard smile.

"You never know what kind of trouble you might run into on the streets. It would be a shame if you came to harm, wouldn't it?"

He shoved her arm away and turned, disappearing into the crowd. Sam couldn't escape the feeling Janus had just delivered a warning—not to her, but to the entire Geminate star nation.

She stood, staring futilely into the crowd, seeking any sign of the man. After several moments passed and it was clear he had truly disappeared, she turned and resumed her walk.

The sun shone just as blue-white and warm as it had earlier, but she couldn't suppress a shiver of apprehension. Something told her the threat that had surfaced a light-year away, around a different star was still very real, and more active than they could possibly know.

A word from LL Richman

Thank you for reading *The Chiral Agent*. I hope you enjoyed the ride. Please join me as I take Micah (and you) through new adventures in a series of fast paced science fiction thrillers.

The following pages contain a preview of the next book, *The Chiral Protocol*.

If you don't mind, please take a minute to leave a short review. Not only would it make this writer a very happy person, your review makes a real difference. It's an effective way you can help keep this series going. The more reviews, the easier it is for new readers to find these tales!

Connecting with you as a reader is also one of the most rewarding things about writing. I'd like to invite you to join my VIP Reader's Group at bit.ly/biogenesiswar. There, you'll receive the latest news about new books and deals, plus receive free content and exclusive excerpts from upcoming books.

PREVIEW:
THE CHIRAL PROTOCOL

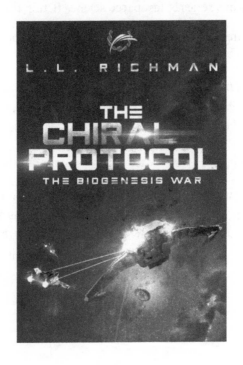

CHAPTER 1

LEAVITT STATION
PROCYON CALABI-YAU GATE, HELIOPAUSE
GEMINATE ALLIANCE (PROCYON SYSTEM)

THE AGENT WAS stretched prone along a section of catwalk, scope held steady against one eye, intent upon his target. The narrow steel walkway felt cool under his lightweight shirt, its raised crosshatch pattern cushioned somewhat by the duffel he'd propped under one forearm.

The catwalk was suspended several meters in the air, welded to the side of a massive arch that rose high above his head. It was one of many that curved upward to form the cathedral-like expanse of Leavitt Station's Concourse D. The catwalk's height provided the perfect vantage from which to observe the people passing below—and to wait for one in particular.

Leavitt was a smart choice for an anonymous meet. As the binary system's lone customs entry point, it was a crowded place, one that provided good cover. It held station just beyond the threshold of Procyon's Calabi-Yau gate.

The fortress was built to withstand the stresses placed on

local spacetime when the gate punched past the surrounding dimensions to access its pair-partner on the other end.

Operating costs, coupled with rigorous policing by the Alliance to safeguard its intellectual property, limited the number of gates built. There were currently only five in existence, each anchored at the heliopause of a stellar body.

Procyon's nearby neighbor, Luyten's Star, was the most recent gate constructed. It also held the distinction of being the one most distant from Sol.

From there, the gates marched inward toward the birthplace of humanity. Sirius was next, followed by Proxima Centauri, Alpha Centauri, and finally, the yellow star around which Earth orbited.

The agent cared little about such things. They got him to where he needed to be in order to do his job, and that was good enough for him. At the moment, that job was to find out why an Akkadian agent was on Leavitt, and to discover who he was there to meet.

Beneath him, ticketed passengers flowed past. They marched in predictable patterns, sparing quick glances at holodisplays spaced along the concourse. The screens served as navigational aids. They announced departure and arrival times, delays, and gate changes.

Citizens of his own Geminate Alliance mingled with visitors from the Coalition of Federated Worlds. Most had some form of luggage floating behind them or slung over a shoulder, filled with purchases bought in far-flung star systems. A few off-duty naval personnel hauled duffels on their way home for a bit of leave.

Savory smells from food vendors three levels beneath him tickled the agent's nose. Very little sound reached him, though, thanks to the structure's nanoacoustics. They worked in concert with metamaterials to dampen the impact such a large mass of humanity had on the cavernous facility. What should have been a loud din was transformed into a soft susurration that enveloped all who transited the concourse.

Given the number of travelers onstation, the agent was lucky to have spotted the Akkadian at all. The man certainly hadn't made it easy. The meet's location—and the agent was certain it was a meet—was obscured by a cloud of light-bending nano. It permeated the short side passageway that had been blocked by an 'under construction' sign, warning visitors to stay clear of the area.

When the Akkadian disappeared into the nanocloud, the agent had been forced to retrieve from his pack the scope he now held. The scope compensated for visual attenuation and allowed him to record the developing scene below.

The station's sound-dampening prevented the agent from recording audio, but he knew the Synthetic Intelligence program embedded in the base of his skull would be able to glean some of what was being said by dint of simple lip-reading. The agent would have to be content with what his SI could capture for now, until opportunity presented itself to detain and interrogate the man.

A woman materialized out of the shadows to stand beside the Akkadian. She looked like she might be a partner of sorts, or perhaps a bodyguard. Her head was on a swivel, her hand hovering near the butt of a weapon holstered by her side.

The two stood quietly, waiting. The agent waited, too.

It wasn't long before a third joined them. The agent's jaw tightened as he saw the uniform the man wore—that of a Geminate Alliance naval officer. The missing lieutenant, by the holopips on the collar.

Traitor, or spy? the agent wondered.

His gaze sharpened as the AWOL transport pilot handed a case over for the Akkadian to inspect.

Traitor, then.

The agent shifted to keep the case within the scope's sights as the Akkadian propped it against a nearby wall and lifted the lid. The man's shoulder partially obscured the case's contents, and the agent moved once more to get a better view.

For one brief moment, he could clearly see the hazard icon

emblazoned on the three sealed metal cylinders resting within. He readjusted the scope to try to capture the serial numbers embedded in the icons, but a hand obscured them as the lid closed. What he'd managed to capture would have to do.

The agent used his neural wire to interface with the Synthetic Intelligence in his skull, ordering it to initiate a data upload to the Special Reconnaissance Unit's headquarters element, back on Ceriba.

The wire's evanescent wave nanocircuitry connected him directly to the Ford-Svaiter node held in orbit around Leavitt by a Starshot buoy. It was one of many such buoys seeded throughout the Procyon binary system. Their placement allowed for near real-time communication to anyone, anywhere within the system.

Not that the agent understood how it all worked. He couldn't care less about quantum tunneling, or photons as evanescent waves, nor how they allowed for instantaneous transfer of information. It was enough to know that his encrypted transmission would be intercepted at the other end by people who would know what to do with the information he held.

Sudden action through the scope had the agent readjusting his focal length once more. He caught a brilliant flare of light, indicating the edge of a plasma blade. The Akkadian had pulled a weapon on the traitor. He slashed, and the knife bit deep into the pilot's throat.

The agent had seen enough. He lowered the scope, intent on breaking it down and storing it back in its case, when his own internal alarm went off.

He hadn't registered the woman's absence. He'd been so focused on the contents of the small case the courier was handing over that he'd missed her sudden head turn, the sharp look she shot his way as her eyes searched the truss overhead. Had he seen, he might have guessed the truth—that light had reflected off his scope's optics, drawing her attention.

It was a rookie mistake.

A soft scraping alerted him that he was no longer alone on the catwalk. He dropped the scope and rolled, reaching for his weapon just as he felt an impact against the base of his head, below his right ear. His skull, reinforced with a stacked lattice of single-layer magic-angle carbyne, or MAC, was virtually impenetrable, although the momentum transferred by the impact hurt and it bled like hell.

His hand scrabbled for the weapon as he kicked out, noting as he did so that his transmission had been cut off. Whatever he'd been hit with must have had a suppression web attached to it.

His foot met air as the Akkadian woman sidestepped. He flung the duffel he'd been using to prop the scope at her head, and twisted, reaching to reacquire his weapon.

A soft click and a whoosh sounded as he did. His brain catalogued the sound as that of a pressurized cartridge powering a flechette pistol at the same time searing pain traced its way across his lower back and up through his bicep.

His arm flopped uselessly beside him, victim of the vaned, pointed-steel projectiles the weapon had fired. A nauseating agony settled where his kidney had once been before the nano reserves controlled by his SI implant began triaging his body. Blessed numbness descended as pain-blocking medication was pumped into his system.

The stimulant that automatically triggered on the heels of the anesthetic was intended to provide the necessary boost to help him evade his opponent and get to safety. It might have been effective had another round of the tiny metal arrows not torn through his back.

His mind distantly registered that the pool of warmth spreading beneath him was his own blood. He commanded his body to move—and realized he was paralyzed.

His head rolled to one side, his cheek coming to rest against the cold deck of the catwalk, the woman's form blurring as he blinked away the blood dripping into his eye. She crouched beside him, nudging him with the barrel of her weapon as if annoyed that he was taking so long to die.

The agent's SI flashed a warning onto his retina that his wounds required immediate intervention. He wheezed a laugh at the obviousness of that statement. Like he could do anything about it at the moment.

The woman stood, holstered her weapon, and turned to walk away. As her steps receded from his hearing, he heard the *plink* of something dropping nearby, but could not turn his head to see what it was.

A deep chill settled into his core, and he found his mind wandering. An image of his wife and son drifted across his consciousness, a vague remorse coloring his thoughts.

His eyelids fluttered closed, his body succumbing to the injuries inflicted. As he drew his last breath, a single tear slipped from the corner of one eye, trailing across his cheek and dripping onto the catwalk to mingle with the ever-widening pool of blood.

CHAPTER 2

Citizen General Che Josza hadn't seen the inside of the State Security building in months. Eight and a half, to be exact.

The last time he'd walked its halls, he'd been brought before the minister of state security, Rin Zhou Enlai, to explain his failure to acquire the Alliance materials stolen from Luyten's Star. The minister had allowed him to keep his position as the leader of the Junxun, but had reduced his rank from general first-class to general third-class.

The demotion made his job difficult, doubly so since his humiliation was public record. Anyone in the Junxun could access it.

The Junxun, or military training regimen, was compulsory for all citizens. Its curriculum was Che's creation. All Akkadians of age were required to spend the first year of their adult lives under his tutelage. It was a crucible of indoctrination, a way to forge young minds and bodies into the perfect weapons the State could wield.

Che had a talent for finding the most gifted among them, but his skills had been sorely tested in recent months.

His students did not know of his sins; they only knew he'd been demoted. Some took this to mean he was unworthy, as life had not yet tempered the hubris of their youth. They'd not faced their first real trial, did not understand that sometimes a battle was unwinnable. These were the ones who tried him and found him wanting.

It was difficult indeed to refine the edge of the carbyne blade when the blade itself refused to cooperate.

Rin Zhou knew this, of course. It was part of the punishment she had meted out. He thought he'd accepted it with stoic equanimity, gratitude even. His behavior since that time had been exemplary. He'd carefully avoided the spotlight, toed the line, rendered his obeisance with dignity and respect. Or so he thought.

He strode down the cold, stark corridors, keeping pace with the guard sent to escort him to the minister's chambers. The escort symbolized another privilege that had been stripped from him during his demotion, as only generals first-class were granted clearance to enter the State Security Building unescorted.

Outwardly, his countenance remained impassive. Inwardly, his mind worked feverishly to figure out what he'd done, where he'd gone wrong.

He could think of nothing.

Che's thoughts drifted to his small holdings, just outside Central Prefecture—all that remained of his fortunes since his fall from grace. He wondered if he'd be returning to his home, or if that, too, would be stripped from him.

Perhaps this time, his luck had finally run out.

What luck? he asked himself bitterly. *Surely what little I had abandoned me on that suns-cursed station in Procyon nine months ago.*

The imperialist bastards who ran the Geminate Alliance had

waged an aggressive campaign against the small tactical team he'd led that day.

It should have been a simple extraction. An in-and-out job. Retrieve a valuable sample case filled with research material carefully culled from deGrasse torus. Bring it back to Akkadia, where it would be used to further the empire's goals.

His decision to oversee the operation personally was one he deeply regretted. Had he stayed behind on Eridu, he could have distanced himself from the operation, cast blame upon the ones who led in his stead. But this was a high-profile case, one that held the minister's complete attention.

He'd rolled the dice, thinking it was a sure bet. He'd lost. The stolen material had slipped through his fingers, and he'd been left to bear the burden of responsibility.

Part of him had been surprised to come out the other end with his life. Another part recognized that Rin Zhou was harsh, but fair—more so than any of her predecessors he'd worked with during his career. She knew, as well as he, that the weak link in the operation had been the sleeper agent they'd activated.

Clint Janus was both a narcissist and a sociopath, and just a little bit unhinged. The man had nearly cost Che his very best agent, Dacina Zian, his Fierce Dagger.

The assassin he'd assigned to Janus as his handler was very nearly lost to him—and for what? An egocentric scientist whose goals only aligned with his motherland when he found it convenient.

Che allowed a small, grim smile to play about his lips. His Dacina had taken care of that last. She'd run Janus through a deep indoctrination program during their return voyage. The man would not soon slip his leash.

Small comfort, at this point. His mind returned to his current problems and he wondered anew why he still lived.

Likely, she thinks death would be too much of a mercy, he thought with asperity. Living with shame in Akkadian culture, to lose face… Death was preferable.

His musings crashed to an abrupt halt as they stopped before the minister's office suite. The Synthetic Intelligence embedded in his skull proffered his security token to the SI that stood guard over Rin Zhou's chambers. Once accepted, the doors slid silently open.

The guard retreated, leaving Che alone to face his minister.

His pulse thundered in his ears, testament to the tenuous nature of the situation. He stepped forward, the doors sliding shut behind him.

The minister stood before a floor-to-ceiling expanse of clearsteel windows, looking out over the hazy skyline. Beyond her, Che could just make out the silver ribbon of the planet's main space elevator glinting in the distance.

Rin Zhou looked up as he halted just inside the entrance. With an impatient wave of her hand, she motioned him forward.

He found his feet responding instinctively to the unspoken demand. "Minister," he murmured, head bowed.

"Citizen General," she said. "Your premier has need of your services once more."

He looked up at that. His surprise must have shown; it brought unexpected humor to her eyes.

Lips twitching slightly in amusement, she asked, "Not what you anticipated?"

Che chose to be candid. "No, Citizen Minister. Given my circumstances...." He let his voice trail off, and she nodded her understanding.

Rin Zhou waved him to a low table where the setting for a ritual pour had already been laid. He settled into the cushion she indicated and waited for her to join him. To his utter shock, she picked up the steaming carafe of water and began the service herself.

"I...." His voice trailed off.

They were in uncharted territory.

He swallowed, his gaze locked on her hand as it wove gently over the freshly-ground coffee, swirling the water in smooth arcs. He tried again. "Citizen Minister, please. Allow me." His lifted hand froze as she brought her free hand up sharply.

"Is it not true that all Akkadians are equal?"

"I—Yes, but...."

How does one refute the party line to one's superior? Everyone knew some were more 'equal' than others. There would always be the need for leadership, and yet—

"As Minister of State Security, *all* Akkadians are in my charge," Rin Zhou continued, tone mild. Her eyes cut sharply to meet his. "Even those who have fallen and are working to atone."

He inclined his head respectfully.

There was nothing he could say to that, nothing at all.

Rin Zhou finished the ritual pour and sank gracefully into the cushion across from him. He waited for her to pick up her own cup, hand waving gently across its surface to release its aroma. It was customary to inhale prior to the first sip; it prepared the mind to properly appreciate the drink.

He followed suit, his hand bringing the coffee's bouquet wafting to him. He breathed the bean, his hand lifting the cup.

"You said the premier has need of me," he began carefully, after his first swallow. "How may I be of service, beyond the training of the Junxun?"

Rin Zhou sipped thoughtfully, taking her time before she replied. Her mouth moved, tongue rolling the coffee around to experience its full flavor profile before swallowing. When her words came, they weren't an answer to his question. Instead, they posed another, more disturbing one.

"How far would you go, Che Josza, to restore your honor, I wonder?" she mused. "Would you embark upon an unsanctioned mission, one the premier would surely disavow, should news of it reach his ears?"

Che's hand stilled, cup halfway to his lips. Very carefully, he set the cup back down. His hand smoothed the fine linen serviette lying to one side of the ritual place setting, his mind racing.

The minister was well aware of his service record. She knew Che was an exceptional tactician. The number of complex, high-risk missions he'd successfully completed on the people's behalf were known only to a select few, due to their sensitivity.

The recent, more public failure that had forced his demotion hadn't been his fault, and yet he'd been made scapegoat. It had been necessary at the time to lay the blame at his feet, for to cast the blame on the one truly responsible would have meant burning two very high-value assets embedded within the Geminate government, and the cost had been deemed too high.

It was Che who had ended up paying the price. Was the minister's question, then, a way by which he might publicly 'redeem' himself, and reattain that which he had lost?

"I would take on any task, regardless of its difficulty, if it served the people." His words came slowly as he measured each one out. "My life is Akkadia's. It would be an honor to spend it in her service, Citizen Minister. I would hope you know that."

Rin Zhou nodded, and he saw satisfaction blazing in her eyes. "Good," she said, the flat of her free hand coming down to slap sharply against the table's surface.

The action triggered a series of preset functions the room's Synthetic Intelligence was programmed to execute. Che suddenly found himself cut off from both the planetary net and the encrypted people's military subnet.

They were alone, he and the minister, encased in a provisional SCIF.

The silence, as it was said, was deafening. Sensitive, Compartmentalized Information Facilities were invoked only in the handling of extremely classified material.

What am I getting myself into? The thought flitted through his head as she began to speak.

"As you know, the premier is closing in on his two

hundredth birth date."

She lapsed into silence, one brow raised expectantly.

Che considered her words, turning over what he knew of the premier. This was the man who had wrested control from the floundering of the colony's original settlers when it had become clear that the financial impact of the Calabi-Yau gates was decimating Eridu's economy.

The man had singlehandedly forced Akkadia into a new world order. He'd marshaled the disenfranchised, the desperate, and the homeless into an army, overthrown those who held office, and established martial law.

The new Akkadia was a world where everyone was equal and each citizen worked toward the betterment of the colony—or they were quietly disappeared. Only the strong survived; the premier hammered that into the minds of impressionable youth, along with the maxim that hard work and service to the homeland were what made life sweet.

The premier's brute force approach had been harsh, but the planet had survived. More, the military under the premier's guidance had become aggressive and expansionist, appropriating privately held business concerns that worked nearby asteroid mines. The monies that came from such ventures funded the struggling colony until Eridu's infrastructure adjusted to the totalitarian regime the premier had put into place.

His advanced age was something no one ever spoke about openly, but there had been much speculation about who would succeed him, and when. He had a daughter, Yachi. The woman cut her teeth on statesmanship, learning the art of political warfare at her father's knee. Everyone knew she was destined to be her father's successor, next in line for the premiership, but had assumed a peaceful transfer of power would ensue at some point.

Che jerked his head back, eyes narrowing. "Yachi will challenge?"

Rin Zhou shook her head slowly. "There will be no

challenge," she said slowly. "There is another whose aspirations eclipse hers."

Che's brows drew down. "Who?"

"The ministry has already intercepted two assassins who were foolhardy enough to accept a contract for the premier's life." Rin Zhou gestured to his cup as she lifted her own. "We interrogated them. It turns out they had been hired by Asher Dent."

Che rocked back on his cushion in surprise. "Your predecessor's son."

Rin Zhou nodded.

"But Dent chose to run for Akkadia's seat in the Coalition's General Assembly. He has power, influence."

The minister nodded again. "That does not negate a bid for premier."

"He's the minority leader for the Coalition of Worlds. He's made no secret of his ambition. His stated goal has always been to become council president."

Rin Zhou smiled. It did not reach her eyes. "His *stated* goal, yes."

Che gestured ineffectually with one hand. "Why would he try for the premiership when he could hold sway over far more than just one world? Council president would bring him much greater influence than Akkadian premier."

Leaning forward, the minister clasped her hands around her steaming cup. "He doesn't see it that way, I'm told. Power within the council is a much different thing than the authority of the premiership. Here, on this planet, the premier's word is absolute. The General Assembly, on the other hand, was established with a set of checks and balances. The president's position can be overruled, his decisions questioned."

Reluctant understanding flared.

"I see," Che murmured. "You're right, of course. But what does any of this have to do with me?"

"Power has always been something Asher sought. He craves it. It was seared into his brain, branded there by his parent at a very early age." Rin Zhou lifted her coffee's stir stick and began to draw it through the hot liquid in a lazy figure-eight. "In order to ensure Yachi inherits her father's position, we must act preemptively."

"You intend to back her?"

Rin Zhou looked directly into his eyes. "She will need a great deal of guidance. Advisors she can trust."

Everything came into focus with sudden clarity. Rin Zhou wasn't concerned about preserving Yachi's rightful place; she intended to make the woman her puppet, to rule from the shadows.

The only question now was, would Che back Rin Zhou's power play, or not?

Che sipped at his drink as he thought through everything he'd been told. It was no secret that Rin Zhou had a hand in ousting the previous minister of state security. If Dent were to succeed in his bid for premier, Rin Zhou's career—most likely her life—would be measured in days, if not hours.

For better or worse, Che's own career was closely tied to that of Rin Zhou. If she went down, he certainly would, too.

"What do you propose?" he asked.

Something shifted in Rin Zhou's expression, her eyes gleaming in the soft glow of her office's muted light. It caused the hair on the back of Che's neck to stand on end.

"An operation that will assure Akkadia's military supremacy while dealing our sister colonies a crippling blow," she stated. "A success of such magnitude, orchestrated by the premier's daughter, would make Yachi untouchable."

And there it was. By crediting Yachi with the success, Rin Zhou was cementing her position within her fledging regime, all but assuring her own career path.

On its heels came a troubling thought.

But am I witnessing history repeat itself?

Asher Dent's own father, the man who'd held the office prior to Rin Zhou, had thought to attempt an equally daring gambit. He'd failed, and the woman before him had been instrumental in his removal from office. And yet....

"What kind of operation?" he found himself asking.

"The Alliance has been experimenting with the samples brought back from Luyten's Star. I have a team working to acquire them."

Che nodded, unsurprised. He waited while Rin Zhou took another sip. When she didn't continue, he asked, "What do you intend to do with the samples, Minister?"

"I intend for *you* to put them to good use. Make me a weapon. Conscript scientists, conduct experiments to optimize its tactical effectiveness. Document their work. It must be swift, and it must be deadly."

Che jerked his head in a nod of obeisance, unable to do more at the moment. His mind was swimming. He had so many questions, all vying inside his head to be the first posed, but he waited to see what else she would say.

"One thing." Rin Zhou's words had him raising his brows in silent question.

"If we are to defeat Asher, we must proceed with great caution. He has informants everywhere. No whisper of this can reach him."

Che considered this. It would be difficult indeed to bury such an operation while using Akkadian resources. Even within the ranks of the Junxun, his own formidable army, there was a robustly healthy rumor mill. There was no way to guarantee he could keep it from them, and still make use of their vast resources.

He nodded slowly, thoughtfully. "You're saying this would have to be completely off the books."

Rin Zhou's gaze never left his face. "A black operation, yes. Select a handful of your most skilled warriors, but be very careful who you choose. You must be very sure they can be trusted. Outside of those people, the rest must be sourced from outside Akkadia. Nothing of this operation can be traced back to this ministry."

They sat in silence for long minutes, Che turning the

problem over in his head. "I'll need to secure a laboratory for the research and experimentation," he murmured.

Rin Zhou lowered her chin. "It cannot be housed within Akkadia's borders."

Che inclined his head, acknowledging that truth.

"There is a place," he murmured finally. "An abandoned laboratory, deep in the dust belt of Proxima Centauri." He knew his eyes held warning as he added, "Even though it is several dozen AU from Shang, it's still squarely within An-Yang territory."

"Then I suppose anyone using that facility would need to proceed with care to ensure they are not discovered," she said mildly.

She set her cup aside and rose in one smooth motion. She waited for Che to join her before continuing.

"You have fifteen days. Once you have achieved your objective, contact me. I will make sure arrangements on this end are ready."

He paused before braving a final question. "Fifteen days, Citizen Minister?"

Rin Zhou's look froze him in place. "You have your orders. I trust you can meet the deadline without any problem?" Her tone held censure.

"Of course, Minister," he hastened to reply. "I live to serve."

* * *

Rin Zhou stood motionless until the doors slid shut behind Che Josza. She ordered the SI inside her head to bring up the security feed as she moved to her desk.

She watched as Che was escorted from the State Security grounds. The citizen general's demeanor was impeccably proper, rendering the required salute to a former peer, despite the other man's subtle rebuff.

Her mouth tightened. She understood better than most what necessitated the rebuff; none who served the premier dared to be friendly with those whose names were under a cloud, for fear the association might reflect poorly on their own careers.

Rin Zhou hated that she'd had to demote Che, one of her most brilliant and capable generals, and yet the situation had dictated no less. It was why she'd chosen him for this particular operation. Che had always done as ordered.

Given his current situation, he was more motivated than most. The opportunity to redeem himself was one he would not refuse.

He would deliver the weaponized material, meet the deadline. And fifteen days from now....

She dismissed the feed as Che disappeared into the crowded streets below, and returned her attention to the intelligence report that had put today's events in motion.

Coalition Defense Summit, October fifteenth. Host: Geminate Alliance, Hawking Habitat.

Her eyes scanned the list of high-ranking military and intelligence personnel that would be attending. They were all key people from powerful governments, including one Asher Dent.

A strike at that event would not just eliminate her own personal threat. It would bring the rest of the settled worlds to their knees.

CHAPTER 3

NATIONAL SECURITY AGENCY
ST. CLAIR TOWNSHIP, CERIBA
MYR (PROCYON B)
GEMINATE ALLIANCE

THE PLAYBACK OF the feed sent by the agent on Leavitt Station ended abruptly.

Duncan Cutter, director of the Alliance's National Security Agency, turned from the holoscreen to regard the woman seated across from him. They were in a Sensitive, Compartmentalized Information Facility—a SCIF—beneath Parliament House.

"Pilot's body was found. No trace of the Akkadians." Colonel Tala Valenti turned from the frozen image on the holo to meet his eyes as she added, "Our agent's been found, too."

The economic spate of words was classic Valenti. The woman had a lean, muscled warrior's build, as befit the head of the Special Reconnaissance Unit.

"Alive?"

The question came from the only other person in the room. Admiral Amara Toland led the Navy's Advanced Research Agency. Her presence here was at Valenti's request.

The colonel's lips compressed into a thin, hard line. "No," she told Toland.

"Who was it? Ladue?" Duncan asked.

Valenti nodded.

Duncan's jaw tightened. Ladue was one of Valenti's best men, highly skilled at technical surveillance and sensitive site infiltration. He'd supplied the images they had just seen, of the pilot passing the vials to a known enemy.

"He was a good agent." Duncan scraped his hand across the stubble lining his jaw and swore softly. "I'll get in touch with his family. Damn, but I hate those conversations."

"He died under my command." Normally taciturn, Valenti's voice held rare emotion. "I can do it."

He shook his head, giving her a brief, non-smile.

"I know you can, and I appreciate the offer. It's ultimately my responsibility, though." He nodded toward the frozen image on the screen. "How did this happen?"

"The pilot, or Ladue?" Valenti asked.

Cutter lifted a hand. "Either. Both."

Valenti's eyes returned to the screen. "Pilot was listed AWOL a week ago."

"Akkadian asset?" Duncan asked sharply.

It was Toland who answered. Shaking her head, she said, "I don't think so. He had a known gambling problem, and I think they blackmailed him into it. He certainly paid for his sins," she added, with a glance toward the frozen image of the dead body, its throat slit.

"And Ladue?" Duncan's gaze shifted from Toland to Valenti.

The colonel nodded to the SCIF's holodisplay. "Takeko," she ordered, "display file Leavitt Three-Five."

Duncan kept his expression neutral as Valenti addressed the Synthetic Intelligence implanted inside her head. He wasn't entirely comfortable with the concept of SIs being embedded within active military personnel.

"We'll wall the SI off," the Navy's chief scientist had assured the intelligence subcommittee when the initiative was first

proposed. *"Think of it as being confined to a miniature SCIF inside the brain."*

The argument was a persuasive one.

Duncan sent a quick glance around the secured room where they sat. This particular SCIF was not only secure, it was fortified. A foreign agency would have to overcome insurmountable obstacles to breach it.

The analogy resonated with the subcommittee, and they'd approved limited deployment within the Alliance's defense command. The SI implants had been green-lighted just a handful of weeks ago. Colonel Valenti was one of the program's first recipients.

{Image Leavitt Three-Five.} Valenti's SI projected its voice over the SCIF's audio feed, and the holoscreen lit up once more.

A different visual appeared on the display, this one, with the watermark of NCIC, the Navy's Criminal Investigation Command.

{This was taken today by NCIC investigators, at oh-two-forty-seven, local time. Leavitt Station, concourse D.}

All thoughts of SCIFs and SIs fled when Duncan realized what he was looking at. The camera panned across the downed agent's slumped form, his slack hand resting beside a partially disassembled sniper's scope.

The recording changed angles, and suddenly, Duncan was looking at the crosshatched surface of the catwalk where Ladue's body lay. He could see a pool of reddish-brown staining its surface.

Ladue's blood.

Beside it was a small, round object. Valenti reached out, and with a gesture, highlighted it. That portion of the image sprang forward, revealing the object in greater detail.

An assassin's bead.

"They found him," Duncan stated heavily.

"It would seem so."

Valenti did something more with the display, and the feed

reverted back to what Ladue had sent to NSA headquarters. She scrubbed through it until she came to a closeup of the case held in the pilot's hand.

"I suppose it's too much to hope there was nothing of value in those metal cylinders," Duncan murmured. "What did they steal?"

Toland took up the narrative. "Those cylinders are protective vaults. Each one holds a glass vial with material from the CID. They were reported missing earlier today."

Her gaze shifted from the case and its contents back to Duncan. Her expression was grave. "Those vials belong to Major Moran."

Duncan felt the blood drain from his face. His eyes jumped back to the frozen visual. "Project Rufus?" he asked.

"Yes," Toland confirmed. "Those vials contain chiral material, held in suspension."

Duncan whispered a low curse. *Chiral material.*

Few outside those involved in the first exploratory mission to Luyten's Star knew what had been found there. The star system annexed by the Alliance a few years earlier was uninhabited and boasted a lone planet.

Vermilion was a super-earth, orbiting the red dwarf in a 3:2 resonance just inside its goldilocks zone. It also harbored a secret so shocking, the Alliance had immediately interdicted the system.

That secret was naturally occurring chiral life.

The concept of chirality dated back to pre-diaspora Earth, when scientists first realized that the building blocks of life all had a certain molecular structure. Each molecule had a mirror-image twin, but just as a right-handed glove would not fit on a person's left hand, none of these mirror-image molecules could sustain life.

The preference biology had for one 'handedness' over another became known as chirality, based on the ancient Greek word *kheir*, meaning 'hand'. The phenomenon was present in every living organism.

In the twenty-first century, chiral molecules were found in interstellar space. Humanity expanded into the solar system, and their exploration of other worlds revealed the same thing: native organisms everywhere all shared the predilection for left-handed life.

By then, it was understood that cosmic rays interacting with a planet's atmosphere induced a magnetic polarization in early developing biological organisms, forcing the dominance of left-handed life. Still, scientists hoped to one day stumble upon a sector of space that had been spared the influence.

The red dwarf that was Luyten's Star proved to be just such a breeding ground. The star had a history of emitting circularly polarized flares.

The right-handed photons that bombarded the system's lone habitable planet influenced its developing life in much the same way cosmic rays had done elsewhere in the explored galaxy. They created chiral life.

Such a discovery had rocked the scientists at the Navy's Advanced Research Agency, and they had rushed to study the world teeming with mirror organisms.

 DeGrasse torus, one of three black-site research stations under NARA's umbrella, had been relocated to Vermilion so that Geminate scientists could study it. Amara Toland, a scientist in her own right who held degrees in both condensed matter and materials physics, commanded all three.

The torus had been subsequently destroyed by an Akkadian agent, virtually all hands lost. The admiral had been away from the torus at the time; it was the only reason she was still alive. Duncan knew survivor's guilt still haunted her.

"How did this happen?" he asked quietly.

"The chiral material was on its way from our facility in Montpelier to the Hawking Habitat for a series of planned experiments," Toland said. "It never arrived."

Montpelier was one of the research centers under the admiral's command. This one, unlike deGrasse, was planet-bound, a few hundred kilometers away from their current location.

"Go on."

"The vials were logged out of Level Two containment three days ago. They were supposed to arrive on Hawking today." Her voice turned grim. "Someone swapped packages."

Duncan ripped his gaze from the vials resting inside the case to spear Valenti with a look. "Have you notified the team?"

He knew he didn't need to clarify which team. There was really only one capable of handling a chiral situation, and they all knew it.

Duncan had given Valenti carte blanche when he'd ordered her to create Task Force Blue. She'd assigned Captain Thad Severance to lead it, and had stolen Gabriel Alvarez from NCIC to be his second. Severance had brought along two people from his former recon unit to complete the fire team. Boone was TF Blue's sniper, and Asha, its medic.

In addition, rather than rely on the Navy's Shadow Recon teams to ferry the task force to and from its covert missions, Valenti had retained Jonathan and Micah Case for the job. After a bit of negotiating with Major Snell, the man in charge of Shadow Recon, they'd brought in the remainder of the flight crew as well: Will, Nina, and Yuki filled the roles of crew chief, gunner, and copilot, respectively.

She nodded in response to his question. "Ladue's intel came in at about the same time the admiral contacted me," the colonel said with a nod toward Toland. "I sent Captain Severance a recall message right after. He should be getting it shortly."

"Getting it shortly?" Duncan repeated, feeling a bit confused. "I don't recall them being on an active mission right now."

She shook her head. "They're not. Thad brought Micah and the rest of the crew planetside."

He felt his brows rise. "I can't think of many places where they'd be unreachable here on Ceriba," he murmured, "and I know for a fact you have priority override on their wires."

"I do." Valenti's response was short and to the point. Her next words, however, were a bit mystifying. "Let's just say things are getting a bit hot where they're at right now."

Start the next adventure now, with *The Chiral Protocol*....

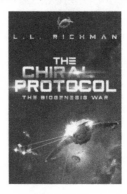

Become a VIP Reader

VIP Reader's Group members get advance cover reveals, exclusive scenes from the cutting room floor, and views from the cockpit. And cats, because the feline overlords insist. Sign up at bit.ly/biogenesiswar.

TERMINOLOGY

ActiveFiber Coating – a coating used to layer the bulkheads of ships and space stations. It has self-healing properties, similar to self-cleaning fabrics used for shipsuits. The fiber is infused with nanobots, which can absorb contaminants within an area, break it down into its constituent parts, and reuse the material.

Branes – can be envisioned as a type of indentation within the Bulk. The universe in which we live is an example of a brane.

The Bulk – the many layers, or branes, that comprise hyperspace, the area of extradimensional space outside the dimension our universe inhabits.

Calabi-Yau Gate – This method of folding space is powered by siphoning dark matter out of a Ricci-flat manifold. The matter is then converted into Casimir energy, which is then used to bend the compactified branes stacked within the Bulk, allowing for instantaneous travel from one location in normal spacetime to another, regardless of distance. The amount of Casimir energy differs, based on the amount and direction of the bend.

Colloid Nano – Colloids are extremely tiny insoluble particles that are so light, they remain suspended in air. When grafted onto nano, colloid nano clouds can be released.

Thanks to brownian motion, the force of the particles in the air around them is greater than the force of gravity attempting to pull them down, therefore they float and are susceptible to the activity of air currents.

Colloidene Nano – A colloidene is made from a colloid particle, but formed just like single-layer graphene. Patterned in a honeycomb lattice, it employs some of the click-assembly techniques used in chemistry.

Pre-loaded common codes, or 'bricks', give nano creation a jump-start. The result is a nanobot, programmed to rapidly alter existing nano to whatever the person controlling it needs it to be.

DBCs – A digital-to-biological converter capable of printing complex, synthetic biological material from detailed molecular diagrams transmitted to it.

DUET Wires (aka "the wire") – DUET is a little-used acronym for communication nanocircuitry implanted in the brain.

DUET stands for Direct Uplink Evanescent Telecom. Much to the dismay of the corporation that invented the tech, that name never took hold. Commonly known simply as 'the wire,' a DUET implant must wait until the brain has reached certain a development level.

A web of nanoscale tendrils is deployed at critical spaces within the brain: information inputs at dendrites, and data outputs at synaptic terminals.

Evanescent (E-V) Nanocircuitry – E-V nanocircuitry is the foundation upon which the DUET system was launched. The core communication unit embedded in the brain makes use of the optical phenomenon of evanescent modes with imaginary wave numbers and a poynting vector of zero to achieve the mathematical equivalent of quantum tunneling for the instantaneous transmission of information.

Ford-Svaiter nodes – F-S nodes use the concept of focusing vacuum fluctuations with parabolic mirrors to induce a quantized field wherein evanescent nanocircuitry can be used to establish instantaneous communication. An F-S node is encased inside a Starshot Buoy. Buoys are seeded throughout a star system in a pattern known as the Starshot Constellation. All inhabited star systems have deployed Constellations.

INS, Interstellar Navigation System – The INS uses pulsars as navigation beacons to generate an interstellar positioning system.

MAC –Magic-Angle Carbyne is the strongest material known in the 25th century. It is fashioned from two single-layer, honeycomb lattices of carbyne, twisted so that they sit at a specific angle relative to one another. MAC is two times stronger than graphene or carbon nanotubes.

MXene – A high-temperature 2D laminar molybdenum carbide material that functions as an ultrafast sieve. Alliance Navy ships are coated in the material. When in motion, the material pulls $H(0)$, ultra-dense hydrogen that dark matter is made of, from the interstellar medium for use as fuel. The $H(0)$ is stored in CNT-reinforced receptacles lining the ship's hull.

No-wake zones – The biggest reason for a no-wake-zone around a space station is because of the amount of neutron radiation generated by a ship's fission drive. A minimal dose of 4.4 GW of neutrons will deliver a lethal dose at half a kilometer in 1/5 of a second. As a result, all ships are manufactured with very thick, effective anti-radiation shadow shields. As a precaution, all ships must maintain mandatory separation when operating fusion drives.

Ricci-flat manifold – a special curvature of space found in the Bulk, also known as hyperspace.

Scharnhorst Drive – Interstellar drive that generates a Casimir bubble. This allows the drive to harness the Scharnhorst effect, a phenomenon in which light travels faster than c. The drive allows a ship inside its bubble to travel at triple the speed of light.

SmartCarbyne – A self-repairing version of MAC, used as the building material for space elevators.

SmartCarbyne Nanofloss – This adaptation of SmartCarbyne is a lattice of ultrafine SC filaments, implanted to reinforce bone, muscle, and sinew. This
military augmentation is usually given to fighter pilots and special operations soldiers.

It was originally adapted for military use to protect pilots in high-g maneuvers. An accelerometer embedded in the pilot's wire controls the deployment of an SC lattice, woven into the soft tissues of vital organs. When experiencing acceleration greater than what the human body can withstand, the SC lattice automatically hardens, protecting the pilot.

Spike – Special operations electronic breadcrumb trail, only useful at short range. Each spike has a unique geometric signature. That signature is contained in the Alliance military database. An app registers the negative space created by each spike on whatever surface it resides. Once a person or item has been spiked, the search app keeps track of the void that particular spike makes, pinpointing its location while it remains in range.

Ziptie – a nano breach application for use on restraining people. Once placed onto exposed flesh the app immediately unpacks itself, blocking an individual's wire from transmitting a call for help, and rendering the victim temporarily immobile.

WEAPONRY & ARMOR

CUSP – Compact Ultra-Short Pulse pistol uses a pulsed, laser-induced plasma to either paralyze, flash-bang, flash-blind, or deliver searing pain, depending on the weapon's setting.

P-SCAR – Pulsed Special Combat Assault Rifle.

RAU-19 – Railgun mounted on DAP Helios attack craft.

Drakeskin armor – A carbyne-reinforced synthsilk skinsuit, used by special operations forces when infiltrating hostile territory.

Drakeskin stealth suit – A Drakeskin suit with a nanoweave embedded into the topmost layer of fabric that is tunable to the environment, providing visible-spectrum stealth. The underlayers are made of metamaterials, which use transformation optics to shield the wearer from view by controlling electromagnetic radiation and guiding incident waves around the wearer.

MAJOR PLAYERS
in the
BIOGENESIS WAR UNIVERSE

The Geminate Alliance – The ships that set out to settle the binary systems of Procyon and Sirius initially formed their own governments, but after the first century of colonization, began the loose governmental alliance known as the Geminate Alliance.

After the invention of the Calabi-Yau gates, this alliance was merged into a cohesive, Parliamentary government.

The Coalition of Worlds – The Coalition isn't a governing body, but rather an alliance of independent star nations, for the advancement of peace and collaboration between the settled worlds. Its members include the Sol, Alpha Centauri, and Proxima Centauri star systems.

Sol's member nations are Terra, Mars, Venus, and the Ganymede and Europa colonies. Alpha Centauri A's star nation is Zoser. Alpha Centauri B (Rigel Kentaurus) is the Akkadian Empire. Proxima Centauri's member nation is the Shang dynasty.

The Coalition's articles state that all eight governmental bodies are equally represented, however, some are unofficially regarded as more equal than others.

The star nations within the Sol system hold the lion's share of influence.

The Akkadian Empire – Akkadia is the Coalition's weakest and hungriest member, due to the hardships the lone terraformed planet, Eridu, suffered. The resulting disparity in both trade and commerce caused a repressive culture to rise up and govern the planet and its people.

Akkadia is known throughout the settled worlds for its oppressive government, and its extensive spy network. A state of cold war exists between Akkadia and the Geminate Alliance, as well as most of the Sol nations.

The Akkadian government is notorious for its tendency to steal the intellectual property of other star nations, appropriating it in commercial endeavors where its conscripted labor force can manufacture and then undercut the owners of the original IP in production.

Akkadian Junxun Tèzhǒng – Akkadia's elite intelligence branch of the State Army, those chosen as Tèzhǒng are sent through a crucible of deep indoctrination that refined its members into surgically efficient killing machines. Most Tèzhǒng operatives focused on a specialty, with the most elite being its assassins.

ACKNOWLEDGEMENTS

The hard sciences are divided into a myriad of niche specialties. In physics alone, there are a minimum of eleven branches, encompassing everything from astrophysics to optics to the one I know best—radiation physics. That number continues to swell as technology advances.

To get it right means leaning on the expertise of others. Special thanks go out to John for checking the chemistry in the book. Any mistakes you may find are entirely my own.

I have a host of beta readers who help me spot inconsistencies, two of which have years of military service under their belts. Their input in this series has been invaluable. Steve and Dawn, thank you so much for your service.

No manuscript of over a hundred thousand words is going to make it to print without the eagle eye of a copy editor and proofreader, I don't care how meticulous a writer you are. For this, I turned to Crystal Wren. Thank you for lending me your keen eye.

Manie, Doug, Marti, and James, your feedback made this story better, and for that I'm grateful.

Lastly, I want to thank Marty for keeping the cats fed and the food coming. You're the best!

ALSO BY LL RICHMAN

You can always find the most up to date listing of book titles
on LL Richman's Amazon Author Page.

The Biogenesis War Series

The Chiral Agent

The Chiral Protocol

Chiral Justice

Chiral Agent/Chiral Conspiracy audiobook set

Chiral Protocol/Ambush in the Sargon Straits audio set

The Biogenesis War Files: The Early Years

Operation Cobalt

Ambush in the Sargon Straits

The Chiral Conspiracy

Want updates?

Join my reader's group to hear news of upcoming books, behind-
the-scenes glimpses of life with a physicist, and views from the
cockpit. And cats, because the feline overlords insist. Sign up at
bit.ly/biogenesiswar.

ABOUT THE AUTHOR

L.L. Richman has a diverse background, balancing a career as a film director with evenings spent running a linear accelerator.

Physics is a big part of Richman's life—particularly radiation physics. Whereas most people keep plates and cups in their kitchen cabinets, Richman's are filled with radioactive materials, lead-lined gloves, and a Geiger counter.

A self-proclaimed 'NASA brat,' some of Richman's earliest memories are of following her father through the Johnson Space Center, of being inside Mission Control (but not while it was active), of fast planes and astronauts.

Richman went on to become a pilot, and can often be found flying a Piper Cherokee, or photographing Deep Sky Objects (DSOs) late at night.

For more information on upcoming releases or the latest news on space science and technology, like LL Richman's Facebook page, or join the Biogenesis War Friends and Fans group.

CPSIA information can be obtained
at www.ICGtesting.com
Printed in the USA
LVHW040007030922
727460LV00001B/23

9 781737 363606